Behind Mt. Baldy

The Army Cadets

C.R. Cummings

Also By
CHRISTOPHER CUMMINGS

The Boy and the Battleship

The Green Idol of Kanaka Creek

Ross River Fever

Train to Kuranda

The Mudskipper Cup

Davey Jones's Locker

Air Cadet

Below Bartle Frere

Bowling Green Bay

Airship Over Atherton

Cockatoo

The Cadet Corporal

Stannary Hills

Coast of Cape York

Kylie and the Kelly Gang

Beyond the Barrier Reef

*Behind Mt. Baldy

The Cadet Sergeant Major

Cooktown Christmas

Secret in the Clouds

Mischief at Mingela

The Word of God

The Cadet Under-Officer

Through the Devil's Eye

Barbara in the Bush

The Smiley People

Barbara at her Best

Barbara's Bivouac

Behind Mt. Baldy

The Army Cadets

C.R. Cummings

DoctorZed
Publishing
www.doctorzed.com

Third Revised Edition Published 2020 by DoctorZed Publishing

DoctorZed Publishing books may be ordered through booksellers or by contacting:

DoctorZed Publishing
10 Vista Ave
Skye, South Australia 5072
www.doctorzed.com

ISBN: 978-0-6489748-4-0 (hc)
ISBN: 978-0-6489748-3-3 (sc)
ISBN: 978-0-6489748-2-6 (ebk)

National Library of Australia Cataloguing-in-Publication entry

    Author: Cummings, C. R., author.

    Title: Behind Mt. Baldy/ Christopher Cummings.

    ISBN: 978-0-6489748-4-0 (hardcover)

    Series: Cummings, C. R. The army cadets.

    Target Audience: For young adults.

    Subjects: Adventure stories, Australian.

    Military cadets--Queensland--Fiction.

Cover design © Scott Zarcinas

Printed in Australia, UK & USA

DoctorZed Publishing rev. date: 20/11/2020

Special Thanks
to

Warwick Hamilton
Former Major in the Australian Army
and
the Australian Army Cadets.

Also

Ashley Barker, then a Cadet Under-Officer
and now Warrant Officer Class 1
in the Australian Army
and
Tracy Beatty, then a Cadet Under-Officer

Who were the staff in June 1991
for a seven day 'Senior' Cadet Field Exercise.
This was the first of a series of 21 week-long 'Senior'
Exercises written and conducted by the author.

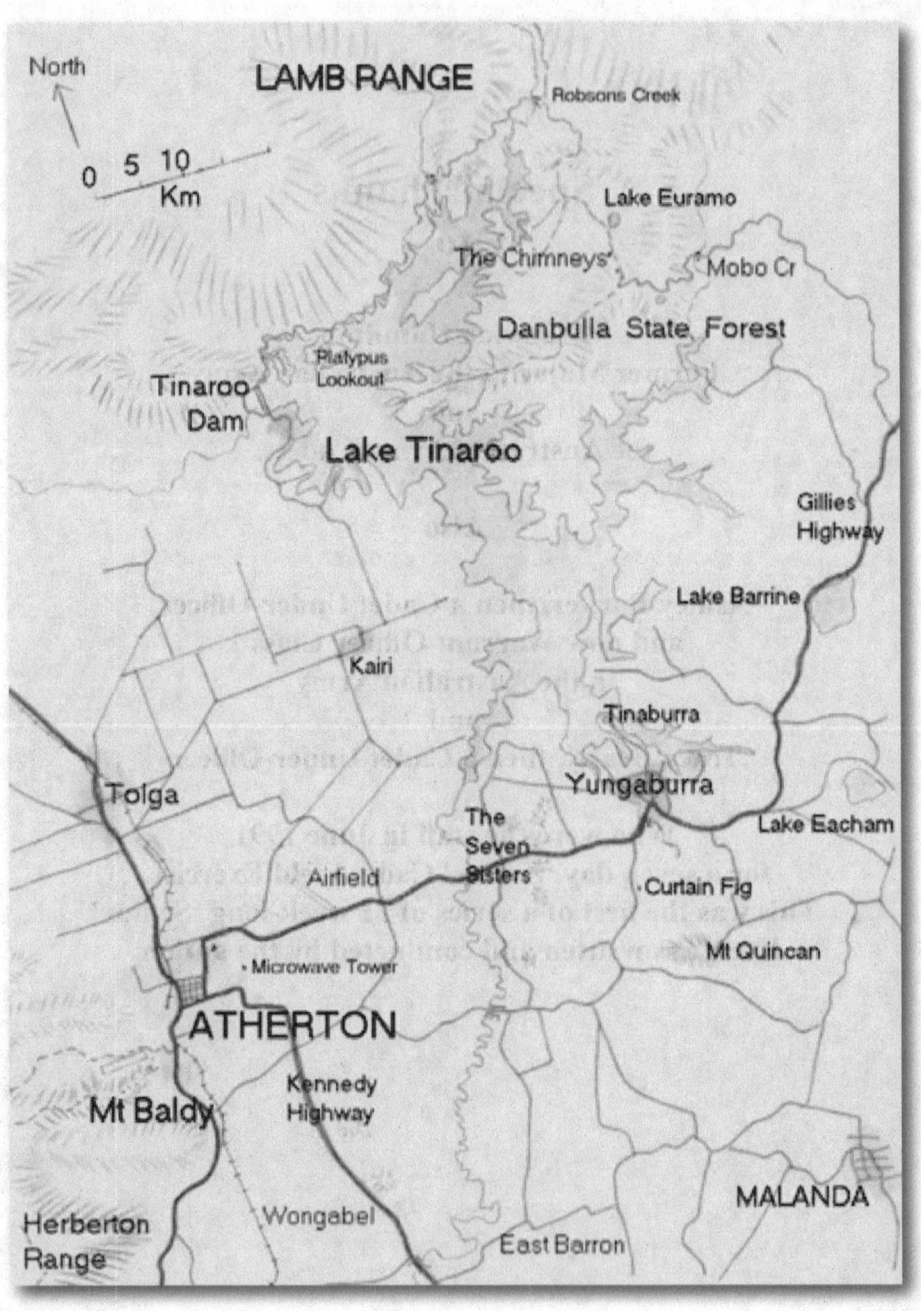

Chapter 1

KEEP OUT OF TROUBLE

Cadet Corporal Roger Dunning, 15 and feeling quite apprehensive, took his pack from the boot of the car and looked anxiously around. He and three of his friends stood on the lawn at the southern end of the massive concrete Tinaroo Dam in North Queensland. They were about to start what promised to be a gruelling 100 kilometre hike.

I hope I am up to this, he thought.

His OC, Captain Conkey, stood nearby. "Now, you guys keep out of trouble," he said, looking at each of the four army cadets in turn.

"Yes sir, we will," Cadet Warrant Officer Class 2 Graham Kirk assured him.

Captain Conkey stroked his chin thoughtfully. If there was trouble to be found, then this lot would find it. In the three years he had known them they had been involved in half a dozen hair-raising adventures.

But they were good kids.

He wouldn't have agreed to their going off on this hike unsupervised, and in uniform, if he didn't trust them. Nor would Graham have risen to be the Company Sergeant Major unless he was very reliable as well as very capable.

Cadet Sergeant Peter Bronksy smiled. "We can't get into trouble just walking along roads and tracks sir," he pointed out. "It's not as though we are heading off into the wilderness."

"You might be," Captain Conkey replied with a grin while pointing vaguely at the jungle-clad mountains to the north of the lake.

Roger, chubbiest and youngest of the four, cast a worried glance in that direction. That was the Lamb Range. From previous experience he knew it was very rough. He turned to Captain Conkey, and asked, "Where are we going sir?"

"I told you. You won't know till you get there. It's about a hundred kilometres and you should cover it in five days. All you have to do is find the clues I have put out and go where they tell you," Captain Conkey replied.

Peter looked at the map in his hand. "Why not tell us now, for safety sake?" he asked with a neutral face.

Captain Conkey laughed. "Nice try Sergeant Bronksy, but that wouldn't test your map reading. You'd probably just take a short cut and sit around," he replied. He had planned the route so that they could easily go the wrong way unless they were careful with their navigation. That wouldn't put them in any danger. It would just mean they would walk a lot further.

Sergeant Stephen Bell took off his glasses and polished them with his handkerchief. "What'll we do if we get lost sir?" he asked.

"You backtrack till you find yourself and then go on."

Roger frowned. "What if we can't find one of the clues, sir?"

"Just search more carefully. You'll find them," Captain Conkey assured him.

"But what if someone else finds the clue first and takes it?" Roger persisted.

Captain Conkey shook his head. "That's unlikely. I've hidden them where no casual tourist would look for them," he assured him. "But if you really do get stuck then give me a call. You've got my phone number?"

"Yes sir," Graham and Peter chorused.

The thought of further inconveniencing Captain Conkey bothered Roger. Captain Conkey was a teacher at their school, and he had already given up the previous week, the first week of the June holidays, to run a 7 day 'senior' cadet field exercise. "Will you have to come far if we call sir?" Roger asked.

Captain Conkey shook his head. "No, not too far. My family is staying with my parents in Mareeba this week." Checking his watch he said to them, "Anyway, it is ten o'clock, so you'd better get going. You've got a nice day for it anyway."

Roger looked up. It was a beautiful day. There wasn't a cloud in the sky. It was winter on the Atherton Tablelands, but the day was warm enough for them not to need jackets or pullovers.

Graham picked up his basic webbing and swung it on. "Packs on," he said.

Roger picked up his webbing and took a deep breath. This was his last chance to change his mind, but in his heart he knew he couldn't back out. *If I do my friends will look down on me; and I will despise myself,* he thought. So he swung the webbing on and fastened the belt buckle. Then he picked up his pack and was dismayed at its weight. *This is really going to test me!* he thought.

The four boys were all members of an army cadet unit from Cairns. They were about to start a five-day expedition, to complete the tests for their gold badge for the Duke of Edinburgh's Award Scheme.

Graham, Peter and Stephen had all been in the cadets for three years. Roger had only served two years. By the accident of his birthday being in February he was a year behind at school and in the cadets. Stephen was only two months older. All four were 15 and had been mates for years. They had been on many other camps and expeditions as a group and did almost everything together.

All four had just completed the 7-day Senior Exercise during which Graham, Peter and Stephen had qualified for the prestigious Adventure Training Award. Roger, being only a 'Second Year', had not been eligible. But he had done part of the exercise during which he had walked about 80 kilometres. That had taken up the first week of the holidays and Graham and Peter had both insisted that it would be excellent preparation for the second week. Roger had reluctantly conceded this, but as they had only had two rest days between the two events he was still feeling sore and worn out.

The boys adjusted their packs and basic webbing and, after a last "See ya sir!" to Captain Conkey, they set off. They walked out onto the bitumen road which led down to the Barron River below the dam. The boys walked in single file on the right-hand side, to face the oncoming traffic. Captain Conkey had briefed them most particularly on this as he thought cars would be the main danger they would meet.

By the time the boys crossed the narrow bridge over the concrete irrigation channel all were perspiring freely and they had had to step off the narrow road to allow five cars to pass safely. The boys had to wait at the bridge across the Barron for two more cars. They then walked across as quickly as they could.

As they crossed the bridge Graham looked down into the clear water gurgling over rocks. "Looks nice. Makes me feel like a swim."

Stephen shook his head. "Be bloody cold," he replied.

"Suppose so."

A swarm of kids appeared along a track on their right and began clambering into a tour bus. The younger children gaped at the heavily laden cadets in their camouflage uniforms.

"Bloody busy," Stephen said.

Peter laughed. "It is the school holidays," he reminded.

The road now wound steeply uphill through savannah woodland. The effort of walking up it told within minutes. Their speed slowed, faces reddened, breath came in deep gasps, sweat beaded their faces. Despite his best efforts, Roger began to fall behind.

Stephen looked back. "Come on Roger, keep up," he called, unable to keep the irritation out of his voice. When the expedition had been proposed he had not wanted Roger to come. "He'll slow us down. He'll break down. He's just a fat little slob," he had said angrily to Peter and Graham.

Hearing that had really hurt Roger's feelings, but it had also made him determined to try. He had appealed to be allowed to join the hike and Graham had supported him.

While Peter had also voiced some doubts, he had supported Roger. "He's a lot fitter than he used to be," he'd said. "And he managed to get through the Senior Exercise without breaking down."

Now, on the first big hill, Roger began to wonder if Stephen might have been right. Looking up he saw with dismay that the road wound on steeply for hundreds of metres. Already his pack felt as though it was filled with lead. With five days food and cold weather clothes and a sleeping bag in it the pack was bulky and heavy. The weight dragged at his shoulder muscles and he worried that he had miscalculated again.

But Roger wasn't ready to give up yet. Gritting his teeth and forcing his muscles to greater effort he tried to catch up. He saw Peter glancing back and wondered if he was regretting having agreed to let him come.

I'll show Steve! Roger thought, pushing himself even harder.

But the effort was too much. Roger felt his heart rate going up and he began to gulp in deep breaths. Then his stomach heaved and a wave of nausea welled up. Unable to keep walking he stopped and leaned on a tree, gasping for breath.

Peter stopped and was about to speak when Roger suddenly vomited. The sound made Graham and Stephen stop and look back. Roger's stomach heaved again. He leaned forward to avoid soiling his clothes. A stream of yellow liquid gushed out onto the leaves and grass.

Stephen shook his head and disgust showed on his face. "Bloody hell! We haven't even got up the first hill," he snorted.

The scornful look just added to Roger's misery. But he was so queasy he was unable to make a reply. Then he spewed again. He felt awful. His eyes went out of focus. He clung to the rough trunk of an ironbark to steady himself. His body trembled and he wasn't sure if he was shivering or sweating. Several cars went past. A person yelled something. Roger didn't hear what it was, but the tone was derisory. Embarrassed, he clung to the tree and spat into the long grass.

Roger was hotly aware of Stephen's 'I told you so' face and felt sorry he had let Graham down. He was aware Graham was now beside him. Then his stomach heaved again. Nothing much came out, mostly mucous. He wiped his mouth and felt miserable.

Stephen jeered. "Not many carrots in that, Roger," he called.

Roger looked at the mess on the leaves and his stomach churned again. This time nothing came up.

Peter gave a wry smile "That was that bottle of passionfruit soft drink you gutsed back at the kiosk," he observed.

"A few greasy chips too," Stephen laughed.

Roger dry-retched again and glared at Stephen.

"Shut up you blokes," Graham ordered. "Here Roger, give me your pack." He unclipped the heavy pack and swung it clear. "Let's get to the top and have a blow."

Graham took Roger's elbow and started him walking up the road, holding the pack in his right hand.

A hundred paces further on they came to a flat area at the north end of the dam wall. Half a dozen cars were parked there and there seemed to be lots of tourists.

Graham looked around, then said, "You right for a bit more Roger?"

Roger nodded. He felt more upset than sick. "Yeah, I'll be okay. Give me back my pack."

"In a minute. Let's just get away from all these tourists."

The bitumen ended. A dusty gravel road led off northwards between a mountainside covered with dry savannah woodland and the lake. The boys trudged on along it.

"This do?" Peter asked, indicating some large rocks beside the waters of the lake.

Graham shook his head. "No. We will go a bit further. Where we can get down to the water easily," he replied.

He grasped Roger's pack against his chest and plodded on. The road was only a few metres above the level of the lake and not 10 metres from it so the boys could see out across the water through a thin screen of trees. On the other side of a long, narrow bay a few hundred metres wide was a tree clad peninsula. Among the trees were the buildings and tents of Camp Barrabadeen, a Scout camp. There were vehicles and people visible there. Several small boats and canoes lay on the distant beach but there were none on the water.

At Graham's insistence, the group walked on for a couple of hundred paces.

"Here's a good spot," Peter said, pointing down to the right. Roger saw that a rough foot track led down to a small sandy beach. Graham agreed. The boys turned off and walked down onto the edge of the beach. Here they dropped their packs and unbuckled their webbing.

"Wash your face and rinse your mouth out Roger," Graham said. He dropped his webbing and stretched. "Aaah! That's a relief," he said. "This stuff weighs a ton."

Peter agreed. Stretching to ease his muscles he took out his map and studied it. "It's a bit of a worry. We've only been walking for thirty minutes. We have only walked a kilometre and a half, if that," he said.

"And we have to cover about twenty kilometres a day," Stephen reminded.

It was a sobering thought. They sat down while Roger splashed his face. They were all experienced hikers and were carrying the bare essentials.

"It's the five days food," Peter pointed out.

Roger sat beside them wiping his face.

"Feeling better?" Graham asked.

Roger nodded. "Yes thanks. I'll be OK. I just ate too much junk food at the kiosk," he replied.

"You always eat too much," Stephen commented pointedly.

Roger did not reply. He knew it; and he wished he didn't. Regretting his weakness he looked out over the lake. "This is really pretty," he observed.

It was. The four sat enjoying the view. A gentle, cool breeze made tiny waves ripple on the lake, transforming the deep blue with tiny sparkles. Small waves lapped on the sand.

It feels nice in the sun, Roger thought.

Graham looked at his watch. "We'd better get on," he said. "It's getting on towards eleven."

"We could have lunch here," Peter suggested.

Graham shook his head. "No. We just had morning tea. Let's go on for another hour. That will give Roger's stomach time to settle. Have a big drink Roger," he answered, standing up and swinging on his webbing.

"What a bloody slave driver you are Graham. I'll bet your ancestors used to whip black people in the sugar cane fields," Stephen grumbled. "Every hike's the same, packs on! March! Keep moving!"

The others laughed as they stood up because it was true. Graham was the driving force, which probably explained why he outranked his friends, all of whom got better marks in class.

Roger rinsed his mouth again and took a big drink from one of his four water bottles. Already he felt a lot better. He looked out over the lake and went to take another drink. Then he paused, the bottle near his open mouth. His eyes narrowed.

"What's that in the water?" he asked.

Graham was about to swing on his pack. "What? Where?"

Roger pointed to a long dark object about 20 metres out.

"Crocodile?" Stephen laughingly suggested as he adjusted his webbing to sit more comfortably on his hips.

Graham sniffed. "Don't be silly Stephen. There are no crocs on the Tablelands," he said, shielding his eyes to look.

"It looks like...," Peter began.

"A body," Roger finished, very softly.

"Oh it is not! Now who's being silly?" Stephen snorted.

"It does Steve. It's not a log anyway," Peter agreed quietly.

Roger stared at the thing and felt a cold hand grip his chest and then his stomach. *It does look like a dead body,* he thought. It was hard to tell as the thing was so far out, but he thought he was looking at a man's back and head.

The others were silent now, staring, each obviously hoping it was not true. They all, at different times, had seen a dead person. None of them wanted to see another.

"I'll get up a bit higher," Roger decided.

He unbuckled his webbing and scrambled up onto a mass of black granite which armoured the small headland beside the beach. Graham came scrambling up to join him.

Roger felt his heart sink into his stomach. There was no doubt. He could see what could only be human arms.

"It's a dead body alright," he said quietly.

Graham gulped and steadied himself on the sloping rock to stare. "I can see his hands," he muttered.

"What can you see?" Peter called from down on the beach.

"It's a dead body alright," Roger replied, unwilling even then to acknowledge the reality.

Stephen stood beside Peter, looking very pale and silent.

"We've got to get him out," Roger said.

"Why? He's dead," Graham replied.

"He might not be," Roger answered.

Peter looked thoughtful. "The wind will push it .. er him, ashore somewhere here," he said.

Roger felt awful and knew he had to act. "That will take half an hour or more," Roger replied. "He might not be dead. We've got to get him out."

"He's dead Roger," Graham replied, climbing slowly back down the rocks.

Roger followed. "Drowned people can be saved. We get taught that in Lifesaving. Mouth to mouth and CPR," he insisted. Back down on the beach again he stepped forward into the water.

"What are you doing Roger?" Graham yelled, running over to him.

"I'm going to get him," Roger replied.

"Let the current wash him ashore," Stephen cried angrily, his pale blue eyes blazing.

"No."

Graham flapped his arms helplessly. "Then, then... then at least don't drown yourself by trying to swim in boots and clothes."

"You're right," Roger agreed. He sat down and began unlacing his boots.

Stephen looked aghast. "You're not going to swim out to that .. that thing?" he asked in a strangled whisper.

Roger nodded and went on undressing. Peter joined them. The others stood in silence while Roger pulled off his boots and socks. Then he stood and began to unbutton his shirt. Roger knew he was only an average swimmer, whereas Graham was very good. In his heart he knew he should not be the one to swim out, but he felt compelled to do it. He turned to look at Graham, hoping he would offer to go.

Graham looked sick. Then he said, "I'll swim out."

Relief flooded through Roger, to be replaced instantly by stubbornness. "No. I'll go. You be ready to rescue me though because it will be cold in there and I might get a cramp," he replied.

Graham looked unhappy but agreed and sat to take his boots off. Normally Roger was very self-conscious of his body. His skin was very white, and as he peeled his trousers off he knew with bitter self-loathing that he did look pudgy. To save weight they had not brought bathers, so Roger stripped off his underpants and stood stark naked in the water. That he was willing to do this brought home to him how intense his own determination was. Embarrassed self-consciousness mingled with sickening dread and he nerved himself to act.

Graham hauled off his second boot. "Off you go Roger, I'll be ready by the time you reach him."

Roger said nothing. Breathing deeply he waded slowly in, flinching at the coldness of the water. The water on the surface was quite warm to the touch but half a metre down it felt like it was straight from Antarctica. He shivered, then launched himself forward.

The freezing water took his breath away as he began to breaststroke towards the dark object bobbing in the waves. But it was not the cold which seized the back of his skull in an icy grip. It was stark terror.

For a moment he faltered. He stopped to tread water, his eyes riveted to the bobbing, waterlogged object. It was half awash and now he could see hair moving in the water.

Peter called, "You okay Roger?"

Roger didn't turn. He waved a hand and, gritting his teeth, swam towards the corpse. As he got closer, he saw it was indeed a man, a grey-haired man dressed in a dark brown coat. A hand, the fingers puffy and unnaturally white, seemed to reach towards him.

Roger suppressed a scream, then gasped as a wave washed into his open mouth. He spluttered then swam forward. *Strewth it's cold!* he told himself, his mind still trying to fend off the awful reality. Then he puzzled: *How do I move him... it... what do you call a corpse?*

Roger saw that the body had a grey scarf wound around its neck. He grasped this and went to tow it...him.. ashore. The body moved. Then it suddenly rolled. An arm came over. A clammy hand seemed to grab at Roger's leg. He cried out in fright.

But the man was dead. There was no doubt of that. As the body had rolled over Roger had seen that the left side of the skull was a mangled mass of bone and... and brains?

The scarf was no good. Worse still Roger knew he was getting tired. In his mind he saw the chill black water and ooze deep beneath his feet. *I don't want to drown,* he thought, mastering with difficulty the urge to give up and swim ashore.

Instead, he turned on his side and grabbed the coat collar and began to swim as strongly as he could. His legs kept touching the body. The scarf wrapped around his right ankle. He had to stop and untangle it.

It seemed a long way back to the shore. Roger could see the others standing there but they didn't seem to get any closer. With a feeling of mounting desperation Roger resumed swimming. Just as he felt he would have to give up there was splashing in the water and Graham joined him.

"Okay Roger. I've got him. Not far now."

They floundered into the shallows. Thankfully, Roger felt sand under his feet. He stood up and, helped by Graham, dragged the body up onto the beach.

Stephen turned away and vomited.

Chapter 2

IS THIS TROUBLE?

Stephen continued to retch almost unnoticed by the other three. They stood staring down in horror. Roger stood there shivering, appalled.

At last Graham spoke. "He's dead alright. And you don't need to be a doctor to see he didn't drown," he said.

"You're right there," agreed Peter, bending to look more closely, his face a mask of grisly fascination.

"Is that a bullet hole in his forehead?" Graham asked.

Peter bent closer. "Could be. Don't know. If it is, it came out here, on the left side." He pointed at the mangled mess Roger had already observed.

Roger eyed the evidence of violent death and felt nauseous. "How long has he been dead do you think?"

They eyed the man's skin, all swollen and wrinkled from the water. The sight was so horrible Roger couldn't take his eyes off it. The eyes of the dead man were still open, dilated but dulled.

"Can't tell," Peter decided. "There's no blood."

"Don't bodies sink?" Roger queried. "At least till they start to decompose and the expanding gasses give them buoyancy."

"Aah Roger!" wailed Stephen, who turned away to gag again.

The boys debated this for a while. Then Peter asked, "What will we do?"

"Get dressed first," said Roger, who had suddenly realised he was shivering with cold. A glance at his naked body made him feel intensely self-conscious, and also very aware of his mortal frailty.

The boys were distracted from their problem for a few minutes while small hand towels were dug out of packs. Roger and Graham dried themselves and quickly dressed. Both found their teeth chattering involuntarily until they began to warm up.

"We'd better tell the police," Stephen suggested.

"Yes, at once," Graham agreed. "And we will certainly have to wait till they've interviewed us."

"There goes our hike," Peter said morosely.

"Looks like it," said Graham.

"Is this trouble?" Roger asked.

Graham looked puzzled. "Trouble? I don't see how it could involve us, other than being an unpleasant experience and an inconvenience."

"No. I meant should we phone Captain Conkey?" Roger replied.

Graham thought for a moment, then reluctantly nodded. "Yes. He needs to know. It will annoy him if he finds out from someone else. We will tell the police at the same time. Who feels like a run back to the kiosk on the other side of the dam?"

Stephen put his hand up at once. "I'll go," he volunteered.

"I'll go with you Steve," Peter added.

Graham nodded. "Yes. Both go. Look, don't tell anyone, just the police and Captain Conkey. We don't want a crowd of tourists here."

Peter nodded. "Right you are. Come on Steve." he said. He set off up the track. Stephen needed no second bidding. He fairly sprinted up to the road and did not once look back.

Graham looked at his watch. Ten past twelve. "I reckon we'll have a good half hour to wait, minimum."

"Where's the nearest police station?" Roger asked.

"Not sure. Atherton, I suppose."

"Should we search his pockets for identification?" Roger asked. He walked to the other side of the body to peer at the man's shoes.

"No. Definitely not. Just leave him for the police," Graham replied.

"Should we cover him up?" Roger asked.

"What with? You can if you like. I think I'll just move away a bit," Graham answered. Then Roger saw him shiver. Graham trembled so much Roger worried he had taken a chill from the water.

Graham dug in his pack for his pullover and walked back up the track to sit on some rocks in the sun. "Come up here Roger. We can watch the road and it's out of the wind," he called.

Reluctantly Roger joined him. He couldn't stop looking at the body. "Do you think he was murdered, or did he shoot himself?"

Graham gave him a jaundiced look. "I wish you'd change the subject. How do I know? I'm not a bloody forensic scientist."

"I wonder who killed him and why?" Roger speculated.

Graham kept looking along the road towards the dam. "The others should be back soon. Ah! Here they come now. No. No it's not. It's more than two."

Roger stood up to look. A line of people walking in single file had appeared around the bend. "They're Scouts," he said.

Graham looked horrified. "Crumbs! We don't want them to see this."

Roger bit his lip and nodded. "I'll go and warn them," he said. Without waiting for an answer he strode off along the road to meet the advancing column, now some forty or fifty in number with several adult Scout leaders.

The four friends were also Senior Scouts, and as Roger walked to meet the scouts he vaguely remembered hearing that there was a scout gathering this week at Camp Barrabadeen but as it wasn't for seniors he hadn't taken much notice. Then his face broke into a smile as he recognised the tall, thin man with the moustache and glasses leading the line. It was 'Silver Wolf', the leader of their troop.

The two greeted each other with a Scout salute, Roger a bit self-consciously in his army uniform. He fell into step beside the scout leader and quickly appraised him of the problem.

'Silver Wolf's' eyebrows rose. "The body is on the beach and visible from the road. Hmm! Oh blast! Another car." He stopped and shrilled a whistle. The line of Scouts all stopped and stepped to the side. The car roared past. "Well, road safety comes first. We will just have to hurry them past. I'll just have a word to 'Brown Owl'." He called to a solid man in his fifties who walked up to them.

The man's cheerful smile died at the news. "Oh well. We will just go on," Brown Owl decided.

"I'll stay with these lads till the police come if you don't mind," Silver Wolf said.

Brown Owl nodded. He blew his whistle and waved the scouts on. When they reached the little path Roger and Silver Wolf stopped. Graham joined them. The body was clearly visible, but only if you looked. Roger turned his back on it to talk to the boys to distract them. Some he knew, so he could make smart comments.

The plan half worked. Some of the young boys saw the body and pointed and the rumour 'accident' went along the line but most were too hot and footsore from their hike to care.

As the last boy went past, Silver Wolf turned and led the way to the body. Roger felt very relieved that they now had an adult there with them.

The scout master pursed his lips as he bent to examine the head wound. After a careful look he stood up. "He's certainly been dead a while and shot for sure. But I'm sure I've seen him before. He looks like the old man who drove up to Platypus Lookout yesterday morning. We were just leaving on a nature walk when he arrived. He was driving an old blue car, a Datsun I think it was."

Roger looked up. "Here are the police."

A police car had pulled up on the side of the road. Out of the back climbed Peter and Stephen and from the front two uniformed policemen. The group waited while they walked down.

Both Roger and Graham were surprised to recognise the senior of the policemen. It was Senior Constable Grey, although now he wore the rank of sergeant.

Sergeant Grey grinned at them. "G'day young Kirk. G'day Tubby. I just knew, the moment I heard that four kids on a hike had fished a body out of the lake, which four it would be. How are you?"

He shook their hands and they mumbled hellos. Roger was nettled by that 'Tubby' and kept back a bit.

Graham gestured to the chevrons on the policeman's rank slide. "Have you been promoted sir? I mean sergeant," he asked.

Roger looked at Sergeant Grey and shuddered. He had vivid memories of their earlier meetings during some adventures on the Kuranda Railway two years before.

Sergeant Grey nodded. "Yeah. The powers that be finally realised what potential they were missing," he replied. He turned to Silver Wolf and introduced himself and the constable with him. "This is Constable Widmark. Now let's have a look at this stiff."

They moved over to the body. The policemen examined it for a few minutes and Sergeant Grey questioned the boys on how they had discovered it. When told Roger had swum out and towed it ashore, he gave the Roger an appraising look. That nettled Roger even more with its implication that Sergeant Grey probably thought him fat and soft.

The constable searched the body then stood up. "Nothing Sarge. Not a thing in any of his pockets."

"Looks like it was murder then. Any labels or name tags on the clothes? Look inside the shoes too," Sergeant said. Then he turned back to the boys. Roger and Stephen both kept staring as the constable peeled the coat from the corpse.

Sergeant Grey said, "Now, tell us what you were doing here. I'll have to get full statements from each of you and I will have to do that with your parents or a solicitor or some other such adult there." He looked up at the scout master. "Could you do that sir?"

Silver Wolf assented. Sergeant Grey thanked him and went on, "I can take notes now but they need to be typed up and checked and so on."

Roger pulled a long face. He didn't like the policeman and this would surely spoil their hike.

Sergeant Grey saw his expression. "Why so glum? What's the matter?"

"Because we are on our five-day expedition for our Duke of Edinburgh badge and this will ruin it," Roger replied.

The boys then explained why they were there. Sergeant Grey nodded. "Yes, I see what you mean. Look, don't get distressed. We'll try to get it done as quickly as we can. This case is out of my hands anyway. As a homicide or suspected homicide it's CIB stuff. There'll be some detectives on their way here by now."

"Where from, Sergeant?" Peter asked.

"Mareeba for sure. Maybe Cairns."

The boys did the mental calculation. "That'll be hours!" Roger said.

"'Fraid so."

Graham looked at his watch. "Can we go, or do we have to stay till they get here?" he asked. Roger saw that it was now twelve twenty-five.

"I want you to stay. I'm sorry. While we wait, I'd like you to help me get your stories down on paper," Sergeant Grey said. Then he looked up and frowned. A car full of tourists had pulled up and people were getting out. "Widmark, tell them to push off," he ordered. "Stay up there and keep people away."

The constable stood up and hurried up the track. The tourists were ordered to move on.

"This road is pretty damned busy," Sergeant Grey said, then muttered something about the school holidays as two more cars kicked up clouds of dust. He then asked the boys if they wanted him to contact their parents.

"Oh no! Don't do that!" Roger wailed. "My mum will take me home and that will mean no hike for me."

Silver Wolf spoke up. "I'm sure their parents would be happy for me to witness their statements. They've been in my troop for years."

Sergeant Grey nodded. "That'll do. We'll get handwritten statements today and they can come in with their parents to sign typed copies after their hike."

The boys brightened up at that. Sergeant Grey went to the police car and returned with a plastic folder and writing paper. He then had each boy in turn sit and give his story while Silver Wolf listened. Constable Widmark was told to cover the body and to chase away some more curious sightseers.

While he waited, Roger was a bit amused to see that Stephen kept casting nervous glances at the now shrouded body every minute or so. It gave him some satisfaction after all the jibes Stephen had flung at him over the years. He noted that Stephen looked so pale that his freckles were much more noticeable.

An hour went by. The boys became a bit bored and restless.

Roger felt his stomach grumble. "I'm hungry. Can we have lunch?"

Stephen looked at him with a shocked expression on his face. "Roger! How could you possibly eat near a... near a.." he tailed into silence.

Sergeant Grey thought it a good idea. He told them to collect their gear and move it up to the road and to have lunch.

"More like afternoon tea if you ask me," grumbled Graham. "It's nearly two o'clock. We've lost nearly four hours."

Peter was the last to be interviewed and he had just joined them when two more police vehicles arrived; a car and a Landcruiser.

Three men in suits, obviously detectives, emerged from the car. The police photographer and fingerprint man emerged from the Landcruiser. An ambulance arrived and stopped. More tourist cars began stopping but were moved on.

The boys sat on a rock and watched while Sergeant Grey explained things to the leader of the Detectives. He was a thin man of medium height with a hatchet nose, bristly moustache and close-cropped black hair. Sergeant Grey pointed at the boys and Roger saw all the faces turned to look. That made him feel as though he wanted to hide.

They were called down and introduced.

"This is Detective Inspector Sharpe. He will be in charge of the investigation," said Sergeant Grey.

Inspector Sharpe looked at each in turn and had each state their name. When Roger's turn came, he stuttered from concern.

Inspector Sharpe frowned irritably. "What's that? Speak up boy!"

Roger looked into two hard black eyes which seemed to reach inside his skull, and he shivered. With an effort he swallowed and cleared his throat. "Roger Dunning sir," he said.

"You swam out and pulled the body ashore?" Inspector Sharpe asked.

"Yes, sir."

"That was a brave thing to do. I think these boys have done a very good job, don't you Bob?" He turned to a burly Detective Sergeant beside him, who grunted assent.

Raised voices on the road attracted their attention. Roger looked and saw that Captain Conkey, still in civilian clothes, had arrived. The constable allowed him to park his car and then join them. As he walked down, Captain Conkey looked at them with a mildly annoyed expression.

"I didn't even have time to get home before I hear you are in trouble."

"Oh sir!" Roger said.

Captain Conkey introduced himself. He obviously already knew Silver Wolf and Roger thought he detected a degree of reserve between the two men. That made Roger feel even more uneasy. Over the last year or so his own interest in Scouts had declined as he had risen in rank in the army cadets and that bothered his sense of loyalty.

More than 20 minutes went by while the situation was again explained, and Captain Conkey decided if they could go on with their hike. He asked Inspector Sharpe, who agreed.

"Can we go now, sir?" Graham asked.

"If Sergeant Grey and DS Crowe have all the details, yes. Where are you boys off to?"

"Platypus Lookout to look for a clue," Graham answered, glancing at Captain Conkey as he did.

Inspector Sharpe raised his right eyebrow. "Clue?"

Captain Conkey explained their hike, then concluded, "So they have to go there to search for a clue which tells them where to go next." He looked at his watch and added, "And if you don't mind, I will get going. I have to go to a dinner tonight in Mareeba and before that I will need to phone an Incident Report to the army HQ in Townsville; and I've now driven here twice today."

"By all means Captain. We will be in touch if we need you," Inspector Sharpe agreed.

Captain Conkey looked at the boys. "Now you lot stay out of trouble and I will see you on Friday. Good luck and take care."

"Yes sir," they chorused as he waved farewell and hurried up the track to his car.

Graham looked at the sky and said. "We should make it to Platypus Lookout before dark if we go fast."

Inspector Sharpe nodded and asked, "Would you like a lift?"

Graham and Peter shook their heads. "No thanks sir," replied Graham. "We have to walk the distance."

"Where will you be camping, in case we need to ask you something?" Inspector Sharpe asked.

"At one of the campsites. We've got a permit," Graham said, tapping his map pocket.

Silver Wolf then interrupted. "You just reminded me. I'm sure I saw this man at Platypus Lookout yesterday morning."

He described what he had seen and Inspector Sharpe listened intently while the Detective Sergeant jotted notes. "We will have a look there later. If you boys see anything there don't disturb it and let us know," Inspector Sharpe cautioned. Then he turned back to Silver Wolf. "Do you want a lift sir?"

"No thanks. I'm only going to Camp Barrabadeen." He pointed across the arm of the lake to the timber clad headland. "I'll walk with the boys. It's only a kilometre or so to the turnoff."

The boys moved off up the track, Stephen leading. Roger came last. Graham took off his pullover and packed it while the others pulled on their basic webbing and packs. Silver Wolf joined them. At a call from Inspector Sharpe, the ambulanceman went down with a stretcher.

"The body looks more spooky under that blanket than it did just lying on the beach," Roger commented.

Graham and Peter both looked but Stephen kept his face averted. "Shut up Roger!" he hissed.

"Let's go!" Graham ordered emphatically.

Chapter 3

PLATYPUS LOOKOUT

It was just after 1430hrs when the four boys and the scoutmaster started walking. To Roger's annoyance, cars went past every couple of minutes, raising clouds of dust. The boys began to perspire and the dust stuck to them.

For the first 10 minutes they walked in silence, still oppressed by thoughts of the murdered man, but as they rounded each bend in the road and saw new sights they began to cheer up. Roger made a conscious effort to push the horror into the back of his mind by noting the different types of trees.

At the turnoff to the scout camp, Silver Wolf bade them good hiking and turned off. The boys walked on along the main road. This took them down across the end of a backwater full of dead trees and water lilies, then up over a low ridge.

Roger soon forgot the body in the effort of trying to keep pace with the others. He pushed himself to keep up on the uphill climbs and was ruefully aware that his shoulder muscles were already hurting under the weight of his gear. He tried to ignore the bodily discomfort but that just seemed to make him even more aware of a dozen niggling little irritations: his webbing digging into his hips, a boot rubbing his left heel, a sore little toe on his right foot, his trousers rubbing the soft insides of his thighs.

The boys went down and around the end of another swampy backwater which gave a view out onto the lake but on the next upslope this was cut off by a belt of quite thick rainforest. Graham kept checking the map he carried in his hand and Peter took his out from time to time. Roger couldn't be bothered. It was hard enough just keeping up.

They can navigate, he thought. *They are better at it than me anyway.*

The road wound around the lower slopes of jungle clad ridges, keeping just above the level of the lake. Every few hundred metres it crossed creeks which flowed into gloomy backwaters. The day was fine but in under the overhanging trees there were patches of damp which made the road soft.

Graham pointed to one of these. "There must have been rain recently to make it as wet as this," he observed.

"How much further?" Roger asked.

"About two kilometres," Graham replied.

"Can we stop for a bit?"

"No."

They walked on. Roger began to feel miserable. Hiking hurt. He wondered why he did it. It wasn't as if he didn't know what it would be like. He'd been on a dozen other hikes. He looked at the three packs ahead of him and felt a tinge of jealousy. How could Graham and Peter just wander along looking around them and talking as though they didn't have a care in the world? They didn't seem to even notice the weight of their gear. At least Stephen seemed to be bent forward a bit, head down. Roger then rebuked himself for feeling such malicious pleasure.

It's all very well for them, he thought gloomily. *They have just done their ATA Course and have toughened up.* He had also been on the exercise but because he was only a 'Second Year', and the ATA Course was for 'Third Years', he had not done all the activities.

They passed through more rain forest. A whole line of 4WD vehicles roared past; ten of them, each with one or two people in it, some reading maps and others talking on CB radios. The boys stood in weeds beside the road and waited. Dust billowed, causing Roger to cough and scowl in annoyance. Then they continued on.

Roger suddenly cannoned into Stephen's pack. Stephen had stopped suddenly. "Look out Roger! You nearly knocked me over," he snapped.

"Sorry, what? What?"

Roger's gaze followed Graham's outstretched finger. He and Peter had also stopped.

A red-bellied black snake had appeared out of the weeds a few metres in front of them and was sliding across the road. Roger felt a shiver of fright as he watched it. The snake was at least two metres long and so thick he couldn't have put his finger and thumb around it (not that he would ever want to, even if it was dead!). The reptile was so black and shiny it looked as though it had been polished and the underside was a surprisingly bright red. It moved with what was, to Roger's eyes, appalling speed.

"Isn't it beautiful!" Peter cried. "So shiny."

"Beautiful be buggered!" Graham replied. He hated all snakes.

"We should kill it," Stephen added.

"Against the law, except in self, defence," Peter reminded.

"What with anyway?" added Graham as the snake slithered into the undergrowth. "We'd better watch where we put our feet when we step off the road."

The boys continued on. Roger now found his eyes scanning the weeds along the edge of the road. He walked with his head down, his hands grasping the pack straps to help ease the burden.

They came to another large backwater studded with the grey trunks of dead trees and fringed by reeds and lilies.

Peter pointed at it. "I'll bet you wouldn't have been so keen to swim out and fish a body out if you saw it in there, Roger," he called.

Roger looked at the murky backwater and went cold. The sunshine seemed to darken as though a filter had been placed over it. He did not reply.

"Shut up about bodies!" Stephen shouted. Peter looked back at him in astonishment. Stephen yelled again, "Shut up about it! I don't want to hear anymore. Just forget it can't you?"

"Sorry," Peter replied. He shrugged, then turned and kept on walking. Roger got a glimpse of Stephen's face. He looked very pale.

They walked in silence up into another area of rainforest. It was like a gloomy tunnel with the trees meeting overhead. More cars went past in both directions, distracting them.

After a few more minutes of marching they came to a clearing on their right. Beyond it was a hill covered with pine trees. A gravel road branched off to the right and vanished up among the pines.

"Here's the turn-off to Platypus Lookout," Graham called.

"Can we stop?" Roger called. He was now 10 metres behind Stephen.

"Stop on top. It's only a couple of hundred metres. We will just waste time if we keep on stopping," Graham replied.

Roger grumbled but said nothing. As soon as he reached the bottom of the hill he slowed down. The track seemed to go up at a very steep angle. After less than 50 paces he stopped, his heart pounding from the effort. The others had slowed down but they did not stop.

Roger swore quietly and began to plod up on loose gravel. After another 50 paces he again came to a panting stop. He looked up and wiped sweat from his brow. Graham and Peter were vanishing around the next bend already. After resting for a minute Roger pushed himself on up. Then 50 paces. Stop.

Heart, slow down, he told himself.

Another 50 paces. The gradient began to level out and curve to the right. He paused again, then plodded on. The next section of road was level and he managed to keep going, though puffing badly. There was a gravel pit on the left. Beyond it a road turned off to the left and went down a steep slope. The road to the lookout went straight ahead up another steep pinch.

By the time Roger reached the top the others had dumped their gear and were having a drink. He plodded across a gravel car park to join them, feeling light, headed and with slightly blurred vision. On reaching the others he unclipped his pack and let it fall with a thump.

"Ah! That's better," he sighed. He rubbed his shoulders and flexed his muscles. His webbing was also discarded. "I feel I want to float away," he said.

Stephen curled his lip. "You'll need to lose another fifty kilograms before that'll happen," he replied.

Roger said nothing, but the jibe stung. He bent to take out a water bottle.

"Let's find this clue," Graham said. He set off at a run, followed by Peter. The hilltop was crowned by a massive granite boulder the size of a house. Smaller boulders lay studded around it and a track with steps led up to a lookout on top. The clearing was ringed by pine trees. The two boys raced up the path, followed by Stephen.

Roger had a long drink and felt a bit better. He put his water bottle back and walked up the track. It was only a short distance, but he was puffing by the time he reached the top. A safety rail surrounded the flat top of the huge rock. The other three were standing looking out to the south.

"Find it?" Roger asked as he joined them.

Peter shook his head. "Nothing up here. Must be hidden somewhere else," he replied.

Graham was busy orientating his map. "Not much of a lookout," he grumbled, indicating the tall pine trees which almost blocked the view. Roger looked. He could see glimpses of Lake Tinaroo, also the small conical volcanic hills called the Seven Sisters, and a few other landmarks he recognised. The view to the north and east was grander but closer; the jungle covered ridges of the Lamb Range. Just looking up at them made him shudder. Memories of that terrifying ride over those mountains in Willy Williams' home, made airship the previous year flooded into his mind.[1] He shook his head and looked away.

Graham looked at his watch. "Nearly four o'clock. We'd better find this clue."

The boys filed back down the stairs. A dirt foot track went left around the rock.

Graham pointed along it. "You go that way Roger. Stephen, you look around the front of the rock. Pete, you and I will search amongst these trees." He indicated the nearest pine trees. Smaller boulders studded the ground which had a thick tangle of lantana and other undergrowth on the edge of the forest. Several distinct foot tracks led into the trees.

Roger began looking around each boulder and each tree. He even peered up into the branches. There were a few pieces of litter discarded by tourists; food packets and chocolate wrappers, but nothing that looked like a clue.

Stephen yelled from the front of the rock, "Here it is. I've found it!"

Roger hurried around to the edge of the clearing. Stephen had scrambled up a steep little mound overgrown with bushes to look behind a large broken slab of rock halfway up the side of the big boulder. As Roger arrived Stephen slithered down, holding the clue in his hand.

It was an oblong of bright yellow cardboard in a plastic bag. On it were printed, in black felt pen, the words:

MOUNT BALDY
THE CHIMNEYS

Graham and Peter came running to join them. They all looked at the clue.

"What does it mean?" Graham asked.

Stephen shrugged. "We go to those places I suppose," he replied.

"But which one?" Peter asked.

"The closest one first, then the other," Roger suggested.

---

[1] Read *Airship over Atherton*, by C.R. Cummings

29

Graham agreed. "Yes, but where are they? Let's look on the maps." He pulled out two maps and spread them on the grass; the ATHERTON 1:50 000 and BARTLE FRERE 1:100 000.

"Look at this one Roger," Graham said, passing him the TINAROO 1:50 000 he had been using.

The boys knelt over the maps and began to pore over them. "Be systematic," Graham ordered. "Go up and down the columns of grid lines."

Roger began to do this, starting on the left of the map. As his fingertip slid up and down his eyes skimmed the names. He found it wasn't as hard as he'd expected. Much of the map was dark green for jungle with hardly any words printed on it. The Tinaroo Dam took up a large area as well. When he found Platypus Lookout he changed his pattern. He began to follow the main Danbulla Forestry Road eastwards. The words slid past his eyes: Kauri Creek, Pine, Tower, Robsons Creek, numerous small tracks, Coi Creek, Lake Euramo, The Chimneys.

"Here it is. The Chimneys!" Roger cried. He pointed to show the others.

"Over in the Danbulla State Forest near Lake Euramo," Graham noted. "That's a fair way. Let's see. It's... hmm…" He roughly measured the distance. "Seven grid squares in a straight line. Be more than twice that along the road. We won't make that tonight."

"What about Mt. Baldy?" Peter asked.

"Don't know. It's not between here and there so it must be further out," Graham said.

Roger looked up. "There's a Mt. Baldy near Atherton. My aunt's house is near the bottom of it."

"Atherton Map," Graham called, snatching it from Peter.

"Yes, there it is, right near Atherton." Stephen jabbed his finger down.

Graham fitted the 1:50,000 maps together. "Gosh! That's a long way."

"So we obviously go to The Chimneys first," Roger said. "Otherwise the shortest way to Mt. Baldy is to backtrack through Tinaroo."

"Hope you are right," Peter said. "It's a long way round the lake."

Graham snorted. "Not that far. We've done it before, on that Senior Exercise with the Navy Cadets last year."

Roger had been on that 8-day exercise and had found it equally enjoyable but painful. During it the army cadets had done a night route march from near Coi Creek to Camp Barrabadeen, 16 kilometres in darkness so black they had trouble staying on the road. The others exchanged stories about it and Graham's enthusiasm annoyed Roger.

Stephen chuckled, "That was when you had your sights on that female navy cadet, Tina," he said to Graham.

Peter nodded. "And she went missing, kidnapped by those bird smugglers."[2]

"And she gave you the flick in favour of Andrew Collins," Stephen added.

"Bite your bum!" Graham snapped.

Roger knew that losing Tina to his rival, also a navy cadet, had hurt Graham. To change the subject he said, "I wonder if Mt. Baldy is the end of our hike?"

"Could be," Graham replied, biting his lip and studying the distance.

"I hope we don't have to climb it," Roger added.

The others laughed. "Do you good," Stephen said.

"Here comes a car," Peter said looking around. They all waited and a minute later a white police car appeared, followed by another.

"It's those cops," Stephen said.

The boys stood up. Graham began folding the maps. The cars were parked at the side of the clearing and five police got out and walked towards them: Inspector Sharpe and his two Detectives and Sergeant Grey and his constable.

Inspector Sharpe spoke first. "Hello, kids, did you find anything?"

"Only our map reading clue," Graham replied, holding up the yellow cardboard in its plastic bag.

Inspector Sharpe nodded. "Fine. Have you got far to go?"

"About twenty kilometres. We won't make it today," Graham said.

"Did you find anything else, any clues which might help us?"

"No sir."

"Would you mind helping us look? I've sent for more men, but they won't get here much before dark."

The boys looked at each other. Stephen looked doubtful. Graham frowned. But Roger didn't see how they could refuse. He answered. "Yes sir, we'll help. It doesn't matter where we camp. What do you want us to do?"

---

[2] Read *Cockatoo*, by C.R. Cummings

Stephen glared at him, but Roger ignored him. He did want to help the police solve the mystery. "Do we know who the man is yet, sir?" he asked.

"No we don't. The body has been taken into Atherton and the doctor will start an autopsy. But we don't know who he was, or why he was killed, or who killed him. All we know is that he was an old man; eighty or ninety at a guess, and he was shot."

They were organised as a line across the centre of the car park and began to slowly walk forward, searching as they went. 10 minutes of thorough looking in every cranny and around every rock, tree and bush uncovered nothing. By then the line had become ragged and they were in the edge of the forest.

It was quite gloomy under the dark pines but there was still a lot of undergrowth. Mostly this was knee high grass or ferns but with clumps of other bushes and the odd boulder. The ground sloped downhill. Roger began following a faint path which seemed to peter out. He looked into the forest and shivered.

This place gives me the creeps! he thought.

Then his eye noticed some crushed weeds. He bent to look. No doubt about it. Someone had trodden on the plants while walking into the forest. He was about to call out when something else caught his eye in the grass. His heart suddenly beat faster, and he sucked his breath in sharply.

"Inspector! Sir! Over here!"

They all came at the run, crowding round. Roger held out his arms. "Keep back," he instructed, then he pointed. "Someone trod on that plant sir, and there," he bent to part the grass, "is a cartridge case."

The Detective Sergeant came forward and picked up the shiny brass case using a twig and popped it into a small plastic bag. He held this up for Inspector Sharpe to study.

"9mm Parabellum," Inspector Sharpe grunted. "Now we are getting somewhere. Okay, line up again and look very carefully for more clues, tracks, cartridge cases, blood stains and so on."

The group lined up again and began walking slowly downhill through the pine forest. Almost at once Roger pointed to another crushed fern. Then another.

"Good boy! Keep going. We will track them," Inspector Sharpe said.

Peter called, "Here's a track too. Someone's run down through here."

They waited while Inspector Sharpe looked. "Either the murderer or his victim, or possibly an accomplice," he said.

They went slowly on. Roger felt very excited. His heart thumped and his eyes scanned eagerly. They went downhill for about a hundred paces before Stephen called out. He was back behind them a few paces pointing at a tree trunk at eye height.

Fresh sap oozed from a small hole in the tree trunk. It had trickled down, red-gold in colour, and congealed.

"Is that a bullet hole sir?" he asked.

Inspector Sharpe came and squinted at it. "Could be. Got a knife? Have a go at digging in there but try not to scrape the bullet if it is one. We'll keep going."

Stephen licked his lips and seemed to go pale. He looked around. "I... I don't want to stay here on my own," he said.

Roger looked around. It was quite gloomy and spooky. But still he felt some scorn for Stephen and it made him feel happier.

Inspector Sharpe looked irritated. "Constable, help dig out the bullet," he ordered.

"The old man must have run down here with someone chasing him," Roger suggested.

"Could be. Let's keep looking," Inspector Sharpe agreed.

Roger went back to searching. Broken twigs, pieces of crushed weed, flattened grass, showed the direction. They went on down a steeper slope and through several clumps of lantana for another hundred metres.

Then Roger's senses noted a change. He paused and looked more carefully. "Sir, here. Another cartridge case!"

He pointed to his feet. While it was being picked up, he went on to something which had attracted his curious eye. As he bent to look at a splintered scar a few centimetres long on the side of a tree, his nose, and then his ears, made him look beyond it. A swarm of flies was buzzing above the ferns. Roger looked more closely, wondering what the black coating on the grass and ferns was. Then he froze and for a moment could neither move nor breathe.

Nausea welled up and he gagged. Panting with fear and swallowing to hold down the rising vomit he turned and caught Inspector Sharp's eye and beckoned. "Sir," was all he could whisper.

It was dried blood.

Inspector Sharpe nodded grimly. He called the others in. "We will search the area shoulder to shoulder on hands and knees but avoid that area." He pointed at the area of crushed and soiled grass and ferns.

"Is... is that blood sir?" Peter gasped.

"Yes, it is."

"Oh my God!" Peter gasped. He looked quite sickly. Graham looked grim. By then Roger had regained control of his stomach. He looked down, then pointed.

"Another cartridge case, sir. And it's different."

So it was, slightly longer and the brass was a different colour.

"Two guns," the Detective Sergeant grunted as he picked it up.

"They went down that way, dragging the body," Roger said, pointing along a line of crushed ferns and grass.

"God Roger, you're a bloodhound today!" Graham cried.

Roger grinned but it was more of a sickly grimace as there was so much dried blood that no tracker dog was needed.

They followed the trail easily for a hundred metres till they came to the reeds on the edge of the lake. Half a kilometre away was the peninsula with Camp Barrabadeen on it and, in the distance, beyond the tip of the peninsula, the buildings at Tinaroo Dam were visible.

"Probably where they chucked the body in," Inspector Sharpe said.

"Why didn't they bury it, or weight it down with stones to hide it?" Peter asked.

"Don't know. They may have been in a hurry or thought it wouldn't be found quickly," Inspector Sharpe replied.

Roger looked out over the lake and shivered as his imagination recreated the horrible scene.

Peter also looked out over the water. "That sun is getting a bit low," he said. Roger looked and noted that the sun was dipping behind a shoulder of the Lamb Range to the northwest.

Graham checked his watch. "It's five o'clock. It'll be dark in less than an hour. Can we go and find somewhere to camp while it's still light, please Inspector?"

"Yes. Off you go and thank you. You've all been very helpful, especially you," Inspector Sharpe said, indicating Roger. Then he went on, "Sorry. I've forgotten your name."

"Roger sir, Roger Dunning."

Chapter 4

NIGHT BY THE LAKE

The three boys went back up the hill past the murder scene until they came to Stephen and the constable, who was still gouging at the tree. Stephen asked where they were going.

Graham answered, "The Inspector said we can go. We're going to find somewhere to camp."

"Not around here!" Stephen replied, his eyes flicking anxiously around.

"Alright. We'll walk on. There's another camping area a few kilometres on. We should reach it before dark if we step it out," Graham replied.

Roger groaned inwardly. Step it out! Besides he wanted to stay here to help look for more clues. But the others obviously didn't. They said goodbye to the constable and walked up the hill to the lookout.

Once there they were on the march in two minutes. Roger barely had time to pull on his webbing and pack and have a drink before the others, led by Stephen, were moving.

And step it out they did. They went down the hill to the main road so fast Roger slipped twice and was lucky not to have a fall. He called out for them to slow down, but in vain. At the T Junction halfway down the hill they turned left. Roger had expected them to go right to the campground nearby but could only shrug.

Maybe they don't want to camp so near the murder scene, he thought.

The sun was gone from the clearing at the base of the hill. All of their side of the mountains was now in shadow but, as yet, the air wasn't cold. Led by Stephen the boys turned right onto the main forestry road and marched briskly along.

Roger quickly fell behind. His aches and pains rapidly returned and he was soon plodding, puffing and sweating freely. Graham and Stephen vanished around a bend a hundred metres ahead. Peter looked back, then halted till Roger reached him.

The two walked in silence. Roger's shoulders ached and he could feel sore leg muscles, a pinched right little toe, rubbing on his left heel, chafing inside his thighs and soreness around his hips but he said nothing. Instead he gritted his teeth and concentrated on putting one foot in front of the other a fast as he could.

He paid no attention to the scenery. Most of the time there was little to see, just a tunnel in the rainforest, but a few times they passed across the heads of bays and inlets of the huge lake. Only two cars passed them.

It slowly got darker and darker. The sky overhead went from bright blue to indigo. Roger began to fear they would have to spend the night camped in the rainforest just off the road. They had done that on previous hikes when they had miscalculated, and he had not enjoyed it. Now he glanced into the jungle, which looked all spooky in the twilight, and knew he didn't want that.

"I wonder how much further," he grumbled.

"Another kilometre or two I'd say," Peter replied.

"Graham and Stephen could have waited for us," Roger complained.

Peter made no answer. The two continued their march. Darkness seemed to close around them so that it became difficult to see far into the jungle, or to make out details. The road became a grey ribbon. Roger started to worry about snakes.

They come out at night to hunt, he thought unhappily.

He told himself it was winter and most snakes went into hibernation. Then he remembered the red-bellied black and was twice as scared.

At each bend Roger hoped to see the other two waiting. He and Peter rounded the next bend. To Roger's dismay another gloomy straight a few hundred metres long stretched ahead. It was now too dark to see his watch or read a map. He wondered where he had packed his torch.

"Some sort of a clearing ahead," Peter said. They plodded up to it.

To Roger's relief they got a view out over the lake to the south. As they came out of the tunnel of jungle, the twilight seemed to be drawn back and, in the distance, there were even the last rosy tints of the sun on some hilltops. A turnoff led down to the right into a picnic area.

This was a small peninsula a couple of hundred metres in extent. Most of it was a lawn of mowed grass dotted with a few large trees. Several cars and tents were scattered across it. Roger didn't say so but he was very glad there were other campers there.

Stephen called to them from a toilet block built in the edge of the forest. He pointed to some trees out on the lawn where Graham was erecting his shelter. Roger plodded the 50 paces and, with a loud sigh, dropped his pack. He eased off his webbing and just stood for a minute, trembling slightly.

"Roger, where's your hutchie?" Graham asked. "There are only these two trees. We can put up two between them."

Roger just wanted to lie down but he knelt at his pack and fumbled with the straps. Graham had tied a nylon rope from the corner of his 'Shelter Individual', a sheet of camouflaged plastic nicknamed a hutchie, around one tree at chest height. Then he proceeded to clip Stephen's shelter to his to make it a double. To the other end Peter attached his hutchie. This was tied to the other tree.

Within the time it took Roger to pull his shelter out of the top of his pack Graham had pulled each corner of the hutchie into position and fastened it to the ground with a thin steel tent peg. The shelters now formed a long A, shaped tent. Peter tightened the cord holding his shelter and then took Roger's from him and began to clip it to his. Roger just sat down and leaned back on his pack. He stretched out his legs and groaned.

Graham came to help Peter. "Don't just sit there, Roger. Put your pullover on or you'll get a chill," he said.

Roger closed his eyes and swore under his breath. He felt exhausted but he did not dare say so for he knew Graham would pour scorn on him with comments on what a short distance they had come. Sometimes Graham could be a real pain.

Just because he can walk 20 or 30 kilometres in a day! But he was right. Roger felt the cooling sweat was giving him a distinct chill.

With an effort Roger rolled over and sat up. He groped in his pack and extracted his pullover. By the time he had struggled into it Graham and Peter had joined their hutchie to the first one. Stephen came back from the toilet, which reminded Roger he badly needed to go.

Twilight was closing in fast and the toilets were already hidden in the black wall of the jungle. Roger found his torch and struggled to his feet. Hobbling painfully he made his way to the building. It was quite dark inside and he did not linger, but after washing his face he felt better.

On the way back to the campsite Roger noted there were five other groups of campers, but none was within 50 metres of them. All seemed to have pressure lanterns or electric lamps and the sound of music and voices made a hole in the darkness. The smell of steak sizzling on a barbeque gave Roger sharp pangs of hunger.

By the time Roger re-joined the others Graham and Stephen both had their hexamine stoves alight. The flames gave a cheerful and homely feeling. Roger picked up his gear and dumped it so as to face the others, forming a rough circle. He sat down on the bedroll end of his pack and began digging in his webbing for his stove and mess tins. He opened the metal stove, scored a square of hexamine with his knife and then neatly broke it in half. Feeling much happier he lit it with a match, then placed it in the stove. The smell of the burning chemical was something he loved. It made him salivate at the thought of food.

The flame flickered brightly in the gentle breeze. He poured water into a mess tin and placed it on the stove to heat. Then he rummaged in pouches and pack for his Milo, condensed milk and food.

Stephen spoke up, interrupting the companionable silence. "What's that you're heating Graham?"

"Braised steak and onions," Graham replied, scooping the contents of a can into his mess tin.

"Looks like it's already been eaten and passed through," Stephen said.

Roger glanced across as Stephen shone his torch onto Graham's food. It looked a disgusting brown mess.

"Reminds me of the German Concentration Camp joke," Peter chipped in.

"Which one?" Graham asked, stirring the mess and quite unperturbed.

Peter changed his voice to give a Germanic accent. "Today ve haf der gut news and der bad news. First der bad news. There is nothing to eat but horse manure. Now der gut news. Zere is plenty of it."

Graham and Stephen both guffawed loudly. Roger smiled even though he'd heard it before.

"What are you eating Roger?" Graham asked.

Roger held up a can. "Beef meatballs and onion gravy for starters."

"For starters. You mean you've done your usual trick of bringing twice as much food as the rest of us," Peter asked.

"No," Stephen cut in, "it's the onions. They're for starters, essential for all farters."

Roger smiled. He was used to their jibes and they were his friends. He poured hot water into his cup canteen to make Milo, squeezed condensed milk into it, then sucked the tube before recapping it. Already he was starting to feel better. The hot drink made, he opened the can of food. After pouring a small amount of water into the mess tin he emptied the can into it and began to heat his meal.

After stirring the food he sipped at the hot drink. "Ah! That's better. I needed that," he murmured.

The meal proceeded for about half an hour. It was completely dark by then. There was no moon and apart from the lights of the other campers there was only the twinkle of some distant farmhouses far across the lake.

Roger cleaned his mess tin and put on water for another cup of Milo. He then took off his boots and socks and began to examine his feet by the light of his torch.

"Roger! What a pong!" Peter called.

"Nearly got a blister on my heel," Roger replied, examining the pink flesh critically.

Graham had begun measuring distances on the map, using the edge of a piece of paper to follow the curves in the road.

"How far have we walked?" Roger asked as he took out a roll of Elastoplast.

"About ten kilometres," Graham replied.

"Not too bad, considering," Peter commented.

"Where do you think Captain Conkey planned on us to be tonight if we hadn't... er.. hadn't been delayed?" Roger asked.

Graham looked at the map. "Probably at The Chimneys," he decided.

"That looks a long way," Stephen said.

"About another twelve or thirteen k's. Four hour's easy walk. We lost about four hours don't forget."

"I'm glad we did," Roger said. "I don't think I could have walked much further."

"You should be fitter," Peter chided.

"I know it," sighed Roger.

Stephen cut in. "Don't you break down on us Roger, and spoil our chances of covering the hundred k's."

Roger felt anger rise. "I won't. Don't worry. I'll make the distance. As I get fitter I'll get better."

"Tomorrow will be worse," Peter cautioned. "The second day is always more painful than the first. It's not until about Day Four that your body adjusts and your muscles get into the swing."

Roger agreed. From hard experience he knew that. He poured another cup of Milo, stirred it and leaned back against his pack. A cold breeze was now coming off the lake. He wrapped his hands around the metal cup for warmth and sipped.

"I wonder who murdered that man?" he asked.

Stephen seemed to spring to his feet. "Shut up Roger! Don't talk about it!"

"I was just..."

"Well don't! Just don't, do you hear!" Stephen cut in.

"Okay. Sorry."

Graham and Peter exchanged glances and looked uneasily at Stephen. He seemed to suddenly sag and he sat down.

"Sorry," Stephen mumbled. "It just got at me." He began to rummage in his pack.

Roger had a long swig from his cup, feeling both embarrassed and nettled. But he was curious! *I really want to know who had murdered the old man, and why,* he thought. He went back over the day's events in his mind, staring absently out over an arm of the lake at the wall of black jungle beyond.

"Do you think it will be cold tonight?" Peter asked, changing the subject.

"No cloud. Lots of stars. Could be. But we are beside the lake and that will help keep the temperature mild. Mr. Conkey explained it in Geography," Graham said. He went on to talk about differential heat transfer and continental climates. Roger decided he was doing that in the hope that the others would forget the body.

Roger finished his Milo. He pulled on his socks and settled to munch a chocolate. It was only about 8pm but he felt very tired. They had all been awake since 5:30 that morning and it had been a wearing day, on the nerves, if not on the body.

Peter made the first move. "Bed for me. I'm buggered."

Graham agreed. "Good idea. If we have a good early start we might make up some lost time."

They dragged their gear into the shelters, unrolled their bedding and prepared for sleep.

"I need a hip hole," Roger grumbled. Being on a lawn in a camping area meant he couldn't dig one.

"My head's downhill," Peter complained.

"Then turn around," Graham suggested.

"No. Then I'd have my nose too close to Stephen's smelly feet."

After a few minutes of joking and wriggling they settled down.

Roger snuggled into his sleeping bag in an attempt to avoid a persistent cold draught which seemed to seek out the left side of his neck. Then he tried to relax and go to sleep.

But sleep would not come. He was aware of all his aches and pains, but that wasn't the real problem. It was the body. He couldn't get the dead man out of his thoughts. Again he relived every moment of the day.

As he speculated on what it must have been like for the old man as he ran for his life down through the pine forest, Roger realised his hands hurt because he was gripping his sleeping bag so tightly. He tried to relax, to think of something else, but he couldn't.

The thought came to him so suddenly he half sat up. If the old man was shot in the forehead, he must have turned to face his pursuers (there were two men after him for sure). Roger sank back down and mulled over the scene.

They emptied his pockets and dragged the body to the lake. If... He drifted off to sleep.

Lights went out. A radio was turned off. A few voices. A car door slammed. Silence settled on the picnic area, other than the lap of the waves and the wind in the trees.

* * * * *

Roger started to run. But he couldn't. The weeds seemed to cling around his ankles. Anxiously he looked behind. Two men in black were flitting through the trees, coming towards him at an appalling speed. Fear surged. Frantic to get away he turned and tried to run again.

"No!" he murmured in a strangled groan. "No! No!"

The voice wasn't his. It penetrated his dream. Other voices intruded; Graham's voice. *Graham will save me from the men in black,* Roger thought.

"No!" the voice shouted.

Roger sat up, his hair on end from fright. A torch shone. Stephen was sitting up beside Graham, his eyes wide and staring.

Graham's voice came again. "Wake up, Steve. You're having a nightmare."

Peter groaned and sat up too. Graham shook Stephen, who started a scream which suddenly cut off.

"Where am I?" Stephen gasped.

Graham turned his torch away. "In your hutchie with us Steve. You were having a bad dream."

Roger struggled into a sitting position. He switched on his own torch. Stephen slumped and hugged himself. He looked thoroughly scared.

"The body!" he began. "It came up out of the lake, just a hand, clawing the way they do in the movies. You remember that movie?"

They all did. Roger felt a thrill of terror and swung his torch nervously around. He got another fright. The air was white!

"Fog!" Peter said.

A fog so thick they could hardly see from one end of the double shelter to the other had rolled in off the lake. They shone their torches out into it and talked about the fog because they couldn't bring themselves to talk about nightmares. Or at least Roger couldn't, and he suspected the others felt the same.

The clammy, moisture laden air made Roger shiver.

Peter swore. "Oh blast and bugger. The fog is all condensing on the underside of the hutchie and dripping on us."

"We need a fire," Graham commented.

Roger looked at his watch. 0200hrs. *Middle of the... mind don't say it!...* The mind did... *the Graveyard Watch.* He shivered again and shone his torch out into the fog. *We will never see anyone who is creeping up on us in this mist,* he thought. He tried to tell himself he was being stupid. Why would anyone bother to creep up on them?

Stephen was obviously feeling a bit embarrassed at his performance.

"I'm going to make a brew. Anyone else want one?" he offered.

Graham and Peter both said 'no' but Roger suddenly felt thirsty. And he needed to go to the toilet badly.

"I'll join you," he said. He slipped out of his sleeping bag and pulled his boots on, then crawled out of the hutchie. Stephen crawled out, dragging his webbing.

"I'll just have a leak," Roger said.

He turned and began walking in the direction of the toilet, his torch cutting a dazzling pattern in the thick fog. He glanced back and saw the black shape of the hutchie and the dim glow of Stephen's torch.

After 20 paces Roger stopped. He knew he didn't have the courage to go all the way to that toilet up in the darkness of the jungle. For a minute or so he stood uncertainly, listening. Then he turned off his torch and stood staring anxiously into the darkness.

Without the light the fog seemed to close in and to physically envelop him. He seemed to have trouble breathing. With mounting alarm he looked rapidly in all directions. The glow of Stephen's torch steadied him.

I can't just sneak back, he thought unhappily. And he did need to do a pee, urgently.

So he stood there and did it, eyes searching around him in fear, half-ashamed at his cowardice and half-ashamed at his poor hygiene. As soon as he was finished Roger turned his torch on and walked quickly back to join Stephen.

"Don't sit down, the grass is soaked with dew," Stephen warned. He was crouched over his stove.

Roger joined him, sitting on his pack. He dug out his own stove and got it alight. The flames were very welcome, but nothing could be seen beyond 10 paces. It was eerie.

The two boys stayed up for nearly half an hour talking quietly. Roger nibbled some more chocolate and then they made their way back to their sleeping bags. Both Graham and Peter were asleep, Peter snoring softly.

Roger took off his boots and slid into his sleeping bag again, then lay back, sure he would not sleep a wink. He listened to Stephen adjusting his bedding.

Chapter 5

DAY 2 STARTS WELL

"Wake up, Roger!"

Roger groaned. He tried to roll over to escape the hand shaking him. Graham's voice came again. Reluctantly Roger opened an eye. He saw Graham grinning at him.

"Breakfast time, up you get."

"Bugger breakfast!"

Graham pretended horror. "What's this? Roger doesn't want food!"

"Is it cold?" Roger asked, lifting his head to look out of the tent. It was light but everything was still enveloped in the fog.

"No, it's quite mild," Graham replied.

Peter and Stephen appeared at the entrance of the shelter. Stephen towelled his head and called in, "Come on, Roger. Get up or we'll chuck you in the lake."

"What's the time?" Roger said, hoping for a few more minutes in bed.

"Ten past six," Peter replied, crouching to move into the shelter. A shower of cold drops fell on Roger.

"Oy! Don't make it rain," he wailed. He looked up. The inside of the plastic was coated with droplets.

Reluctantly, Roger crawled out of his sleeping bag and pulled on his socks and boots. The cold leather soon woke him up. He got out and stood up. As he stretched, he was instantly aware of all sorts of twinges and aches from the previous day's hike. He wasn't really looking forward to the day's march.

Graham struck a match and lit a hexamine tablet. That seemed to break the spell. Roger looked around. He could just see cars and other tents but no other campers seemed to be awake yet.

"Go and wash your face. That'll wake you up," Peter suggested.

"No thanks," Roger replied. But he did need to go to the toilet, so he trudged up over the wet lawn to the toilet. When he came back a few minutes later he found Graham and Peter were busy rolling up their bedrolls.

"Looks like another fine day," Peter said, indicating the cloudless blue sky which was being revealed as the fog thinned.

"Probably be hot later," Graham said.

Stephen had just packed his sleeping bag. He looked out of the shelter and called. "Come on Roger. Roll up your bedding so we can drop the hutchie."

"Aren't we going to wait for the sun to dry it?" Roger asked.

It was Graham who replied. "No. We can be on the road by seven thirty if we move and then we can make up some lost time."

Graham pulled out his tent pegs. That done he hauled the sheets of wet plastic off onto the grass. Peter went to help him. Stephen then unpegged the other shelter and dragged it off, exposing their bedding. Roger didn't complain. It was the routine in their cadet unit and it was easier to pack up then. He consoled himself with the thought that they weren't 'tactical', in which case everything would have been pulled down and packed before First Light.

Wondering why he inflicted such experiences on himself Roger knelt and rolled up his bedding and stuffed it in the bottom of his pack. Next, he took the wet shelter Graham handed him and proceeded to fold it up. As he did, he thought of what Captain Conkey had said during Senior Exercise: 'If you don't enjoy rolling up a wet hutchie at two in the morning, don't join one of the combat arms of the army. You will hate it!'

Roger could only agree, not that he had any intention of being a regular soldier when he left school.

Having packed the hutchie in the top of his pack he placed the pack face down on the wet grass. Then he lifted over his webbing beside it and sat on the pack to light his stove. A cup of hot Milo cheered him up. He followed this with a tin of ham and eggs and two muesli bars. Then he heated another cup of Milo.

The other boys all included a shave as part of their morning routine. Roger surreptitiously ran his hand over his chin but it merely confirmed what he knew. It would be another week before his downy fur needed a scrape. It gave him a twinge of jealousy, particularly for Graham and Stephen, both of whom seemed to sprout several millimetres of bristle overnight.

Instead Roger concentrated on eating and then on washing his mess tins and cup. To do this he walked down to a small beach on the edge of the lake and crouched to scoop up some sand to scour the utensils. It was only then, as he felt the relative warmth of the water, that he remembered the horrible events of the previous day.

Instantly his entire body seemed to be covered in goose bumps. He looked out over the still water of the lake. The mist seemed to steam and roll in wisps and Roger was seized with the irrational fear that another body would reach up out of the dark water and drag him in. As quickly as he decently could he swished the sand and water out of his mess tins and stood up.

Roger found he didn't want to turn his back on the lake, but he forced himself to do so, knowing it would look silly to his friends if he walked backwards. Quickly he returned to the others, trying to appear calm but uncomfortably aware that his heart was thumping hard. In spite of the morning chill his forehead and hands went sweaty.

Luckily, none of the others seemed to take any notice. Stephen headed for the toilet, so Roger followed him to do his 'Number Two'. By the time Roger came out of the toilet the first rays of sunlight were touching the tops of the trees across the bay. The fog had thinned and other campers were up and about. A few hardy souls could be heard splashing in the shallows.

Despite the relative coolness Roger peeled off his pullover and packed it, another of their cadet unit's rules: No matter how cold no jackets or pullovers when marching. "You will just sweat and have wet wool," Captain Conkey had said. "When you stop take it out and drape it over your back and chest to stop a chill."

After 15 minutes, the four boys stood with webbing and packs on beside the toilets. From a tap they refilled their water bottles (four each) and had another big drink. As soon as he heaved his pack on Roger was instantly aware of his sore shoulders and stiff muscles. He couldn't avoid several groans as Graham started marching.

The boys went up to the main road and turned right. It was a lovely morning, cool and pleasant. In under the rainforest the mist was still trapped, and big drops of condensation spattered down in a steady shower which made the road surface quite moist and soft.

Roger felt easier as his muscles warmed up and lost their stiffness. He still found it an effort, but he kept up with the others. They were all in a good mood and Graham and Stephen kept cracking silly little jokes.

Half a kilometre further along they crossed Downfall Creek, a real little jungle stream which gushed noisily under the road through a culvert. The road then went east. The sun reached the treetops overhead and the mist evaporated without the boys really noticing. After 15 minutes march, they came to a belt of pine trees which seemed to go on and on. These were only half-grown and had a lot of secondary growth. The first car of the day went past.

Soon after 8 o'clock they stopped for a few minutes to adjust their gear and to have a drink. The march resumed. Another picnic area was passed.

Roger looked as he plodded on. That campground was also dotted with cars and camper's tents. The irritating and insistent buzz of a high, powered speedboat engine came from somewhere out on the lake.

Rainforest on the right, pine forest on the left. A curve to the right and a narrow concrete bridge over a crystal clear stream flowing swiftly over a sandy bed. Roger didn't need to ask Graham its name. The tourist signs told him.

KAURI CREEK

There was a mowed picnic area and toilet on the left and then the road went uphill. Ahead loomed a conical hill clothed in pine trees and crowned with a forestry firewatcher's tower. It was all very pretty but Roger only had eyes for the slope. The road curved sharply back to the right and the angle of ascent sharpened abruptly. Roger soon felt the strain. In spite of his efforts he fell behind and began puffing and perspiring. His calf muscles started to burn. The road curved back to the left but went on climbing.

There was a road junction on the crest and the others waited there for Roger. Graham pointed behind Roger as he reached them. "Quite a view. You can see right over the lake to Bones Knob and Tolga."

Secretly Roger couldn't give a damn about the view, but he dutifully turned and looked. "Can... puff... can you... puff... see Mt. Baldy from... puff... here?" he asked.

Graham and Peter both looked concerned. They pulled out Silva compasses, ruled pencil lines on the map and checked the Magnetic bearing then stood to look in that direction.

"No. You can't," Graham replied.

Roger nodded. He didn't care. It had given him a couple of minutes to get his breath back. They waited while two more cars went past, one in each direction, before starting again.

It was then downhill for over a kilometre, with the sun in their faces. Both sides of the road were pine forest.

"I don't approve of all this pine forest," Graham said.

"Why? We have to have timber," Peter asked.

"We do, but not pine trees. We can buy them from all those places like Canada and Finland that have them everywhere. We should plant native hardwoods like Blackbean and Cedar."

Stephen disagreed. "But they take too long to grow. Pine trees grow in about twenty years."

"Doesn't matter. It's a State Forest. The Government doesn't need the money. It can afford to wait. It's wrong to plant rainforest country with a temperate needle leaf. Mr Conkey says pine trees will grow on poor soil and if they are planted on good soil they ruin it."

"Oh bull!" Peter snorted.

"He said so."

Roger chipped in. "He's right, but in this case they didn't clear the rainforest to plant pine trees."

Peter turned and waved his arms. "So how did they all get here Roger?"

"A lot of this area was cleared as dairy farms back in the 1920's. Mum told me. I had a great uncle and a great aunt who had a farm near Danbulla. There used to be a town called that but it's now underwater in the middle of the lake."

"When was that?" Stephen asked.

"Don't you read?" Peter said. "It was on the sign on the lookout at Tinaroo. The dam was built in 1950... er 1950 something or other."

"1959," Graham provided.

"Yes, so then the Forestry Department replanted some of the old farms," Roger concluded.

"Still say it should have been with native trees," Graham replied.

The argument took them all the way to the bottom of the hill. They passed a road going off to the left and came back into rainforest country. At the bottom of the hill they crossed a swampy creek on a causeway.

After that there were more uphill stretches. The uphill grades weren't all that high or steep, but Roger began to feel the strain. As he plodded along with head down, he took out his map and studied it, hoping to find they didn't have too far left to walk. His watch told him it was just on 0900hrs.

"What about another blow?" he called at the others. They were drawing ahead again.

Graham answered. "Not yet. We'll go to Robsons Creek."

Roger looked at his map. To his regret he noted that was at least a kilometre and a half. The map also told him they were passing the extreme northeast corner of the lake, but it was hidden by a belt of very thick jungle. Particularly unpleasant looking jungle too, he noted, seeing the palm fronds and dangling tendrils of the lawyer vine or 'wait-a-while'.

The others drew slowly ahead. There was another fairly steep uphill slog. The road was quite muddy and lined with weeds. Roger found he was sweating hard and panting by the time he crested the rise. The road went gently down and to the left and came to a concrete bridge.

ROBSONS CREEK proclaimed a sign. A hundred metres beyond was a triangle of pine trees with short grass under them. A gravel road went off to the left. The others had already dropped their packs and sat down.

Roger walked over and joined them. "If you reckon we were supposed to cover that yesterday afternoon I'm bloody glad we didn't," he said, flopping down.

Graham finished drinking from his water bottle and wiped his mouth. "Never mind. We've got off to a good start today. We've covered at least six kilometres and we haven't been going for two hours. Fourteen or fifteen more to go and we've covered the day's quota."

Roger groaned.

Peter laughed and added. "And then we need to push on a few more to make up for yesterday. Cheer up Roger! Here, have a lolly."

Roger took the fruit jube and sucked it. He closed his eyes and mentally checked over his physical ailments. He didn't want to spoil it for the others by breaking down.

Peter pointed up the side road. "This is the road up to the top of the Lamb Range isn't it?"

Graham nodded. "Yes. To Mt Edith. I went up there once with Captain Conkey, Lieutenant Maclaren and Warrant Officer Howley."

Stephen looked up from polishing his glasses. "This is where the search HQ was when they were looking for you and Willy last year Roger."

Roger shuddered at the memory of that nightmare ride. He had tried to grab his friend Willy's runaway home, made airship when it flew past the top of Lambs Head and had been dragged over the cliff. To save his life he had hung on to a rope and endured a truly terrifying ride across the mountains until it caught in a tree at the top near Mt Haig. Willy had climbed off and the airship had been blown away with Roger still aboard. All he could do was sit on the bicycle seat and cling on through a whole night of fear as it drifted all over the tablelands until finally being rescued at Atherton.

They discussed that adventure for a few minutes. Roger then lay back and closed his eyes, trying to ease his sore muscles.

Stephen's voice broke into his thoughts. "I hate to spoil your rest old son but there's a large leech moving up your left boot."

Roger sat up with a jerk. If there was one thing he hated with a passion, it was leeches. He looked at the repulsive thing as it wriggled its way up onto his trousers, nose, tail, nose, tail. How quickly it moved!

"So much for the mite, tick repellent," Peter said. They had all treated their uniforms with anti, mite fluid before the hike.

"It's a leech, not a tick," Graham laughed.

"Bloody thing!" Roger grabbed it and held it squirming between his fingers. He tried to crush it but the tough, rubbery body defied his efforts. He rolled it into a ball between his finger and thumb and flicked it off into the grass.

"There's another one on your right boot now," Graham said.

Roger stood up and scraped it off, then stamped on it, to no avail, the leech kept moving.

"It's all that hot flesh that attracts them," Stephen said.

"Quality blood you mean," Roger retorted.

He took out his water bottle and had a long drink. Then he stood in the road and looked around. *The jungle is certainly thick,* he noted, thankful that their hike did not require them to go into it. *I had enough jungle last week,* he thought, remembering the Search Exercises they had done during the Senior Exercise. That had been in the Kuranda State Forest, 50 kilometres further north.

Then Roger's gaze wandered down the tunnel of trees along where the road ran straight for several hundred metres.

"There's a black car parked down there. What a funny place to park," he said.

The others looked idly along the road. The car was at least two hundred metres away, parked in a patch of shadow but once seen it was obvious.

"Probably someone pinching orchids from the State Forest," Stephen said.

"Or nature lovers," Graham suggested.

"In this!" Peter laughed, "With all that 'wait-a-while'?"

"Not those sort of 'nature lovers'," Graham replied. "Come on. Packs on! Time we were gone. Steve, you've got a leech on your collar."

They stood up, checked each other for leeches, then pulled on their gear. To Roger it seemed to be even heavier than before. He found all his sore muscles had gone stiff during the short halt so the first few steps were a painful hobble.

They trudged along in single file on the right of the road. The effort of getting back into their stride kept them all silent.

As they drew close to the parked car Roger eyed it curiously. For some reason it made him feel uneasy. A fleeting thought crossed his mind that they would find another body in it but he could see no shape slumped over the wheel.

Just as Graham drew level with the car they heard voices in the jungle and 10 metres ahead of them two men dressed in black walked out onto the track.

That the men were surprised was obvious. They stopped in their stride with mouths agape. The first man, who had a hard, thin face and close, cropped fair hair let drop a compass which hung on a cord around his neck and his hand flashed to his pocket. The second man, also thin but with a black moustache and black hair was carrying a rifle. He threw it up ready to use and uttered a cry.

The boys stopped in shock. The sight of the rifle pointing at him made Roger go cold with fright. For a moment he could not move or speak. Then he joined the others bunched behind Graham, who had stopped facing the men.

"Army?" the first man asked in a hard voice, his hand in his pocket.

His eyes rapidly scanned them. Roger had the distinct impression the man was about to dive for cover.

"No... no... Cadets," Graham managed to say.

The first man spoke out of the side of his mouth in a foreign language. The only words Roger understood were 'Bruno' and 'Cadets', only pronounced in a hard, European way with a K. The second man lowered the rifle but still held it in both hands and looked suspiciously at them.

The first man forced a smile. "You are not soldiers? You are Kadeten?" He could see they were unarmed. He ostentatiously pulled a handkerchief from his pocket and wiped his brow. "You startled us. Gave us fright, you know."

"Sorry," Graham replied. The four cadets stood uncertain what to do.

The first man kept talking. It seemed obvious to Roger the man was very nervous and guilty about something. The memory of his dream the previous night seemed to swamp his consciousness and ice, cold needles of fear stabbed down through his skull into his brain.

The man gestured casually. "We have the rifle in case of the wild pigs. You need to be very careful of them you boys." He gave a short, forced laugh and pushed the handkerchief back into a pocket, which Roger could see bulged with something else. From a shirt pocket the man extracted a cigarette packet. As he fumbled for a lighter, he turned and said something in the foreign language to the other man. The second man nodded, unsmiling, and walked over to the car and unlocked it.

Graham was now speaking, and he was angry. "You shouldn't carry guns in a State Forest. It's against the law. And I don't like people pointing guns at me. I should report you."

Roger wished Graham wouldn't antagonise the man. He noted the man's eyes narrow, even though he kept a smile on his face. Worried that Graham would say something else Roger pushed forward and took Graham's arm.

"It's alright," he said to the man. "We are just on a route march. We've got another twenty kilometres to go. We are sorry we gave you a fright." He forced a smile even though he was so scared he was worried he would lose control of his bowels. Despite his fear he managed to turn and smile at the other man, who had placed the rifle in the car and stood with the car door open.

Graham went to speak but Roger cut him off. "We have to go. Good day," he said. Roger then started walking. The man stepped aside. Roger didn't dare look back but to his relief the others followed him. Then he had to fight down an urge to run, an urge his more rational mind told him was ridiculous. Weighed down as he was he knew he wouldn't even be able to raise a lumbering trot.

"Roger, what the...?" Graham began.

"Shut up! Keep walking!" Roger hissed.

Graham did as he was told. After about 50 paces Roger glanced back. Both men were standing watching them. Neither was smiling. Roger walked even faster, feeling very scared and defenceless.

They had only covered another hundred paces when a car door slammed behind them. Roger glanced back and saw that both men were now in the car. Its engine roared to life.

By now the road was curving to the right. An overgrown track went off on their right and on that side the jungle gave way to open pine forest. The sound of the car came towards them.

"Wave! Smile! Look friendly," Roger ordered.

He forced a grin with muscles that felt like old rubber as the car drew level. The men looked hard at them, then the driver's teeth flashed in a grin and the car accelerated away, to vanish around the next bend.

Roger suddenly turned down the side-track. Graham let out a surprised exclamation. "Roger, you're going the wrong way!"

"I know. Follow me. Into the jungle, quick!"

Roger turned and pushed his way into the jungle and didn't stop until confronted by a tangle of vines and wait-a-while 10 metres in. Then he dropped his pack and turned to face the others.

"I'll bet those men are the murderers," he said..

Chapter 6

WHAT WERE THEY DOING IN THE JUNGLE?

Roger pulled out his notebook and wrote down the car's registration number and make. The other three stared at him in surprise.

Roger repeated himself. "Those men murdered the old man. I'm sure of it."

Peter shook his head. "Don't be silly Roger. You're just imagining things."

"I'm not! Have you ever seen two blokes look more worried and guilty in all your life?" Roger replied heatedly.

Graham nodded. "I certainly think they acted suspiciously. When that bastard pointed that rifle at me I thought he was going to drop me. He pushed the safety catch off."

"I saw that," Stephen added.

Roger went on, "And that first man. I'll bet he had a pistol in his pocket. Did you see how his hand went to it?"

"He had something there that made a lump," Peter confirmed. "They thought we were soldiers."

Roger nodded vehemently. "Yes. They were foreigners, Europeans of some sort. I don't think the one with the rifle even spoke English."

"What language was it?" Stephen asked.

"Search me. It wasn't German anyway," Graham said. Both he and Stephen learned German at school. Peter and Roger both studied French.

"That second guy," Roger went on. "His name was Bruno."

"I didn't know he was a mate or yours Roger," Peter quipped.

"It's no time for joking Peter! It's not funny. I'm going back for a look."

The others again looked surprised.

"Why? What for? Let's just get out of here," Stephen said.

"Because when the blond man pulled his cigarette packet out of his shirt pocket, he dropped something. I want to see what it is," Roger replied.

He went to pass them to get back out on the road.

"Hang on Roger. We'll come too," Graham said, unclipping his pack. Peter and Stephen did likewise. The packs were placed on the old track.

"What if they come back?" asked Stephen, voicing the fear in Roger's mind.

"So what? We have every right to be here. They won't bother four of us without a good reason," Roger said.

"I agree," Peter added. "They won't know if we are alone or not. Soldiers go around in armies, don't they?"

Roger led the way back out onto the road. As he did he was amazed how fast his heart was beating and how dry his mouth felt. On reaching the road he cast a look in the direction the car had gone. Then he headed back the way they had come as fast as he could walk. The others followed, also casting nervous glances behind them.

Even before he reached the place Roger could see the object. He went straight to it and picked it up. He held it in the palm of his hand as the others crowded round.

It was a metal badge, shaped like a shield. The base colour of most of it was shiny black but it had a raised silver rim. On the face of the shield were the letters KSS in silver. The bottom portion of the shield was red. The whole thing was only about 5 centimetres high and 3 or 4 wide.

Roger turned it over. There was a pin fastener on the back.

"A badge," Stephen said quite unnecessarily.

"What's it made of? Aluminium?" Peter asked.

Roger weighed it in his hand, then shook his head. "No, heavier. Might even be silver."

"Any writing on it?" Graham asked.

The badge was passed around and carefully examined.

"Here's a number on the back," Peter noted. He read it out. "One, three, two, zero, zero."

Graham took the badge and also weighed it in his hand. As he did his usually cheerful face clouded with concentration. "These letters. Very Germanic. See the shape of the two 'S's'? Straight lines, not curves. Like the Nazi SS used."

"But you said they didn't speak German," Peter reminded him.

"No. It's odd. It's not just a souvenir or something. Why would the man be carrying it?" Graham asked.

"Identification?" Peter suggested.

"They were both dressed in black," Roger reminded. "Maybe it's a uniform?"

"What, Nazis here at Tinaroo Dam? More than seventy years after World War Two! Get real Roger," Stephen snorted.

Roger shrugged. "I wonder what they were looking for?" He walked to the edge of the jungle where the two men had emerged. There was no sign of any track but the jungle wasn't too thick.

Graham joined him. "Here, have your badge. That first bloke was walking on a compass bearing."

"Where would they have been?" Peter asked. He pulled out his map and they all looked at it. Robsons Creek was only a couple of hundred metres away and the lake about a kilometre.

"From the lake?" Stephen suggested.

Graham shook his head. "Nah! Why bash through the bloody jungle when there are roads going right to the water, like the one where we dumped our packs," he said.

"I'll bet they were hiding something," Roger said.

"Like what?" Peter asked.

"Murder weapon? Bloodstained clothes maybe," Roger replied.

"Oh Roger! Stop talking about murder," Stephen said. Then he paused, mouth open, before adding, "or... or another body?"

The boys turned as one to look into the shadow of the rain forest. The place suddenly took on a very sinister aspect.

"I wish you hadn't said that Stephen," Peter said quietly.

There was silence for nearly half a minute.

"We have to look," Roger said.

"But where?" Peter asked.

"I don't know! In there," Roger pointed.

Graham pulled out his compass. "We can't just walk away from this. We'll have a quick look, but only for 10 minutes. We are losing time again. Form an extended line 10 paces apart. We will go in on due West. If you get separated due East will bring you back to the road."

At that moment Roger had another awful thought. "What if there are more of them, in there?"

The others looked at him, Stephen with undisguised dismay.

Graham shook his head. "No. Those two came in their car. They're gone. Let's go or we'll be seeing phantoms next."

"He does live in the jungle," Peter said.

"Who?" Roger asked as he pushed a vine aside.

"The Phantom, you know, the Ghost Who Walks," Peter replied.

Roger sniffed. "Don't be silly Peter. Not now."

The boys lined themselves out and began walking slowly into the rainforest. Roger tried to look everywhere. As he moved slowly forward his eyes scanned tree trunks for bruising, palm fronds for damaged leaves or stems, and the black, rotting leaf, mould for tracks. There didn't seem to be anything unusual.

They went into the jungle for about a hundred metres. To avoid trees, vines, fallen branches and clumps of wait-a-while they had to weave to and fro but Graham kept them roughly on course with his compass. It was a skill they had been trained at in cadets so presented no new experience or technical difficulty.

"That'll do," Graham called, looking at his watch. "Turn around and we will go back. Try to follow a different route."

Roger wanted to keep searching. He found it frustrating as well as exhilarating. He also found he was sweating profusely and had a scratch on his right hand and had tipped a stinging tree with the little finger of his left hand. He didn't remember seeing one but as he made his way back he noticed the furry, heart, shaped leaves in time to avoid a worse sting.

Back on the road they stood uncertainly for a moment. Stephen took the initiative. "Come on. We are supposed to be on a hike. They probably weren't doing anything. Let's go."

They made their way back to their packs. Once there, Roger had a big drink, draining his second water bottle. He felt oddly frustrated but knew he could not explain quite why.

Graham looked at his watch. "Twenty to eleven! Come on. Packs on! Let's march!"

"Packs on! Let's march!" echoed Roger in a resigned voice. Reluctantly he hoisted on his webbing and pack. On the way out to the road his foot caught in a vine, nearly tripping him. Then his pack caught in another, pulling him sideways. He swore and wrenched himself free and stumbled out into the open.

Graham set off as fast as he could go.

"Bloody hell!" Roger swore and lurched after him.

The road curved around to the left, up over a low hill then down over another narrow concrete bridge before winding up over a steeper ridge. Thick jungle with lots of secondary growth hemmed them in. There wasn't a cloud in the sky and the sun blazed down on them.

"This is supposed to be winter," grumbled Roger, wiping drops of sweat clear of his eyes.

"Could be worse. It could be cold," Peter reminded.

Somehow Roger managed to keep up as they slogged along. He found himself counting paces. Then he called 'The Step' to himself, "Left, Right, Left, Right, Left!"

The road wound down across another narrow bridge. They passed a cattle yard full of beef cattle and several overgrown side roads. At the next bend to the left a side road went off on the right into a clearing among more pine trees.

Peter gestured towards it and said, "That's where we had the pretend fort in last year's Senior Exercise."

Graham pointed along an overgrown road which led into the jungle on their left. "That is where we rescued the girls from a camp."

"That's when you fell in love with Tina, the navy cadet," Peter teased.

"Oh I did not! She's Andrew's girlfriend," Graham replied hotly.

They fell to discussing how Tina had gone missing, kidnapped by the bird smugglers. Andrew Collins had saved her in quite dramatic circumstances. As they talked, Roger could only listen enviously. He had not been allowed to take part as he had only been a 'First Year' cadet at the time. Being those few months younger could be really annoying!

The road went down across another bridge. Coi Creek read a sign. Then the road began to climb up a long slope with pine forest on both sides. Roger slowed down and fell behind. A car came from behind and left dust hanging in the still air. As it went past Roger stared at it anxiously, but it contained a family with small children and he relaxed again.

At the crest of the rise a well, graded road led off on the right. The sign indicated it led to School Point Campground. The others waited there for Roger to catch up. As soon as he did Graham set off again.

"What about a blow?" Roger asked.

"No!" Graham was adamant. "We should have reached 'The Chimneys' yesterday. We will stop there for lunch. It's only another two kilometres."

Half a kilometre further on, another good road led off on the right.

This one led to Fongon Bay Campground. The main road went steadily uphill. One the left was rainforest and on their right a forest of mature pine trees which were clear of undergrowth. Buildings came into view ahead on their right. These turned out to be an old school and some huts. Graham just kept walking.

A few hundred metres further on a gap opened up in the jungle on their left. Graham led the way across the road and stopped. Below them lay a small lake, half-covered with reeds and lilies.

"Lake Euramo. It's a volcanic crater lake," he said.

"I know. I've been here on picnics," Roger said grumpily. "In a car."

They had all been there before with parents on sightseeing trips showing relations the Tablelands, so they didn't linger. Roger was feeling quite down by this time. His shoulders ached, his feet hurt, his chafing was starting to bother him again, his muscles seemed hot and he had a headache. He was in quite a bad mood.

A few hundred metres along another large clearing opened up on the right. A couple of large trees stood in lawn and two brick chimneys stood beside a side-track.

"Two Chimneys," Graham called back to cheer him up.

"I can count," Roger snapped. He was fast losing interest. All he wanted to do was stop and lie down.

They walked to the shade of a large tree on the lawn between the derelict chimneys and the main road. Packs were dropped and Roger lowered himself with much sighing and groaning. He pillowed his head on his pack and closed his eyes.

"Eleven forty, five. That's not too bad," said Graham. "We can have lunch. Till twelve thirty. Then we must push on. Let's see if there's a clue here."

He walked off towards the old brick and concrete chimneys, obviously all that remained of some house, followed by Peter and Stephen. Roger just lay there feeling sore and sorry for himself.

Stephen found the clue almost at once, stuck up the rear flue of the left, hand chimney. The three walked back to Roger with their find.

"We found it Roger," Stephen called.

"Good," replied Roger without looking round.

"Oh cheer up mate. It's not that bad," Graham said, sitting down beside him.

Roger felt a bit churlish but didn't reply. Peter sat on the other side. "Have some lunch Roger. You'll feel better."

"And you'll have less to carry," Stephen added.

Graham made a point of reading the new clue aloud. "Four words again. High School, Curtain Fig."

In spite of his mood Roger couldn't help being interested. He opened his eyes and reached out. Graham passed him the clue. As before it was printed by hand in black felt pen on bright yellow paper and placed in a plastic bag.

Roger looked at it and asked, "High School? Which High School? Where's the nearest High School?" He tried to sort out the small towns which dotted the Tablelands. He had been driven across the Tablelands often enough but the layout and road network was just a maze to him.

"There's certainly one in Atherton," Peter said.

"And Malanda. Remember playing against them at the Sports Carnival?" Stephen reminded.

"All you noticed were the legs of their girls' basketball team," Graham said with a grin.

"So did you!" Stephen replied hotly.

Peter chuckled. "I wondered when girls would re-establish their normal supremacy in Graham's mind," he commented to the nearby tree.

Graham ignored his friends 'dig', being busy unfolding and smoothing the 1:50 000 scale maps. With a groan Roger rolled over and got to his knees to join the others studying the maps.

"The Curtain Fig is near Yungaburra," Stephen said. "My dad took me there once."

"We've all been there," Roger sneered, "a dozen times. Every time relations from the south come to visit."

They all looked at the map in the vicinity of Yungaburra. Peter jabbed with his finger. "There it is."

Graham bent to look closer, then checked a symbol on the map legend. "Yes. That's it."

"How far is it? It looks a long way," Roger asked, his eye following the circuitous route.

Graham did some measuring. "Fifteen kilometres in a straight line. About thirty-five or thirty-six along the road."

"Thirty-six kilometres! We can't do that in one day!" Roger said.

"Yes we can. We should be able to do about thirty," Graham replied.

"You might be able to," Roger retorted.

Peter interrupted. "If we have to we can camp along the way somewhere. We've come about twelve kilometres so far, so we can do another twelve today."

"Don't forget we may have to go into Yungaburra to see if there's a High School," Stephen said.

"No we won't," Roger said. "We can ask someone along the way."

"Good thinking," Graham said. "Now, let's have some lunch."

They dug around in their packs and began their meal. Roger opened a tin of sliced peaches.

"Roger, I hope those peaches aren't like the ones you took on that hike to Kuranda?" Peter asked.

Roger snorted. It was an old 'in, group' joke from when they had found he was carrying a large tin of peaches 'in heavy syrup'. He scanned the label. "No Peter. But what puzzles me, is why the clues have two places on them. Does it mean we have to go to the other places eventually?"

"Probably," Graham surmised, in between wolfing down Vienna sausages from a tin.

The sound of a car coming from ahead drew their attention. Roger spooned peaches into his mouth, then looked up as the car drew closer. The car was white so the faint worry which had surfaced subsided. Then he jumped to his feet, spluttering and dribbling juice.

"Sgmrsh... Iths... It's the Inspector!" He began to wave and yelled out as the car drew level. "Inspector!" (Inspector who? His mind tried to recall. Ah yes, Inspector Sharpe). The name came to mind when he saw the face with a moustache looking at him through the car window. For a moment he thought the police hadn't heard him, but the car began to slow and it turned off onto the side-track.

Stephen scowled. "Oh Roger! Why the bloody hell did you do that?" he asked.

"We've got to tell them about the two men," Roger replied, half-oblivious of Stephen's disapproval in his excitement.

"They may have nothing to do with the murder," Stephen said.

Graham joined in. "Roger's right. Even if they haven't, the police should know."

The police car drove back and stopped. The three detectives climbed out. All had discarded their coats in the heat and Roger felt a distinct thrill when he to saw they wore pistols in shoulder holsters. Inspector Sharpe removed sunglasses as he came over to them.

"Hello lads. Lunch time eh? Nice spot for it. How's the hike going?"

"OK Inspector. But we saw these two men," Roger said. He then described the incident. The attitude of all three policemen at once changed. They listened intently. Then Inspector Sharpe began to ask questions.

"What time was that? About ten thirty. Where?"

They showed him on the map. Graham made a quick sketch map on a page of his notebook, added the six figure Grid Reference, and tore the page out.

Inspector Sharpe nodded his thanks. "Make of car? Good. Did you get its number?"

Roger pulled out his notebook and gave it.

"Good boy!" Inspector Sharpe said.

At such praise Roger didn't even resent being called a boy.

Inspector Sharpe turned to his companions. "Foreigners in black with guns wandering around the jungle, eh? I think we need to locate our friend Bruno and his mate and have a chat with them." He turned back to the cadets. "Thanks for this. This could be our most useful lead yet."

Chapter 7

INTO THE JUNGLE

When Roger heard that, he felt a deep glow of satisfaction.

Inspector Sharpe smiled at him, and said, "You lads have been our biggest help so far and this lead may well crack the case. I think you deserve to know why I think that." He looked at each in turn, then he went on. "We know who the dead man was. His name was Boris Krapinski, and he was European. The doctor in Atherton who did the autopsy recognised him as one of his patients. Mr Krapinski migrated to Australia about seventy years ago as a refugee after World War 2."

Roger couldn't help exchanging a glance with Graham. The mention of World War 2 reminded him of the badge in his pocket and slid his hand in to hold it while he listened.

Inspector Sharpe went on, "He was what was called a 'Displaced Person' and came from Kosaria. We've contacted the Kosarian Embassy in Canberra for more details, but his neighbours and former workmates have given us an outline. Apparently, he served as a soldier in the Kosarian Brigade with the British 8th Army in the North African and Italian Campaigns; you know, fighting the Germans under General Rommel."

Inspector Sharpe paused to see if his young audience had enough history to follow him. They all nodded, so he went on.

"After the war he was one of those people who didn't dare go home because the Communists had taken over, probably because they would have been imprisoned or shot, so he migrated to Australia."

"Curiously, although he lived in Atherton all those years he was never naturalised, that is, he didn't become an Australian citizen. I say curiously because there are quite a number of Kosarian migrants on the Tablelands and most have taken out citizenship."

"He worked with the Forestry Department as an ordinary worker for over forty years. That's why we are here in the Danbulla State Forest. We've just been talking to the Forestry blokes at the barracks up the road. The interesting thing is that we were just on our way to Robsons Creek because of something they told us."

Roger was amazed, and his face must have showed it because Inspector Sharpe nodded and said, "Yes, one of them said he was driving back from Tinaroo on Saturday just before lunch and he saw Mr Krapinski come out of the jungle just beside the bridge at Robsons Creek. He was carrying a shovel. The man stopped to talk to him. They'd worked together for years and he just asked casually how he was getting on in his retirement and what he was doing with the shovel."

"He said Mr Krapinski was very abrupt and unfriendly and just got in his car and drove off. The forestry bloke was a bit miffed but thought that maybe Boris was digging up plants, which he shouldn't do in a State Forest, so he forgot about it till we called this morning."

Inspector Sharpe went on, "So now you can see why, when you mentioned Robsons Creek and two men with guns searching the jungle, my ears pricked up. It all looks very odd."

Roger asked, "It was murder, was it sir?"

"Yes. Shot in the head. We didn't get the bullet, but we got the one out of the tree. And yes, there were two guns fired at the murder scene."

"Gosh!" Roger said. His mind raced with possibilities.

Peter broke in. "You said the man lived in Atherton sir?"

"Yes. He lived alone. His wife died some years ago. We searched his house yesterday afternoon. That raised our suspicions too, didn't it Sgt Crowe?"

The hard, faced, solid detective nodded and sucked his teeth. "It certainly did, sir."

Inspector Sharpe explained. "We got there at about four p.m., but we were too late. Someone else had beaten us to it. The place had been searched. And I mean searched! All the carpets rolled up, cupboards emptied, wall panelling ripped off, floorboards torn up."

"What were they looking for?" Graham asked.

"We don't know. But whoever they are they must want it pretty badly. They must have spent hours ransacking that house."

The Detective Sergeant snorted. "And the bloody neighbours never heard or saw a thing!"

Peter cut in. "Whatever they were looking for, it must be hidden in the jungle back at Robsons Creek."

"A treasure maybe!" Roger cried. He could not keep the excitement out of his voice. This was so interesting!

Inspector Sharpe smiled. "Maybe. Whatever it is, it's worth committing murder for. We are going there now to organise a full, scale search."

"Can we help?" Roger blurted out.

"Roger!" Stephen and Graham both cried.

Inspector Sharpe laughed. "Thanks son, but you've been a big help already. You've got a hundred-kilometre hike to do. How much have you done?"

"Only about twenty kilometres," Graham answered.

Roger felt annoyed and deflated. He didn't want to walk a hundred kilometres. He wanted to solve this mystery. Then he remembered. "Oh sir, we also found this badge. The blond man dropped it." He pulled out the badge and passed it to the Inspector. Inspector Sharpe held it carefully between finger and thumb by two corners. While the three Detectives examined the badge Roger described how it came into their possession.

Inspector Sharpe looked very thoughtful for a minute. He pursed his lips and wrapped the badge in a handkerchief held on his left palm. "I will take this. We might get a fingerprint off it."

Roger flushed with shame. *What an idiot I am!* He hadn't thought of fingerprints.

Inspector Sharpe saw his look. "It's alright ,Roger. You've been a big help. Now, finish your lunch and have a nice hike. See you later."

He turned and walked back to the police car with the other two detectives. Roger realised he was still holding his half-eaten tin of peaches in his left hand and felt a bit embarrassed.

What a goose I am at times!

The police drove off and the boys sat down and fell into animated discussion of all they had just been told.

"Told you they were foreigners!" Peter said.

Graham laughed. "Well you'd know, with a name like Bronsky!"

Peter bridled. "That was my Grandad. Anyway he was a Russian, not a Kosarian. And besides, what would the Aborigines call you, you Scottish reject!"

Stephen stopped the dispute. "Where's Kosaria?" he asked.

"Eastern Europe somewhere; the Balkans," Peter replied.

"It's one of those little countries squashed in near Serbia, Bulgaria and Greece," Graham added.

They all accepted this without dispute knowing that Graham had an encyclopaedic memory for such things.

"Isn't it interesting?" Roger asked. "I think it's the most interesting thing I've ever been involved in. I'd love to be there when they find the treasure."

"Treasure!" Graham snorted. "Old Boris probably got bumped off for playing around with his neighbour's wife."

Peter laughed. "At his age! Ha ha ha! That's what'll happen to you. How's Rosemary getting on these days?"

Graham scowled. Rosemary, who was in Year 10, was obviously a sore topic with him at that moment. "Come on Roger, eat up. Time we were moving."

Roger bristled. "Just because Rosemary dumped you for that yob Nigel in Year 12 you don't have to take it out on me by marching me to death."

Graham sucked his teeth and muttered but said nothing. Peter and Stephen grinned. Roger kept on eating, deliberately taking his time.

"Rosemary?" Stephen queried. "I thought you had your sights set on Barbara Brassington."

Graham made a wry face and shook his head. "No. I suspect Barbara might be a bit too tough for me," he said. "Anyway, she's a corporal and I didn't think I should be going against the OC's policy of no fraternizing across the rank levels if I am the CSM."

At that Stephen laughed. "I'll bet you would have been right after her if she'd given you any encouragement!"

Roger formed a mental picture of Barbara. She was a long, legged, busty redhead in his class but also a corporal like himself in the school cadet unit. He knew that she had paired up with Graham in a kayak for a couple of weekend 'commando' exercises back in March but didn't think it had gone beyond that. Graham's face tended to confirm this when he gave a wry grin. He shrugged but did not answer.

Nearly 10 minutes later, they hoisted on their packs and started walking. Roger looked back in the direction of Robsons Creek. How he wished they were walking that way! He would even walk fast if he could be there in time to help solve the mystery. With a sigh he turned his back and set off after the others.

The road ran wide and straight for a kilometre. It was hot and dry and a passing 4WD full of tourists threw up the dust. Within a hundred paces Roger was perspiring and all his aches and pains had come back.

After passing through another belt of jungle they came to the Forestry Barracks; two lines of sheds and huts facing each other across a hundred metres of open grass. There were several vehicles parked there but the boys saw no-one.

The road then began to climb quite steeply and curved right. They passed into shade with the tree canopy meeting overhead. The leaves on the trees and bushes all looked drab with a coating of dust. Roger soon slowed to a crawl. Graham kept stopping and looking back impatiently. That annoyed Roger but he made the effort to keep plodding on.

The road wound around several curves and continued to climb for half a kilometre. To Roger's intense relief he saw sunlight ahead on a level space. Here a side road went off to the right and the main road doubled sharply back on itself to the left.

"The Python Road," Peter said.

Graham nodded. "That's the one we went down to get to the lake during the exercise last year." The friends briefly discussed the exercise with the navy cadets while they paused to get their breath back and to have a drink. Then they resumed marching along the main road.

The road ran almost level along the crest of a ridge. The ground dropped away steeply on either side. Large trees again formed a cool tunnel of shade. Roger wanted to ask for a halt to catch his breath but kept silent. Slowly his breathing slowed to near normal and the sweat began to chill on his soaked shirt.

From time to time Roger got a glimpse out through the trees of other jungle covered ridges and of distant mountains but he didn't have the energy to pull out his map all the time in the way Peter and Graham did. He had faith they wouldn't get lost. They were good at navigation. Roger felt a twinge of envy.

They are good at lots of things. And they aren't all pudgy and unfit! he thought wistfully.

Graham called to the others. "There's that old timber road we followed last year when we went to capture the fort."

Roger looked up and saw an overgrown logging track going up a rise on the left. It vanished into the forest. The main road went right, snaking around the side of a steep hill with moss covered cuttings on the left and a drop into the green tangle on the right. The rainforest down there looked most uninviting.

Once again, the others halted to wait for Roger. He wasn't far behind, so they said nothing but the looks on their faces hurt. Roger pursed his lips and forced himself to walk faster.

The road curved left, then right, then left. As they trudged around that curve Roger thought his heart was going to stop. He found he was walking in a state of such mental turmoil that later he could only remember snippets.

There was the black car!

And not two men in black with guns but four!

The men were standing in a group looking at a map spread on the bonnet of a red and white 4WD parked on the right in front of the black car. Two of the men were the pair they had met previously. Another had a round face and glasses and had a shotgun slung over his shoulder. The fourth was much older with a hard, hatchet face and close, cropped grey hair.

At that moment the man with the glasses saw them. He gave a guilty start, (or was that just imagination?) and went to unsling the gun. All the others turned in surprise and Roger saw the blond man put a hand out to stop the man with the glasses. He shook his head and said something, but the boys were still too far away to hear.

Roger felt an urge to turn and run. Instead he just plodded on behind the others. He wanted to call out to Graham to tell him to act naturally but by then they were too close.

He found himself muttering "act naturally, act naturally!" and had to make a conscious effort to will himself do so. He didn't know whether to look at the men or not but found it impossible to look away.

Graham waved. "G'day. How's it goin'?" he called to the men. Roger was filled with admiration for the tone of breezy nonchalance Graham used, or did he not understand the situation! These are the killers! And there are four of them, with guns, or at least two had them. The older man and blondy appeared unarmed.

The older man wore knee length leather boots, obviously highly polished despite a sheen of dust. The men looked hard at the boys and for a moment, as they came up to them, Roger feared... he didn't know what. He just feared!

Then the blond man gave a smile and said, "Hello boys. How goes the hike? It is hot is it not, ja?"

"Too bloody hot!" Graham replied with a grin.

"Nefer mind. It is down der hill from here," the man said.

By then the boys were level with them. To Roger's intense relief Graham didn't stop. As he passed the men Roger managed a feeble grin, but he was panting for breath and his heart seemed to be hammering at a hundred times his normal rate.

The one called Bruno said something in the foreign language and the other three laughed. It was an unpleasant sound and Roger felt a flush of embarrassment and anger. He was sure they were laughing at him.

Graham just kept on walking. The road had a couple of curves in it but not enough to hide them from the men for several hundred metres. There had been a spur going down on the right with a timber track along it at the point where the men were parked but after that there were high cuttings on the left and a steep drop on the right.

"Keep walking, act normal!" Roger whispered urgently. He was managing to keep up with the others.

"Calm down Roger," Peter called back. Stephen turned his head to look back.

"Don't look back," Roger hissed.

They trudged on. The road began to go slowly downhill. At a sharp bend to the left Roger risked a glance. The men were out of sight.

"Stop here! They can't see us now," he called.

The others stopped and turned to face him.

"It's them!" Roger gasped.

Peter grinned. "No!"

"Don't clown Peter! It's those men. And did you see? All in black, and with guns. We've got to tell the Inspector!"

"Calm down Roger," Graham said. "How are we going to tell the Inspector?"

"By telephone?"

Graham shrugged and gestured at the surrounding jungle. "It's a fair way to the nearest phone."

"How far?" Roger demanded.

Graham looked at his map. "Five or six kilometres. Not till we get out of the Danbulla State Forest."

Roger's heart sank. Then he brightened. "There must be one back at the Forestry barracks."

"Sure to be. But how are you going to get back there? Are you going to cut through the jungle on a compass course or walk back past those men?" Graham asked.

"Is it far?" Roger asked.

Graham again studied the map. "No. Only about a kilometre in a straight line."

Roger bent to look at the map. "Where are we?"

Graham indicated their location. Roger bit his lip, then said, "See how the road wriggles around this hill next to us. Couldn't we cut across back onto the road there?" He pointed to where he meant.

Stephen cut in. "This is stupid. Come on. Let's go on with our hike. We're behind time already."

Roger turned to him in surprise. "But Steve we've got to tell the police."

"We already have. They've got their car number. They'll get them. Let's get out of here." Stephen turned to keep walking.

"No!"

Roger was adamant. He stood there trembling with excitement and dripping sweat. "We've got to tell the police."

Graham met Peter's eye and nodded. "Roger's right Steve."

Stephen stopped and turned back. "Well you bloody well tell them. I'm sick of this. I just want to get on with the hike!"

"Not so loud," Graham cautioned. "Keep your voice down."

Stephen sneered. "You're as bad as Roger. You think those men murdered that man too."

"As a matter of fact I do," Graham replied evenly.

Peter interposed. "They do look mighty fishy. Or I mean like fish out of water. What are they doing here, in the middle of the jungle?"

"Probably just stealing orchids from the State Forest!" Stephen snapped.

"Or looking for someone else to shoot?" Peter said.

Roger shivered. The blond man certainly looked like he was capable of shooting someone, and so did Bruno.

"We've got to do something," he urged.

"Yes, but what?" Graham asked.

Peter spoke first. "We could start by having a look at what they are up to."

"That's a good idea," Graham cried. "We could sneak back through the jungle and watch them."

Roger went cold with fright at the thought of that but felt his whole being concentrated on the desire to do just that. "What about telling the police?" he asked.

"Let's have something to tell them first," Peter said.

"Couldn't we do both?" Stephen asked. "Two go to watch and two go to get the police?"

Graham hesitated. Then he shook his head. "No. Better if we all stick together."

"Remember what happened when we split up at Stannary Hills that time," Peter said.

"Don't remind me!" Roger cried. He went cold at the memory.[3] "Come on. Let's get going."

Graham grabbed Roger's arm. "Hang on. Let's plan this." He studied his map. "We will get off the road here and go up to the top of this hill and dump our packs. It isn't far."

"Come on. Let's go. I want to know what these men are up to," Roger urged.

Graham turned to look back along the road, then led the way to where the end of a cutting allowed them to get off the road. Compass and secateurs in hand he led the way up into the jungle.

---

[3] Read *Stannary Hill*, by C.R. Cummings.

Chapter 8

ROGER IS DETERMINED

Roger found the slope much steeper than he expected. He and his friends had to grab at trees to help haul themselves up the first 20 metres. The jungle wasn't too thick but there were still enough small trees and vines to impede their movement and to catch on their packs and equipment. It was also very dry so the leaves and deadfall underfoot rustled and crackled.

After about a hundred paces Graham stopped. The hill still went on up. "We'd better dump our gear. We are making too much noise," he whispered as the other closed up on him.

Roger looked around. He could not see the crest of the hill but he could just see the road down on their left. He felt a worry that was almost a physical itch, that the men would drive off before they got there.

They took off their packs. Stephen dropped his with a thud and earned a glare from Graham and Roger.

"What about our basic webbing?" Peter asked.

Graham hesitated, then said, "Better leave that too."

"That's against Captain Conkey's orders," Stephen reminded.

The rule in their unit was that cadets in the bush always had a map, matches, water and one meal. That meant basic webbing. This was basic safety in case they got lost or injured, but Graham shook his head, and said, "I know. But it's more important we don't make a noise and aren't seen. Those blokes have got guns don't forget."

"I haven't forgotten," Stephen said, looking a bit pale.

Roger felt the same. He was remembering not only the body they'd fished out of the lake but the kid he'd seen shot by a .22 in a gang fight two years earlier. He presumed Stephen was remembering the same incident, but he was so excited he pushed the emotions to the side of his consciousness. His whole being seemed to be tingling.

As he unbuckled his webbing, he asked, "What's the plan?"

Graham pointed. "We will just creep along the side of the hill where we can see the road until we can get a look," he said.

"Should we all go?" Stephen asked. "Won't four make more noise?"

Graham answered. "A bit more, but we are safer in a group. Come on. Have a big drink and let's move."

They began walking slowly along the side of the slope. Without their gear it was much easier to weave around obstacles and slip through between trees. Only their boots made a noise in the deadfall. Graham risked going fairly fast to begin with as they had two hundred metres to backtrack. They went down into a small re-entrant choked with ferns and wait-a-while and this took a couple of minutes to find a way around.

As they went on around the slope, they got a clear glimpse back along the road. To his consternation Roger saw the men open the doors of their vehicles and get in. Motors roared into life.

"Blast! They're going to drive off!" he hissed. The boys began to move as quickly as they could, knowing they would not be heard above the vehicle engine noises.

For a few seconds, a thick clump of undergrowth hid the vehicles from view. The sound of them moving off came clearly to them.

"They're not coming this way," Peter said.

The boys stopped to listen. The engines did not accelerate and there was no sound of gear changes, but the noise began to get fainter. Graham and Roger both broke into a run, or as near a run as they could manage through the tangle of dry undergrowth on the slope. Graham leaped a fallen log blocking his path. Roger couldn't clear it but sprang up onto it.

Crack!

The log snapped and Roger sprawled into the leaf mould. He swore and scrambled to his feet. By this he was so excited his vision seemed blurry. A thin vine at ankle height caught his left foot and he fell again, heavily this time, striking his face on a tree trunk. He felt blood rush in his nose but ignored it and sprang to his feet. Ahead was another dip, with thicker undergrowth. They crashed through this and up a slight rise.

Graham suddenly stopped and lay down. Roger slowed and went forward at a crouching run and joined him. Peter and Stephen were still well behind them. Roger saw that he and Graham were on the edge of the cutting and could see down to where the vehicles had been parked.

"Oh they've gone!" Roger wailed.

"Shh! Listen," Graham said. The sound of a motor came to them. "They've gone down that old timber track."

"Both of them?"

Graham shrugged. "Don't know. One for sure, the four-wheel drive."

"What's down there?" Roger asked.

Peter and Stephen joined them. Graham pulled out his map and peered at it.

"There's no road marked," he said.

Roger leaned over to peer at the map. "Where are we?"

"Here." Graham put his finger on the map.

"None of the timber snig tracks are marked," Peter said.

"It must run down this spur line." Graham traced it with his finger. It was one of about five roughly parallel ridges which ran south from the main ridge to end in an arm of Lake Tinaroo. The whole area was a network of small creeks and covered in rainforest.

"What on earth are they doing down there?" Peter asked.

"Hiding something?" Graham suggested.

"Looking for treasure," Roger answered with conviction.

Stephen snorted. "Treasure! Your imagination's taken over Roger," he commented as he turned to laugh at him. Then his expression changed to concern. "Jeez Roger! You've got blood everywhere."

Roger put his hand to his nose and it came away covered in blood. He realised it was trickling down his chin and red droplets were spattering on the dead leaves. He pulled out a handkerchief. "It's okay," he said. "It's only a blood nose. I tripped. What will we do now?"

"First we will check if both cars went down the track. Then we should tell the police," Graham replied.

"Here comes a car," Peter cautioned. They listened to an approaching vehicle. A white Landcruiser came into view from the west and drove straight past.

"Just tourists," Peter observed as the vehicle went out of sight.

By this time Roger had staunched the flow of blood. He pulled out his water bottle and washed his face. His nose now felt all stuffed up and his handkerchief was a bloody mess. A few drops still trickled and dripped and he could taste the blood on his lips and at the back of his throat. He ignored it.

"Come on," he said, leading the way down onto the road.

The four walked quickly but cautiously forward to where the vehicles had been parked. Roger stopped, looked down the side-track then scanned the ground. "Both vehicles have gone down there," he murmured, pointing to where the wheel tracks showed in the dust.

"I wonder if they dropped anything else?" Peter asked.

Their eyes quartered the ground. There was nothing. Roger walked across to get a better look down the side road. It went gently downhill along the spine of the ridge but curved to the left 50 metres on. There was no-one in sight and no sound. He began walking down it.

"Roger! Where are you going?" Stephen called after him.

Roger turned and hissed furiously. "Ssh! They'll hear you. I'm going to see what they're up to."

"Don't be a fool! What about our hike?" Stephen replied angrily.

"Bugger the hike. It can wait. This is more important," Roger replied.

"Shouldn't we go and tell the police?" Peter temporised.

"Tell them what? We haven't seen what these blokes are up to," Roger replied.

Graham looked at his watch. "Two o'clock. We should be getting on," He said. Then he added, "Besides, I'm not at all keen to go looking for armed men in the jungle."

To Roger it appeared that Graham's sense of responsibility was warring with his spirit of adventure. "Just a little look," Roger replied.

"We promised Captain Conkey we'd keep out of trouble," Graham replied. "I'm the senior rank don't forget and I'm responsible for your safety."

"Why don't two of us stay here and watch while two walk back to the Forestry Barracks to contact the police?" Peter suggested.

Graham hesitated. He bit his lip in indecision.

"I'll stay and watch," Roger said.

"So will I," Stephen replied.

Graham gave in. "Alright. Pete and I will go back. If we don't meet you here, then we will RV on top of the hill where our gear is. And for God's sake don't let them see you."

"We won't. Get going. Hurry up," Roger replied.

Graham and Peter turned and set off at a brisk walk. Stephen turned to Roger. "Where will we hide, up on the bank?"

"I'm going to follow this track for a bit, just to see where it leads," Roger replied.

"Roger! You said we would hide and watch."

"I will too. I don't want to be seen," Roger replied. He glanced around. Graham and Peter had vanished from sight.

It will take them about twenty minutes to reach the Forestry Barracks, so I have perhaps twice that long, he calculated. Now he was gripped by an intense curiosity. *I just have to know!* he told himself. After a check of his watch he started walking cautiously along the track.

"Roger!" Stephen hissed, fear evident on his face and in his voice.

"You stay here and hide if you want to," Roger hissed.

He wiped sweaty palms and swallowed. His throat felt suddenly dry. He knew he was scared. He also knew he was being stupid, but he couldn't stop himself. So he continued walking.

Stephen swore quietly and began to follow. They moved slowly and carefully, scouting as they had been trained to do. Their eyes searched through the undergrowth ahead, then flicked down to scan for dead sticks in their path. There was a fair amount of leaf, litter but otherwise the track was clear.

On either side of the track the ground dropped steeply away. Some of the jungle was very thick. In other places it was relatively open. Roger strained his ears but could only hear the normal jungle noises; wind in the leaves, an occasional bird, a few rustles in the leaves as lizards scurried away. The most obvious noise was his own heartbeat which seemed to boom like jungle drums.

Roger swallowed. He was very scared. But he couldn't turn and go back now. *Stephen will despise me even more if I do,* he thought.

Off in the distance, in the direction they were heading, Cockatoos began their raucous screeching. The two boys stopped and looked at each other. Roger nodded with satisfaction. The men must have disturbed the birds.

Reassured, Roger went on, Stephen following reluctantly 10 paces behind. The track curved left, then slightly uphill and back to the right. At the curve, a side-track went off to the left. Roger walked to it and looked.

This was an overgrown snig, track. It went downhill very steeply. Stephen joined him. "We'd better not get lost. We should make a sketch map," he whispered.

Roger nodded. "I'll scout. You make the map."

Stephen agreed. As a sergeant he was better trained to do this. It was a skill Captain Conkey made the NCOs practise every year. He pulled out notebook and pencil then took compass bearings both ways along the main track then down the side-track. After jotting these onto a rough sketch he moved to follow Roger.

Roger went on along the main track for another 50 paces. It continued to climb gently and curve back to the left. As he reached the bend he froze. His heart thumped wildly and he had to force himself to edge forward. He could see the back of the black car.

With rapid but cautious steps he went across the track to the right and into the trees, making more noise than he intended. From there he could also see the back of the 4WD. Both vehicles were parked on the track, one behind the other.

Moving very cautiously from tree to tree he edged forward. He heard Stephen following and glanced back. Stephen's eyes asked the question. Roger shook his head. No-one in sight.

"Write down the make and number of the 4WD," he whispered. Stephen nodded. He still had his notebook in his hand. To get a clear view of the number plate they had to creep forward level with the black car and only 5 metres from it.

By then Roger was sure no-one was there but he kept moving cautiously just in case there was a guard somewhere out of sight. They went on past the vehicles and within 10 metres found another track angling downhill on their right. It was also partly overgrown. They crept into the V where the two tracks joined.

Roger peered through the bushes along the main track. The reason why the vehicles were parked where they were became obvious. A large tree had crashed across the main track.

Probably blown down by that cyclone in February, Roger thought.

Waving Stephen to follow, Roger stepped out onto the side-track and looked down it. It was quite steep and curved out of sight to the left. Stephen joined him and took a compass bearing.

As Stephen was writing it down Roger's heart seemed to stop. His hair stood up on the back of his neck. He found he could not speak so grabbed at Stephen's elbow.

Two men had appeared at the bend in the track below them, men in black.

Roger kept his grip on Stephen and pulled him sideways as he moved to the nearest big tree, on the downhill side of the track. He thought he was going to be sick or faint, but he managed to somehow watch where he was going and keep his eyes on the men.

The boys slipped behind the big tree and began retreating down the slope looking for better cover. Roger looked around. There were no large trees for 10 metres, just lots of small saplings, then a wall of wait-a-while. He heard Stephen break a twig and turned to shake his head and gave the signal to get down.

After another anxious look around for better cover Roger crouched behind the biggest tree. This had a small prickly palm at its base which gave some extra cover. He felt sure the men hadn't seen them because they had been searching the ground.

As he crouched there, Roger noticed that the tree had a thick layer of moss growing on it and a small liana wound twice round it. He crouched, peering through the palm fronds, and tried to control his trembling.

For a time he couldn't see the men but then he heard them. They were speaking in low voices in the foreign language. Roger didn't dare move. *I hope Stephen has a better hiding place than me,* he thought, breaking into a sweat of anxiety as he did.

Then he saw one of the men.

It was Bruno. He was carrying his rifle and a shovel. Then the blond man came into view. Roger was surprised. The man was wearing headphones and was using a metal detector which he waved low over the ground along the sides of the track and around the trees on the other side of the track. Roger also noted with a spasm of anxiety that the man was wearing an automatic pistol on his belt.

The two men came closer and closer, talking quietly and searching very carefully. From time to time one or both would leave the track and search around the trees. Roger swallowed and began to sweat.

If the men search this side of the track like that we must be discovered, he thought anxiously.

His mind filled with a desperate picture of trying to run downhill through the jungle with bullets thudding into the trees, and into him. He was quite sure the men would shoot them and would bury their bodies in the jungle where they would never be found.

At that Roger nearly lost control of himself. His vision went hazy with black dots dancing before his eyes and it was with difficulty he controlled his bladder.

The men were quite close by this, only 10 metres away. There was a scuffling noise in the jungle behind Roger. The blond man turned to look, then said something before resuming his search. A wave of hot and cold swept over Roger. He heard the scuffling again and risked a sideways glance.

It wasn't Stephen, just a Scrub Turkey. To his dismay he realised he could see the top of Stephen's back behind a small dead log. *Oh my God! I hope they don't see him,* he prayed. Roger turned his head carefully to keep watching the men.

They were right opposite him now. Only 5 paces away. He could see every detail and hear every word. The men clearly weren't enjoying themselves and obviously weren't friends. Roger gained the distinct impression the blond man was giving orders to Bruno.

Then the tree blocked them from sight. Roger resisted the temptation to move. He waited till they had gone on a few more metres up the track. Then he had to move. He found his legs were starting to cramp.

I won't be able to run, he thought.

Very slowly he eased himself around, moving leaves and twigs with his fingers then shifting his feet. He ended up half leaning on the tree and half kneeling but able to look around the other side of the trunk.

The two men kept searching until they came to the track junction, which was only about 20 metres away. Roger could just see them. When they got there they stopped searching and stood together in the middle of the track. The blond man took off the earphones and pulled out his cigarette packet and lit a cigarette. They began to talk, looking idly around.

Roger heard a faint rustle behind him. He looked back and saw Stephen cautiously lift his head to peer over the log. Roger met his eyes and shook his head while pointing to where the men were. Stephen nodded and lay still.

Roger was in a real state. If the men searched their side of the track the same way they had just searched the other they must be found. *Should we try to creep away?* he wondered.

After a careful study, he decided it could not be done without them being seen or heard. They would have to take the risk and stay.

Chapter 9

WHAT ARE THE MEN SEARCHING FOR?

Roger eased himself around into a more comfortable position so that he was sitting with his side against the tree. Very slowly he stretched and rubbed each leg. The two men made no move to leave. As the tension eased Roger became bored. He shivered. An occasional rustle indicated that Stephen was also changing position.

As the minutes ticked by a new worry came to Roger. He looked at his watch. It was a quarter past three; over an hour since Graham and Peter set out for the Forestry Barracks.

They must surely be back by now, he thought unhappily. *They will be worrying about where we are.*

He risked another look. Bruno had sat down but otherwise nothing was changed. Was it possible they could sneak away undetected? There was doubt and that made Roger stay where he was. He saw Stephen peering at him. From his eyes and a pointed finger Roger guessed Stephen was thinking the same thing. He shook his head emphatically.

More time passed. Roger became bored and stiff. The sweat dried and he realised he was thirsty. A noise in the leaves caught his attention. A large centipede was trekking along but it wasn't headed for him, so he ignored it. The call of a whip, bird sounded down the slope. A tree trunk rubbed against another as the wind moved it. It was all very peaceful.

The sound of different voices roused Roger. He looked up through the trees and saw the other two men appear. They joined the blond man and Bruno. A discussion began which Roger could hear quite clearly but of which, because of the language, he could not understand a word.

What was plain was that the old man with the hard face was the boss. It was also obvious there was disagreement. The blond man pointed down the side-track with emphatic gestures and did a fair amount of gesticulating. Bruno and the man with glasses made almost no contribution.

It then occurred to Roger that this was their chance to creep away. He looked around to check the best route. It would have to be downhill southwest, which was away from the road. Stephen had his head up and was watching the men. Roger was about to attract his attention when the men began a real argument.

The old man began to shout. Roger was so astonished at the reaction of the other three men that his withdrawal plan slipped out of his head.

The three men had formed a single line and stood at attention!

The old man continued to speak but lowered his voice. It sounded pretty venomous whatever it was. Roger studied the situation anew. The men had heads up, shoulders and elbows back and their hands flat against their trousers, fingers pointing down, as though they were soldiers being dressed down by an angry superior.

It was so unexpected in that context Roger actually gaped. Who were these men? Or what were these men? And what were they doing here in the Danbulla State Forest? Searching for something that was buried Roger assumed. But what?

The old man snapped a command and the other three relaxed their positions. The blond man dug into a pocket in his trousers and extracted a plastic bag with various articles in it. One of these was a notebook. It was taken out and the older man carefully leafed through the pages and read it.

Roger could clearly see the lines of concentration on their faces. Then both men took out compasses and took bearings which seemed to be off to his right. A map was opened and studied. There was more discussion. This ended abruptly with the old man turning and walking back the way he had come. The other men followed, the blond man first shrugging and pulling a wry face to Bruno behind the old man's back.

The four men detoured through the rainforest around the roots of the fallen tree. For a moment this brought them clearly into view through a gap in the trees. To Roger's relief they vanished from sight over a low knoll.

Stephen rose to his knees, then to his feet, brushing leaves off as he did so.

"Let's get out of here," he hissed.

Roger shook his head. "I want to see where they go."

"Don't be stupid Roger. If you get seen..." Stephen didn't finish the sentence. Neither said anything for a moment but Roger was determined.

"I'll be okay," he said.

"You're mad. Besides Graham and Peter will be wondering where we are."

"Then you go back and tell them."

"No. That's even sillier. We must stay together. Come on!" Stephen replied.

"No. I'm going to follow them," Roger said with finality. He began walking uphill through the jungle. Stephen shook his head and swore softly, took off his glasses and cleaned them, put them on, then followed.

Roger made his way to the place where the men had vanished from sight. A faint footpad showed their route. This led up onto the main timber track but here it was in more open scrub and was overgrown with waist high grass.

The men had trampled a path which was easy to follow. 10 metres further on it crested a low knoll. Roger walked up to the rise, every nerve alert. Here another side road went off downhill on the left. Trampled grass led in both directions. Roger paused, unsure which way to go.

The screech of cockatoos told him. He moved forward a few paces and could just see over the rise. What he saw made him stop and crouched behind a bush.

The timber track went downhill for about 50 paces then entered a large clearing at least a hundred metres long by half as wide. Beyond this it tunnelled back into a forest of tall white eucalypts further along the ridge. The cockatoos were in the eucalypts. The clearing had been bulldozed as part of the timber hauling many years before and was now either bare red clay or small bushes.

Near the closest edge of the clearing three of the men stood with their backs to Roger while the blond man paced deliberately on a compass bearing. He was counting aloud and suddenly stopped and turned to face the others. They at once began walking to join him.

Stephen had joined Roger by this. "What are they doing?" he hushed.

"Counting paces. I told you it was a treasure hunt. Look. Now they've got their metal detector to work," Roger replied.

They watched as the man with the glasses quartered the ground systematically with the detector. He stopped from time to time and Bruno dug but only threw aside several small rusty metal objects. After circling up to 10 metres from where the blond man stood the operator stopped. He took off his earphones and shrugged.

There was some discussion. Then the old man gave quick orders. Bruno set to work chopping at a bush. The man with the glasses and the blond man both began walking back towards the boys.

"Here they come! Quick, into the trees," Roger hissed. He pushed at Stephen to move and keep down. His heart had leapt into his mouth and the adrenalin pumped.

The boys moved on hands and knees as fast as they dared. Roger paused to reach behind him to stand the tall grass back up then followed Stephen. They just had time to push into the undergrowth amongst the closest trees when they heard the men's voices.

Roger gestured to lie down. "This'll do. Keep still!" he hissed. They lay flat, hearts thumping.

The men walked up over the rise talking angrily. They looked neither left nor right and were clearly in a bad mood. As they went past Roger shuddered with relief. From where he lay he got glimpses of the men as they skirted the fallen log. To keep them in sight he moved and raised his head. He could just see part of the 4WD beyond the track junction.

The men went to the vehicles and the boys lost sight of them but heard doors open and close and metallic noises.

Stephen tugged at Roger's sleeve. "Come on Roger. Let's get out of here," he whispered, pushing his glasses back up his nose with one finger.

"Not yet. This is interesting. Let's just creep down through this thick patch to see if we can get a clear view of that clearing."

Stephen shook his head but followed him as he began a careful crawl down around a thicket of spiky palms. Suddenly he gripped Roger by the ankle.

Roger froze but no explanation was necessary. The two men were returning from the vehicles. The boys were now a good 10 metres in from the old road and quite safe from observation. They waited till they heard the men pass down into the clearing before continuing to creep forward.

"Ah!" Roger breathed. He had found just the spot. At that point as the slope dipped again yet another old snig track went off down to the right. Here there were thick bushes on the bank above it and a clear view out into the clearing. The boys crouched behind them and peered through their leaves.

"Digging a hole," Stephen observed.

"Yes. They must have found it," Roger replied. Once again he was a, tingle with excitement. The men had brought machetes and another shovel and mattock. They began to clear the bushes and then marked out an area indicated by the old man.

Bruno then began loosening the hard, red clay with the mattock.

"He's not enjoying that," Roger sniggered.

Stephen didn't reply. After a while Bruno stood aside and the other two shovelled the loosened soil away. Roger glanced at his watch. It was ten to four! Reluctantly he decided it was time to go. But he did want to be there to see the treasure unearthed!

He was just about to tell Stephen when Bruno handed the mattock to 'Glasses' and, on the instructions of the old man, picked up his rifle and began walking back up the track.

For a horrible moment Roger thought they must have been seen or heard but as he watched he decided that Bruno had been sent on another errand. He waited till Bruno passed from view then whispered to Stephen. "When he comes back, we will get out of here."

"About time too," Stephen replied.

They lay and watched the digging. The old man just stood and looked on. The other two took turns. That it was very hard digging was plain from the slow progress and the size of the clods hacked loose. Both diggers discarded their shirts and sweated freely.

"Bruno's taking a long time," Stephen muttered angrily.

"Yes he is," Roger replied. He looked at his watch again. 1610hrs; 20 minutes. Where could the man be? What could he be doing? A horrible suspicion formed in Roger's mind that Bruno might be stalking them. This caused such a flutter of panic that for a minute or two he couldn't think straight. He forced himself to calm down.

Stop it you coward! he told himself. *Be logical. If those men thought we were here, they would take much more direct action.*

He turned to Stephen. "Let's go. We will find out what he's doing."

Roger again led the way. He crawled back for 20 metres until positive they could not be seen from the clearing. Then he slowly rose to his feet, his joints protesting and sore muscles stiff. Then, careful step by careful step, he made his way around the side of the hill to near the roots of the fallen tree.

What he saw at once relieved and dismayed him. Bruno wasn't stalking them. He was sitting on the bonnet of the 4WD with his rifle cradled across his lap, looking back along the track towards the main road.

Stephen crept up beside Roger. "What can you see? What's going on?" he whispered.

"Bruno. He's sitting there on sentry duty. At least he looks like he's on guard. Strewth, I hope Graham and Peter don't come looking for us," Roger replied.

"We will have to go round him," Stephen replied. Roger nodded.

Stephen now took charge. He set his compass for West, then began slowly making his way down the steep slope in that direction.

It was difficult to move silently. There were so many dead twigs in the leaf mould and Bruno was only 50 metres away. Step by step the two cadets edged downhill, gripping small trees for support, avoiding vines and spiky bushes. They had to weave around fallen logs and through a patch of wait-a-while.

Here Stephen got caught up. He avoided the more obvious thicker tendrils but a thin one caught the back of his shirt. He stopped almost at once but not before the bush had been pulled and leaves set rustling. The two cadets froze.

Had Bruno heard them?

After a moment Stephen eased backwards. Both knew what to do. Never pull at wait-a-while! The curved barbs just dug in deeper and the vines are too strong for a human to break. You have to take the tension off then roll gently away. Roger helped by gripping the offending tendril in his fingers, ignoring the sharp pricking.

The slope got steeper as they went down and the undergrowth became thicker with more and more wait-a-while. Stephen stopped. "We are heading into some sort of a creek. Do you think we've come down far enough?"

Roger looked back. He estimated they were only about a hundred paces down the slope, perhaps 50 metres.

"No. Twice that distance at least. Keep going," he murmured.

They resumed their slow descent.

Further down Roger got snagged by wait-a-while. The barbs hooked the sleeve of his shirt. He stopped and backed up, then peeled the tendril off. It came clear of the cloth with a ripping sound. Roger let go of the tendril, but it swung from the palm frond overhead. Instinctively Roger put his hand up to ward it off. At the same moment his right foot slipped on the rotting vegetation underfoot.

"Ow! Bloody thing!" Roger cried softly.

He pulled away and stepped back, into another hanging tendril.

"Hold on Roger. I'll help. You've cut your hand," Stephen said.

Roger looked. Four holes in the skin on the outside of his right palm suddenly had drops of blood appear. These overflowed and a sticky red trickle ran down the fingers. Roger put his hand in his mouth and sucked. The smell and taste of the blood made him nauseous.

"Not your day," Stephen observed as he unhooked the tendril.

Roger mumbled some swear words then followed Stephen on down the slope. They seemed to be well away from Bruno by this, over a hundred metres but Roger insisted they go on down for another hundred paces.

"Better to be sure than sorry," he grunted. He was irritated and uncomfortable. By now he felt tired, sore and very thirsty and he was eaten up by curiosity about what the men were digging for. The blood trickles on his hand dried up and he forgot about them.

The compass bearing took them out of the re-entrant and down the side of a steep spur, line. They crossed the spine of this and halted for a moment to look. An overgrown snig track went on down it. A trampled plant showed that the men had been down it.

"This will do. Let's head north to the main road," Roger said.

Stephen pulled out his map and a pencil and they made a guess where they were.

"About forty-five degrees for about 300 metres, say 500 paces, should do it," Stephen decided. He put the map away and set his compass.

Roger nodded agreement. He was well aware that the Cadets used the same system as the Australian Army, navigating by mils with 6,400 mils in a circle, but he also found working in degrees mathematically simpler and just as accurate for navigational purposes.

They continued their detour, pushing through a clump of huge, broad, leaved plants that were taller than them, then past a tree with huge moss-covered buttress roots, then past another tree caught in the parasitic embrace of a strangler, vine. The bearing led them steeply downhill.

It became so steep they had to use both hands to grip the smaller trees as they went down. Several large clumps of wait-a-while caused detours of 10 metres or so. Both boys were sweating freely and became grimy around the hands and neck. A huge butterfly with brilliant blue wings fluttered past.

The bottom of the slope was a small creek bed. There was no running water, just damp leaves and moss-covered rocks. Down there the boys were in the shadow of the next ridge by then and it was quite gloomy. The far side of the small watercourse was so steep they had to look around for a way to haul themselves up.

Stephen dragged himself up into a thicket of small saplings with difficulty. Roger went a few paces up the creek bed towards an easier place.

"Aah!" he cried aloud.

Before he even looked, he knew what it was. Fierce waves of sharp pain lanced from his left, hand up his arm.

Stinging Tree! He swore, then cried again and waved his left hand in the air. The blasted bush was obvious when he looked for it. He had brushed one of the heart-shaped leaves with its distinctive serrated edge. There were several stinging trees there he now saw. The thousands of tiny white poison bristles were plain to see.

The pain was intense. Roger gripped his wrist with his right hand while tears flowed down his cheeks. His vision blurred and he hopped around. It took a real effort to stop crying out again. Stephen stood further up the slope waiting. He looked sympathetic and Roger knew there was nothing he could do to help.

If circumstances had permitted Roger would have tried to remove as many of the tiny white bristles as he could. He could see them, like unshaven hairs, stuck in the palm of his left hand. The outside of the little finger had collected the most. Sticking plaster gently eased on might have removed some when it was pulled off; or careful plucking one by one with tweezers. But there wasn't time (and his tweezers were in his pack).

As the first waves of pain subsided Roger wiped his eyes, swore again then gritted his teeth and reached up to a tree to pull himself up the slope. That hurt too as the bristles were driven in or broken off and he knew he would feel the sting for months to come.

Every time I wet my hand or it gets cold, the tiny poison barbs will activate, he thought morosely.

Trying to ignore the stabbing agony, he hauled himself up to join Stephen who murmured. "I said it wasn't your day!"

"Just lead on. Aw, bugger it hurts," Roger replied through clenched teeth.

He checked his watch. It was nearly five o'clock! Worry helped push the pain aside. What were Graham and Peter doing all this time?

Chapter 10

A LONG WAY FROM HELP

For 15 hot and sweaty minutes, Roger and Stephen finished their climb up through the jungle. They emerged from a particularly thick patch of wait-a-while onto the main road. Stephen was in front. He crawled up the steep slope and took a cautious look over the top.

"We are just around the bend from the track junction I think," he whispered.

Roger, feeling hot and flushed, made his way painfully up to join him. He wasn't sure if that was from the stinging tree or the start of heat exhaustion. The two cadets climbed up onto the road and looked at the steep slope of the cutting opposite them.

"Which way will we go? We can't climb that," Stephen said.

"Just walk around to where we left Peter and Graham," Roger replied.

"Their guard might see us," Stephen reminded. He took off his glasses and gave them a worried polish.

"Not if he's still at their vehicles," replied Roger. By this time he was too sick and sore to care very much.

Stephen shrugged. He didn't feel like arguing. The two began walking along the road. There was no breeze and everything was very still and quiet. The treetops had sunlight on them, but they were in the evening shade.

They slowed as they rounded the corner where the timber track joined but there was no sign of anyone. As they reached the actual junction, they became even more cautious and went forward a step at a time till they could see down the side-track. It was deserted.

"Pssst. Hey! Pssst."

Roger jumped with fright and looked around at the soft noise. At once he saw Graham and Peter. They were up on top of the cutting opposite. He nudged Stephen and pointed.

"Oh, thank God! Come on," Stephen said.

The pair walked quickly along the road to where the cutting came down to the small re-entrant. Peter and Graham met them there.

"Where the hell have you two been?" Graham hissed angrily.

"We went to have a look; to see what the crooks are up to," Roger replied.

"You what!" Graham gasped. "You pair of bloody fools! We've been sitting here nearly an hour worried sick."

"Sorry," Roger replied. "But it was worth it."

"What did you see?" Peter asked.

Stephen replied. "The men are searching for something."

"They're digging up the treasure right now," Roger added.

"Not all of them," Peter answered. "Your mate Bruno walked out to the track junction not 10 minutes ago. He had his rifle."

Roger felt ill at the thought of how close they had come to disaster. "He's on guard," he replied.

"Well you are damned lucky he didn't see you," Graham replied. "He stopped and looked down the slope where you two came from. Then he took something blue off the back of a tree beside the turnoff, looked at it and walked back down the track."

"Took something blue?" Roger asked. He had to swallow to prevent the words coming out as a croak.

"Piece of paper, I think. It was hard to tell," Peter replied.

The boys were standing just in the edge of the trees at this point.

"Should we move further in?" Stephen asked.

"I need a drink. Let's go to our webbing," Roger replied.

"What about watching the turnoff?" Stephen asked.

Graham shook his head. "We will hear their vehicles if they start up." He looked at his watch. "It's five twenty. It will be dark in half an hour. We'd better have tea while it's light and plan our next move."

"Why? What did the police say?" Roger asked.

"We didn't get to contact them. There was no-one there. All the buildings were locked. Come on. We can talk about it later," Graham replied.

Graham led the way back through the scrub above the road. A few minutes of scrambling along the hillside brought them to where their discarded gear lay scattered on the ground. Roger and Stephen both took out water bottles and drank greedily.

"Where will we go?" Peter asked.

"To the top of the hill. There's a good spot to camp," Graham replied.

"Is it out of sight and sound of those men?" Stephen asked.

Graham nodded. "Yes, it is," he replied.

"Not too far. We want to be able to hear if they drive off," Roger said.

"We'll be able to," Graham said. He swung on his gear and started up the slope.

The twilight was setting in fast, so they walked quickly, making no effort to be silent, other than talking softly. After about 50 paces the rain forest opened out to be mostly tall, thin trees with almost no undergrowth and a carpet of dry leaves.

The top of the hill came into view after another hundred paces. By then Roger was sweating and puffing. He was sharply reminded of the stinging tree sting after grabbing a sapling to haul himself up the slope.

The crest of the hill levelled out and they came out onto an old timber road. This was thickly carpeted by leaves and obviously had not been used for years. The line of the road was quite clear as no undergrowth grew on it. Roger assumed this was because the overhanging tree canopies blocked most of the sunlight.

Peter looked around. "This is what we want," he said.

"I think I know where this old road joins the main road," Roger added.

Graham pointed ahead. "Just down there. We came up it half an hour ago," he replied.

Peter nodded and added. "This is the old road we walked along during Senior Ex last year, when we went to attack the pretend fort."

Stephen agreed and they began to discuss the exercise. Graham stopped them when both took off their packs. "We won't stop here. We will camp just along there, in that bit of a dip."

He led the way a hundred paces westwards along the old track to where it ran onto a low bench cut. An old bulldozer scrape in a small hollow right on the crest of the ridge provided a convenient flat space.

Graham dropped his pack and looked around in the gathering gloom. "There's another old track just there. It runs down the spur to where we were watching. We will camp here. The men won't hear us if we talk but we will still be able to hear their vehicles."

"Can we light our stoves?" Stephen asked.

Graham nodded. "Yes. They won't see us from anywhere on the main road. And I don't think the smell of the hexamine will carry that far.

We should be safe here. I don't think they suspect we are anywhere in the area, unless they saw or heard you two."

"I'm sure they didn't," Roger replied, looking to Stephen for confirmation. He nodded.

Peter suddenly pointed to Roger's hand. "You okay Roger? What's wrong with your hand?" he asked.

"Which one?" Roger replied ruefully holding up both hands. He recounted his minor injuries as he eased his gear to the ground.

"I hope it was worth it," Graham said.

"It was," Roger replied. He then sat on his pack and proceeded to describe what he and Stephen had seen. While he talked, they all pulled out hexamine stoves and lit them. The flames gave a cheerful glow which helped restore their spirits.

Roger put on water to boil and had another drink. Two of his four water bottles were then empty. He shook one ruefully then said, "I tell you, when I was standing in the middle of that track and I saw them two blokes come around the corner I nearly wet meself."

Stephen added his comments. "We had to lie in the bloody leaves for nearly a bloody hour and now I'm starting to itch."

"Pair of bloody fools," Graham repeated, but he and Peter were intensely interested in the story.

By the time Roger had made a cup of Milo it was quite dark. The air was very still, with no breeze. Through a gap in the tree canopy he could see there were no clouds. It was very quiet, apart from a few insect noises, crickets and the like.

"I haven't heard a car for a while," Stephen observed as he stirred a mess tin of meat and onions.

"No. There hasn't been one since we left you about two o'clock," Peter replied. "We hoped one would come along so we could hitch a ride but none did."

"What happened?" Roger asked. The sweet Milo tasted wonderful.

"We walked back to the Forestry Barracks no trouble," Graham replied, "but there was no-one there. We looked around, then sat down and wondered what to do. We thought of phoning but all the buildings were locked and we didn't feel like breaking in."

"So what took you so long?" Stephen asked.

"Well, we sat there for half an hour hoping someone would come along. Then we walked back to the old house beside the road, you know, near Lake Euramo, but it was deserted."

"Then what?"

Peter answered. "We thought of walking to Robsons Creek but decided it was too far," he said.

Roger shuddered at the thought of that much effort and drained the last of the Milo.

Graham continued. "We sat for another fifteen minutes hoping a car would come along, tourists or something. But none did."

"And we tried to come up with a story in case the car was the crooks," Peter added with a grin.

Graham went on, "Anyway, we just started walking back to here at quarter to four. We came up this track and went down that overgrown one there which I guessed led to the road junction. When we got there, we looked around for you and got really worried when we couldn't find you."

"I went and checked the gear," Peter added. He had opened a tin of corned beef and was eating it cold.

Roger took out a tin of Chinese sweet and sour pork. It was now so dark he put his torch in his mouth so he could see while he opened it.

Stephen swallowed a spoonful of food and then asked, "What will we do now?"

Graham answered. "I thought we might walk back to the Forestry Barracks again. The men should have come back from work after five. They should be there now."

"Who's going? All of us?" Stephen asked.

"No. Only two. Two can stay and watch; or rather listen," Graham replied. "I'll go. Who wants to come with me?"

Roger had a sudden yearning to see electric light and other people. To his own surprise he said he would go.

"You sure Roger?" Graham asked doubtfully.

"Yeah. I need more water anyway."

"Don't wear yourself out. We're going to have to step it out tomorrow to make up lost time," Graham reminded.

On hearing that Roger mentally groaned but he merely nodded.

Stephen ate another mouthful then asked, "How far have we come so far?"

"About twenty-five kilometres," Graham replied.

"So we now do seventy-five k's in three days?" Stephen said.

Roger grimaced. "Steady on. It's not a bloody death march," he snapped.

There was an embarrassed silence for a moment. Roger stirred the food heating in his mess tin. The others busied themselves with cooking and eating.

The warm food helped restore Roger. His left hand still throbbed and there was a lump in the glands under his left armpit, but the intense sting had subsided. He drank some more and ate a couple of biscuits. As he munched them, he wondered why on earth he inflicted such pains on himself. *I'm certainly not a masochist,* he told himself. But he knew why he came on hikes. These were his friends, and he had a deep need to belong to the group.

Stephen spoke next. "Will we light a fire?" he asked as he wiped his mess tins clean with toilet paper.

Graham shook his head. "No. Better not. The glow might show in the trees and it will spoil our night vision," he replied.

"What about sentries?" Peter asked.

Graham thought for a moment. "I suppose we'd better, only one person though."

"Why bother? Those blokes don't know we are here, and they won't come blundering about the jungle in the dark," Stephen replied.

"Maybe not. But it's better to be sure than sorry. Besides we need to be sure we wake up early," Graham answered.

"How early?" Roger asked. He hated early rising.

"Six o'clock. So we can be on the road by seven," Graham replied.

"I still don't reckon we need a sentry," Stephen persisted. "We will get too tired. My watch has an alarm."

Roger spoke up. "Yes we do. What if the crooks drive off tonight or early in the morning? And how will we meet the cops when they arrive?"

Graham said, "Roger's right. Sentry duty it is. Two hours on. Let's see. If we start at eight, that's in fifteen minutes, we should all get about six hours sleep. That's enough."

Stephen grumbled but accepted this. "What's the roster?"

"You and Peter work one out while Roger and I walk to the Forestry Barracks. We should be back by ten," Graham replied.

"Then the police will arrive and we will be up half the night," Peter said.

"Too bad. It's got to be done."

"Will we put up hutchies?" Roger asked. He had turned off his torch after packing his stove and eating gear. With no fires or torches it was very dark. He literally could not see his hand in front of his face. He tried it. It gave him a very claustrophobic feeling. A hutchie might not keep anything out but it gave the illusion of security.

"No," Graham answered. "No hutchies. It won't rain and there won't be any dew under these trees. We'd better get going. Come on Roger."

"Just a minute Graham. Who else needs water bottles refilled?" Roger asked.

Peter and Stephen both did so Roger took these and hung them on his webbing. He put this on and took out his torch.

"Can we use a torch?" he asked. He had no desire to walk without a light two kilometres along a jungle road knowing that the snakes would be out hunting. He also knew Graham well enough to guess that he had planned on doing just that, despite a keen fear of snakes.

Graham considered, then grudgingly conceded. "Aw. okay I suppose. The crooks aren't likely to see us. Let's go."

The two set off down the old road in the direction of the Forestry Barracks. Both held their torches low so their beams shone on the ground a couple of metres ahead. They had to take some care as there were a few small washouts and the odd fallen branch. Another 2 minutes walking found them on the main road where it ran due west along the ridge top.

Even though there were gaps in the tree canopy it was still very dark. Graham stopped for a moment and turned off his torch.

"Sssh! Let's listen for a moment."

The two stood silent. Roger reluctantly turned off his own torch and felt so oppressed and threatened by the enveloping blackness that he had to fight down the urge to turn it on again.

Apart from the gentle sighing of the wind in the trees there was not another sound.

Roger had an intense feeling of isolation.

Graham grunted with satisfaction. "Good, let's move."

"What will we do if a car comes along? Do we flag it down or hide?" Roger asked as they began walking side by side, torches once more on.

"Flag it down," Graham replied.

"What if it is the crooks?"

"We tell them one of us has got sick and we are going to phone his parents."

"What sort of sickness?" Roger asked.

"Oh I don't know, the flu I suppose."

"What about a fever, say from ticks or something like that," Roger suggested. He was feeling a bit feverish himself and had broken into a gentle sweat.

"Good idea."

They walked in silence for a few minutes. A sudden scuffling in the leaves made Roger stop in fright.

"What's that?" he cried, shining his torch around. The beam exposed a large rat which stared in surprise before scampering out of sight.

"Only a bandicoot," Graham laughed.

"I thought it might have been a wild pig," Roger replied.

"Shut up Roger. Stop thinking about things or you'll put the wind up yourself," Graham advised.

Roger bit his lip and made no reply as they continued to walk. It was easy to say and hard to do. *And easy for Graham. He's brave,* he thought.

After less than 10 minutes, they reached the road junction where the road switched back on itself and went down the north side of the mountain. Roger found it easier going and said nothing. The two just tramped quietly along. There were several more minor frights from unidentified nocturnal creatures and once the swish of dark wings overhead. At length the road straightened out and they emerged from the tunnel of rainforest.

"It isn't much further is it? It's just along here somewhere isn't it?" Roger asked, looking eagerly ahead for the first glimmer of electric light.

"Stop for a minute and turn off your torch," Graham commanded.

Roger did so and they stood silently. The straight road became visible as a grey blur bordered by pitch black.

"What's wrong?" Roger asked, sensing Graham's concern.

"I think we are going to find no-one home again. The barracks is just on our left and there isn't a light to be seen," Graham replied.

Roger felt a surge of dismay and a quite irrational spasm of fear.

"What will we do?" he asked.

"Go and have a look."

Chapter 11

THE JUNGLE AT NIGHT

Graham turned on his torch and resumed walking. Roger hurried to catch up. Both shone their torches off through the trees to the left. Roger saw they were pine trees and could just discern a building but neither torch was powerful enough to light up things more than a few metres away.

After 2 minutes walking, the beam of Graham's torch pointed out the turnoff and entrance to the barracks yard. The row of buildings began beside it, all black and silent.

"Maybe they've gone to bed," Roger suggested. He felt very disappointed and worried.

"Fair go Roger! It's only eight p.m. More likely they've gone to town."

"Will we wait?"

"For half an hour maybe. Let's have a look around," Graham replied. He led the way in through the open gate and walked up a short flight of steps onto a timber veranda. He shone his torch on the door of the building and in a window.

Roger felt very uneasy about it. "Come on Graham, let's go back to the others," he said. To his shame his voice had a distinct quaver in it. By an effort of will power he mastered it. "I don't like this. It's spooky and we could get into trouble for trespassing."

"Rot Roger! Let's fill our water bottles anyway. There's a tap just there," Graham retorted. He clumped down the steps and walked to a tap at the corner of the building.

Roger followed and they stood and filled all the water bottles and had a drink. As they did the wind moaned in the pine trees and Roger found the silent buildings very threatening. A feeling of intense isolation crept over him as it occurred to him that the nearest house where there would be people with electric light and a telephone was probably 25 kilometres one way or 10 kilometres the other, and all through the jungle.

Graham sat down on the steps, took out his map and studied it using his torch.

Roger looked over his shoulder. "What will we do Graham?" he asked, trying not to let the nervousness (or was it just plain funk!) show.

"I suppose we could walk to one of these farmhouses out to the southeast. It would only take a couple of hours if we stepped it out," Graham replied.

The thought of 'stepping it out' was bad enough for Roger but the prospect of those seemingly endless kilometres through the dark jungle was more than he wanted to face.

"It's not that urgent is it? I mean, it can wait till tomorrow can't it?" he said.

"I thought you wanted these crooks caught Roger."

"I do, but it's not an emergency and the police will soon pick them up when we give them the descriptions and vehicle numbers," Roger replied. In his heart he knew that the march Graham was contemplating would be a real ordeal. He also knew Graham was quite capable of it. On other occasions he had done just that. That got Roger thinking about the previous year at Stannary Hills when Graham had walked much further than that, at night, and with a damaged arm and injured ankle, to save Peter and Stephen from some thieves.

In an attempt to dismiss this idea Roger said, "Besides, our torches wouldn't last that long." He blushed, knowing it sounded lame, so he cast about in his mind seeking for further good reasons.

Graham grinned and folded his map up. "OK mate. We won't go. We will just go back to the others and make an early start instead. Come on."

Roger felt simultaneous relief and shame. He knew Graham guessed he was scared but also sensed that it didn't affect their friendship.

They made their way back out onto the main road and began the walk home. The darkness was just as frightening and the steep uphill stretch reduced Roger to a sweating, panting wreck but he didn't stop. He forced himself on. All he wanted was to get back to the safety of their camp. In part of his mind he knew the safety was illusory but the place still represented sanctuary.

By pushing himself he managed to keep up and even to recover his breath a little on the stretch along the ridge top.

God it's dark! he thought, dismayed by the whole situation.

He heaved an audible sigh of relief when the beam of Graham's torch lit up the overgrown turnoff of the old road. They went up it in silence. The stiff climb for two hundred metres again made Roger's heart hammer at an alarming rate and his breath was coming in hot gasps by the time they reached the camp.

Stephen sat on guard. Peter was asleep.

"Anything happen while we were away?" Graham asked.

"Not a thing. Did you contact the police?"

"No. Nobody home," Graham replied. He gave a brief description of their walk. Peter stirred and rolled over.

Roger eased off his webbing. All around his waist was sore from chafing and where the equipment had dug into his too ample flesh. Ruefully he rubbed it while looking for his pack. While the others talked quietly he cleared sticks and leaves away to make a bed, space. Then he dug a hip-hole and unrolled his bedding. Thankfully he sat down on it.

"Can we have a brew?" he asked.

"Yes. I'm going to," replied Graham who was engaged in the same chores.

"What about boots?" Roger queried.

"You can have one if you like. I'm going to have coffee," Graham replied.

"What do you mean? Oh. I get it. I meant, can we take our boots off?"

"No. We are in the presence of the enemy I reckon," Graham replied.

Roger had expected this and he didn't grumble. In their cadet unit when they were 'tactical' with an Opposing Force they slept fully dressed and with their boots on.

The boys prepared supper in silence so as not to wake Peter. The glow of flames was wonderfully heartening to Roger and the warm, sweet drink restored some of his spirits. He pulled a chocolate from his pack, broke off four squares and passed them to the others. Stephen thanked him but declined. Graham loved chocolate and accepted.

Roger then packed his stove and cup and stretched out on his sleeping bag with his pack for a pillow. As the perspiration dried, he felt a bit chilled, but was aware that it wasn't really a cold night. Over the next 20 minutes he lay silently, popping squares of chocolate into his mouth and savouring them as they slowly melted.

Sometime later he was shaken awake by Graham. He opened his eyes, then tried again before realising it was so dark it made almost no difference.

"What? What is it?" he asked muzzily.

"Roll on your side. You were snoring. You'd better get into your sleeping bag too. It's getting a bit chilly," came Graham's voice, quiet but reassuring.

"Sorry. What time is it?" Roger replied.

"A bit after midnight," Graham answered.

Roger was amazed. They had returned to camp at 9:30 pm. "Strewth! Isn't it dark."

Graham chuckled. "Too bloody right!"

"I'm on sentry next, aren't I?"

"Yeah. In about three, quarters of an hour. Go back to sleep."

Roger squirmed into his sleeping bag and was amazed how stiff and sore his muscles were. He had trouble getting back to sleep, but he lay quiet and pretended to be. Once again, he drifted into a deep, dreamless sleep, to be roused at 0100hrs by Graham.

Roger sat up and rubbed sleep from his eyes. It was still pitch dark, with no moon and no wind. He assured Graham he was awake, then had a drink and rubbed his eyes with wet fingers to help freshen up. Groaning softly at his sore muscles he got out of his sleeping bag and stood up. It was just cold enough to need a jacket, so he extracted this from his pack and pulled it on.

Then he stood for a while flexing his legs. Graham fidgeted for a while as he made himself comfortable and then almost complete silence settled. Roger listened in wonder. Even the usual small night noises: crickets, lizards, frogs and so on, seemed absent.

Once again Roger had the impression of being very isolated and the knowledge of the men in black less than half a kilometre away added to a deep feeling of concern. (He refused to concede it was fear.) One consequence was a continual shifting of position to look and listen in different directions.

As he stood there, Roger went over in his mind the events of the last two days. He also gently rubbed his chafed skin and sore muscles. Not knowing who the men were or what they were searching for now nagged at Roger's mind as insistently as his bodily aches.

So they were Kosarians. Well, maybe not, but Boris Krapinski was a Kosarian. That idea led to the presumption that they were the murderers. Roger was sure they were but uneasily recognised this feeling of certainty was not based on real proof and he was, possibly, being unjust.

But the guns, the black clothing, the odd behaviour and the police interest? It all looks very suspicious, he thought. *And who, or what, are the KSS?*

Roger had a wristwatch with a small light in it. He checked the time: 0145hrs. *It's going to be a long night,* he mused. He sat down to massage his thigh and calf muscles, then had another drink.

So the two hours of his duty slowly passed, the thoughts and fears going round and round in his head. Nothing disturbed the night and the other three slept on, stirring from time to time to change position. Roger became bored and tiredness began to drag his eyelids down. Aware that he was in danger of nodding off he shook himself and washed his face. Then he stood up again to stop dozing off.

At last 0300hrs came round. Roger walked carefully the 5 paces to where Peter slept. As he did his boots crunched on the dry leaves and Graham stirred and looked up. Roger shook Peter awake and waited until he assured him he was ready and wouldn't go back to sleep.

"Anything happen?" Peter asked.

"Not a thing. Don't forget to wake Stephen at five o'clock," Roger replied.

"Don't worry about that," Peter replied with a soft laugh.

Roger groped his way back to his bedding and thankfully slid into his sleeping bag. He was asleep in minutes.

Roger was so tired that he slept soundly for the next three hours with only an occasional movement to ease his discomfort.

He was shaken awake by Peter. With an effort he opened his eyes and rolled onto his back. It was still dark.

"What is it?" he asked, dimly aware that Graham and Stephen were awake too.

Peter answered. "Six o'clock. Time to get up."

"But it's still dark!"

Graham spoke. "Tough! Up you get Roger. Roll up your bedding straight away and get ready to move."

"Will we have breakfast first?" Roger asked.

"Yes, as soon as everything else is packed."

"What will we do then, go back to the Forestry Barracks?"

"No. Push on till we come to a farmhouse."

Roger squirmed out of his sleeping bag and rubbed his eyes. By feel he straightened out the bedding on the groundsheet, then rolled it up, kneeling on it after each roll while he dusted off dirt and leaves which clung to the plastic. The bedroll was strapped into the bottom of his pack within a couple of minutes. This was a drill they often did on cadet exercises, so he had no difficulty with it. Then he stood and stretched.

At once all his aches and pains returned and he became aware his left hand was throbbing from the stinging tree. He didn't feel at all like a forced march carrying a pack. After going to the toilet he washed his hands and instantly regretted it. The water activated the poison barbs of the stinging tree which were now embedded in his flesh and they stung!

As waves of pain shot up his arm he moaned and muttered and fluttered his hand in the air. It was just starting to get light and he could see the shapes of the others.

"You okay Roger?" Stephen asked.

"Yeah. Just that bloody stinging tree."

The others were sympathetic but there was nothing they could do to help. Roger sat on his pack and held the sore hand as the pain slowly subsided. Graham removed a boot, powdered his foot and placed on a clean sock.

"Phew! What a pong!" Peter chided.

"Washing day if we pass a creek," Graham replied. He sniffed at his shirt. Roger noted that his own sweat soaked uniform had a definite reek to it.

After seating himself on his pack Roger took out his stove and a tin of steak and kidney. It was still quite gloomy so the flare of the match and the flicker of flames cheered him up. The smell of sulphur and then of hexamine made him instantly feel hungry and happy.

Things aren't so bad after all, he thought. In fact, apart from his sore hand and a few scratches, aches and pains, he felt okay.

As he opened the can and emptied it into a mess tin to heat they discussed the events of the previous afternoon and night. This re-awakened Roger's interest.

"I'm bursting to know what those blokes are looking for," he said.

"Is that what it is? I just thought you ate too much," Stephen replied. He looked tired and grumpy.

The jibe hurt but Roger ignored it. "I wonder if they've dug the treasure up yet. Do you think we should go and look? I thought two of us could stay and watch while the other two went to phone the police," he suggested.

Graham looked up from his cooking. "Fair go Rog. You took an awful risk yesterday. Besides we've got our hike to get on with. Don't you want to do that?"

"Not particularly," Roger replied.

Stephen looked up from his cooking. "Then why the bloody hell did you come with us? You've been a bloody drag right from the start, moaning and dropping behind. You're too bloody fat and unfit and..."

Graham cut in. "That'll do Steve. Let's not fight among ourselves, and keep your voice down or those blokes might hear us," he said.

"Bugger them!" Stephen snapped back. "I don't care about them. They won't bother us if we mind our own business."

"We shall, once we contact the police. That will be the end of it," Graham replied.

Peter stopped drinking coffee and spoke up for the first time. "Should we phone the OC at the same time? He told us to keep out of trouble remember."

Graham shook his head. "No. I don't think so. We haven't been in trouble yet. We've just been delayed," he replied.

It was fully light by this and a brightness through the leaves to the east heralded the sunrise. A kookaburra woke the echoes with its laugh. Then cockatoos began screeching down the ridge. Roger had just placed a mess tin of water on his stove and picked up the other mess tin to start to eat. He paused, spoon halfway to his mouth.

"Hear those cockatoos? I'll bet those men have just woken up."

"If they're still there," Stephen said.

"We didn't hear them leave," Peter said. In the distance there was the sound of a sharp but unmistakable 'crack'.

"Gunshot!" Graham said.

They listened for a moment. The screeching of the cockatoos grew louder, then rose and fell indicating the birds had taken flight. Then the awful racket receded as the birds flew away southwards.

"One of those blokes took a pot shot at the cockatoos I reckon," Peter said.

Roger was indignant. "But it's against the law to shoot in a State Forest. And cockatoos are protected," Roger said indignantly.

Graham gave a dry laugh. "So are men. I reckon if you've murdered a bloke, you wouldn't be too worried about shooting a few birds."

Stephen pushed his glasses up and looked up. "Give it a break Graham! You're as bad as Roger. We don't know those blokes are murderers. We've no proof. They might be just pinching orchids," he suggested.

Peter laughed softly. "Orchids grow in trees Steve. Why are they digging that hole?"

Stephen didn't answer. The conversation lapsed while they finished their breakfast. Graham kept looking at his watch and Roger knew he was going to start urging them to move. He wiped his mess tins and packed them and the stove. Then he stood and cleaned his teeth. While the others shaved Roger turned his back and unbuttoned his shirt and the waistband of his trousers. For the next 2 minutes he searched himself for ticks and leeches. He was appalled at all the bruises and chafing he found but there were no ticks.

After that he combed his hair and gave his face a rinse. Taking care, he wiped a smear of tick repellent around the openings in his clothing. Then he was ready to go. The others soon finished their packing. Graham checked his watch again. "Nearly seven o'clock. Everyone ready? Then let's move."

Reluctantly Roger swung on his webbing and pack, causing the stinging to start in his hand again. The friends stood for a minute adjusting their gear and settling it comfortably. Stephen bent and picked up his hat.

"Aaargh!" he cried, throwing the hat down.

The others turned in surprise.

"A spider!" Stephen said. "A bloody great spider in my hat."

"Spider!" Roger snorted. He was closest so he bent and picked the hat up and looked inside it. Then he turned it over. If there had been one he couldn't see it. "It's gone now," he said, handing the hat to Stephen. The incident gave him malicious pleasure, which he instantly regretted.

Graham gave a wry smile then turned and started walking.

Chapter 12

THE MORNINGS WALK

G raham began walking and they followed him. He went back the way they had come up the previous afternoon, walking along the old road then turning off to go down the slope through the rainforest.

Halfway down the hill the sound of a motor starting up made them stop.

"Is that them? Or just a car on the road?" Peter asked.

Roger listened, then cried, "Them for sure. Come on! Let's get down closer to the road so we can see." He quickly pushed his way around Stephen.

"They're on the move early," Stephen commented.

"They must have dug up the treasure and are getting away, quick!" Roger replied. He tried to run but kept getting snagged by trees and vines. Then his right foot caught and he almost tripped, only saving himself by clutching at a vine. The result was that he stumbled and cannoned into a tree, bruising his right shoulder. The others came pushing down through the jungle behind him.

Graham called, "Slow down Roger, you'll break something."

But Roger didn't. *I have to know,* he told himself.

Regardless of bumps and scratches he went on blundering down the slope. He heard the engine noise change, then die away, then increase in volume, then die and rise several more times.

It was the 4WD and it was on the move. Roger began to get glimpses of the road below him but he was too far from the turnoff to see that.

If the vehicle goes back towards Danbulla we won't see it, he thought.

When Roger was only about 20 paces from the road, the engine noise abruptly grew in volume and the vehicle came into view around the bend to his right. Roger stopped behind a tree and watched. He could just see through gaps in the jungle.

It was the men in black alright. Roger saw the hawk-faced old man sitting in the passenger seat as the 4WD went past. It was followed almost at once by the black car with the blond-haired man driving. Bruno sat beside him. The men were still all dressed in black. The men in the vehicles did not look up into the rainforest and both vehicles quickly vanished from sight heading downhill to the east.

"They've got away!" Roger wailed.

"Doesn't matter. The cops will pick them up," Graham replied.

"They might not," Peter suggested. "They could go down the Gillies Highway and be in Cairns in less than two hours. They could go the international airport and fly out of the country in three hours, say by ten o'clock. We'd be hard pressed to reach a phone before then."

"We will hitch a ride with the first car that comes along," Graham replied. They went on down the slope and stepped out onto the road.

"I want to see what they dug up," Roger said.

Graham gave a wry grin. "They'll have it with them Roger."

"Yes I know, but I still want to see."

Stephen wasn't amused. "Don't be bloody silly Roger. It will waste half an hour while we walk back there," he said irritably.

"I still want to see," said Roger stubbornly.

Graham looked at his watch. "We can't afford the time."

Roger was adamant. "You go on. I'll catch up. I'm going back to look."

Stephen sneered. "You! Catch up!" he cried.

Roger ignored him. He swung off his pack and, forgetful of his sore hand, dumped it in the bushes beside the road.

Stephen swore, and said, "This is bloody ridiculous! We'll never finish this bloody hike. I'm going on. Bugger Roger!" He looked at the other two. Peter shrugged.

Graham took off his hat and ruffled his hair, then shrugged and said, "You two go on ahead. We will catch you up."

Graham's pack joined Roger's in the weeds, and he strode off after him. Peter shook his head and Stephen started to criticise Roger and then Graham for allowing Roger to come.

Roger did not look back. He walked as quickly as he could, unhappily aware that he had caused friction.

"I can't help it. I've got to know!" he told himself. It was further back to the turnoff than he realised, at least three hundred metres and several bends. He heard footsteps behind him and glanced back to see Graham. Seeing him gave Roger a spurt of gratitude and affection.

106

When the two friends reached the track junction, they paused for a moment to listen. Roger was puffing and sweating, and the excitement seemed to press against the sides of his head and narrow his vision. All he could focus on was the old timber track. He began walking along it as fast as he could.

Only when he rounded the bend near where the vehicles had been parked did he slow down. There was no-one there, but a litter of empty food cans and other refuse marked where the men had eaten a meal. The sight of such antisocial leftovers roused Roger's ire.

Bloody grubs! he thought angrily.

He turned to Graham and said, "Bloody poor guests these. Just walk in and turn the place into a pig sty!"

Hoping to find a clue Roger bent to look at a tin but it was only a normal can of ham purchased locally, nothing foreign about it. Even so he carefully picked it up.

"Are you going to tidy up?" Graham asked.

"No. I thought it might be useful for fingerprints," Roger replied. He extracted a plastic bag from his basic pouch and slid the can into it.

"The cops can come here and get this stuff," Graham pointed out.

"Yeah, I know, but you never know," Roger replied. He looked around the area where the vehicles had been parked but saw nothing else of interest. Then he led the way past the track junction to the fallen tree.

"That's where Stephen and I hid," he said, pointing down the slope. The memory made him get goose bumps as awareness of what an appalling risk they had taken sunk in.

They made their way past the fallen tree, over the low rise and down into the overgrown clearing. Roger walked straight to the newly dug hole. Even before he reached it he could see they would find nothing and his disappointment was strong.

The hole was less than a metre deep and about 2 metres in diameter. Around it the clay was spread and trampled. A scattering of cigarette butts marked where the old man had stood watching.

Graham frowned. "Well this doesn't look very exciting," he said.

"It doesn't look finished," Roger replied. "It looks like they just stopped and left it." He scanned the disturbed soil for some sign of regularity which might have indicated where a box or container had been prised out but there was none.

"So what was it?" Graham asked as they discussed this.

"Search me," Roger replied. "But it looks to me as though they didn't find anything."

"Or if they did, it wasn't very big, and now they've got it and gone on. Let's get going ourselves," Graham said. He turned and walked back the way they had come.

Roger turned regretfully and followed, his eyes searching the shrubbery for any clue. Seeing nothing he sped up to catch up to Graham, who was striding along.

In less than 10 minutes they were back where they had dumped their packs. Peter and Stephen sat there waiting for them. Stephen gave Roger a sour look and muttered. "Bloody waste of time and energy. You'll be complaining you can't walk any further in a few minutes Roger."

Graham snapped at him. "That'll do Steve. I wanted to look too. It's only just after seven thirty so we haven't lost much time."

"Twenty minutes, two kilometres," Stephen replied angrily. He got up and pulled on his pack.

The boys set off in silence with Stephen in the lead, then Peter, Graham and Roger. It was another cloudless day and they passed through patches of sunlight and dappled shade as they walked. The road went steadily downhill and had several tight bends in it.

After about 10 minutes rapid walking Roger spoke up. "We are going the same way as those men went. What do we do if we see them again?"

"For Christ's sake Roger! Give it bloody rest," Stephen retorted.

"Calm down Steve," Graham interjected. "It's a fair question. We just act normal and say we camped up a side-track, which we did."

Stephen muttered something and conversation lapsed again. Roger's feelings were already depressed when he also realised his body hurt. Stephen had been right. He did feel as though he didn't want to walk any further. He bit his lip and hitched up his pack, then grimaced as pain shot through his left hand. Once again, he'd forgotten his stinging tree.

Determined not to give Stephen another chance to imply anything Roger forced himself to keep up and tried looking around to take his mind off the pain. In a bar of sunlight he noted several butterflies whose wings were a brilliant blue. He saw a bright green caterpillar on a leaf. Beside the road he noted strangler vines, lawyer vines and assorted dangling lianas.

By pushing himself he managed to keep up.

After a while the walking became mechanical and the various pains blurred into a dull overall ache. The road went on downhill, winding through dense rainforest along the side of the ridge. There was no view other than along the road. The jungle hid everything else. Roger became bored with it.

The road turned north, crossed a small creek down which water gushed noisily; then it curved right to a clearing where there was a car park and a National Park sign.

MOBO CREEK CRATER, it said.

Roger pulled out his map and located it. It was another of the extinct volcanic craters which dotted the Tablelands. Having been there on car trips with family he wasn't particularly interested.

Peter pointed to the walking track that led off down steps into the rainforest. "I'm going to have a look," he said.

"We haven't got time," Graham replied.

"If we have time to walk back to look at a little hole dug by treasure hunters, we have time to look at a big hole dug by nature," Peter replied evenly.

He turned off and headed for the walking track. The others came to a stop. Roger stood, chest heaving, wondering if he should drop his pack.

Peter dumped his so Roger did likewise and followed the others.

All four went down the walking track and Roger had to agree with Peter that the detour was worth the effort. The track led down to a most delightful pool with a crystal-clear jungle stream flowing in from the left under a little footbridge. Another stream plunged over a waterfall into the pool on the far side.

The cadets washed their faces and had a drink.

"I vote we have a swim," Graham said.

"No. Too cold and take too long," Stephen replied.

"What about washing clothes?" Peter asked.

"No!" Stephen answered. "We've all got a spare set. We can't keep stopping like this. We've only come three kilometres. We are a whole day behind."

"We still need to change, and I think we should have a bath," Graham persisted.

"And I don't," Stephen snapped.

"We do pong a bit," Peter said mildly.

Stephen glared at him but said nothing. Peter turned to Roger. "What do you think Roger?"

"Well, I, er," Roger stammered. He didn't want to cause more problems with Stephen. Hoping to find an excuse he looked back up the hill. "Somebody might come," he said at last.

"We will go downstream a bit," Graham said, pointing that way.

"Our packs are at the top," Roger said. He didn't want to take sides against Stephen.

"Oh! So what? It's only a hundred paces," Peter said in exasperation.

"Anyway I'm going to have a wash. You others can go on and I'll catch you up," Graham said. He set off back up the track.

The others followed in silence. The track with its numerous steps got Roger's heart really pounding and despite the cool of the jungle shade he started to sweat profusely. At the top Graham grabbed his pack and set off down at once. Peter followed. Roger picked up his pack but Stephen kicked viciously at the gravel, swore and sat down.

Roger hesitated, then asked in a conciliatory tone, "You coming down, Steve?"

"Bloody swim! This is stupid! Here we are halfway through the third day and all we can do is stop at every excuse. We have only just covered one good day's walk and we keep wasting time!"

Roger stood uncertain whether to stay or go. He wasn't sure what to say so he said nothing. Stephen looked up and their eyes met.

"Go and have your bloody swim!" Stephen spat.

"You may as well join us," Roger replied, trying not to get upset.

Stephen looked away, sniffed then looked at his watch. The sunlight lanced down on them. Roger wiped sweat from his face.

"Come on Steve," he persisted.

Stephen got up and swore again. Then he grabbed his pack. "May as well. We aren't going to make this hundred kilometres. We may as well just give up and enjoy ourselves." Muttering angrily he set off down the path.

Roger followed, worrying that he had done more harm than good. They found Graham and Peter undressing on a tiny beach 20 metres downstream where the water gushed and gurgled over boulders.

Graham pulled off his boots and looked from Stephen to Roger. He gestured upstream to the waterfall and pool. "This reminds me a bit of that pool above Stoney Creek Falls where we had the swim."

Roger shuddered and broke out in goose bumps. It did too. He didn't want to be reminded of that terrifying experience during a hike to Kuranda two years before.

The boys spent the next half hour having a swim, rinsing their dirty socks and dressing in clean camouflage uniforms. The water was ice cold so they didn't stay in long. Roger was acutely self, conscious of his physique and painfully aware of all the bruises, chafing and scratches which mottled his white skin. The cold water made the stinging tree bite throb with agony.

When Stephen went off into the scrub for a while Peter asked, "What's wrong with Stephen? He hasn't said a word, he just scowls."

Roger related their conversation. Graham's face clouded with concern. He looked at his watch. "Strewth! Nine fifteen. Doesn't time fly when you're having fun. We'd better get a move on."

Stephen returned as they quickly dressed. "What's the hurry?" he asked.

"We need to get moving," Graham replied reluctantly.

Stephen curled his lip. "That's what I said. We've wasted nearly an hour here."

"Half an hour," Graham replied defensively.

"More, three quarters," Stephen snapped back.

"What does it matter? We all needed a wash, and I feel much better," Peter replied.

Roger finished tying his damp socks to the back of his pack and looked at his friends. It upset him when they argued.

Stephen persisted. "You're right. What does it matter? We can't finish in time. I've had this. I've hated nearly every minute of it. It's the worst hike I've ever been on. I think I'll just phone my parents to come and get me when we find a phone."

The mention of a phone reminded Roger of the need to contact the police. He opened his mouth to remind the others but thought better of it. The four stood in uneasy silence for a minute.

Graham spoke at last. "Suit yourself. I still reckon we can do it. It's worth a try."

"It isn't. It is bloody impossible!" Stephen replied, almost shouting as his temper flared. He grabbed his webbing and put it on. The others did likewise and followed him back up the path, Peter shaking his head to caution the others to say no more.

They climbed back up the track with its hundred or so steps. With the pack this got Roger's heart really pounding but he refused to fall behind. The march was resumed in silence. It was nine thirty.

The road wound on through the jungle. If anything the forest looked greener and lusher than before and there were patches of road that were quite damp and even soft enough for their boots to sink in a few centimetres. After 15 minutes walk, a patch of sunlight appeared ahead as they rounded a bend. A bridge with a white signpost stood beyond it. The sunny area was an old gravel pit, half-overgrown with long grass and lantana. The sign said: MOBO CREEK.

Graham consulted his map and his watch. "We've come about four kilometres since we started," he said.

"Is that all? It seems further," Roger said. He instantly regretted the utterance and felt sure he had seen Stephen's lip curl in disdain.

The road now levelled out and went back into a tunnel of jungle, the gloomiest they had yet been in. Roger realised he was getting sick of rainforest, sick of the feeling of being closed in; of not being able to see far.

As they rounded a bend just beyond the bridge, Peter asked. "The road's quite soft and muddy. Has it rained do you think?"

"No," Graham replied. "It's just the dew dripping from the trees in the morning I reckon."

Ahead of them stretched a vista of several hundred metres of dark shadows. This was lighted by a couple of patches of sunlight. Roger plodded along at the back, peering into the gloomy tangle on either side.

"It looks a bit damp in there," he said.

"We're on flat ground here," Graham pointed out.

"Oh do tell!" Peter laughed.

"Does that mean no more hills?" Roger asked.

Graham shook his head. "'Fraid not. Look at your map," he replied.

At that moment they were just coming into a small clearing. The sunlight was able to shine through onto the road. This had caused a growth of lantana on both sides. On the right a snig track went off into the jungle.

Peter indicated the turnoff, pointing at the ground. "Pretty soft here, judging by these wheel tracks."

They all glanced down at where deep wheel ruts went off through churned up mud and grass.

Stephen, who was leading, suddenly stopped, causing the others to cannon into each other.

"What the?" Graham began.

Stephen pointed.

Not 10 metres up the side-track and clearly bogged was the black car.

"The black car! It's them!" Roger said in a hoarse whisper.

He had forgotten about the men but now interest and excitement gripped him again.

113

Chapter 13

THE BLACK CAR

For a few flustered seconds, the cadets stood and stared. Roger had to make an effort to focus his eyes and channel his thoughts.

Peter spoke first. "The men aren't here. I wonder where they are?"

Roger pointed along the track. "Searching the jungle again, I'll bet," he said.

"Where's the other vehicle, the 4WD?" Graham asked.

Roger pointed. "Up the track. I think I can see wheel tracks," he said. To get a better look he stepped forward, but Graham grabbed his sleeve.

"No Roger. We aren't going to look," he said firmly.

"What will we do?" Roger asked.

Peter answered. "Tell the police."

"Will we all go?"

Graham bit his lip. "Do you think we should do what we did yesterday and leave someone to watch?" he queried.

Stephen now spoke up. "No. Let's get going, all of us. We will never finish this hike otherwise."

"I thought you'd given up?" Graham asked.

"I have! This is stupid. Come on. Let's get going," Stephen replied. He was so hot his glasses started to fog up. Angrily he pulled them off and began to wipe them, his eyes blinking myopically as he did so.

Roger faced him. "You go. I'm staying to watch. I'll stay on my own if I have to."

Stephen put his glasses back on and shook his head, then waved his arms in exasperation. Graham interrupted. "Let's not have an argument standing here where anyone can see us down that track."

Roger looked. He could see at least a hundred metres along the track to where a patch of sunlight indicated a clearing of some sort.

What drongos we are, he thought. *We mustn't let those men see us.* He started walking, at the same time beckoning the others to follow.

They did so, all striding along as fast as they could go. Roger went along the road for another 50 metres and stopped in the shade on the other side of the small clearing. He then pointed into the jungle on the left. "I'm going to hide my gear in here and find a spot where I can watch the track junction. You others go and get the police."

"Let's just keep going," Stephen persisted.

Roger shook his head. "No. I'm staying. As you said, the hike is finished so now we should help the police," he replied firmly. He kept glancing nervously back towards the track junction and into the surrounding rainforest, fearful that the men might suddenly appear and see them.

Graham took command. "We won't debate this. Roger's right. Our duty is to help the police. We can always do the hike next holidays. Roger, you and Peter stay here. Steve and I will go for the police."

"Leave your gear here," Peter suggested.

"Good idea. Let's get off the road in case those blokes come out," Graham said. He led the way into the rainforest on the side opposite the track. The ground here was reasonably open and quite flat. The sound of running water became louder as they made their way in. Once they were about 50 paces in and hidden from the road Graham stopped and dropped his pack.

"This will do. Dump your gear."

They did so. Graham pulled out his map and jotted down the estimated Grid Reference in his notebook. Then he pointed to a farm marked in the open country about two and a half kilometres further on to the Southeast. "We will go to this farm. If they don't have a phone, we will go on along the main road to the next one."

"What if a car comes along?" Stephen asked.

"We will flag it down."

"What if it's going back in this direction?"

"Doesn't matter." Graham checked his watch. "Just on ten o'clock. We should be there by half past but don't expect us back before about eleven thirty."

"What will you do when you get back?" Roger asked.

"I'll leave that to the police."

Peter then suggested that one of them be beside the road around the next bend along to stop the police before they drove in. "They might want to surprise them. Otherwise you could drive past that side-track before you realised it," he said.

"Good idea. One of you be there waiting for us from eleven fifteen on," Graham agreed. "Come on Steve, big drink and then let's hoof it."

They all had a big drink. Then Graham and Stephen set off. Roger stood and watched as they went. They paused to look cautiously up and down the road before stepping onto it. Within seconds they had vanished from sight.

"Now let's find a good possie," Roger said, tingling with excitement.

"Let's refill all the water bottles from this creek first," Peter replied.

Reluctantly Roger agreed. They took out Graham and Stephen's half full bottles as well and made their way to the small stream. It was a typical jungle creek, crystal clear, cold and fast flowing. Once that was done Roger took a packet of jellybeans from his basic pouch, popped a couple in his mouth, pocketed the rest and began making his way carefully through the jungle in the direction of the track junction.

As he crept forward Roger became aware of pains in the chest. He realised he was holding his breath. The excitement made the blood pound in his ears and his mouth went quite dry. He developed a maddening desire to do a pee.

After a few minutes he came to the belt of lantana and was able to find a place which gave him a view across the main road and straight along the side-track. He was confident he was well hidden, so he crouched down to watch.

Peter crept up to join him. "Can you see anything?" he whispered.

"No sign of the men," replied Roger.

The two boys sat and waited. They were just back from the edge of the sunlight. It was hot and there was no breeze. Roger looked up. Still no clouds. He watched the ants streaming up a nearby log. There were orange tinted fungi growing on it.

Boredom and frustration rapidly replaced the initial excitement. Peter checked his watch. "Half past ten. They should have reached a phone by now."

Roger nodded. "I'd love to know what those blokes are doing," he murmured. He had to blink and wipe his eyes. The bright sunlight and shadows were affecting his eyesight and he felt drowsiness creeping up on him.

Peter gestured to the left. "We'd better start moving back. It will take us ten minutes to get to the RV," he said.

Roger shook his head. "In a few minutes. We might see something and be able to report, ah! What was that?"

Quite clearly to their ears came the distant clank of metal on metal.

"Sounded like a shovel hitting something," Peter suggested.

"That's what I thought. Oh! I'll bet they've found the treasure and are digging it up," Roger said. He squirmed his toes in his boots with excitement.

"Come on!" Peter hissed, indicating his watch.

Roger shook his head. "You go. I'm going to have a look and see what the men are doing," he replied.

"Don't be bloody stupid Roger! Come on," Peter persisted.

"No! It's not far. I'm going to have a look. Wait here if you don't want to come. I've got to know," Roger replied. He rose to his feet, ignoring pains in his knees and leg muscles.

Peter reached forward to restrain him but Roger side-stepped and started slowly walking through the scrub to his right. Peter swore softly and hissed at him to come back then stood and began to follow, his face red with anger.

Roger skirted a large clump of ferns and wait-a-while then made his way to the edge of the road. He was 20 metres to the right of the track junction and could no longer see the black car. He paused for a moment to listen and to study the jungle opposite. Then he walked quickly into the open and across the road.

"Don't run! Don't run!" he murmured to himself as his legs seemed to want to take control. He had to consciously control himself as he had been taught to do on fieldcraft exercises. *If I run, my boots will drum on the ground and my webbing will thud and flap,* he reminded himself.

Thankfully, Roger stepped into the shadows between two large trees. His heart beat wildly and he stopped to search ahead and to wipe sweat from his eyes. He looked back and saw Peter gesticulating furiously and angrily at him. In return he beckoned then began to cautiously walk forward.

The rainforest here was quite flat and very damp underfoot. The leaf, litter was all sodden and squashy. Away from the zone of sunlight along the road there was very little undergrowth. Roger could see at least 50 paces and was worried to discover that the black car was easily visible to him on his left, which meant he was visible from it.

About a hundred paces ahead was a much thicker belt of scrub which masked his view. Luckily, there was very little wait-a-while, but for cover there were only the occasional fern or dead log. Because of the sodden ground he was able to walk quickly with very little noise.

Roger walked on a route which edged to his right, away from the side-track. He could discern the change in light and vegetation pattern which marked its course. Ahead of him loomed the wall of thicker scrub with a brightness behind it which indicated a clearing. As he flitted forward from tree to tree, he realised that the wall of scrub was just that. It was a windrow of felled timber overgrown with a tangle of vines and weeds on the edge of a clearing.

The sound of voices made him stop. Tingling with excitement, he crouched down behind a tree and looked. The voices came from beyond the wall of scrub. Even more carefully now Roger crept forward, edging further to the right. The ground underfoot changed to actual mud, a black ooze into which his boots sank. Mosquitoes began to attack him. The voices grew louder.

The men were arguing. Roger made himself go forward. His curiosity was so intense he felt that he just had to see! He found a place where he could see between two trees and through a gap in the felled logs.

Beyond the logs was a muddy clearing about 20 metres across surrounded by the tangle of logs and scrub. In the centre was a large muddy hole like a bomb crater, half-filled with brown water. There were several other holes nearby.

Digging in one, stripped to the waist, was Bruno. Nearby stood the man with the glasses, or without at that moment, as he was wiping mud or sweat off them while scowling. The blond man was arguing with the old man. The blond man had taken off his jacket, rolled up the sleeves of his black shirt and had a pick over his shoulder. Roger was thrilled to see that both he and the older man wore black leather holsters on their belts.

Even as Roger watched, the men reached some sort of decision. He couldn't understand what they said but Bruno clambered out of his muddy hole, cursing and obviously not too happy.

It looks like they are packing up. I'd better get out of here while I can, Roger thought. He turned and began to move carefully back the way he had come.

Within 20 paces he knew he had a problem, as he could hear the murmur of voices moving to his right to where the muddy clearing connected with the snig track. He walked quickly to the next big tree and stopped to look that way.

Around the end of the tangle of logs and scrub appeared the blond man and Bruno, walking side by side. They were obviously walking along the track and were only 50 paces away. Luckily, they were engrossed in their conversation and busy watching where they put their feet.

Roger bit his lip and stayed behind the tree. The two men were carrying shirts and tools and were muttering angrily. All Roger could do was stay put and watch. They went past him towards the car. Unsure where the other two men were Roger remained still.

The sound of a vehicle door opening beyond the wall of scrub told him that the 4WD was parked there. Roger looked around, wondering if he should try to re-join Peter, or stay where he was.

The sound of vehicle engines in the distance came to him. Through the trees he glimpsed the blond man stop to listen. He and Bruno were almost at their car. Roger could just see it. Then the 4WD's motor burst into life. A door slammed, gears grated and the vehicle roared into view, churning through mud almost up to its axles.

Over the noise of its motor, Roger heard a shout and was dimly aware of other motors. He peered around his tree and saw that a white Toyota Landcruiser had turned in off the main road and pulled up right behind the black car. Then he saw that the blond man was running back up the track yelling. Blue clad figures sprang out of the Landcruiser.

The police!

Things happened so fast that Roger had trouble later sorting them out. He got a glimpse of Bruno dropping the tools he was carrying and raising his hands; and the blond man diving behind a tree. The 4WD stopped. Its doors opened. The driver went out the far side and the old man scrambled out on Roger's side.

A loudhailer boomed.

"This is the police. Stop!"

There was a sharp *crack!* Roger winced and gripped the tree.

That was a shot!

Another shot!

The loud hailer boomed again, telling the men to drop their weapons and to come out. For the next minute there was a babble of shouts and more shots, some from different guns and not all in the same direction.

Roger froze, unsure what to do. He saw the old man's face twist in fury as he pulled out an ugly looking black automatic pistol. Roger gaped at him, transfixed with fear.

More shots. The old man suddenly dived behind a rotting log and lay flat, not 20 paces from where Roger crouched. The loud hailer boomed again. More shots.

A bullet struck a nearby tree with a vicious thud. Roger went cold with shock and realised that the police were shooting his way, but not at him. There were more yells and another shot, followed by a cry of pain.

In spite of his fright Roger peered around the bole of the tree. He saw the blond man lying on his back twitching, his legs scrabbling at the leaves. Two police rushed forward. Roger recognised them as the plain clothes detectives. They levelled pistols on the blond man. One bent and scooped aside the man's pistol.

Then two uniformed policemen ran along the track to the other side of the 4WD and re-appeared with 'Glasses'. He was spreadeagled on the bonnet, searched and handcuffed. One policeman began hustling him towards the main road. The other, who Roger now recognised as Sergeant Grey, came around to his side of the vehicle and looked into it.

Aghast, Roger realised that Sergeant Grey didn't know the old man was only a dozen paces behind him. Roger looked and saw the old man had raised his head. He had something in his left hand and the pistol in his right. Fearing the old man was about to shoot, Roger yelled in a frightened, high pitch squeak, "Sergeant Grey! Look out behind you!"

Sergeant Grey spun round and dived behind a tree. The old man's head jerked around in surprise. He saw Roger at once. Their eyes locked and Roger seemed to be transfixed by the hatred which blazed from them. The man rolled on his back and swung his pistol, and Roger dived flat.

Crack!

The bullet splintered the side of the tree only centimetres from Roger's face. He lost control of his bladder.

The loudhailer boomed again. Inspector Sharpe's voice, Roger realised as he writhed in the mud in fear and humiliation. Still he managed to roll quickly aside and noted that the old man had rolled back behind the log.

Inspector Sharpe's voice boomed and echoed through the forest. "Put down your gun and come out with your hands up. You haven't got a chance of escaping. We have you surrounded."

Roger lay flat, almost frozen with fear. There was a moment of tense silence. Then the old man uttered a curse in his own language before calling out in accented English. "Don't shooten. I surrender."

The man scrabbled at the leaves for a moment then put the pistol on the log and got to his feet with his hands in the air. Sergeant Grey sprang up and doubled across to cover him.

Inspector Sharpe appeared, tie askew, white shirt plastered with mud and sweat, pistol in hand. He took the old man's pistol then covered him while Sergeant Grey searched and handcuffed him.

Then Sergeant Grey looked around and called out, "Right, you can come out now Tubby."

Shaking with reaction and burning with hurt over the name Roger rose slowly to his knees. His legs felt weak and he seemed to see things through a haze. He stood up and found he was trembling so much he needed to lean on the tree for support. Then he remembered he had wet himself. He flushed with shame and looked hastily down.

To his enormous relief the front of his uniform was plastered with mud and was so soaked that it wasn't obvious. Sergeant Grey walked over to him and grabbed his hand.

"You saved my life then Roger Dunning. That was a bloody brave thing to do."

Roger got even more embarrassed and hoped Sergeant Grey wouldn't smell anything. He mumbled for a moment, then shook his head and muttered, "It was nothing."

"Nothing be buggered! I owe you son and I won't forget. You okay?"

"Yes. I'm okay," Roger replied. It was only his pride that was hurt after all. Sergeant Grey turned and began walking back towards the others. Roger followed, feeling as though things weren't real.

As he reached the log he stopped and looked down.

"Sergeant, the old man had something in his left hand. He hid it here before he got up."

Sergeant Grey spun round. He bent and scooped at the leaves and picked up a plastic bag containing some notebooks and other items.

"Ah! Very interesting. Good boy!"

Roger looked at the old man and was appalled by the look of pure hate on the man's face.

Inspector Sharpe called. "Are there any more of them Tubby?"

Roger blushed at the 'Tubby' and felt a surge of resentment. "No sir, only four; and I am Corporal Dunning."

He regretted his tone of voice even as he spoke but was now shaking with emotion.

Inspector Sharpe looked at him sharply, then chuckled. "Sorry Corporal. It should be Sergeant after this don't you think Sergeant Grey?"

"I do indeed sir, although I suspect he was exceeding his CSM's orders a bit. Weren't you supposed to be hiding safely the other side of the road?"

Roger bit his lip. "Yes, sergeant. But I just had to know what the men were doing."

"And what were they doing?"

"Searching for treasure," Roger replied.

Chapter 14

THE IRON CLAW

Inspector Sharpe raised his eyebrows. "Treasure, eh! You sure?"

"Well, er, no sir," Roger stammered. He felt a bit silly. "But it must be. They've been walking up and down with metal detectors and digging holes in the jungle."

"Digging holes! Where?"

"In there," Roger pointed.

At that moment a loud groan of pain interrupted them. Inspector Sharpe looked to where a Detective was administering first aid to the man who had been shot. Peter knelt beside the man, holding an open Medical Kit.

"How is he?"

"Not too good Sir. He's hit in the lung I'd say."

"We'd better get him to hospital. Sergeant Grey, get on the radio and call an ambulance. Tell them you will meet them on the way, then get going. Use our car. Widmark, you drive. Stay with that fellow. I want him guarded. Does he have a name?"

The detective quickly searched the wounded man's pockets. He extracted a notebook and wallet, then felt again and slid his fingers into a breast pocket. He pulled out a black and silver metal badge.

"Another one of those badges with KSS on it sir."

"Let me see," Inspector Sharpe ordered. He made his pistol safe and put it in his shoulder holster, then moved over and took the badge. Roger followed him out of curiosity. Inspector Sharpe turned it over.

Roger looked at the badge. "It's got a number on it too," he said.

They all peered at it. The number 18041 was stamped into the metal.

"Sir," Detective West called.

He held up the collar of the man's black shirt. Pinned under the lapel was another badge. It was diamond shaped, made of black enamel about 3 centimetres long. On it was what looked like a silver hand.

They crowded to look, and Peter said, "It looks like a gauntlet. An armoured glove like medieval knights wore."

"Yes. No! Look at the fingertips," Roger replied.

The silver gauntlet had its fingers in a grasping attitude and the tips were sharp points.

"Like talons or claws," Peter commented.

"An Iron Claw," Inspector Sharpe said grimly.

"What does it mean, sir?" Peter asked.

"I'm not exactly sure, but I'll tell you what I know in a minute. What's his name Crowe?"

"It says Helmut Boltoff here sir," DS Crowe replied. He passed the wallet to the Inspector.

"Right, let's get Mr Boltoff into the car and off to hospital. Will you lads give a hand?"

Both Roger and Peter nodded and moved to help lift the wounded man. At that moment two running figures thudded into view. Sergeant Grey reached for his revolver.

It was Graham and Stephen, both crimson with effort.

"What happened sir? We heard shots," Graham gasped. They both looked down at the wounded man in horror.

"Yes, but it's all over," Inspector Sharpe replied. "Thanks for the call. We got here just in time. Sorry we couldn't give you a lift."

"Why not?" Roger asked.

"We came from Tinaroo. Your friend there stopped us just in time," Inspector Sharpe said, pointing at Peter, who was helping to put the wounded man in the police Landcruiser.

For the next few minutes the friends stood aside until the police vehicle drove off. Inspector Sharpe then said, "Okay Sgt Crowe, you and West caution these three, then search them one at a time. Separate them and handcuff them." He wiped sweat from his face with his handkerchief then turned to face Roger. "Okay boys, show me where the men were digging."

Roger slapped at a mosquito on his arm as he led the way along the muddy track. Curiosity gnawed at him so he asked, "Sir, what is the 'Iron Claw'?"

Inspector Sharpe did not reply, and Roger glanced across at him, fearing he had asked something he shouldn't. Inspector Sharpe grunted with disgust as he squelched through the mud then replied, "I'll tell you in a moment. Let's look at where they were digging first."

They came out of the cool shadows into a clearing. The open space seemed very hot in the bright sunlight. Roger wiped sweat from his eyes. The group arrived at a muddy hole and stopped. Roger just stood and looked at it. A feeling of intense lethargy seemed to engulf him. Now he just wanted to lie down and sleep. He closed his eyes against the glare and shivered.

Suddenly a hand seized his arm.

"You okay Roger?" Graham asked.

Roger blinked and shook his head to clear it. "Yeah. Just a bit tired."

"I thought you were going to fall over," Graham replied.

"I think I'll sit down for a minute," Roger answered, aware that he felt dizzy. He walked unsteadily over to a log in the shade and sat on it. While the others searched, he slumped there, rubbing his eyes and yawning. The search didn't take them long.

Inspector Sharpe pulled a wry face. "Well! There isn't much to see. I think we might do a detailed search later, but only if we need to. I had enough jungle this morning at Robsons Creek. Strewth it's hot! What the devil are these Iron Claw types looking for?"

Roger looked up but it was Stephen who spoke first. "Who are the Iron Claw sir? You said you'd tell us."

"Yes I did. Alright, let's sit in the shade."

The boys settled in a silent group on the log while Inspector Sharpe mopped his face with a sodden handkerchief. Then he said, "Okay, what I tell you now, you must promise to keep to yourselves, at least until all this is published. I'm telling you because you've been so helpful, and it was your handing me the KSS badge yesterday that gave us the clue."

Was it only yesterday! Roger thought. He was wide awake now.

The Inspector went on, "We had identified Boris Krapinski and then ascertained he was a migrant from Kosaria; was in fact still a Kosarian national. We informed various government departments... er like Immigration, and also the Kosarian Embassy in Canberra."

"After you handed me the KSS badge I phoned them again in case they knew anything about it. I knew instantly that I was onto something when the fellow at the other end went silent, then gasped 'KSS' in a sort of strangled voice. Then he repeated it – said, 'KSS, here! In Australia!' He then asked me to wait and a couple of minutes later told me he would call me back."

Roger listened to this enthralled. He forgot his aches and pains and flicked a leech off without being aware of it.

Inspector Sharpe saw he had their attention, so he continued. "The Kosarian Embassy phoned me back about half an hour later. They told me they were very worried about KSS agents being in Australia; and particularly in North Queensland because their Deputy Premier is out here on a tour. They sent me a fax on these KSS types. It's in my briefcase but I can give you the gist of it."

He pulled a face. "This will be a bit of a history lesson I'm afraid. It seems that Kosaria was part of the Turkish Empire until sometime in the 19th Century. After their war of Independence they suffered several revolutions and coups. Usual reason: Who is going to be boss. It seems there are two families who battled it out. The Dragovitch clan won and their man became king. In 1895 there was a revolution and General Paul Grabovitch..."

"Grabovitch!" Graham chortled.

"Shh!" Roger nudged him.

Inspector Sharpe frowned but went on, "The General took over and had himself crowned King Paul I. In 1904 he was murdered in another coup and the Dragovitches came back, with King Peter the fourth (I think). During World War I Kosaria was overrun by the Germans and Austrians. The Grabovitches had taken their side and Paul's son, the Archduke Paul, came with them and was crowned as an under-king of the Austrian Kaiser."

Inspector Sharpe paused to check they were with him then went on, "As you know Germany and Austria lost the war. King Peter came back with his army and Paul fled with the Austrians. He went into exile, first in Switzerland and then in Spain where he died in the 1920s. His son, also called Paul, continued to claim the throne. Is this all getting too confusing?"

"A bit sir," Graham said.

"Oh please go on," Stephen cried.

"Yes, well. This Prince Paul made friends with people like Benito Mussolini, he was dictator in Italy, and Adolf Hitler. When the Nazi Party gained control of Germany, sometime in the 1930's."

"1933," Stephen put in.

Inspector Sharpe nodded. "Then Prince Paul moved to Germany

where he gathered Kosarian supporters. He set up a political organisation modelled on the Nazis. The German SS, the guys in black uniforms with the 'Death's Head' badge, provided money, training and guns. Paul set up the Kosarian Schutzstaffel, the KSS, the Shooting Squadrons I think is the rough translation."

Stephen nodded. "Yes. When Hitler set up the National Socialist Party to begin with, he had an armed group called the Sturm Schutzen, Assault Riflemen. That was to try to get some of the prestige from the storm troops of 1918. But later he set up the mob with the black uniforms, the Schutz Staffeln," he explained.

Roger looked at him, surprised. *I didn't know Steve knew all that stuff,* he thought.

The Inspector nodded. "That sounds right. Anyway the KSS went to work to secretly undermine King Peter's government, using all the usual Nazi dirty tricks, murder, blackmail, bribery, sabotage and so on. They extended their secret organisation into Kosaria."

"In April 1941, the KSS staged a coup, aided by German paratroops. It coincided with the German invasion of Yugoslavia and Greece. The German Army took over. King Peter fled with his loyal bodyguard. We know who one of them was; he was Captain Boris Krapinski."

"Boris, a captain!" Roger gasped. He tried to imagine the sodden corpse as a fit, young soldier half a century before.

"Yes. Captain. And a hero I gather. He helped the Royal Family escape, so the Kosarian Embassy said," Inspector Sharpe added.

"So he fought against the KSS?" Peter asked.

"Yes."

"That's why they murdered him then," Stephen blurted out.

"Come off it Steve," Roger snorted. "Why wait seventy-five years to do it?"

"Why then?"

Inspector Sharpe cut in. "Good question. Am I boring you or will I go on?"

Roger nodded. "Oh please go on Sir."

"Right. The Germans made Prince Paul their 'Reichsschutzer', some sort of puppet governor, they wouldn't let him crown himself king. Then resistance to the Germans, and the KSS, developed in Kosaria, Partisans or guerrillas, led by the Communists."

The boys nodded so Inspector Sharpe continued. "In 1944 the Russian Army, Communists then, defeated the Germans and drove them out of the Balkans. As the German forces retreated Prince Paul and his cronies went with them and vanished. Most were never caught, and it was rumoured that many escaped to live in South America, in Brazil, Paraguay and Argentina. It was believed that the KSS had ceased to exist as an organisation, until yesterday."

There was silence for a moment. Then Stephen spoke in a hushed voice. "Real live Nazis. Here! On the Atherton Tablelands!"

Peter spoke up. "That old guy. I'll bet he's one of the originals."

"Possibly is," Inspector Sharpe agreed.

Roger itched to know more. "Is that all we know sir?"

"No. It isn't. The paper they sent me included details of how the KSS used to be organised, their ranks and badges, and so on. I didn't memorise them. They are all in German anyway."

"German? Those blokes weren't speaking German," Stephen asked.

"No. Apparently most Kosarians speak Serbo-Croat; a few speak Greek or Turkish but most educated Kosarians speak German," Inspector Sharpe explained.

"Do you think there are more of them sir?" Graham asked.

"There could be. Their basic squad size was nine."

"Nine! We've only got four!" Roger cried.

"Do you think they are dangerous?" Stephen asked.

Inspector Sharpe gave a short laugh. "Yes, very! They murdered Captain Krapinski, or at least I think they did. They carry guns, and they use them! Ask Roger."

Roger remembered his shameful terror and could only nod.

Stephen then asked, "But they are the KSS. Who are the 'Iron Claw'?"

The Inspector stroked his chin thoughtfully for a moment before replying. "The KSS were modelled on the German SS. It had different branches or departments. One was the 'Waffen SS', who were soldiers of a particularly repulsive and brutal kind, but still soldiers. The KSS was organised in a similar way. The whole organisation in World War 2 had about 3000 men. About 1500 of these formed an army regiment. Their duties included Palace Guards, guarding key installations and helping the police."

"Another branch was their Secret Service group. Because of their badge they were called the 'Iron Claw', although their correct title was a long German name with the acronym KGSD. The Iron Claw were an elite group of a few hundred. All of its members were veterans, of the rank of corporal or higher."

"So the Iron Claw were something like the GESTAPO and worked closely with them. They provided secret police, spies and Special Action Teams. The Special Action Teams carried out espionage, sabotage, assassination, kidnapping, torture and interrogation. Real murderous thugs."

"They recruited all sorts of strange and repulsive personalities. Many were sadistic bullies and brutes. Quite a number were convicted murderers. Allegedly many were sexual deviates, you know, homosexuals and so on."

"Nice types," Peter said, his face showing his distaste.

"Yes," Inspector Sharpe went on, "Their Special Action Unit consisted of a HQ and nine Special Action Teams, each of nine members. Each S.A.T. was commanded by an officer and included specialists such as signallers, Intelligence and Interrogation specialists, demolition experts, snipers and so on. They were all skilled in the use of weapons and trained at things like parachuting."

Graham spoke up, "And you think that is what we have here sir, a Special Action Team of the Iron Claw?"

The Inspector nodded soberly. "It's a distinct possibility."

"But what are they doing here?" Stephen asked.

"Looking for something that Captain Krapinski hid," Roger replied

"Correct. But what?" Inspector Sharpe replied. "Come on, let's go back and see what these gentlemen in black have to say."

Chapter 15

THE DIARY

Inspector Sharpe led the way back along the track. Back at the vehicle Det. Sgt Crowe was busy searching the 4WD. Detective West stood guarding the three men. They were handcuffed and sat along the side of the track.

"Find anything?" Inspector Sharpe asked.

"Yes sir," Detective West replied. He bent down and lifted up the collar of the old man. Pinned underneath was another 'Iron Claw' badge. The old man looked up and glared at them.

Det Sgt Crowe pointed to another man. "That fellow over there has one as well, and both of them had KSS badges in their shirt pockets," he said, holding up two of the badges. "This man had nothing on him." He pointed to Bruno.

"Any identification on them?"

"Not on him sir, but on the other two, yes."

Sgt Crowe pointed. "The bloke with the glasses is Otto Dorkoffsky," he said. "He has a Queensland Driver's Licence. The old man is Nitro Klotovitch and he has a Paraguayan Passport."

"Paraguay. That fits," Inspector Sharpe nodded, taking the plastic bag with the documents the old man had tried to hide. He began to spread them on the bonnet of the 4WD. There were some credit cards, a notebook and several strips of light blue cardboard with numbers on them.

He held up a credit card. "Boris Krapinski," he said grimly. "I think we have our murderers alright."

That earned more hostile glares from the prisoners. Inspector Sharpe put down the cards and picked up one of the strips of blue cardboard. "What are these I wonder?" he asked.

"Grid references?" Graham suggested.

"They might be clues telling these men where to dig sir," Peter added.

"You could be right."

"Ah hah! Good! Ah, yes!" Inspector Sharpe picked up a small book. Roger squirmed with curiosity. "What is it sir?"

"The Diary of Boris Krapinski. I think we have certain proof that these men are the murderers." Inspector Sharpe walked over to the old man and held up the pocket diary for him to see. "This was in the plastic bag you tried to hide. Where did you get it?"

The old man gave him a stony glare and looked away. Inspector Shape went to 'Glasses' and repeated the question. Roger saw 'Glasses' return a blank stare. Inspector Sharpe moved on to the third man and tried again. The man shook his head and said nothing.

"What is your name?" Inspector Sharpe rapped. The man looked at him calmly but did not reply.

"His name is Bruno sir," Roger said.

Bruno's eyes swivelled to focus on Roger and seemed to bore into him. Suddenly Bruno began to shout in a foreign language and tried to get to his feet. Roger couldn't understand a word of the torrent of abuse the man screamed at him, but its meaning was clear. He felt sick inside and had to resist an urge to flee; actually stepped backwards several paces before he realised it. By a conscious effort he made himself stand his ground.

Detective West grabbed Bruno and pushed him down, but he kept shouting. He was so enraged that spittle flecked his lips. As Bruno paused to gasp for breath the old man spoke sharply to him in their own language. Bruno slumped down and hung his head.

Inspector Sharpe snarled at the prisoners, "Keep silent all of you. Speak when you are spoken to; and don't make things worse for yourselves by making threats."

He went over to the man with glasses. "Now Mr. Dorkoffsky, you tell me what is going on."

Dorkoffsky looked up and said something in the foreign language. Inspector Sharpe flared with anger and stood over him with hands on hips. "Don't give me the 'no spik da English' crap Dorkoffsky. You've got a Queensland driver's licence and you've lived in Yungaburra for years."

Dorkoffsky said something, a swear word by the way he said it. Then, in excellent English he said. "I know my rights. I wish to speak to a solicitor. I have nothing further to say."

Inspector Sharpe tried again but none of the men would speak. He swore angrily and slapped a mosquito on his face.

"Right, let's have those badges off these fellows. Put them in plastic bags with their names in with them," Inspector Sharpe ordered.

"Can't sir," replied Sgt Crowe. "Our gear was in our car and there's none in the 4WD. I looked."

"I've got some sir," said Roger. "In my webbing. I'll just run and get them."

"Good boy Roger. Do that."

Roger ran quickly out and across the road to where their gear was hidden. He was so keen to help he didn't notice how much he was puffing when he got back. He held the plastic sandwich bags open. Inspector Sharpe took the badges as Sgt Crowe handed them to him. He examined each closely, before popping it in the plastic sandwich bag. Roger stared at the badges, fascinated. Graham wrote KLOTOVITCH on a page of his Field Message Notebook and tore it out. This went into the bag with the badge.

One badge was Rhomboid shaped metal with pin fasteners on the back. It was black enamel with silver edging and what looked like silver leaves on it.

"I wonder what it means?" Stephen asked.

"I've got a sheet in my briefcase in our car with the KSS badges on it," Inspector Sharpe said. "We'll soon know." He took the two packets from Graham. "Okay, Crowe, you and West load these three into the 4WD. West, you drive it. Crowe and I will drive these vehicles. And when we get back, keep this quiet. I don't want the media people getting hold of it yet. Don't answer any questions; and tell the Senior I want it kept under wraps for the moment."

As the two detectives moved to start putting the prisoners in the 4WD Graham spoke up. "What about us Sir?"

"Sorry boys. I want you to come with me. This time I need a more detailed statement."

"So that's the end of our hike?" Graham said sadly.

"It was finished on Day One," Stephen snapped irritably.

"How far have you got?" Inspector Sharpe asked.

"Only about thirty kilometres," Stephen sneered. "We should have covered sixty or seventy. We would have to do that in just over two days now."

Graham spoke up. "We can still do it. It's only midday now. We've got about five hours of daylight left today. We can do twenty kilometres in that time."

The idea of walking that distance before sunset dismayed Roger but he held his tongue rather than attract derision. To his relief Stephen spoke up. "Ah! Don't be stupid Graham," he replied.

"Just a minute," Inspector Sharpe interrupted. "It's not up to you. I'll decide. You will need to inform your captain and your parents, and I need full statements." He looked from one glum face to the other then spoke again, "You really do want to go on with your hike, don't you?"

"Yes sir, please sir," Graham replied. He looked at the others. Peter nodded. "What about you Roger? Do you feel up to it?"

Roger really just wanted to say no and go home but found himself saying "Yeah. I can do it."

"What about you Steve? Do you still want to drop out?" Graham asked.

Inspector Sharpe interrupted again. "Where are you heading? Where is your next clue?"

"The Curtain Fig Tree. It's near Yungaburra," Graham replied. "It's about twenty-five kilometres from here."

As Roger heard this he groaned inwardly. *Twenty-five kilometres!* he thought ruefully. *Bloody hell!* He wished he had the courage to speak up against it but feared Graham's contempt.

"Can you make that?" Inspector Sharpe asked.

"We can try. If you'll let us," Graham answered.

"I meant, can you make it by dark?"

"Probably not sir."

"Well, I will be in Yungaburra later. I've got to go to Atherton first. Then I'm going to search Mr Dorkoffsky's house which, as you heard, is in Yungaburra. If you could make it to there by about 5pm that would be fine."

"We can try," Graham replied eagerly. Again Roger groaned inwardly but said nothing.

"Show me the route you intend to follow," Inspector Sharpe ordered. Graham pulled out his map and did so. It was just along the main roads.

"Right. Don't leave that route. If you aren't there by 5pm wait beside the road and we will pick you up. We can drop you at the same place early tomorrow morning if that doesn't break the rules for your hike."

"That will be fine sir," Graham beamed. He turned to the others. "You coming with us, Steve?"

Stephen pulled a face. "Yeah. I'll come as far as Yungaburra anyway. But I reckon when I phone my oldies about this they'll just come and get me."

Roger suddenly felt his spirits fall. "So will mine," he said.

"That's the plan then," Inspector Sharpe said. "Oh, and remember what I said about not saying anything to anyone. It might be a good idea not to speak to people at all. And, just in case, don't accept a lift from any strangers."

Roger felt a sudden chill. "Do you really think there might be more of these 'Iron Claw' types Sir?"

"Could be. Just be careful. Now, give us a hand to get this car out of the bog."

About 5 minutes later the boys were on their own, the sound of the vehicles receding in the distance.

Graham glanced at his watch. "Okay, let's grab a quick lunch and get going," he said.

"Come on Roger," Peter called.

"Be with you in a minute. I'll just have a leak," Roger replied. He walked back up the side-track a few paces.

As he stood there he looked around at the scene of the action. It reminded him of that awful day in Year 8 when the leader of the Swamp Rats gang had been shot. At the memory he shuddered and shook his head. He found he was trembling, and a wave of goose bumps ran up his back. It made him glance behind him, suddenly very conscious he was alone.

His eye caught something at the base of a tree. Curious, he finished his business and walked over to it. It was a black jacket, almost invisible on the rotting deadfall. It had been dropped or thrown there.

Roger's heart leapt. *It must belong to one of those men!* he thought as he bent down and picked it up. Out of curiosity he looked under the collars.

Yes!

An Iron Claw badge under one lapel and under the other a black lozenge with a silver border and a silver stud on it, like a miniature 2nd Lieutenant's 'pip'.

Roger felt the pockets then unbuttoned them. In the left one was a KSS Badge and a Passport, Paraguayan. Roger flicked it open and there was a photo and the name MILAN JABLONSKI. In the other pocket was a notebook; a small book with pages of letters and numbers in groups of four. Stuck between the pages were two folded sheets of paper.

He unfolded these and stared at them. One was obviously a coded message because it had headings in boxes and the text was typed rows of the jumbled letters. He'd seen the same sort of thing at an army cadet signals exercise.

The other page was also a Signal Form but the message on it was typed in words. He tried to read it but gave up. German? He wasn't sure.

Bubbling with excitement he hurried after the others, out onto the main road and along it. He met Graham coming back.

Graham looked anxious. "I wondered what you were doing," he commented.

"I found this. Look. It's that other man's jacket. And it's got a code book and a secret message," Roger said. He thrust the Message Forms at Graham.

"Secret Message!" Graham began. Then, as he studied the form his expression changed. "You're right. It is. Gosh! I wonder what it says."

"It's in German, I think," Roger said. He dimly remembered lessons in Year 8.

"Yes, it is," Graham agreed. "Ooh! I wish I'd paid more attention in class."

"We'd better give it to the Inspector."

"We will. Tonight. Come on."

When they joined the others Roger told his story again and they all looked at the badges, passport and signals.

Graham urged them on. "Come on! Eat and let's get going. It's twelve forty-five already."

Roger pushed the signal into his map case then had a big drink and sat down. All of a sudden, he felt quite drained and really regretted having said he would walk.

Ruefully contemplating the pain to come, he packed the black jacket in his pack and dug out a tin of peaches.

Chapter 16

THE MARCH CONTINUES

Twenty minutes later Roger groaned audibly as he hoisted on his pack. The cadets made their way out onto the road and continued their trek. Roger felt the strain right from the start. His muscles ached. He was chafed and tired; and he was worried the others could smell his wet uniform.

Graham, as usual, set off at a cracking pace. Roger had to force himself to stride it out to keep up. Soon he was sweating freely and hating every step. He was also starting to develop a real loathing for the rainforest. The road was damp underfoot and that made walking harder as mud stuck to his boots. The jungle met overhead and induced that claustrophobic feeling of walking in a never, ending tunnel of gloom. The rainforest on the right had never been cleared and had almost no undergrowth. It appeared to be just a mass of trees with black trunks which gave the impression of all being the same height and thickness. Even the rotting deadfall was black.

"There's a car coming," Stephen called.

"Will we hide?" Roger gasped in alarm.

"Don't be silly, Roger. You've got those crooks on the brain."

"Besides, it could be the police looking for us," Peter added.

The boys all moved over to the right-hand side of the road. A car came into view behind them, an old station wagon. It drove slowly because the road was badly potholed. As it drew level Roger turned to look. There was an elderly couple in it and the old lady gave a cheerful smile.

"Good on you boys!" she called.

Stephen waved. The car drove on out of sight, leaving Roger feeling slightly foolish. The boys marched on.

Soon Roger settled into the rhythm of marching. As his muscles warmed up the soreness went away. Only the chafing at hips and shoulders still intruded noticeably. After about 20 minutes, Roger heard Graham call out. He looked up. Bright sunlight showed a few hundred paces ahead.

"That's the last of rainforest," Peter said.

"Thank God! I'm sick of the stuff," Stephen said.

Roger was puffing too much to say anything but could only agree. The damp from his perspiration had inflamed his stinging tree bite and he couldn't resist scratching at it.

They came out onto a bitumen road with open pasture on the left and rainforest on the right. Roger's spirits lifted and he stared out over the rolling hills, his eyes almost aching with relief at being able to focus at more than 50 paces.

After a few minutes they passed a grassy car park. A family with a van were there. A sign said:

CATHEDRAL FIG

"Is that the Curtain Fig?" Peter asked.

"No. Don't think so. Wrong name," Graham replied.

"We'd better check. We'll look silly if we walk all the way to Yungaburra if the next clue is here," Peter cautioned.

"Good idea," Roger said, coming to a standstill.

"No Roger, you keep going. I'll go and check and catch you up," Graham replied.

Roger groaned but began walking again. Without Graham leading they slowed down to a nice steady plod. Roger kept looking behind and saw Graham reappear in the distance and set off after them.

A small tourist bus rattled past, forcing them into the long grass beside the road. Graham gradually overhauled them. He caught up as they came to a road junction and farm.

"Nothing there," he reported. "This is the farm we rang up at," he added.

The friends stood in a perspiring group while they discussed this. Peter pointed along the dirt road which led off east across the open country. "This is the road we came along on Senior Ex last year," he said.

Graham nodded. "We walked from Gordonvale along the Mulgrave and then up Robsons Track. That was a great exercise." The three older boys then exchanged reminiscences about that exercise, leaving Roger feeling quite left out. For once he was glad when they started marching again.

The road curved around the farm buildings and southwards away from the jungle. It went down to a small bridge and then wound its way over open farmland. In spite of his pain, Roger thought it looked pretty.

Within 10 minutes he had lost interest in the scenery as he plodded up a kilometre-long slope. Several times cars rushed past, forcing them to step into the long grass. There seemed to be no breeze and there was no shade. Roger began to wish they would pass through some rainforest.

The road curved and dipped down a long slope to a narrow bridge. Roger struggled to keep up. He wished Graham would slow down but he didn't dare suggest this. A glance at his watch showed it was 1330 hrs. They had been marching for nearly 50 minutes.

Perhaps Graham will go by the book and give us the ten minutes in the hour to rest? he wondered hopefully.

No such luck. Up another long hill. Into the sunflowers to avoid a shiny blue car driven at high speed by a young man with a black moustache. *Trying to impress his girlfriend!* Roger thought resentfully.

Another narrow bridge and a wait for another car to rush across, also far too fast for safety. Bloody tourists! Up a slope through more open fields, some brown and poorly maintained, others green and dotted with black and white dairy cows. Down to yet another narrow bridge. Past a farm with magnificent flower gardens bordering the road. Past a derelict barn on the right.

A swarm of tiny finches flashed across the road at their approach. A car came from behind. Why do they all drive so fast? Uphill past a row of pine trees which threw a little shade. Another farm and dogs barking. By this time Roger was just marching mechanically. His legs and feet seemed numb and his hips and shoulders just a general misery. Sweat poured out of him. He began to fall behind and had to battle with himself not to call out asking for a rest.

The road seemed to wind uphill between walls of head-high grass until it reached the crest of a long ridge. Here it passed to the right of a low hill and out to the right there were glimpses of half the Atherton Tablelands.

Suddenly they stopped. Roger came to a standstill and blinked sweat from his eyes. Graham was dropping his pack!

"Okay, ten minutes. This is the junction with the Gillies Highway," Graham said.

Roger looked around. He was astonished they, he, had walked so far. It was just on 1400hrs. "How far have we come?" he asked.

"A bit over seven k's," Graham replied with a grin. "That's good going for an hour and a half."

Roger dropped his pack and webbing and felt as though he would float away. He flexed his arms and rubbed his sore shoulders. A slight breeze sent a pleasant cooling sensation down his sweat soaked back. He sat on his pack and had a long drink.

At that moment a car, a white sedan, arrived at high speed from along the highway and pulled up with a scatter of loose bitumen. Two men in it peered out, the closest one pointing to the road sign with his left hand and waving a map in the driver's face with his right.

Roger looked up out of curiosity and felt a thrill of fear run through him. Both men were dressed in black!

The pointing man suddenly saw the cadets sitting beside the road. His face went hard and he clenched his teeth. He turned to look at them. Then he and the driver exchanged words and bent to the map. Roger couldn't help staring. The nearest man was in his forties with big shoulders, a large squarish head and a roll of fat on the back of his neck.

The car suddenly leapt into motion and sped off down the Danbulla Road. Roger pulled out his notebook and began to write.

"What are you doing, Roger?" Peter asked.

"Writing down that car's make and number."

"Whatever for?"

"Didn't you see? Those men were both dressed in black."

"Oh, come off it Roger!" Graham snorted. "You've got Iron Claws on the brain. Give it a rest. The cops have arrested the murderers."

To Roger's surprise Stephen spoke up. "I think Roger's right. The Inspector did warn us about strangers, and he did say the KSS used to be organised in groups of nine."

Graham had no answer to this. Instead he looked sulky, then took out his water bottle and had a drink. Then he hoisted on his webbing. "Let's keep moving before our muscles stiffen up," he said.

Roger just wanted to lie down but he made the effort to stand up. "Ouch! Too late. I'm stiff already," he groaned. All his muscles seemed to be tense, like hard rubber. With an effort that made him groan he swung on his webbing and pack.

Graham was already on the move. He began striding down the right-hand side of the two-lane highway. At least it was downhill for a half a kilometre, but Roger could see the road went up over another long, open hill. Once again it took a few minutes for the stiffness to ease out of his aching muscles. By then they were at the bottom of the slope and all their muscles had to painfully 'change gears' to begin the upward slog.

It wasn't very pleasant. Cars and trucks raced past at high speed, often too close for comfort. Some vehicles tooted their horn and people in a few yelled derisory taunts and obscenities which made Roger feel very self, conscious and embarrassed.

As they plodded up the next slope the four strung out until Roger was a good 200 paces behind Graham but only fifty behind Stephen. He kept grimly on, trying to think of something nice, rather than of his chafing and sore knees.

What his mind kept returning to were the events of the last two days. Try as he might, he could not shake the horrifying visions of the sodden corpse, or of the men in black lurking in the jungle.

The cadets reached the crest of the ridge. A secondary road went off on the right. The highway curved left along the crest. Away down to the right sunlight glinted on an arm of Lake Tinaroo. Beyond it was the dark jungle covered mass of Python Ridge where they had spent the night. Beyond it was the distant mass of the Lamb Range where he had endured his terrifying airship ride. He looked away.

I've had enough of this place for a while, he thought.

Instead he looked left to where, 20 kilometres away, Mt Bartle, Frere, Queensland's highest mountain, heaved its jungle covered bulk above the rolling pastures to cover half the distant horizon. That got his mind going back to the January a year and a half before when he and the others had spent two weeks searching the jungle there for a gold mine. That had culminated in them being rescued from the rain sodden jungle by helicopter.[4]

I must have rocks in the head to keep coming on expeditions with this lot, Roger mused, remembering the fear he had felt as the cyclone had lashed their jungle camp.

As the friends got closer to a belt of trees ahead these developed into a wall of solid jungle. Roger pulled out his map to confirm his memory.

---

[4] Read *Below Bartle Frere*, by C.R. Cummings.

Yes. It was the patch of jungle around Lake Barrine. The boys passed a farmhouse. A gravel road went off on the left. They passed another farmhouse and then the jungle was right beside them on the left. Traffic whizzed past. Roger felt he was in a sort of nightmare.

As they passed the turnoff to Lake Barrine Graham stopped and waited for the others to catch up. "Anyone want to go to the shop?" he asked.

"Where?" Peter asked.

"At the kiosk down at the Lake."

"Fair go!" Stephen replied. "That's a couple of hundred metres, and downhill all the way, which means uphill coming back. It will add half a kilometre to the walk."

Roger said nothing. He just stood bent over to ease the weight of his pack, while trying to recover his breath.

"You go if you like," Peter said. "Leave your pack and I'll wait here."

"Okay. Do you want anything? Steve? Roger?" Graham asked as he dropped his pack.

"No thanks," Stephen replied. "I'll keep walking. This is ridiculous. You keep talking about doing this hike but you are forever stopping for every silly little reason."

"It's okay. I'll catch up," Graham replied. "Anyway, it's nearly time for another rest."

"How far have we come from the Danbulla turnoff?" Stephen asked.

"About four Ks," Graham replied. "Do you want anything?"

"Get me a soft drink," Peter said.

"Roger?"

"Yes please," Roger replied. He was debating dropping his pack or sitting down but knew that was weakness. He dug out some money and passed it to Graham. "I'll just keep going."

It took an effort to make that first step, but he pushed himself. Stephen started walking too, following a few steps behind. Roger didn't look back. He just put his head down and gripped his pack straps with both hands to ease the weight.

The main road ran through jungle with a mowed verge a few metres wide. The traffic raced past. Roger found it most unpleasant. As he plodded along, he saw the back half of a large brown snake slide into the weeds just ahead of him, but he did not change his pace. Some instinct

141

told him it wasn't going to attack, and he was too tired to get excited. He just warned Stephen. The snake slid along near them for half a minute before vanishing into the weeds.

As the road curved slowly left they came into an area of shade which went on for over a kilometre. Roger just plodded on, feeling more like a zombie every minute. He was just coming to open country again when Peter and Graham caught them up.

Graham called, "Pull up you two and have a drink. It's time for a break," He was grinning and striding along as though he didn't have a care in the world. That nettled Roger and he shook his head in annoyance. He looked at his watch; nearly twenty past three.

"How much further to go?" he asked, taking the cold can of soft drink from Graham. He opened it and poured the refreshing liquid down his throat. "Aaah! That's good!"

Graham consulted his map. "About seven Ks I reckon. Another hour and a half."

Seven Ks! Roger thought. His gloom must have showed on his face.

Stephen clapped him on the shoulder. "Cheer up Roger. We've walked about fourteen since lunchtime. You are going well," he said.

This unexpected statement made Roger look at Stephen. He didn't know what to say and wasn't sure if Stephen was giving him a compliment or teasing him. In reply he gave a weak smile and nodded, then quaffed some more soft drink before holding the can out.

"This is good. Want some Steve?"

"Thanks. Yes." Stephen took the can and drank a mouthful, then handed it back. Roger drained the last few drops and felt a pleasant glow inside.

After a few minutes they set off again, the empty cans crushed and placed in basic pouches. It was a long downhill slope through open farmland for the next kilometre. As they trudged along Roger looked out over the rolling country. On the next rise was another dark belt of rainforest, the Lake Eacham National Park. In the middle distance the bulk of Mt Quincan, and the Seven Sisters, a line of ancient volcanic scoria cones, stood in a line across their front. In the far distance a low lava dome topped by a microwave tower marked the site of Atherton, largest town on the Tablelands. Beyond it, barring the western horizon, was a line of jumbled and rugged mountains, the Herberton Range.

One of them is Mt. Baldy, Roger thought.

He could not identify exactly which mountain peak it was, but it cheered him up to be walking directly towards it as he was sure that was the end of the hike.

Near the bottom of the hill Roger remembered his packet of jellybeans. He put a hand into his damp pocket and fumbled around until he extracted two. They were all sticky, but he didn't care. He glanced at them.

Just my luck, two black ones!

Then it was uphill for nearly a kilometre. They were now marching straight into the afternoon sun and the stench of diesel fumes from several big trucks made him feel a bit queasy.

At length they reached the road junction on the crest and got glimpses of sunlight glittering on water off to their right. It was another arm of Lake Tinaroo. The boys halted for a minute for a drink.

"We've come a fair way," Peter said, indicating the lake.

They all looked out and in the middle distance to the north was the dark mass of Python Ridge and beyond it, blue with distance, the mass of the Lamb Range. They couldn't see the actual town or dam at Tinaroo but could work out where it was. Roger was amazed at how far it did look and felt a sudden surge of accomplishment.

"Let's go," Graham said. "Still five or six kilometres to go and it's nearly four o'clock."

Roger lumbered into painful motion. Now he didn't care how much it hurt.

I'm going to walk this if it kills me! he told himself.

Chapter 17

MORE QUESTIONS THAN ANSWERS

The sun was now low in the west, just above the mountains beyond Atherton. Roger was up with the others, but the effort had cost him and he knew he was near the end of his strength. At 1710hrs, the four sweat-soaked boys rounded the bend on the edge of the small town of Yungaburra.

As they walked past the state school, Peter asked, "Where will we go? Will we wait here for the police?"

"Let's go to the shop," Graham suggested.

"The Inspector said to wait beside the road," Stephen reminded.

"What's the difference? It's not a very big town. The cops will find us," Graham replied.

"Where are we sleeping?" Roger asked. He felt so tired he just wanted to lie down.

"There's a caravan park down by the lake," Stephen said.

"That will do. Oh! Here come the police," Roger replied.

The Police Landcruiser turned into view from a side, street. Sergeant Grey was driving. He pulled up and grinned at them. "Right on time. Did you walk all that way?" He looked at Roger.

Roger nodded, too tired to speak.

Sergeant Grey nodded approval. "Bloody well done young Roger! Chuck your gear in the back. Some of you will have to get in there. Just pretend you're a bunch of crims. You look like a mob of ne'er do wells anyway."

Roger took off his gear with a sigh of relief and climbed into the rear of the vehicle. Graham and Peter followed. Stephen hopped in the cab. Sergeant Grey started up and did a U, turn.

Stephen took off his glasses to polish them. "Where we going, Sarge?" he asked.

"Dorkoffsky's place."

Graham leaned forward. "We need to find somewhere to camp for the night," he said.

"You can doss down there, or, if the Inspector doesn't like that, at the station."

"Can we have a hot shower?" Peter asked.

"Sure. We've done our search in the house. We are searching the garage and garden shed now."

"Doesn't anyone else live there?" Stephen asked.

"Apparently not. It's a four-bedroom house, almost new. Dorkoffsky lived on his own, only moved into it a few weeks ago."

A couple of minutes later, they pulled up in the driveway beside a modern house down near the edge of the lake. The house was built on a slope so that the front door was also the entrance to the upper level of the two-story building. Roger climbed out and stretched. He had stiffened up and could hardly walk. Even so he was struck by the beauty of the setting. The back lawn ran down to the lake, which was like a mirror. The afternoon sun lit up rainforest on a hill across the water. A line of ducks sent a ripple of Vs in their wake.

The detectives were searching a shed at the back of the house. Inspector Sharpe was there. He looked up and gave a wave but went on probing a garden bed.

Sergeant Grey spoke. "Grab your gear and dump it in this room."

He led the way down past the side of the house and around to the back of the house. Here there was a concrete patio. A sliding glass door opened into a bedroom. The room was carpeted and the bed made but was otherwise bare. The lights were already on and it was all so clean and civilised Roger hesitated to walk in while wearing his muddy boots and filthy clothes. So he dropped his gear on the patio and so did the others, before following Sergeant Grey in.

Sergeant Grey pointed. "There's a shower just there. Keep yourselves in this area for the moment except to use the phone. The Inspector wants you to call your captain and also your parents. But he doesn't want you to say much. Just tell them you are okay and safe then give the phone to me. So far the news media haven't got wind of any of this and the Inspector wants it kept quiet for the moment."

"Why's that sir?" Graham asked.

"I'd rather not say."

Stephen frowned. "Are there more of them and he wants to catch them too?" he suggested.

"He has his reasons. Now, who's first on the phone?"

Graham put his hand up. "I'd better call Captain Conkey first."

Sergeant Grey led him through an internal door and up a flight of stairs. This led to the lounge, dining room and kitchen which were level with the front lawn.

Roger turned to the others. "I'm first in the shower."

Peter wrinkled his nose. "Good idea."

Roger flushed, unsure just how badly he smelt. He went out onto the patio and dug into his pack for his soap, towel and clean underwear. The first thing he saw when he opened the top was the black jacket he'd found. He pulled it out and looked around for the Inspector. None of the police were in sight.

He shrugged and put it down and kept unpacking. His muscles hurt so much he could hardly bend his legs. He also extracted his other uniform and looked at it. It was already dirty from two days walking. *I'll have to wear it,* he thought unhappily, knowing he had nothing else. With a sigh of relief he sat on the concrete and began to unlace his boots.

Stephen came out and began to rummage in his pack. "There's a washing machine and tumble dryer in the next room. I'm going to wash my uniforms," he said.

"Do you think we should?"

"Why not? The police want us here, so it's only fair," Stephen replied.

Roger decided he would definitely wash both uniforms. He had a spare T-shirt and could wear his first pair of trousers. Taking his clothes and toilet gear Roger went through to the bathroom. Peter had gone upstairs to the phone. It was all very modern and clean and made Roger feel even dirtier. The tiles felt smooth and cold under his bare feet.

Roger quickly undressed and was appalled at what he saw in the mirror. His whole body seemed to be blotches of red and black on white where chafing and bruises had marked him. He felt utterly exhausted and his legs trembled.

Quickly he adjusted the temperature in the shower and stepped in.

Oh! Bliss! Aaah! It hurt!

First the water and then the soap stung his chafing and scratches. Then the stinging tree bite began to throb. Tears came to Roger's eyes, but he persevered and soaped himself. Slowly the sharpness went out of the pain and he seemed to itch all over. He washed the soap off then saw some shampoo on a shelf. For a moment he hesitated and then picked up the bottle.

As he was lathering his hair there was a knock at the door. Peter called, "Roger, do you want a hamburger or fish and chips? Constable Widmark is going to the shop to buy tea for the police."

"Two hamburgers please."

A few minutes later, Roger had towelled himself dry, dressed in T-shirt and trousers, combed his hair, and cleaned his fingernails and teeth. His whole body seemed to smart and glow, but he felt much better.

Stephen knocked. "Can I come in?"

"Sure. I'm finished," Roger replied. He gathered his belongings and went to the laundry.

Here he began tossing things into the washing machine, carefully emptying the pockets as he did. It was a chore he did at home and his mother had trained him well. He fished his plastic map case out of the trouser pocket and at once saw the signal in German.

Cripes. I'd better get this to the Inspector in case it's important, he muttered.

He shoved it into his waistband, turned the washing machine on and went to get the jacket. On going outside, he was surprised to find it was now quite dark and that it was already getting quite cold. He picked up the jacket, went inside and closed the sliding door, then went upstairs. Here he found himself in a very pleasant lounge room: polished floor with rugs, leather settees and armchairs, sound equipment, TV and a bookshelf which had been emptied, its contents stacked against the wall.

Inspector Sharpe, the other detectives, plus Sergeant Grey and Peter and Stephen were there. Graham was in the shower. Stephen was on the phone, and as Roger came in he handed it to Sergeant Grey. Inspector Sharpe was seated talking to Det Sgt Crowe. Roger hesitated, unsure whether he should be overhearing any of it.

Inspector Sharpe looked up. "Yes Roger? What is it?"

"Excuse me sir. After you left, I found this jacket, and this message was in the pocket." He held them up.

Inspector Sharpe took the jacket and looked at it while Roger described where he had found it. DS Crowe pointed to the black metal badge with the silver 'pip' and silver edging.

"Untersturmfuhrer," he said.

147

"Yes. Where's that info sheet on the Iron Claw? What else have you got there Roger?"

"This message, sir. It appears to be in German."

"That's a bloody lot of good!" snorted Inspector Sharpe, taking the message. He looked at it, grunted and passed it to DS Crowe. "Anyone speak German? What about you kids? Do you learn it at school?" he asked as he looked at the Code Book and rough copy.

Stephen nodded and answered, "I do, and so does Graham, but we've already looked at it. It's a bit beyond us. Maybe if we had a dictionary."

Peter sat up. "Might be one among those books." He went over to the bookshelf.

Roger went to help him. As he knelt, he cried out in pain. "Ow! Ow! Aaah! Oooh! Cramp!" he moaned.

He rolled on the carpet clutching his right leg. As always with a cramp the pain was so intense and sudden that it quite shocked him. Stephen pummelled it for a couple of minutes and the pain slowly subsided.

Peter pulled a book from the stack and held it up. "Here we are: A German-English dictionary," he said.

Stephen bent and picked up another book. "Look, here's a *History of Kosaria*."

While still lying on the floor massaging his leg, Roger looked. It was only a small book. On the black cover was a white eagle with a crown on its head being blasted in two by a yellow lightning bolt coming from a red star.

Stephen flicked through the pages. "It's in English," he said.

"Here's Widmark with the food," Inspector Sharpe said. "Here, you kids have a go at translating this for us." He passed the message to Roger, who sat up.

Stephen picked up the dictionary. "Let me help," he said.

"Have a bath first."

"Yeah. okay. You phoned your Mum yet, Roger?"

"No," Roger replied. He didn't want to phone her. He was sure she would say he had to come home.

At that moment Constable Widmark walked in with a carton full of takeaways. Inspector Sharpe turned to the boys.

"You boys have your shower first, then eat. Roger, you phone your parents."

"Yes, sir. I'll just get my clothes out of the washing machine so someone else can use it," Roger replied. Then he groaned because as he got up he found all his muscles had gone stiff. He had to hobble across the room and down the stairs.

Graham was in the laundry in shorts and T-shirt. "I've just chucked your stuff in the dryer Rog, to make room for mine. Has Captain Conkey arrived yet?"

"No. But the food has," Roger replied. He turned and made his painful way back upstairs, followed by Graham. They got their hamburgers and went over to the sofa. Roger hadn't realised how hungry he was, and he devoured the two hamburgers in a few minutes. Then he sat back and wiped his mouth and fingers with a paper napkin.

"Ah. That's better!" He leaned back and closed his eyes.

It was a horrible dream. The vines in the jungle kept reaching out to grab at him, to trip him up and to slow down his frantic flight. The men in black were getting closer. He... He woke up to find Captain Conkey, dressed in civilian clothes, sitting opposite him.

Roger rubbed his eyes and sat up.

"Good sleep Roger?" Captain Conkey asked.

Roger blinked and looked around. Peter sat beside him reading the History of Kosaria. Graham and Stephen were seated at the table, heads together and writing. All the police had gone except Constable Widmark who also sat at the table, pen in hand.

Roger looked around for a clock. "What time is it? Have I been asleep long?"

Peter answered. "A couple of hours. It's getting on for nine O'clock."

Roger turned to Captain Conkey. "Have you been here long sir?"

"Only half an hour. I'll just wait till you've all been interviewed and for the Inspector to get back," Captain Conkey answered.

"Where's he gone sir?"

"To Atherton to ask some questions I think."

Constable Widmark came over and sat in an armchair, notebook on knee. "Okay. Roger is it? I'll get your statement now if I may."

"Can I have a drink and go to the toilet first?"

"Sure."

It took Roger over half an hour to make his statement and even then it was just a bare recounting of the facts. Captain Conkey listened attentively, half-horrified and half-pleased. He then said, "You lads have done very well; but CSM..."

"Sir?"

"Didn't you promise to keep out of trouble?"

Graham looked crestfallen. "Yes, sir. Sorry sir. We did try."

"It's Roger's fault sir," Stephen offered. "He kept crawling around the jungle finding things."

By now Captain Conkey had heard the full story. He shook his head in wonder. Graham turned to him. "Can we go on with our hike sir?"

"How far have you got?"

"About halfway. We've got about fifty kilometres to go. We can do that in two days. We did half that much after lunch today."

"I'll ask the Inspector what he thinks. If there are more of these characters, it could still be dangerous."

"How sir? We will go our own way now."

Stephen spoke up. "You'll have to ask my mum sir. She isn't very happy about all this."

At the mention of mothers Roger felt a twinge of guilt. He had avoided phoning his parents and he didn't want to.

Captain Conkey tugged at his chin for a moment then asked, "Are you sure you want to go on?"

Graham nodded enthusiastically. "Yes sir, we do; don't we?" Graham cried, looking around at the others for support.

Peter spoke up at once. "I do."

"Steve?"

"Yeah. May as well. If Mum will let me."

"Roger?"

Roger would have dearly loved to say no. His aching muscles and tiredness all called on him to say so, but his pride would not let him. Even the moment's hesitation had brought the beginnings of a sneer to Stephen's lips.

"Yeah, I can do it."

"Good on yer!" Graham commented.

Headlights flashed on the front windows and a car pulled up. Inspector Sharpe and DS Crowe came in.

"You got all the statements, Constable?" Inspector Sharpe asked.

"Yes, sir."

"Good. You can head off home." He turned to the table. "How's your translating going?"

"Bit slow sir but we are getting there. It says..." Graham began.

Inspector Sharpe held up a hand. "Tell me when you've got it all." He turned to Captain Conkey. "They've been an enormous help these lads, especially young Roger here."

Roger flushed with embarrassment. Inspector Sharpe then turned to Peter. "Do you mind if I have a look at that book?"

"Here sir. It's quite fascinating," Peter said. He passed the History book to the Inspector who sat down in an armchair. He said, "Get us some coffee Crowe. Do you want some Captain?"

"Thanks. Yes. Then I'd better be going if you don't need me anymore. I've got to drive all the way to Cairns," Captain Conkey replied.

"Are you happy your boys are okay? Do any of the parents want them to come home?" Inspector Sharpe asked.

To Roger's surprise Captain Conkey said no. He said he had spoken to them all on the phone, even Roger's mother, and assured them the boys were all safe. "The boys want to know if they can continue with their hike?"

Inspector Sharpe rubbed his chin. "They should be safe enough. I mean, it's hard to imagine how there could be any more problems, involving them that is."

"Okay then. I'll call all the parents again to see if that is alright," Captain Conkey replied. He got up and went to the phone.

Roger struggled painfully to his feet and went to the kitchen. "I'll make the coffee sergeant," he offered.

"Good lad. You can help. See if there is sugar in there."

They made coffee and carried it out. Roger joined Graham and Stephen at the table. Graham had printed out the German message in ink, in block letters, using every third line as they'd been taught to do in cadet signal training. On the second line he was printing in pencil the translations.

Stephen was thumbing through the dictionary and muttering to himself. "Wegweiser, Wegweiser. Umm..." He read what it said, "Signpost."

Graham wrote it down then said. "Okay. 'Nahe zu das Strassenknottenpunkt'."

"Strewth! What a mouthful. No wonder they lost the war. It took them so long to get their orders out," Roger quipped.

Stephen sat up and spoke in a mimic of 'War Comic' German. "Ve did not lose der War! Ve came second!"

"That'll do you idiots," Graham laughed. "Nahe zu das!"

"Near to; near to the; near the...now what the devil is a Strassenknottenpunkt?"

Roger leaned over to watch. Stephen turned the pages to 'St' and ran his finger down the column. "Strassen, Street. No 'Strassenknottenpunkt'."

"Don't forget German often puts different words together," Roger suggested.

"Shut up Roger. We know that. We've been at this for over an hour. Now, 'knotten'." Stephen began flicking over pages.

Roger felt a bit hurt. He was only trying to help. He looked up. Graham met his eye and smiled. "Here Roger, read this. It's about the KSS."

Roger took up the two-page document and read it quickly, only half hearing Stephen saying "Street, Knotting, Point."

"Road Junction," Graham replied.

Roger turned the page and saw the second sheet was a page of diagrams of the KSS badges. He quickly scanned it and caught his breath. "Inspector Sharpe Sir. That old man, his rank badge says 'Standartenfuhrer'. That's a Colonel. He must be important."

"You're right Roger. We think he's right up near the top. And our mate with the glasses, Mister, or I should say 'Herr' Jablonski is an 'Untersturmfuhrer', a 2nd Lieutenant. I think he is a Special Action Team Leader."

"So why is the Colonel here? Are there more than one of these Action Teams at work?" Captain Conkey asked, coming over to look at the diagrams.

"Possibly, but I suspect not," Inspector Sharpe replied. "From the information I have, their organisation is probably under strength. The Kosarian Embassy told me an hour ago that Klotovitch was a colonel during World War 2."

Peter chuckled. "So he hasn't been promoted in well over half a century," he said.

"I hope I get promoted faster than that," Roger said.

They all laughed. Inspector Sharpe went on, "It probably means they have just begun to rebuild their organisation."

That puzzled Roger so he asked, "But why sir? What are they doing here in North Queensland?"

Inspector Sharpe took a sip from his coffee then said, "I wish I knew. Perhaps you can all spot a clue for me. I've just read bits of this." He held up the history book, "and I don't know if it's important or not. I'll read some of it to you and see if it rings any bells."

Chapter 18

A SHORT HISTORY

Inspector Sharpe settled back and turned a few pages of the book. Captain Conkey finished his coffee and looked at his watch.

"If you'll excuse me Inspector. It's ten thirty and I might just be home by midnight."

"Certainly. Thank you for coming. I hope I won't need to bother you again."

Capt Conkey rolled his eyes. "So do I! Well, goodnight kids. Now this time, keep out of trouble!"

"Yes sir," the boys chorused.

Captain Conkey went out into the night and Inspector Sharpe began. "I won't read this word for word. It's too long and boring. I'll just pick the main points. Now, you've all found Kosaria on the map? There's the atlas. You'll find it wedged in there near Albania and Greece. It's only a little place, about 100 kilometres north to south, and 150 kilometres across. About 1.2 million people live there, 90 per cent are Slavs, 8 per cent are Greeks, and 2 per cent are Turks. Of which 92 per cent are Eastern Orthodox Christians, 5 per cent are Roman Catholics and 3 per cent are Moslems. Most speak Serbo-Croat, which is the official language. German is the second language and is taught in most schools, hopefully better than it's taught here."

Graham and Stephen pulled faces but said nothing at this little dig.

Inspector Sharpe went on, "It's a poor country, all mountains and forests. Most of the people are peasant farmers and the capital city is only about half the size of Cairns, with a population of about 65,000. It's a primitive place. It still uses steam locos on the railway and mules and horse drawn wagons are common. Kosaria is the poorest country in Europe and has the last communist government in that part of the world, which doesn't help the economy. But then you kids wouldn't remember the communists and what a threat they were when Russia had a communist government."

"Yes we do, sir. We learn about it at school," Roger said.

Graham spoke up. "Peter's grandparents. They were Russians and had to flee the country so the communists wouldn't shoot them."

Inspector Sharpe eyed Peter with interest. "Is that so? Are they still alive?"

"Yes, sir. They live in Brisbane. Grandpa's ninety and Omma's eighty-nine."

"That's good. Now, let's get back to Kosaria. The place used to be part of the Byzantine Empire. They were the last country in the Balkans to be conquered by the Turks. Apparently, they withstood several attempts at invasion. I'll read this bit."

"Prince Theodore was prepared to submit, to the Turks that is, in 1457, but the Archbishop Joris persuaded him to fight. The small Kosarian army met a huge Turkish host on the Field of the Black Crows. The Turks attacked and quickly broke the Kosarian Centre. The Kosarian Standard Bearer was cut down and the Kosarians began to lose heart and give ground. Seeing this, Archbishop Joris rushed forward and picked up the flag. The Turks slashed and hacked at him with their scimitars. A terrible blow severed his right leg and he fell, but managed to keep the flag aloft."

"Inspired by his example the Prince led a counter, attack. The Prince's horse was killed and he fell heavily, losing his sword. The Turks closed in for the kill. Theodore seized the first thing which came to hand as he scrambled to his feet. It was the leg of Joris. With this he flailed the enemy and held them off."

"The Kosarian soldiers rushed to the Prince's aid and drove the Turks back. The Turkish general, Ahmed the Fat, was killed. Panic seized them and they fled. By then the Archbishop had died from lack of blood but his dead body still held the flag aloft."

Stephen spoke up, "Strewth! What a gory tale."

"Yes, isn't it? There's more to follow," said Inspector Sharpe. He went on, "Archbishop Joris was canonised as a Saint. His thigh bone became a holy relic. It was preserved in a case made of gold and glass and was placed on the altar of the Cathedral in Dragavia. That's the capital city."

"Sir, Sir!" Roger called excitedly. "That's what the men are looking for: the Thigh Bone of St Joris!"

Inspector Shape smiled. "Maybe Roger. But listen, there's more. Ten years later the Turks tried again but were again defeated in a battle at the

Pass of Monastria by Prince Michael Dragabog, who carried the Thigh Bone of St Joris into battle."

Stephen chortled. "Dragabog!" he muttered.

Inspector Sharpe frowned at him and went on, "Then, in 1491 the Turks, led by Abdul the Damned, invaded. Prince Constantine assembled his army but, before the detachment bringing the Thigh Bone from the capital could find a way to cross the flooded Draga River, the Turks attacked. The Kosarians were defeated."

"The country became a Turkish province. The Turks searched long and hard for the Thigh Bone but never found it. It was hidden by hermit monks in the caves of the Vulture's Peak."

"For over 300 years Kosaria suffered under Turkish misrule and oppression. It was not until the war between Austria and Turkey in 1788 that they rose in revolt. The Turks put down the revolt with great cruelty. Many Kosarians believed that their failure was due to not having the sacred thigh bone."

"The country remained quiet until 1804 when the neighbouring Serbs began to rebel against the Turks. Most Kosarians were afraid to rise in revolt but a bandit chief, Black George Dragavitch, managed to make himself ruler of one valley in the Black Durmitor Mountains. His strength grew only slowly and was only a few hundred men."

"In 1821 the Greeks to the South also rose against the Turks. The Turks withdrew many of their troops from Kosaria. Black George decided the hour had come and rallied the peasants to his banner. They attacked the Vulture's Tower, which commands the main road in from the north, but they were betrayed and suffered a terrible defeat."

Inspector Sharpe paused to take a sip of coffee then turned the page. The boys sat silent. He read on, "Black George fled to the rugged slopes of the Dragavista Mountains with a handful of survivors. They were given refuge by the Monastery of the Black Monks. One of the monks, Friar Silios..."

"Siliarse," Stephen quipped.

Inspector Sharpe raised an eyebrow and frowned again before going on. "Friar Silios revealed to Black George that the Thigh Bone of St Joris was hidden in a locked room behind the altar. Black George demanded the relic, but the Patriarch Nicodemus refused, saying prayer was the only way."

"In a fit of rage, Black George struck the patriarch, killing him. He then had the altar demolished and the door broken open. He found the Thigh Bone but most of his men refused to follow him, terrified that such sacrilege would turn God against them."

"It seems that this was the case, for soon after the remnants of the band were almost wiped out in a Turkish ambush. Only Black George and two others escaped and while they were hiding one of them, Driblos Nurkovitch..."

The boys snickered over the name 'Driblos' but said nothing to interrupt. Inspector Sharpe read on, "...betrayed him to the Turks. The Turks captured both Black George and the Sacred thigh bone. Black George was executed in the traditional Turkish manner by impalement and left for the crows to peck out his eyes."

The boys winced at hearing the gruesome manner of his death, then Inspector Sharpe said, "Anyhow, where was I? Ah yes, the loss of the Thigh Bone was a shattering blow to the hopes of the Kosarians. But not all gave up. It fell to the 17-year-old son of Black George, the handsome Peter Dragavitch to avenge his father. In a daring raid he... oh, er... I'll just leave that bit out... er..."

"Oh sir! We aren't little kids. Is that a juicy bit?" Stephen asked.

Inspector Sharpe eyed him coldly. "If you mean does it involve women. Yes, it does. He er... became friends with the slave girl, Fatima, who let them in to the Black Tower."

"Black Tower," Peter said. "These guys certainly like black."

"Shut up you blokes," Roger called. Normally he found history boring, but this was fascinating.

"Alright. Peter got into the Black Tower, which was the Turkish stronghold overlooking the capital. Here's a photo." He held the book for them to see. "He killed the governor, Osman Pasha, and recaptured the Thigh Bone.

"The Turkish reaction was so barbaric and ferocious that the civilised nations of Europe were moved to protest. Despite the suffering, Peter became the hero of the Kosarian people. He fled to the Dragavista Mountains in Western Kosaria and began a guerrilla war.

"This went on for thirty years. During that time, Peter was able to drive the Turks from the whole mountain range. He was helped in this by a rival guerrilla group in the Black Mountains on the east side of the capital. This group was led by Paul Grabovitch. Both leaders claimed to be the rightful Prince of Kosaria, although they were little more than bandit chiefs.

"Peter was the stronger and more popular. During the Crimean War he managed to free more of the country and declared himself to be king. No other country recognised this claim, but many Kosarians did.

"In 1858 Peter I died. His son was crowned Peter II by the Patriarch of the church but still no nation recognised this. A three-sided struggle against the Turks and the Grabovitch clan dragged on. It was a dirty little war of ambush, murder and betrayal."

Inspector Sharpe paused for a moment. Roger had a flood of stark memories. *Ambush, murder, and betrayal!*

Graham spoke. "Well, we've seen that first hand. The murder bit anyway."

Inspector Sharpe read on, "Yes. In 1874 the Bulgars rose in revolt against the Turks. Serbia and Montenegro also declared war on Turkey. A Serbian army appeared on the northern border; Serbia claiming that Kosaria was rightfully part of their territory. To unite the people to oppose this extra threat Peter made an alliance with Paul Grabovitch. To seal the alliance he had his son Peter III marry Paul's daughter Olga.

"With the forces of the two factions united they were able to block the Serbian Army at the Vulture's Pass. Then in 1877, on that same plain of the Black Crows, they utterly defeated the Turkish army. The Turks were driven from the entire country. The Kosarians ascribed the victory to the Thigh Bone of St Joris, which the King had carried throughout the campaign. Other historians suggest the real reason was that the Turks had withdrawn most of their troops to face a Russian army in Bulgaria."

Graham gestured across to Peter. "Pete's great grandad. The family have always been troublemakers."

Peter laughed and turned to Inspector Sharpe. "What Graham means is that I come from a long line of freedom fighters," he replied.

"Yes, I'm sure. I'll go on. In the peace treaty which ended the war Turkey conceded the independence of Bulgaria, Serbia, Montenegro and Kosaria. The last Turkish troops withdrew in 1878. Peter II was now recognised as the King by the Great Powers.

"In 1893 Peter II died and the 18-year-old Peter III came to the throne. He was a good king and very progressive. He introduced a Parliament with limited powers. He also had the first railway built. This work was done by German engineers and with German government aid. German technicians settled in Kosaria to run the railways.

"However, a proposal to introduce a written constitution and a proper parliament precipitated a crisis. This move was opposed by conservative elements whose leader was Duke Paul Grabovitch, grandson of 'Prince' Paul and brother of Queen Olga. He was the colonel of the Iron Guards Regiment. On the night of 17 June 1895, Paul led a coup. His regiment attacked the palace. The Kings Guard was wiped out and the king murdered.

"However, Queen Olga refused to support her brother. At the time she was expecting, and Paul ordered her shot so that no rightful heir could be born. His younger brother, Alexander, refused to allow this and he was supported by the Archbishop Constantine, who arrived at the palace.

"Queen Olga was allowed to leave with the archbishop. They at once boarded a train and left the country. Too late Duke Paul discovered that the Thigh Bone of St Joris had vanished from the cathedral. He suspected the archbishop had taken it, but his agents were unable to locate the queen. When the archbishop returned, he was tortured but made no statement.

"Paul declared himself King. He began to rule the country with an iron hand. All possible opponents were arrested and many just vanished. Taxes were increased. The army was built up with German weapons and German Instructors.

"Meanwhile, Queen Olga gave birth to a son, named Peter (the fourth). Paul next made a secret deal with Greece. In 1897, he led his country into a war with Turkey, hoping to gain half of Macedonia. The Greeks simultaneously attacked the Turks from the south. The Turks defeated both attacks then counter-attacked. Only the intervention of the Great Powers saved Kosaria from another Turkish invasion.

"Paul denied the defeat was due to his poor tactics and leadership and said it was because Queen Olga (and her son, Prince Peter) who was living in Paris, was withholding the sacred thigh bone just when the country needed it most.

"King Paul's unpopularity grew when he again increased taxes. There was much official corruption and his family and friends were given top government jobs. He became even more unpopular when he took... oh. Perhaps I shouldn't read this," Inspector Sharpe paused.

"Oh sir!" Stephen said. "How can we understand if you leave bits out? It might be the vital clue."

Inspector Sharpe made a wry face. "I doubt it. It's just sordid. King Paul took a mistress, an Austrian actress named Magda, who was already notorious for immoral behaviour. This adulterous behaviour scandalised the majority of the ordinary people as Paul was married to a Hungarian countess, Queen Draga, who was expecting another baby.

"Queen Draga and her ten-year-old son, the Archduke Paul, were sent away and the actress installed in the palace. Queen Draga went into exile in Budapest with her son. Back in Kosaria matters got steadily worse until, in 1903, there was another murderous coup. This was led by General Radomir Ritnik, the army commander. During the coup King Paul and his mistress were shot and their bodies mutilated."

"Nice people!" Peter commented.

"Yes, we've seen that," Inspector Sharpe commented. He went on. "General Ritnik invited the 17-year-old Prince Peter to return as King. He did so and was crowned King Peter IV. During the ceremony, the Thigh Bone of St Joris was brought in by an honour guard of Officers of the White Eagle Regiment and restored to it its place in the cathedral."

Graham interjected. "This bloody bone gets around."

Inspector Sharpe frowned and read on, "Peter was a good king and did much to improve the country. He reduced taxes, cleaned out the corrupt officials, sent away the German officers and reduced the army. In particular he disbanded the Iron Guard Regiment and made the White Eagle Regiment the Royal Guard.

"Unfortunately for Kosaria, it had troublesome neighbours. When the First Balkan War broke out in 1912, she was attacked from all sides. Greece, Bulgaria, Serbia, and Montenegro had all made a secret treaty to attack Turkey but in the process they all tried to grab a bit of Kosaria. Attacked on four fronts, the Kosarians fought bravely but were forced back. After desperate fighting the Serbs, Montenegrins, and Greeks were halted but a Bulgarian division reached the outskirts of the capital. Only a heroic counter-attack by the Royal Guard, led in person by King Peter carrying the sacred thigh bone, managed to hold them.

"Then circumstances turned their way. After a short and uneasy truce the Second Balkan War broke out in 1913. In this all of the former allies fought each other as well as Turkey. Even Romania joined in to attack Bulgaria. The Kosarians took the opportunity to mount a counter, offensive. By brilliant generalship, Ritnik was able to drive all of the invading armies from Kosarian soil, but at heavy cost.

"Kosaria, however, had no chance to recover from these exhausting wars as World War 1 broke out in the following year. In 1915, Kosaria was attacked by the Bulgars. The Kosarians allied themselves with the Serbs and Montenegrins. In a series of desperate defensive battles they were able to defeat the Bulgars in the rugged Dragavista Mountains.

"Then, in October 1915, a combined German-Austrian Army Group, led by Feld Marschall von Mackensen, defeated the Serbians. In December 1915, the German and Austrian forces broke into Kosaria through the Vulture's Pass, despite a stubborn defence by the outnumbered and outgunned Kosarians. General Ritnik was able to save most of the army by a brilliant delaying defence, which allowed time for the regiments facing the Bulgars to fall back to help defend the capital.

"The Kosarians fought on grimly against a German army with vastly superior artillery but, as the first snow began to fall, they had to make a bitter choice. The Serbian army on their left flank had begun to retreat and, if they did not fall back with them, the Kosarian army would be surrounded and annihilated. The king decided to abandon Dragavia and save the army.

"The Royal Family, Treasury, the Thigh Bone of St Joris, and thousands of civilian refugees joined the troops in an agonising retreat over the frozen mountains of Albania. German and Austrian forces pushed hard against their rear guards.

"As the army struggled to cross the flooded Narga River by the only bridge, a regiment of Austrian mountain troops cut into the middle of the column and blocked the road. In a howling blizzard, General Ritnik led a desperate counter-attack using the Royal Guard Regiment. They were able to re-open the road but Ritnik was mortally wounded. The army managed to cross the river in time.

"The retreat went on in a blizzard. Austrian ski troops harried their flanks. King Peter stayed with the dying Ritnik, personally commanding the rear guard. Snow and bitter cold killed thousands. Others died to bullets, hunger and disease. Ritnik died just as the army reached the sea.

"British and French ships evacuated the survivors under fire and took them to safety in Corfu or Malta. Among those rescued were the

Royal Family and most government ministers. They had with them the Thigh Bone of St Joris, and the Crown Jewels. But, sometime during the retreat or evacuation, the treasurer, Slimo Nikoffovitch, went missing. So also did the Treasury of over one million gold coins. Some said they last saw him at the battle of the Narga River. Others thought they saw him disembarking from a French troopship at Bizerta in Tunisia."

Inspector Sharpe stopped reading and looked up.

"Gold!" Graham cried.

"A million gold coins," Peter gasped.

"Why, they must be worth… must be worth millions," Roger added.

They all laughed.

"Is that what these men are after then, gold?" Stephen asked.

Chapter 19

IS IT THE GOLD?

Inspector Sharpe shook his head and made himself more comfortable. "Could be. It would make more sense than an old bone. Are you bored? You can go to bed if you like."

"No, sir. Keep reading. This is gripping stuff," Roger said.

Stephen agreed. "More interesting than our boring old history: bloody convicts, goldrushes and depressions."

"We fought in the First World War too," Graham defended.

"Have the debate later," Inspector Sharpe said. "I'll go on. It is still during World War 1. With the invading German and Austrian armies came the Archduke Paul. He was established as King of Kosaria, but owing allegiance to the Kaiser of Austria, with a palace guard of Austrian Imperial Grenadiers. Here's a photo of him arriving at Dragavia Railway Station and being met by the German General Von Blotwitz."

"Blotwitz!" Stephen snorted.

Peter frowned. "You're a blot. Clot rather. Shut up and listen Steve," he chided.

Inspector Sharpe nodded agreement and resumed, "In 1916 the remnants of the Serbian and Kosarian armies were re-armed by the British and French and then shipped to join the allied army at Salonika in northern Greece. Where's that on the atlas, Graham?"

Graham showed them.

Inspector Sharpe read on, "The Kosarian army played a small but important part in the Salonika Offensives of 1917 and 1918, which led to the defeat of the Bulgars. The Germans, defeated in France by the allies, withdrew their troops. The Austrians went with them. The Serbian and Kosarian armies followed them north.

"When the Germans and Austrians pulled out of Dragavia in October 1918, King Paul and his supporters went with them. King Peter returned to his capital amid great rejoicing. There followed 20 happy years for Kosaria. King Peter set about improving his country. He established a democratically elected parliament with real power. He built schools, hospitals, roads, and bridges. There was peace and prosperity. People called him 'Good King Peter'. There was much joy when he married a beautiful exiled Russian Princess, Princess Kalia. Here's a photo of her."

Graham whistled. "Strewth! She's a stunner alright."

Inspector Sharpe smiled and went on. "There was more rejoicing when a son, Peter (the fifth) was born in 1938. A daughter, Princess Karena, was born in 1940.

"But trouble was brewing. Paul II had gone into exile in Spain. Before the war, Paul had married a German Princess, Helga of Zeitheiligen, and they had a son, Paul III, who was born in 1912. When Paul II died in 1929, the young Archduke Paul declared himself to be the rightful King of Kosaria. However, he remained living with his mother in Germany.

"For a number of years Paul made no active moves to secure the throne, but when the Nazi Party, led by Adolf Hitler, became the government of Germany in 1933, he joined their organisation. In Germany in 1934, Paul set up a secret organisation from Kosarians who supported him. This included a political party modelled on the Nazis, and the Kosarian Schutz Staffeln, the KSS, similar to the German SS who armed and trained them. Well, we already knew that bit as we've met some of these chaps, haven't we?"

The others chorused agreement. Inspector Sharpe went on. "The KSS had its own Secret Service Branch, the 'Iron Claw'. They infiltrated secretly into Kosaria and prepared to take over the government by force. In preparation, they carried out murders of selected leaders loyal to King Peter and spread deliberate lies about the Royal Family; that they practised witchcraft, and that both the King and Queen had secret lovers and so on."

"I wish I had a secret lover," Stephen said.

His friends scoffed and laughed. Inspector Sharpe eyed him speculatively. "How old are you Stephen?"

Stephen went red and took off his glasses to polish them. "Er, fifteen, sir. Old enough."

"Hmmm. Technically, yes, legally no. Let's get on with this story. Before dawn on 6th April 1941, the KSS struck. Special Action Teams attacked the Palace, Army HQ, Police HQ, the Radio Station, government offices, and the countries only airport. Iron Claw murder squads began killing selected important people in their homes."

As Roger listened to this, he felt a chill of horror. "What disgusting animals!" he cried.

Inspector Sharpe nodded grimly and read on. "At first light, German paratroops were dropped in to assist the KSS. This was part of a simultaneous attack by two German Army Groups on Yugoslavia, Kosaria, and Greece." He turned the book to show photos of aircraft with black crosses on them, and of parachutes scattered across the sky.

Stephen pointed to one of the aircraft. "I've got a model of one of those," he said, "That's a JU 52, the transport plane with three motors."

DS Crowe turned and growled. "I wish you kids would shut up. We'll be here all night otherwise."

The boys fell silent, all secretly afraid of the tough looking man. Inspector Sharpe resumed reading.

"By treachery, the KSS managed to penetrate the palace, but the Royal Guard fought bravely. There was desperate fighting in and around the palace which went on for over an hour. The Germans then landed glider-borne troops in the nearby park and these tipped the balance in favour of the attackers. The King, Queen and baby Crown Prince were trapped in the East Wing of the palace, which was on fire.

"At that critical moment, help arrived. As soon as the first German attackers had been identified, the British Ambassador had called for assistance from the British forces that had moved into Greece. The commander of the British 1st Armoured Brigade, the formation which was the corps covering force, at once ordered the nearest squadron of the 4th Hussars to the area. At 0800hrs, a troop of armoured cars led by 2nd Lieutenant Ponsonby-Smythe, arrived in the capital after driving from the border."

Graham couldn't help himself. He broke into an exaggerated imitation of an English officer. "By Jove! Ponsonby! In the nick of time too!"

"Jolly good show!" Peter replied. "Stout chap, Ponsonby."

Even DS Crowe laughed. Stephen added. "It reminds me of the joke about Ponsonby and the Burmese Princess."

"That will do!" Inspector Sharpe said severely.

Stephen grinned. "Oh sir! We know all the jokes about when The Regiment was in India."

"I don't doubt. But this story is in Kosaria, so let me get on with it. The British armoured cars were led to the palace by a captain of the Royal Guard. The King, Queen and Crown Prince were bundled in and driven to safety. The survivors of the Royal Guard then fought their way clear.

"Only then was it realised that the baby Princess Karena and her nurse were not with the group. A counter-attack was launched by the Royal Guard but failed with heavy loss of life." He paused and looked at the boys. "You have probably guessed who the captain was. It was Boris Krapinski. He led the counter--attack to try to rescue the princess but was badly wounded. He was carried to safety in one of the British armoured cars."

There was a moment's silence. Roger felt somehow that he had been honoured to have touched such a brave and loyal man, even if only in death. He felt an unaccustomed constriction in the throat.

Inspector Sharpe resumed, "The British armoured cars, with the Royal Family, plus survivors of the Royal Guard and remnants of other loyal army units fought their way out of the capital and withdrew to Greece, only just ahead of a German Panzer Division which had smashed its way in from Bulgaria.

"In Greece, the royal family were driven to Athens, then evacuated by sea to Egypt on the British cruiser HMS *Orion* and the Australian cruiser HMAS *Perth*."

Graham spoke up. "My Grandad was on *Perth,* sir. He was a lieutenant then."

"Was he, eh? Did he survive the war? *Perth* was sunk by the Japanese in Sunda Strait only a few months later."

Graham nodded. "Yes, sir. He was transferred to a corvette and fought around New Guinea. He lives in Mareeba now."

"Good. Well, that is the Royal Family safe, except for the Princess Karena. She was never seen again. As part of the coup, the KSS sent a Special Action Team to the cathedral to seize the Thigh Bone of St Joris. They shot down the ceremonial guard of five officers who always guarded it, as well as two priests and a dozen people who were at morning Mass.

"However, as the KSS were leaving the cathedral, they were counter-attacked by a squad of Royal Guards. There was a savage hand-to-hand battle on the steps and the Thigh Bone of St Joris has never been seen from that day to this."

"The bloody Thigh Bone of St Joris!" Peter groaned. "That has to be what these mongrels are looking for."

"Could be," the Inspector agreed. "Anyway, Yugoslavia, it doesn't exist anymore remember, Kosaria and Greece all come under German control. The Archduke Paul was installed as ruler of Kosaria, but the Germans never allowed him to crown himself King. In reality, he was just a puppet. He was extremely unpopular and the KSS were widely hated for their brutal methods. Resistance to the Germans soon developed. This was led by the Kosarian Kommunist Party under the leadership of Comrade Chairman Slobodan Turderov."

"Turderov!" Stephen snickered.

Inspector Sharpe frowned at him then read on. "By 1943, the Kommunist Partisans had set up an army of resistance and an intelligence network throughout the country. They began a guerrilla war against the KSS and Germans. By early 1944 the Partisans controlled nearly all the western mountains and the Germans could only move freely on the heavily guarded main routes.

"Most Kosarians did not like the Kommunists but supported them because they led the resistance. The Partisans carried out ambushes, raids and sabotage. They also murdered people who did not agree with their politics, including leaders who were loyal to the King.

"As the war began to go against the Germans, Paul began losing support. People secretly changed sides, or slipped into hiding. In October 1944 the Russian Red Army, communists of course in those days, drove the Germans out of Romania and Bulgaria. The Germans began withdrawing their forces from Greece and Kosaria so they would not be cut-off.

"When the Russian advance reached the Kosarian border the remaining Germans withdrew very rapidly. With them went Prince Paul, his remaining KSS supporters, and the Kosarian Crown Jewels."

"Jewels!" Stephen cried.

Inspector Sharpe paused and raised an eyebrow. "During the retreat, the Crown Jewels were lost. The convoy was ambushed in the Vulture's Pass. Treachery was involved because the ambushers knew exactly which vehicle, out of hundreds, was the one carrying the jewels. The trap was sprung in such a way as to isolate it. The ambushers wore Partisan badges and uniforms, but the Kommunists have always claimed it was not their men who did it. They say that it's a lie to cover the identity of the people who really stole the crown jewels."

The boys exchanged glances. Roger spoke their thoughts. "Crown Jewels!"

"The Kommunists claim it was all just a deception and that the KSS actually had the jewels in other vehicles and got away with them. So it may not be the Crown Jewels," Inspector Sharpe commented. He went on, "Kosaria then fell under the control of the Russians, who set up a communist government, led by Turderov."

Peter interrupted. "I hope there aren't any communists involved in this. I don't like them after what they did to Grandpa and Omma."

"Well there are."

"I thought all communist governments fell years ago?" Graham said.

"They did. All except for Kosaria. In Europe that is. Kosaria is the last communist state in Europe."

"I hope I don't meet any," Peter said.

"You very well may if I see you again. One of the officers from their embassy is joining me tomorrow," replied the Inspector. "The Kosarians are very worried about what's going on up here."

Roger sat up. "Why's that, sir? Do they want the treasure?"

The Inspector hesitated, then replied, "You lads don't follow the news do you. The Deputy Premier of Kosaria, their Number Two man, is on a state visit to Australia. He's in Cairns tonight and will be visiting Mareeba and Dimbulah tomorrow, and Atherton and Herberton the day after. Knowing that the Archduke Paul's thugs are here, and murdering people, has the people at the Kosarian Embassy very worried."

Roger frowned. "Why is he here, sir?"

"Usual things, trade and good relations I suppose. Remember, there are a lot of Kosarian migrants living on the Tablelands."

Stephen spoke next. "What happened to the Archduke Paul and the KSS at the end of the war sir?"

"They appear to have fled with the Germans. Their organisation rapidly fell apart as the rats left the sinking ship. Paul was last seen in Zagreb in April 1945 but then vanished. It was rumoured that he escaped to South America in a German U-Boat which sailed from Trieste on 2nd May 1945. Other KSS men have definitely been seen living in Argentina, Brazil and Paraguay."

Stephen grinned. "The *Boys from Brazil*," he said. "We've seen all the movies sir."

Roger nodded. "Paraguay certainly fits. Two of the four we met had Paraguayan passports," he added.

Graham looked puzzled. "Why are there a lot of Kosarian migrants here sir?" he asked.

"Remember what I said about Krapinski a couple of days ago? Thousands fled the country during World War Two. A lot of their army retreated to join ours in Greece. There was a British Empire army there which included the 6th Australian Division and the 2nd New Zealand Division."

"And Ponsonby," Stephen added. They all laughed.

"Yes, and Ponsonby. Our forces were outnumbered about twelve to one. The Germans had four Panzer Divisions against one British Armoured brigade. That's stiff odds, even for Ponsonby. And they had two Austrian Mountain Divisions; and Greece is mostly mountains. We didn't have a chance, so it was a fighting withdrawal back to the sea, then evacuation by the British Navy back to Crete and Egypt.

"A Kosarian Brigade was reconstituted, which served with the British 8th Army in the North African desert and then in Italy. As a result many got to know Australian and New Zealand soldiers. After the war it was not safe for them to return to a Kosaria run by communists who were busy executing any royalists they could lay hands on. So they became refugees and migrated to Australia. It's just coincidence many of them settled here on the Atherton Tablelands. I suppose they liked the place."

"What about King Peter, sir?" Roger queried.

"The Royal Family lived in Egypt until the end of the war, then went to live in England. Over the years there were a number of attempts made on their lives. This culminated in the murder of the King and Queen while they were walking in Regents Park before the Cold War ended. They were killed by agents using poison-tipped umbrellas.

"It was assumed that the Kommunists carried out the murders, but it has never been proven and they deny any involvement. The Crown Prince, who would be Peter V if he is ever crowned, went into hiding and has not been seen in public since."

Inspector Sharpe then said, "Kosaria is apparently in trouble. Their economy is in a mess, there are food shortages and a lot of unemployment.

There have even been riots demanding freedom and democracy. These have been brutally put down by the KOSPAR, the Kosarian Partisans, that is the communist army. The communists are managing to keep control by fear and by force but apparently the place is a powder keg ready for civil war and revolution. The speculation is that when Turdorov dies, from old age if nothing else, then the place will erupt in revolution."

Roger tried to imagine this. He didn't pay much attention to the news and now felt quite ignorant and ill-informed.

Graham then asked, "Do I get this right, sir. There are two rival princes, Peter and Paul, one hiding in Paraguay and the other hiding God knows where, plus the Kommunist government in Kosaria?"

"That's about the size of it."

Graham nodded, looking serious. "So maybe, if Krapinski was a captain in the Royal Guard, then the KSS may not be looking for the Thigh Bone of St Joris or a treasure, but for a person, a Crown Prince, one they would probably like to kill."

The Inspector sat up. "You could have something there. If the Archduke Paul's men, the KSS, are here, perhaps the Crown Prince's men are here too? Perhaps their organisation also still exists?"

"I think it does, sir," Stephen said.

"What makes you say that?"

Stephen held up the captured signal. "This message we have been translating from German."

"Ah yes! What does it say?"

"We haven't quite finished translating it yet, sir. Can we finish it?"

"Yes, do that," he chuckled. "My word, you kids are doing more to solve this case than we are!"

Chapter 20

THE SECRET MESSAGE

Roger sat and watched Graham and Stephen finish translating the secret message. He saw by the clock it was 2315hrs, but his mind was so active he did not feel tired. This was the most exciting and interesting thing he had ever been involved in.

Inspector Sharpe returned and sat talking to DS Crowe. Peter went downstairs to the laundry. Roger fidgeted with impatience while Graham and Stephen worked.

A long 10 minutes dragged by before Graham cried out, "We've finished it, sir."

"Good work. Read it out."

Graham turned and called, "Okay. Hey Pete! Come up here."

Peter came and sat next to Roger.

"All ready?" Graham asked. "Okay, this is a Radio Message Form. The title at the top says that. Then there are these ruled boxes across the top section of the page. The first box says, 'Security Class'. Next to that is written 'Secret'. There is then some sort of reference number system, KSS/SAT/9, 001, 673."

Sgt Crowe looked at it. "For filing in records probably," he suggested.

Graham went on, "Then it says: 'Message Handling Instructions' and a three letter code which we don't understand. After that comes a Date/Time Group. That is written in military style: 170800K JUN."

Peter looked interested. "That is the same system we use. Why would they use that?" he asked.

DS Crowe replied. "Probably because most countries have adopted the American system that NATO uses."

Roger spoke next. "So it was only sent at 8 o'clock this morning."

Graham agreed. "Then it says, 'From' and 'To'. It is from the 'Obersturmbannfuhrer Australie'. That is the Lieutenant Colonel Australia, to the 'Untersturmfuhrer' or lieutenant of detachment or Group, Abteilung, it's hard for me to give it an exact meaning, Detachment Rainforest."

Roger nodded. "That is the man with the glasses," he added.

Graham also nodded. "Yes. Now comes the text of the message. It is actually a message within a message so I will read it all. Don't interrupt me," he instructed.

He then read slowly and carefully while both Inspector Sharpe and DS Crowe made notes.

"Paragraph One. The following message has been overheard or intercepted. It was sent by the General Staff of the Royal Army to Colonel Count Michael Von Krapnoff, Kommandant of the Royal Guard.

"Paragraph Two. The intercepted message says: 'Operation Return' is planned for 19th June. Company Knight is to group at Concentration Place Cloud. Cloud is some sort of nickname, I think. Then it says: 'Red Eagle is still following his travel plan'.

"Paragraph Three. You will meet White Falcon at Legend Hill. In brackets it says: 'This is a codename whose exact location we do not know but it is believed to be a road junction between Malanda and Yungaburra', brackets end. It goes on to say: 'Between two Date/Time Groups: 171800Z and 172400Z JUN. White Falcon will be in a grey Mercedes with three other people including Adjutant Stiltz. You are to guide White Falcon to Concentration Place Cloud. Message ends.

"Paragraph Four. KSS Detachment Rainforest is to secretly observe the meeting, then follow Von Krapnoff to locate his secret hiding place. It is most important that the Royalist HQ be found within the next thirty-six hours.

"Paragraph Five. Major Gostyxz is coming to assist you. He lands at Mareeba Airport on Tuesday at 1600hrs. Meet Gostyxz and have the answers or, there are four dots. Message ends."

There was complete silence for a moment while they all thought hard about what they had just heard. Then they broke into an excited babble of talk. Inspector Sharpe slapped his hand on the table. "Quiet! I will ask questions. You answer them. Now, does the KSS exist?"

"Yes sir," Graham replied. "We know that because we, you have captured some of its members. We have their badges. And we have this message."

"Question Two," Inspector Sharpe asked, writing it down as he did. "Who is the message from?"

"The Obersturmbannfuhrer Australia," Stephen replied.

"Who or what is he?"

Roger put his hand up. "He must be the KSS chief in Australia," he answered.

"Probably. So what else can we deduce?"

"That there are KSS in other countries as well, like Paraguay," Peter offered.

"Yes. Good. Now, who was the message to?"

Stephen held the sheet up. "The... the Untersturmfuhrer commanding Detachment Rainforest," he read out.

"Good. That is Mr Jablonski, currently assisting police with their enquiries. Was he alone?"

Graham shook his head. "No, sir. He had at least three others with him," he answered.

"What is he?"

"A Kosarian?" Roger answered.

"Yes. But that's not what I meant," Inspector Sharpe replied.

"I know," Peter said. "He is the leader of a Special Action Team."

Inspector Sharpe nodded. "That is what I think too. How many men in a Special Action Team?"

"Nine," Stephen replied.

"How many men have we accounted for?"

"Only four," Graham answered.

"No," Roger said. "Only three. One was a colonel, the old guy."

Inspector Sharpe nodded. "That's right, Roger. So there could be six more around. I doubt if there are, but we must plan on that assumption. Now, when was the message sent?"

"Eight o'clock this morning," Graham answered.

"It was a message within a message. The message within was one they had intercepted somehow from their enemies. What does that suggest? How did the KSS get it?"

"Radio intercept?" Peter suggested.

"Possibly," Inspector Sharpe replied.

"Treachery," Roger said. "From a traitor in the royal organisation."

"Have a chocolate frog Roger! That's what I think too, and I even think I know who our treacherous double, agent is. Listen to this. It is from the Diary of Boris Krapinski, which you recovered for us this afternoon," Inspector Sharpe said.

173

He reached into a plastic bag and took out the small diary. Flicking it open at a marked page he read, "13th June. After all these years the White Falcon has called for me at last. I must go. Dorkoffsky gave me the message but I don't trust him. I will lay a trail to check. I will put out the clues tomorrow." Inspector Sharpe closed the diary. "That is the last entry. He was murdered the next day."

"Dorkoffsky," Roger hissed. "This is his house."

"Yes."

Graham looked puzzled. "Did Captain Krapinski put out the clues?"

"We don't know. That may be what these numbers on the pieces of blue cardboard are," Inspector Sharpe replied, indicating them.

"Clues to what?" Peter asked.

"Where to find the treasure of course!" Roger cried.

"Why not lead his people to it, or give it to them?" Peter asked.

Stephen answered that. "Because he obviously feared treachery and he wanted some sort of extra insurance it wouldn't fall into the wrong hands," he suggested. "He said he would lay a trail to check. I'll bet he was going to watch from in hiding who followed that trail."

"Possibly," Graham conceded. "He was right to be careful."

"But not careful enough," DS Crowe added grimly.

They were all silent for a moment. Then Inspector Sharpe ended this speculation by asking, "Who is the intercepted message from?"

"The General Staff of the Kosarian... no... of the Royal Army," Stephen read out.

"Who is it to?"

"Colonel Count Michael Von Krapnoff, Kommandant of the Royal Guard," Stephen read.

"Who do we know for sure was in the Royal Guard?"

"Captain Krapinski," Roger answered. His fingers seemed to curl up as they involuntarily shrank back as he had a vivid flash, back to when he first touched the floating corpse.

"He was. But would they have such an old man in such an organisation?" the Inspector quizzed.

"Yes!" Roger was emphatic.

"So you think the Royal Guard still exists?"

"Definitely sir," Graham said. "Why would there be a signal to its kommandant, this Colonel Krapnoff, if it didn't exist?"

"Good deduction. And nor would the KSS be interested in them otherwise. Now, what do the Royal Guard do?"

"Guard the Royal Family," Peter suggested.

"Guard Prince Peter," Graham said.

"Which Prince Peter?"

"The one who was the baby, whose parents were murdered in London," Stephen said.

The Inspector nodded. "The prince was born in 1941. He could still be alive."

"Yes," Peter answered. "He'd be old, but not ancient."

"Where is he?"

"Here, of course," Roger answered. "Here, on the Tablelands."

"Why do you think that?"

"Because this is where the commander of his bodyguard is."

The Inspector sat in silent thought for a moment, then went on. "What does the intercepted message say?"

Stephen read it again, "Colonel Krapnoff is to meet the White Falcon at Legend Hill at... between those two times, and then guide him to Concentration Place 'Cloud'."

"What are the timings. Read them again."

"Between 171800Zulu and 172400Zulu June," Stephen read. The Inspector jotted them down.

Graham looked at the wall clock. "Oh. We are too late. It's nearly midnight now. We've only got 20 minutes to try to catch them."

Inspector Sharpe looked at the clock and swore. He stood up and walked to the telephone.

"Wait sir," Peter called. "Those timings are in Zulu Time. That is Time Zone Zulu, which is Greenwich Mean Time."

"Good lad!" Inspector Sharpe beamed. "That's ten hours behind us. So what are those timings in local time?"

"Between 0400hrs and 1000hrs tomorrow," Peter answered.

"There is time!" Roger squeaked with excitement.

Inspector Sharpe sat down. "Let's keep teasing this out. Where is the meeting place?"

"Legend Hill. It's a nickname or code name, and is believed to be a road junction between here and Malanda," Stephen read.

Inspector Sharpe snapped his fingers. "Quick, a map."

Graham pulled out his 1:100 000 scale map and unfolded it on the table. They all crowded around to look.

"There are a lot of road junctions," Stephen noted.

Peter ran his fingertip across the map. "On a hill. A road junction on a hill," he suggested.

"That's better. Let's see now. Count them," Inspector Sharpe said.

Roger looked at the web of roads between Yungaburra and Malanda and was instantly depressed. He didn't bother to count. There were at least three routes, all interconnected by several laterals.

Graham did and he said, "There are at least twenty-five road junctions, not counting dead-ends going to farms."

When he heard that Roger felt a stab of dismay.

"But only fourteen are on, or close to hill tops," Peter said. "That's not too bad."

Inspector Sharpe turned to DS Crowe. "Start planning Crowe. How can we get the manpower to watch them all; and to get them in position within three hours?" He turned to the boys. "What else do we get out of this message?"

Roger put his hand up. "Sir, can we help? We could watch a couple of road junctions," he suggested.

"No Roger. Sorry. This could be dangerous, and it's police business. You just go on with your hike."

Roger didn't try to hide his disappointment. It had seemed such a good idea; and he really wanted to help solve the mystery.

Inspector Sharpe went on. "Okay, who is the White Falcon?"

"Didn't I read that the Royal Guard was the White Falcon Regiment?" Graham asked.

"White Eagle wasn't it?" Peter corrected.

Inspector Sharpe picked up the History Book. Roger looked at the cover. Suddenly he jabbed his finger at it.

"The White Falcon! There it is, with a crown on it. The White Falcon is the King."

They all looked at the cover. Inspector Sharpe bit his lip. "I have a sinking feeling you are right. The Crown Prince anyway. He isn't a King until he is crowned, and I suppose that can only be done with the proper ceremony in their national cathedral."

Roger felt a pulse of excitement. "Prince Peter! Here, on the

Tablelands!" he cried. It seemed unbelievable. He'd once seen Prince William in the distance at a Scout Jamboree in Sydney. That was the closest he had ever come to royalty.

Graham added, "He must be important anyway, if a general orders a colonel to go and meet him."

Inspector Sharpe asked, "What else do we know about him?"

Stephen read from the sheet. "He will be in a grey Mercedes with three other men; one of whom is Adjutant Stiltz."

"We should be able to spot that sir," DS Crowe growled. "There can't be that many grey Mercedes on the Tablelands."

Inspector Sharpe nodded. "Yes. It gives us a chance. Bloody hell! Here's me worrying about the Kosarian Deputy Premier's visit and now we've got a Crown Prince swanning around as well. Blast! Why couldn't this just be a simple murder?"

"We will need more men sir," DS Crowe said.

"Lots more. And Federal as well as State. Let's see what we can work out before we hit the panic button. Where is this White Falcon going?"

Graham answered. "Concentration Place Cloud. That's 'Sammelplatz' in German," he explained. "It's a literal translation, but in the dictionary it had 'mil' in brackets after it so I think it means what we would call an Assembly Area."

"Mil?"

"Military sir. It's a military technical term."

"What's an Assembly Area?"

"Where troops from different units group together and get organised for an attack sir." Graham replied.

For a moment there was complete silence. Inspector Sharpe swore softly, then asked, "Where?"

Graham shrugged. "A place called 'Cloud'. It is a codeword. So we don't know where."

"What troops?" asked the Inspector. He now looked very worried.

Stephen read from the message, "Company Knight sir, for a thing called 'Operation Return'."

"A company is about a hundred men isn't it?" DS Crowe asked.

Graham nodded. "A hundred and thirty in our army," he replied.

DS Crowe swore then said, "Christ! Could they have that many men in this Royal Guard?"

No-one answered. It was a sobering thought.

Peter frowned. "I wonder what 'Operation Return' is?" he asked.

Graham flung out an arm in a theatrical gesture and said, "I shall return! You know, General Macarthur in World War Two. In this case I'll bet it is the return to the old country."

Inspector Sharpe looked at him with a grim frown. "I think you've got it lad. These Kosarians have formed a secret army here and probably plan to go back to Kosaria to start a revolution, to try to put the king back on his throne."

"That makes sense," Stephen said.

"It might. But it's bloody illegal. These bloody foreigners have no right to break our laws while having their own political squabbles," Inspector Sharpe snapped, pounding the table.

Roger was puzzled so he said, "But sir, if the Kosarian government are Communists I can understand why they and the Royal Guard are enemies. But where do the KSS come into it?"

"Oh Roger!" Stephen sneered. "We just had pages of it. First Peter, then Paul, then Peter, then Paul! Obviously, the Archduke Paul wants to be the king, so he's sent his men to bump off Prince Peter."

"Yes. I see that," Roger replied. "But then why are the KSS digging holes and searching the jungle? What are they looking for?"

"Something Krapinski hid," Peter suggested.

"But what?"

"The Thigh Bone of St Joris?" Graham answered.

"The gold." Stephen said.

Peter shook his head. "No. The Crown Jewels. You need a crown to have a coronation," he stated emphatically.

"Stop!" Inspector Sharpe said. "We are starting to go round in circles. It's nearly midnight. Let's finish picking this message to pieces. Read the whole thing again Stephen."

Stephen did so and Inspector Sharpe said, "Okay, this Operation Return is timed for the 19th, in two days' time. Tomorrow is the 18th. In fact, it's nearly tomorrow now. So we don't have much time."

"That ties in with this bit where it says the KSS must find the Royal Guard HQ within thirty-six hours," Stephen suggested.

"It could. Let's see. Thirty-six hours from eight o'clock this morning is..."

"2000hrs tomorrow," Peter replied.

"Only twenty hours! Bloody hell! Now, who is this Red Eagle who is still following his travel plan?"

DS Crowe spoke first. "Red, Communist colour. The Kosarian Deputy Premier?"

"Could be. I suppose they would keep close tabs on their enemy's movements. Now, the KSS have been ordered to watch this meeting, then follow the White Falcon. If there are more KSS we could well end up bumping into them when we try to put those road junctions under surveillance," Inspector Sharpe said.

Stephen laughed. "It will be like 'Spy versus Spy'!"

DS Crowe gave him a sour look. "Yes. It is a real worry. These characters obviously mean business. It certainly complicates things."

"It certainly does," Inspector Sharpe agreed. "We don't want any gun play. Also, this Major Gostyxz is coming to help the local KSS lads. He lands at Mareeba airport tomorrow at four pm. He is to be met and they are to have the answer or..."

"Or what sir?" Roger asked.

"Or bloody else Roger. It is a threat. And I think these chaps back up their threats," Inspector Sharpe said.

He made a pistol of his fingers and pretended to shoot it and blow smoke from the barrel. Roger felt his hair stand on end and a wave of goose bumps swept up his back. Krapinski's shattered skull with the hair all...!

DS Crowe gave a mirthless grinned. "He will be easy to deal with anyway," he said. "We will certainly make sure he is met at the airport."

Roger shivered. He would hate to be 'met' by DS Crowe. "I didn't know airlines flew into Mareeba," he said.

"They don't. He has either chartered a light plane or the KSS own one," Crowe replied.

"What will we do now sir?" Graham asked.

"I've got to get on the phone and start wheels turning. There is nothing more you lads can do. I suggest you go to bed."

Roger looked at the clock. Five past midnight. Suddenly he yawned. That set all the others going. The excitement ebbed away, and his mind seemed to shut down as though a battery had gone flat. He realised he was very tired.

Chapter 21

IN THE FOG

As he went to stand up, Roger found that all of his muscles had tightened up. He cried out in pain, then used his arms to lever himself to his feet. There were more stabs of pain and he groaned.

Peter laughed. "Come on, grandad!" he said. "Coming Graham? Steve?"

Graham looked up. "We will just make a neat copy of this message for the Inspector. We won't be long."

"OK."

Roger hobbled to the stairs. Inspector Sharpe and DS Crowe sat hunched over the map, busily making notes. Peter went down into the laundry. Roger followed, a step at a time, thankful there was a handrail.

Peter met him at the laundry door. "Here are your clothes Roger, all clean and fresh." He dumped a warm bundle in Roger's arms.

"Thanks," Roger said. Clutching the bundle he turned and hobbled along the corridor. The clean clothes felt deliciously warm. He turned into their bedroom.

And came to a standstill.

Outside the glass sliding door a man was bending over his pack!

The man was middle-aged, with a solid build. He had a squarish face, tanned skin with many wrinkles in the neck, short, close, cropped grey hair and grey eyebrows.

At that moment the man looked up and saw Roger. *Brown eyes,* Roger noted. Hard, unfriendly eyes. The man abruptly straightened up and walked out of sight.

"Hey!" Roger cried. He tossed the clothes on the bed, walked quickly to the door and wrenched it open. "Hey! There is a man out here!" he called.

Without thinking Roger stepped outside. He was just in time to see the man turn the corner of the house. Roger walked quickly after him.

Away from the light of the room it was quite dark and only as he reached the corner did Roger realise there was a heavy fog. He could just make out the shape of a man walking quickly up the driveway. A streetlight showed as just a dim, golden glow.

Roger started up the driveway, his aches and pains forgotten. "Hey you! Who are you? Stop!" he called out.

The man reached the street and turned right. Roger was 20 paces behind. He tried to run but his muscles began to cramp. When he reached the footpath, he looked along the footpath, just in time to see a ghostly figure pass under the streetlight, to be swallowed up by the fog.

Only then did Roger hesitate. Should he chase the man in the fog and darkness? *What if the man turns and attacks me? What if he has a gun?* he thought.

Those thoughts stopped him and he stood, hopping from foot to foot in indecision. Dimly he was aware of doors opening and of voices behind him. Then the fear hit him. It seemed to wash over him as though he had been doused in ice, water.

He turned and saw Peter running up the driveway. At the front door, silhouetted in the bar of light, were Graham, Stephen, Inspector Sharpe and DS Crowe.

"What's going on?" Inspector Sharpe called as he started across the lawn.

"A man sir. He was looking through our gear. He went off that way."

Peter arrived first and went to run along the street.

"Hold it young fella!" DS Crowe snapped as he ran past. With a shock Roger saw that the sergeant had a pistol in his hand. So had Inspector Sharpe. The fear became solid ice.

"Don't follow him Crowe!" Inspector Sharpe ordered. "Describe what happened Roger."

Roger did so, also describing the man's face.

"What was he wearing?"

"A Coat Man's Field, dark grey long trousers and black rubber-soled shoes."

"Coat Mansfield? What the devil is that?"

"An army field jacket sir, a dark green coat," Roger flustered as he tried to explain.

Graham spoke up. "We've all got one sir. I'll show it to you. It's just army 'Q' Store jargon. The coat and then the type; for men and for field service."

"Ah. I see. Yes. Let's get back to the house. It's damned cold out here. Don't you do that again young Roger! It was a bloody silly thing to do. You could have met a bullet coming the other way."

"Yes, sir. I realise that now, sir," Roger replied. He shivered and peered into the gloom.

DS Crowe slipped his pistol back into its shoulder holster. "Well, now we know there are more of the bastards lurking in the area anyway," he growled.

They went back down the driveway and Roger showed the policemen where the man had been. By then he was shaking with fright and the darkness and fog on the back lawn seemed very threatening.

Inspector Sharpe pointed indoors. "You boys get all your gear inside," he ordered.

When they had done so he locked the door and pulled the curtains across. "Now, you are to stay inside. You are not to leave the house till I say so. Go to bed."

The two policemen went upstairs. Graham and Stephen followed to finish rewriting the message. Roger sat on the bed and trembled.

"You okay mate?" Peter asked.

"Yeah. I just got a fright."

"A good sleep will help."

"Who gets the bed?"

"You have it. You deserve it after that effort this afternoon. That was real gutsy," Peter said.

Roger glowed with pleasure. "What about you blokes?"

"We will sleep on the floor. It's okay with this thick carpet," Peter assured him.

"Sure?"

"Yes. Don't argue."

Roger pushed the clothes off the bed and lay back with a sigh. He closed his eyes and tried to relax his trembling muscles. He found his mind spinning with emotions and thoughts and knew he was over, tired. His mind raced; jumbled thoughts of the KSS and murder and secret meetings. He also began worrying about intruders sneaking in during the night.

Peter turned off the light and arranged his bedding near the glass door. Roger pretended to be asleep but kept opening an eye to check. He despaired of going to sleep but it claimed him gently. He did not even hear Graham and Stephen come down, or their grumbling while they organised their beds.

Roger slept so soundly he hardly moved all night. When he was woken he could not even remember dreaming. His muscles felt very stiff, but he was only slightly tired, with a small headache behind his eyes. He saw that Inspector Sharpe had turned the light on and was shaking Peter. The Inspector was wearing a thick overcoat and looked cold and tired. Roger rubbed sleep from his eyes and sat up. As he did, a groan was wrenched from him as stiff muscles let their displeasure felt.

"Oouch! Oooh! Uh! Hello sir. Good morning."

"Good morning, Roger. Sleep well?"

"Yes, sir. Like a log. Did you?"

Inspector Sharpe gave a short laugh. "Huh! No such luck. I haven't been to bed yet."

Roger woke up abruptly as memory flooded back. "Sir! You've been looking for the White Falcon in his grey Mercedes. Did you find him?"

"Quite right, I have. And no, we haven't seen any sign of him."

The others were awake and listening by this. Graham asked, "What do you want us to do now sir?"

"I'm going to have breakfast, then go out again. Are you lads still set on going ahead with your hike?" Inspector Sharpe asked, turning to look at Roger who was rubbing his calf muscles.

Roger felt put on a spot as the others looked at him too. *Could I do it?* he wondered.

He had made it the previous day when they had marched over 30 kilometres. They had 50 to go and two days: perhaps 25 each day. He set his jaw.

"Yes, sir. We do," he said.

"Good lad. That's the spirit."

Stephen spoke up. "Do you think it is safe sir? That man saw us last night."

"I've been thinking about that. He may assume you are working with the police, but I think it is unlikely he will see you; and even more unlikely he would bother you. I suspect these KSS types must be puzzled about what has happened to Dorkoffsky and his scaly mates; so they'll be worried and be slithering away under rocks."

"Can we help sir?" Roger asked.

"Thanks for the offer Roger, but no. You have been a great help, but this is serious police business. You go on with your hike. Do you know where you go next?"

Graham answered. "Yes, sir. Our last clue directed us to the Curtain Fig Tree."

Inspector Sharpe nodded. "I'm going to lock this place up when I leave. Do you think you could be out of here in half an hour? Say by six thirty?"

"Yes, sir. We can eat our breakfast on the back patio if that's okay?" Graham answered.

"Fine. I will see you before I go."

"I'm going to have a hot shower then," Roger said. He got to his feet with a groan.

In reply Stephen sprang up and pushed Roger. "I'm first! You had the bed," he cried. Caught by surprise Roger fell back on the bed. Stephen pointed at him. "Hold him down while I get my soap and towel," he ordered.

Graham at once grabbed Roger and sat on him. "Tickle him Pete."

Peter joined in. Inspector Sharpe grinned, shook his head and left the room. Roger squirmed and shrieked.

About 20 minutes later he stepped from the hot shower into a bathroom filled with steam and towelled himself dry. He felt much better, almost fresh. He was even looking forward to the day. Well, almost. Ruefully he examined the blue, black blotching of bruises. They appeared to encircle his entire mid-section. His chafing wasn't too bad he decided, and the blisters had mostly subsided.

He pulled on clean underwear and a fresh uniform and felt better. Then he went out into the bedroom. The others had all moved outside. The light in the room had been turned off and the sliding door was open. Roger saw that thick fog still blanketed the back lawn. He collected his gear and carried it out.

The transition from the warm room to outdoors was abrupt. His bare feet met concrete which felt like ice and the first breath seemed to scour its way down his nostrils.

"Cripes it's cold! I'm going back to bed," he cried.

The others laughed. Roger lumped his gear to a clear space on the patio and looked around. The fog was so thick he could barely see the garage a few metres away. The lake at the bottom of the lawn was invisible. It was very gloomy and depressing. He pulled out his pullover and put it on, then sat to put sticking plaster on his blisters.

Graham went in to have a shower and shave. The other two had their stoves alight and were cooking. Roger pulled on socks and boots before digging out his own stove. A cup of Milo, liberally sweetened with condensed milk gave him a lift. Then he had two Weetbix with warm milk. A muesli bar followed.

Graham returned, talking to Inspector Sharpe. The Inspector looked at their cooking arrangements and asked what they were having for breakfast.

"Smells good Peter. What is it?"

"Beef Stroganoff sir."

"What else! Well, I'll be off. I will lock this door and go out the front way. Thank you for your help. I will ask you to telephone me when you finish so that I know that you are safe. Here is the number." He wrote in a notebook, tore the page out and passed it to Graham. "Goodbye then, and once again, thanks for your help. Remember not to mention this to anyone; and beware of strangers. Good luck."

"See you sir. We will be careful," Graham promised.

"I hope you catch all these foreigners," Stephen added.

Roger said nothing. He wished he could go with the Inspector more than anything he could think of. He gave a small smile and turned back to heating a tin of Pork and Beans. The Inspector slid the door shut and locked it.

Stephen said, "I wonder if he will catch these KSS creeps?"

"I hope so. We don't want types like that lurking around our country," Peter replied.

Graham sat down and picked up a boot. "Eat up you lot. It's ten to seven," he said.

Inwardly Roger groaned. "So we have plenty of time. We could sit here till midday and still cover the twenty-five kilometres before dark."

Graham looked up, then burst into laughter. "Quite right Roger. Okay, we will aim at being on the road by seven thirty."

"I wish Inspector Sharpe hadn't locked the house. I need to go to the dunny now," Peter complained.

"You will have to save it till we are in town then," Stephen replied unsympathetically. "There is a toilet in the main street."

"Where do you think the next clue will take us?" Roger asked.

"I reckon Atherton, or near it somewhere," Stephen said.

Graham tightened a boot lace. "That's what I think too. There is a High School there," he replied.

"There is one in Malanda too," Peter reminded.

Half an hour later the friends were crouched over the map studying the route. Graham laid out all the clues on the concrete. "Here is the first one. It says MT. BALDY on top and TWO CHIMNEYS underneath. Then at The Chimneys we got this one, which said HIGH SCHOOL on top and CURTAIN FIG underneath. So we still have to go to the Curtain Fig. Eventually I reckon we must end up at a high school and at Mt. Baldy, here, just west of Atherton."

Roger bent closer to look. "One thousand and seventeen metres. I hope we don't have to climb it!"

"I'll bet we do. You know Captain Conkey," Peter laughed.

"Cheer up Roger. That's the height above sea level and we are about seven hundred metres up now. So it won't be that bad," Graham said. He began folding the map. "Okay. Let's go. Pullovers off!" he ordered.

Roger didn't want to do that but knew it was the right thing to do. No matter how cold it was, if he was wearing a pullover he would sweat and then when he stopped the damp garment would chill. So he nerved himself to the cold and peeled the pullover off. It was stuffed into the top of his pack, ready to pull out as soon as they stopped.

He had only just clipped the pack up again when Graham gave the order, "Gear on."

With reluctance Roger complied, picking up his webbing and swinging it on. The sun was up by this, shining through the fog as a bright orange ball. Roger could see the water of the lake now. The fog had lifted a few metres and wisps of mist streamed up from black water that looked like polished glass. He groaned and hoisted on his pack.

They had to walk uphill for the first few hundred metres and Roger found this very testing as tight muscles warmed and loosened. He soon began to sweat.

By the time they reached Yungaburra's main street 10 minutes later the fog was no more than patches in the shady hollows.

"Not a cloud in the sky again," Graham observed.

"It will be another hot day," Peter grumbled.

"I'm hot already. Stop for a few minutes," Stephen said.

"Good idea. Over near that Bakery. They look like they are open," Roger added.

"Roger! We've only just started," Graham replied.

Stephen sniffed. "Oh yes! Smell that fresh bread!" he said.

That decided them. In spite of Graham's protests they crossed to a picnic table under a tree in the centre of the wide street, dropped their gear, pulled out pullovers and draped them over their backs with the sleeves wrapped around their throats for warmth, then headed for the shop. Peter made for the nearby public toilet.

At the door of the shop Graham grumbled. "But we've only been going for a few minutes."

"So?" Roger replied. "We've covered a kilometre. Twenty-four to go and ten hours to do them in. The slower we go the more likely I am to make it. Besides, I'm hungry."

In the shop Roger purchased a Steak and Kidney pie and a Sausage Roll. Stephen bought a loaf of freshly baked bread which he broke in two to share with Peter. Graham sulked but bought a Caramello chocolate. Stephen also purchased a newspaper.

They walked back to the picnic table. Stephen spread out the newspaper and began to read. Roger took out the warm pie and sniffed it in pleasurable anticipation. It smelt delicious.

Peter re-joined them. "Anything about the murder?" he asked, pointing to the newspaper.

"Not on the front page," Stephen replied. He turned the pages searching. "Nothing on any of the pages. Not that I can see."

They looked, but there was no mention of the previous day's events.

"I wonder if it was on radio or TV?" Roger asked.

"Maybe. But probably not. Remember the Inspector wanted to keep it quiet. He doesn't want to scare the other KSS off, so he can catch them too." Peter reminded him.

Roger nodded. "Yes. I know. I wish we could help."

Graham shook his head. "Forget it Roger. Ask him when it's over. Which reminds me, no loose talk in shops or around town," he said.

The boys sat in silence for a few minutes, eating and watching the lovely little town come slowly to life. Two attractive girls walked past. Graham watched them with open interest, then commented, "They are the third lot of good-looking girls to go past since we got here."

"Maybe we should spend the day here?" Peter said, tongue in cheek.

"Certainly a lot of pretty girls in this town," Stephen added. "Here comes another."

They looked across at a woman walking with a dog. Roger smiled at his friends comments and took another mouthful. He felt stiff and sore but he was happy. *We have reached the halfway point of the hike. I will make it,* he told himself.

He had been scared that he would have to give up during the first two days of the hike. Now it was Day 4 and he felt fitter and more confident.

By 0815hrs the boys were marching out of town. They crossed the small bridge on the western edge of town and turned left at the first road junction. There was already an uncomfortable amount of traffic, locals rushing to work. The route led up a long gentle hill along a bitumen road for three hundred metres. The sun was already hot enough to make them thankful when the road plunged into a tunnel of rain forest.

Apart from a few cars which raced past at high speed it was peaceful and it was easy walking. The road climbed gently and curved, first right, then left. A clearing opened out ahead with a bitumen car park.

"Here's the Curtain Fig Tree," Graham said.

"No-one else here," Peter added.

Stephen snorted. "Bit early for tourists!"

It was quite cool in the shadows. They dropped their gear next to a National Park sign which marked the end of a walking track. This led a short distance into the rain forest to the Curtain Fig Tree. Roger shivered as the cool air encountered his sweaty shirt when he swung off his pack. For a moment he considered getting his pullover out again but then shook his head as he decided it wasn't worth it."

Graham looked around. "Now, where would you hide a clue?"

"Where a tourist wouldn't find it and take it," Peter replied.

"And where a National Park Ranger picking up litter wouldn't see it," Roger added.

Graham took command. "Okay. Let's search. Look behind trees and rocks away from the track. Roger, you do this side of the track. Pete, you and Steve look on the other side."

Roger stepped off the track into open rain forest. There were numerous moss-covered stones amongst the tree trunks but very little undergrowth and only a few vines. He decided he was sick of rain forest. This patch did not impress him. It was cold and water dripped from everything, condensation from the fog.

It was only 50 metres in to where the huge parasitic strangler fig grew, its aerial root system forming the 'Curtain'. A wooden walkway with railings surrounded the tree. All of the boys had been there several times on family excursions, so they gave the giant wonder of nature only a cursory glance.

There was no sign of a clue. They looked behind every tree and rock within 25 metres, then under the walkways. Roger walked over to a large signboard describing the tree. Then an idea came to him. He clambered under the wooden railing and looked at the back of the sign.

"Here it is," he cried, reaching up to extract a plastic packet wedged between the board and an upright. The others crowded round as he returned to the path. They did not need to open the packet. It contained the same bright yellow cardboard with black printing. It said:

MICROWAVE TOWER
RAILWAY TUNNEL

"Microwave Tower! Railway Tunnel!" cried Peter. "Bloody hell. There are dozens of microwave towers around. They stretch from here to Melbourne!"

"And plenty of railway tunnels too. There are fifteen on the Kuranda Railway," Stephen added.

"Don't remind us!" Roger said, remembering that awful day the madman had chased them into Number 15 Tunnel. He didn't like tunnels, or caves, or mineshafts!

"Surely we don't have to walk to Kuranda from here? That must be fifty kilometres in a straight line?" Peter asked.

"Easily fifty. There must be a closer tunnel than that. Wrack your brains. Let's look at the map," Graham said.

He unfolded one map. "Wrong one. Atherton 1:50 000 is the one we need." He unfolded the correct map. A large drop of condensation fell, *splat!*, fair in the middle of the map.

"Bugger!" he swore and wiped it off.

"There are no tunnels between Kuranda and Mareeba," Stephen said. "I know, we just walked it all, on that exercise last week against the Air Cadets."

"Yes. And there are none between Mareeba and Atherton either," Graham agreed. He traced his finger over the map. "Here is the railway from Mareeba coming in through Tolga to Atherton. Then it goes south and up the mountains to Herberton."

"Remember our trip to Herberton on the steam train last year?" Peter asked. "We went through a tunnel then, up on the Herberton Range."

Graham nodded. "We were going to walk up that railway one day."

"That is a private railway isn't it?" Stephen asked.

"Yes, it is," Roger agreed. "It belongs to a company called RailCo and they run the steam train."

"That is a great trip," Peter enthused.

"I loved the steam engine," Graham agreed. He bent closer to the map and traced along the railway line with his finger. "Here it is. 'Tunnel'."

"It's right near the top of the mountain," Roger groaned.

"Herberton Range," Peter read.

"How far is it?" Stephen asked.

"Just a minute." Graham took out his notebook, tore out a page and began measuring distances along what looked to be the shortest route. "What a spider web of roads. It's hard to know which one is the shortest," he grumbled.

Roger began to get a sinking feeling as Graham marked pencil marks at each bend, going round the page more than once. He measured this against the maps kilometric grid.

"You aren't going to like this Roger. It's twenty-eight kilometres."

Roger felt suddenly depressed. "We've already walked over three. That will make it over thirty kilometres!" he wailed. "This is supposed to be a hundred kilometres and we've done about sixty already haven't we?"

"Yes we have. Cheer up. We don't have to do it all today. We can camp somewhere along the way," Graham said cheerfully.

"Then we might not be able to finish tomorrow," Roger said. Suddenly he felt exhausted and depressed. He was already sore and had to hold back tears.

Graham shook his head. "No. We should only have about ten kilometres to go then. I'll bet the last leg is from the tunnel down the main road to Atherton. That's only about ten."

Roger looked at the map. "What about Mt. Baldy?" he sniffed accusingly.

"Bugger Mt. Baldy! We will climb it when we come to it," Graham snapped.

Peter gave a wry grin. "More likely it will bugger us," he observed.

Graham looked irritated. "Enough! Let's get moving. Here's the first tourist bus arriving. Gosh. It's half past eight."

They walked out against a tide of Japanese tourists who gave them curious stares. The boys shouldered their packs and set off Southwest, walking along the side of the road.

Roger now felt very stiff and he began to notice his chafing and odd aches and sore feet. He was dispirited and could feel a headache developing. The day's march loomed as another gruelling ordeal.

Chapter 22

THE ATHERTON TABLELANDS

Nearly 5 minutes walking brought the boys out of the rain forest into open farmland. Tall grass walled the road, allowing only glimpses of the fields beyond. On their left, about a kilometre away, was a large hill covered by a tangle of lantana, weeds and patchy rain forest.

"What's the name of that hill, Graham?" Peter called.

Graham consulted his map. "Mt Quincan."

"I've heard that name. What's a Quincan? Is it some sort of fruit?"

Stephen called from behind. "No, that's a quandong you are thinking of," he said. "A Quincan is an Aboriginal bogeyman; a spirit who comes out at night to leap out and grab you. It's one of their legends."

"The hill is really an old volcano," Graham explained. "Captain Conkey showed us some pictures of it in Geography. There is a swampy crater up in the top at the other end."

Roger eyed the hill with little interest. He kept his mouth shut and concentrated on walking, trying to ignore the many irritations and pains which seemed to grow by the minute. The boys walked up a long, gentle rise. The road curved left so that Mt Quincan remained on their left. Out to the right were open fields dotted with cattle, and a grassy flat covered with a scattering of tall white-trunked gum trees. Beyond were several of the small volcanic hills named The Seven Sisters.

They passed a road junction on their right. Roger glanced along the farm road and saw a white car parked about 50 metres along it, with a man sitting in it. Just a car, or? He wondered. And if so, was it police or KSS? The thought made him feel quite restless.

The traffic on the road they were walking beside in single file was building up too, with a vehicle either way every couple of minutes. This forced them off each time, so they had to walk on the verge which was covered in long grass.

"Look out!" Graham cried.

Roger looked up in fright, in time to see Graham jumping backwards into Peter.

"Snake," Graham added as he grabbed at Peter to stop them both falling over. After a moment Graham stopped jumping up and down and began laughing. "It's okay. Only a Yellow Bellied Black. Bloody hell! He gave me a fright. I nearly stepped on him."

"Probably just sunning himself," Stephen commented.

They went on, Roger now looking anxiously at the grass at his feet, and thankful he was last. Having to keep getting off the bitumen to walk in the grass because of cars made him even more disgruntled and resentful.

At another road junction, this time on their left, a battered and muddy red tractor was parked. A man in greasy overalls was working on the engine. He eyed them for a moment, grunted a surly 'G'day' and put his head back under the engine cover.

After another hundred metres they came to another road going off on their left. BALLS ROAD the sign said. They kept marching. The main road curved right so that Mt Quincan was now behind them. The road crossed the grassy flat which looked like a marsh. They crossed a small bridge over a sluggish creek and began a trudge along a kilometre of straight road with the open forest of tall white eucalypts on their left. The traffic flow increased to dangerous and unpleasant proportions with a car, truck or tourist bus each way every minute or so.

At 0900hrs they reached the junction with the main Atherton-Malanda road. It was bitumen with no shade and a busy traffic flow, so they just kept on marching, turning right towards Atherton.

"We turn off a side road in about two kilometres," Graham explained.

"Can't be soon enough for me. I hate this," Roger growled as he was buffeted by the slipstream of a huge semi-trailer. Diesel fumes filled his nostrils and he could taste it on his tongue. He felt queasy and his headache got worse.

About 25 sweaty minutes later, they reached the turn-off of the East Barron Road. It was a bitumen road but only one lane wide. It went south up a depressingly long hill onto a wide, bare ridge. There was a row of pine trees at the junction but when Graham went to stop Roger surprised him by saying,

"Don't stop. Not here. Go on further and get away from the main road. I'm bloody sick of this traffic."

The others agreed so they tramped on up the long rise for 200 paces before stopping. There was no shade but at least the vehicle noise was now only an annoying buzz. Roger dropped his gear and flopped down, using his pack as a pillow and putting his feet up on a fence. He was soaked in sweat.

"Strewth it's hot! This is supposed to be winter!" he cried.

"I wish there was a breeze," Stephen agreed.

They lay or sat in relative silence for 10 minutes. Roger felt quite drowsy and found the humming of bees, busy amongst the giant sunflowers along the fence, melded with the distant hum of traffic.

Graham nudged Roger's leg with his boot. "Don't go to sleep Roger. Have a big drink. It is time we were moving," he said.

"Bugger it! How far have we come?"

"About five K's from the Curtain Fig I guess."

"So we have already done eight or nine K's and it's only 9:45?"

"Yes," Graham conceded with reluctance.

"Then a few more minutes won't hurt."

So they lay for another 10 minutes before Graham's restlessness goaded them up. Roger had a big drink and rubbed his sore muscles.

The boys resumed walking but at a more leisurely pace. As the road climbed the spine of the ridge, they began to get long views for many kilometres out to the west, north and east. Peter suddenly flung out his right arm to point. "Microwave tower!"

They stopped walking to look. About 10 kilometres to the northwest was a wide, flat hill, the low dome of the extinct shield volcano which Atherton sheltered behind from cold winter winds. On top was the lattice finger of a Telstra Microwave Tower.

"I'll bet that's the one. I can't see another anywhere," Peter said.

"Where is this railway tunnel?" Roger asked, looking west to a wall of mountains, tinged blue by the distance.

Graham took a compass bearing. "You see how there is a long range running from behind Atherton southwards to a gap? The tunnel is at that gap."

To Roger it looked a discouragingly long way off. He nodded, had another drink, slipped a jellybean into his mouth and followed the others as the march was resumed.

After about a kilometre the ridge levelled out. The area was all open farmland and they could see a surprising distance. It all looked very rural and quite pretty. The farms and fields and little patches of woodland made Roger think of pictures he had seen of England. It certainly wasn't the usual dry Australian bush.

The road went on southwards with long straights which Roger found very disheartening. It continued to climb slowly on a long, wide spur which Graham said was an old lava flow from Mt Weerimba, a prominent hill about five kilometres away; another extinct volcano.

They halted again at 1015hrs for another 15-minute rest. Graham wanted to keep it to the army standard of 10 minutes, but Roger refused.

"No. By your calculations we have come eleven kilometres and it is only morning teatime. We only need to do another one and a half by lunch time to be on schedule." He then popped another jellybean in his mouth and turned to look out towards Atherton and that tantalising microwave tower.

To the west, Roger saw that there was another chain of conical hills marking more old volcanoes. They looked to be only about three or four kilometres away. He pulled out his own map to check. WONGABEL the map read. In the distance two outliers of the Herberton Range just near Atherton caught his eye. Both were cloaked in open timber instead of the rain forest which covered the main range. Roger searched the map, then cursed and pulled out the other map. Why did they always have to be near the edge of two maps?

Sure he was right he pointed. "You see the two mountains with grassy tops?" he said. "The one closest to Atherton is Mt. Baldy."

Peter looked and laughed. "That is a pleasure to look forward to tomorrow," he replied.

Roger eyed the line of distant mountains with distaste. The rain forest gave them a dark blue appearance. *Almost black,* he mused.

Tiny wisps of cloud hung over the higher peaks, the only cloud in 180 degrees of sky. He checked the map and saw that they could follow the main Herberton-Atherton road from the railway tunnel to the base of Mt. Baldy. *Thank God for that!* He didn't feel like any more jungle and certainly didn't want to drag himself over any mountains.

Roger looked around to check if he could see where they had been. "It is a pretty view," he commented. "We can see half the Tablelands from here. Look, there is Lake Tinaroo." He pointed to where sun glinted on distant water, about twenty kilometres to the north. He suddenly felt quite proud of himself.

I have walked all that way! He took out another jellybean and stood up.

"Okay. Let's go," he said.

The others stared at him in surprise.

Graham grinned. "Have another jellybean Roger!"

They marched on for another 2 kilometres. Only one vehicle passed them, an old truck driven by a farmer. They came to a road junction and halted. Maps were consulted and Graham took a compass bearing to check.

"This way." He pointed west.

They had to step off the road as a large truck rattled past and headed in the same direction. The road went downhill for half a kilometre and crossed a small creek before going up a steeper hill for the same distance. It then wound between two collections of farm buildings and across another creek. A large area of jungle closed in on their right.

Graham pointed down the slope. "The Barron River is just there in those trees," he said.

They went up a short hill and came to another road junction. Their speed was a good 'Quick March' pace and Roger became aware that he was managing to keep up, and, that while his legs, feet, hips and shoulders were hurting, they weren't as sore as before. The boys turned right and went down slope to cross another small bridge, then up another kilometre-long hill between newly ploughed paddocks.

At ten past eleven they reached the Kennedy Highway and dropped their packs.

"Fifteen kilometres. We are going well," Graham said.

Roger had a big drink and looked around. The mountains were much closer. The section of the range on their side of the tunnel was now only three or four kilometres away. Individual trees could now be seen, and the general bluish colour had taken on a brown-green tinge.

Graham pointed up the slope. "Your airship drifted right across here last year Roger."

Roger looked around with interest. "Did it? I had no idea where I was. It was all fog."

Peter sat up and looked. "You did. We went to that farmhouse with the police at about midnight."

Roger experienced a wave of memories and shivered. "It was

horrible," he said. That unplanned ride on Willy Williams' home, made airship had been a terrifying experience. He carefully dabbed his eyes with water on his fingertips. It made them sting as the dried salt he had perspired was moistened but he felt fresher. It was very hot and there was no breeze.

He looked up. *Not a cloud in the sky, not one!* he thought. To check this he looked around. *No, there are a few wisps of cloud over the mountain tops,* he noted. The largest one, a mere ball of white fluff in the distance, clung to the mountain beyond the pass where the tunnel was.

Traffic was racing past at high speed and with irritating frequency.

Roger didn't like that. He wrinkled his nose at the engine fumes and said, "Let's keep going and find somewhere nicer for lunch."

The others agreed and stood up. As they adjusted their gear Peter asked, "Which way?"

Graham pointed. "Down to that bridge to the right. That is the Barron River. Just across that is a road going off on the left. We take that," he replied.

It was 500 metres to the bridge but in the 5 minutes it took them to walk the distance at least ten vehicles roared past, buffeting them with wind, fumes and dust. The Barron River at this point was barely 10 paces wide and the banks were all choked with bushes, lantana and weeds.

The boys had to wait for a truck to pass before crossing the short bridge, then again for two cars before crossing the highway and starting along the bitumen road heading west.

"Thank God for that! It's a relief to get away from all that traffic," Roger said. The side road curved left, then right. To their left was open pasture, on the right open timber, the trees all magnificent white gums with wonderfully straight trunks. The road also became straight. The bitumen gave way to gravel. Roger eyed it with disfavour and lowered his head to look at his feet as he plodded along. A truck rattled past from the other direction, grey dust billowing in its wake. This set the boys sneezing and cursing.

"Ah yuk!" Stephen snorted. "Are we going to stop soon?" He took off his glasses and wiped off a film of dust.

Graham looked at his watch. "Quarter to twelve. okay. We stop at the first shady spot we come to."

Roger had a drink to wash grit off his teeth. "I need to refill my water bottles soon," he said. He started to feel very thirsty and was aware his headache was coming back. It became an effort to keep going now that the idea of stopping was fixed in his mind. He drained the water bottle. Sweat stung his eyes. His boots felt heavier, his feet very sore.

They boys passed another stand of white gums. There were a few houses scattered in the open bush, just visible over the high blady grass lining the verge. With each step they got closer to the mountains until, at a bend with a road junction they reached the gentle change of slope at their base. Here the road swung to northwest and skirted through open bush along the base of the mountain, the ugly scar of a gravel scrape on their left.

Just after they had rounded the bend a car came racing up behind them. It took the corner at high speed. Roger heard it and glanced back, yelled a warning to the others; and stood transfixed. The car raced past, its tyres thrumming on the corrugations.

It was a grey Mercedes!

With four men in it!

They wore white shirts and ties. *The driver was, don't waste time looking at the driver! Look in the back. Too late! A thin man with grey hair and a moustache?*

"A grey Mercedes!" he cried, watching it vanish around the bend ahead of them. "The White Falcon! We must tell Inspector Sharpe!"

"Did you get the number of the car?" Stephen cried.

Roger felt a flush of shame. "No. I didn't think of it. I was too surprised," he replied in a crestfallen voice.

"It is heading towards Atherton," Graham added.

Roger began to walk as fast as he could. "Quick! Let's find a house with a telephone," he said. He was so keen to do this that he was oblivious to his aches and panting breath.

"Slow down Roger. You'll keel over from the heat. You're all red in the face," Graham said as he strode up beside him.

Roger realised his heart was beating very fast and that black dots were dancing before his eyes. He slowed his pace and suddenly felt dizzy. He felt Graham grab his arm to steady him.

"Stop Roger! Stop!" Graham ordered.

Roger did as he was told, weakly protesting. "But the White Falcon will get away!"

Stephen snorted. "White Falcon! Probably just the local Real Estate Agent showing some prospective buyers a farm," he commented.

Roger bit his lip. He felt silly and ashamed of his weakness. He unscrewed the top of another water bottle and drained it.

Graham nodded with approval. "Drink some more. You look very flushed," he ordered.

"Out of water," Roger croaked.

Peter passed him a water bottle. Roger had a mouthful and passed it back. "I'm okay now. I was just excited. Come on. Let's find a phone before they get away."

"Relax. They will already be in Atherton mate. By the time we find a phone they will be miles away. We will just go on, nice and steady," Graham replied.

They resumed their walk and in 5 minutes a house came into view, a modern brick bungalow of the 5-acre-block type. The boys went in and knocked. A grey-haired lady cautiously answered the door. When Graham removed his hat and politely asked if he could phone the police she assented. He dropped his pack and webbing.

"You blokes stay here. I will do the phoning."

Roger met the lady's gaze. "May we fill our water bottles please?" he asked. He really wanted to be the one to phone but accepted that Graham was the senior; and the lady wouldn't want them all trampling through her home in their sweaty uniforms.

While the lady led Graham inside the others went to a tap to fill all the water bottles. Roger filled Graham's as well. He drank until he felt bloated, then refilled his own.

In 5 minutes Graham was back. "The Inspector wasn't there but they promised to pass on the message," he explained.

Roger felt a sharp disappointment which he knew was unreasonable. But he felt better knowing the message had been passed and after a drink and rest. He was perspiring freely again and realised he must have been getting heat exhaustion. Heat exhaustion! In mid-winter on the Tablelands! He looked up. Still not a cloud to be seen except for the few blobs of cotton wool on the mountain tops to the west.

The boys thanked the lady and walked back out onto the road.

"What about lunch?" Stephen asked.

It was 1240hrs, Roger noted. Only a hundred metres further on two dirt roads turned off on the left amongst a stand of trees: one up the slope and the other through a gate to a house. At the junction was a grassy area well shaded by the eucalypts.

"This will do us," Graham said. "It's not as private as I'd like though."

"It'll do. I'm starving," Stephen replied. He dropped his pack and the others did likewise. Roger sat on his pack and rummaged in his webbing for food, but he did not feel hungry. He decided on a tin of peaches, some biscuits with apricot jam, and a cup of coffee.

"Boots off. Air your feet," Graham ordered.

Peter groaned. "But I will have to move then," he complained in an aggrieved tone.

"Why?"

"Because of the stench from your gungy feet!"

"Bite your bum!"

They all laughed. Roger took off his boots and socks and stretched his toes. It felt better at once. He examined his feet and renewed one piece of sticking plaster but was pleased to note there were no new blisters. Using a spoon he ate the peaches from the tin. Already he felt much happier.

While sipping his coffee Roger pulled out his maps and began to calculate how far they had walked.

Graham swallowed some food and called, "How far do you make it Roger?"

"Eighteen kilometres," Roger replied. He felt proud of the achievement.

"That's about what I reckon," Graham agreed.

"Nearly time to find a camp site then," Roger said.

"Another seven. Let's make it twenty-five."

Roger grimaced. "Till I can't go any more," he said.

Peter sat up. "How far is it to that tunnel?"

"Only six in a straight line," Graham replied.

Stephen leaned over to look at the map. "Which way are we going? Up the railway or along the road?" he asked.

"The road is further," Peter said.

"By a lot. Be all that awful traffic too," Roger replied.

"I vote we go up the railway," Graham said.

"Let's wait and see what it is like," Stephen cautioned.

At 1330hrs they resumed their march. Only a hundred metres further on the road crossed a small creek which was flowing. It was only ankle deep but was crystal clear on a sandy bottom.

"Oh! I wish we'd known this creek was here," Peter said.

"Let's stop and have a wash," Roger suggested.

Graham shook his head. "No. We've only just started again, and we've still got seven kilometres to go. Besides, there are bound to be more creeks running off these mountains," he vetoed.

The others grumbled but continued walking. A large truck roared past powdering them with dust, followed soon after by a car from the other direction. They passed more new houses of the suburban type, crossed another creek and went up over a steep little spur which reduced Roger to heavy panting.

Just over the crest they came to the railway. They stopped and consulted their maps and studied the line. The rails were rusty, and the sleepers were grey from age and weather but there were not many weeds. Another vehicle raced by along the road, throwing up more dust.

"The railway," Graham said emphatically. He turned left and started along it.

Luckily there was a footpath beside the ballast which made walking easier. The line curved right in a gentle climb along the side of the mountain. Dry forest: a mixture of dense stands of she-oaks and more open areas of Eucalypts, closed in their view. The boys could only see along the line with occasional glimpses of the mountains ahead.

As soon as they were away from the road, Roger felt a peculiar sense of isolation. The hairs on the back of his neck stood on end and he had vivid flashbacks to that memorable hike down the Kuranda Railway two years before.

Stephen spoke up. "Remember when we walked down the railway from Kuranda?"

"Shut up, Steve. I'm trying to forget that," Roger replied.

He shivered and looked up the mountainside on his left. It was just ordinary dry bush. Nothing unusual. Nothing to worry about. But he still had the urge to keep looking behind him and wished he wasn't last.

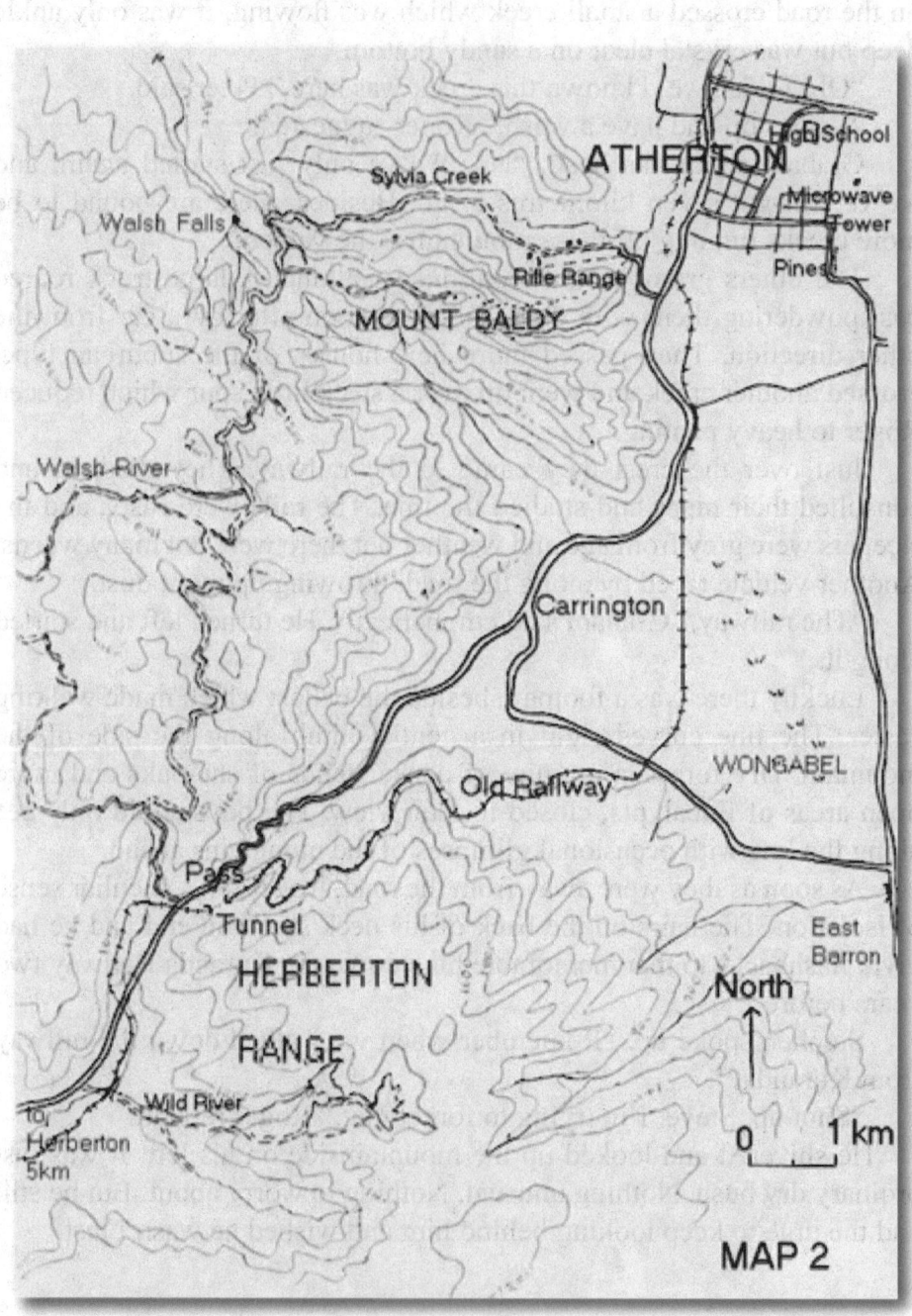

MAP 2

Chapter 23

THE HERBERTON RAILWAY

For Roger, the walk up the railway became a test of willpower. He seemed to quickly tire and was soon walking in a sort of zombie-like daze. Frequent trivial obstacles forced him to keep alert: fallen rocks and clumps of tall grass or small washouts. From time to time the footpath became so narrow they had to walk between the rails but this was annoying as the sleepers were unevenly spaced which made it hard to settle into a rhythm. The timber sleepers also varied. Some were flat and others rounded. Many were half-rotted with crumbling interiors or had split and jagged surfaces.

The cadets crossed half a dozen culverts and small bridges a few metres long, but all the streams were dry. Bare sand and bare rock began to predominate on the surrounding slopes, with grass-tree and straggly, open bush. The railway curved into a small valley where there was no breeze at all, and the afternoon sun radiated from the enfolding slopes as from a reflector fireplace.

At the head of this large re-entrant was a larger bridge, 10 metres long. The map showed the stream to be Carrington Creek. Carrington Falls was the steep rock face on their left but barely a trickle of unattractive slime was the only water flowing down it. The disappointed boys stood on the bridge and looked gloomily at it.

"Let's stop and have a break anyway," Stephen suggested. "We've been walking for an hour."

"Not here," Graham replied, shaking his head. "Somewhere nicer. Over there where the line curves around that spur. We might get some breeze there."

The others reluctantly agreed and followed him. Roger had a big drink and set off in a walk that was almost a stumble. Then he nearly put his foot between the sleepers of the bridge. It gave him a small shock and he told himself to keep his wits about him. Slowly he plodded on for another five hundred metres with his head down as they were walking almost directly into the afternoon sun. He licked his lips and wondered if he would be able to push himself much further. Using the back of his hand he felt his cheeks. They felt very hot, making him worry he was getting sick.

And then a faint breeze cooled his sweat. There was a distinct change and he looked up. They were walking in shade. At first he thought it was just the shadow of the hillside on his left, but he saw, with something of a surprise, that a huge, jungle-covered mountain loomed ahead. The shadow was cast by a cloud clinging to its top.

The boys walked through a long, deep cutting and reached the end of the spur. Graham called a halt. Packs were dropped and they drank deeply. Roger then observed that the mountain to the west was actually on the other side of a valley a couple of kilometres across. Below them lay the Atherton-Herberton Road. It skirted the lower slopes opposite them as it began its climb up to the pass. The floor of the valley was mostly forest with a patchwork of fields and houses. Away to the north they had a long vista out to Atherton and beyond.

Stephen pointed. "I can see the microwave tower at Atherton," he said.

"That's the road to Herberton isn't it?" Roger asked.

"Yes, it is. Remember when we got a lift up it in that old truck?" Graham replied. They laughed at the memory and reminisced.

"I wish I could get a lift up it now," Roger groaned. "I'm buggered."

"We must be halfway up the range," Graham estimated, eyeing the slopes on both sides.

"How far have we come?" Peter asked.

"Since lunch? I reckon about four kilometres."

"Is that all?" Roger said with dismay. "Still, we can stop and camp after another three," he added.

"We may as well push on to the tunnel and get the next clue. That's only about four K's," Graham suggested.

Roger groaned. "What's the time?"

"Just after three. Two hours or so before it gets dark. We could crawl four K's in that," Graham insisted

"I might have to," Roger replied gloomily. Wondering if he could walk the distance he sat down and had another drink. He could never remember being so sore and exhausted in his whole life. He felt like just one huge mass of tingling aches and pains. But it was cooler; and he was amazed he had managed to walk so far. To prepare, he had another drink, draining his second water bottle.

After 15 minutes Graham cajoled them to their feet, and they set off again. For Roger, the next 45 minutes were the hardest so far. He stumbled frequently. His hobble turned into a limp. His shoulders sagged under the weight of the pack and he trudged along bent over and feeling miserable. There was such an accumulation of little pains that tears formed in the corners of his eyes. But rather than give up he bit his lip and pushed himself on, slowly falling further and further behind the others.

The line curved left and ran Southwest. By this time they were completely in the shadow of the mountain opposite. A steady breeze was funnelled up the valley and helped to cool them. The railway went through several more cuttings as it led into another steep little valley. Then it curved sharply back to run north along the side of a steep spur. The country was still open: straggly eucalypts and grass-tree, with tufts of dry, greyish-brown grass growing in sandy soil.

A sharp curve to the left through another steep, sided cutting led them around the end of the spur and back to the Southwest. By this time Roger felt ready to drop. Several times he formed the words calling on the others to stop but some residue of pride kept him from uttering them.

As they emerged from the cutting, he wiped sweat from his face and looked up in amazement. The jungle-covered mountain now towered high above them less than a kilometre away. On their right the ground dropped steeply into a re-entrant, then climbed steeply up to the clouds. Level with them, and only a few hundred metres away was the Herberton, Atherton Road, snaking up the other slope through similar dry bush. Above the road the vegetation gradually changed to an open forest of tall, straight trees, which in turn gave way to rain forest near the top.

Roger watched a car buzzing up through the trees until it vanished over a sunlit saddle ahead. A cold wind blew on his sweaty back making him shiver. He stopped for a drink and felt he could not possibly walk another step.

Graham looked back and saw him. "Come on Roger. Not far now. There's the pass," he called, pointing to the sunlit saddle.

"How far to this tunnel?" Roger croaked.

"Only a few hundred metres, maybe half a kilometre," Graham said.

Roger put his water bottle away and lurched into painful motion.

He had to grit his teeth against the agony of the chafing between his thighs.

The railway went through yet another cutting and curved left. The road rose above their level. A heavy truck ground up it in low gear. Roger looked up to watch it and saw there was a distinct hill covered with trees, right in the middle of the pass. The road went through a cutting to the right of it. The railway seemed to aim straight at it.

Then he realised he was looking at the mouth of the tunnel. He gasped with relief and pushed himself on. The railway still ran on a bench cut with the steep drop on the right, the re-entrant rapidly narrowing to end beside the tunnel entrance. The hill ahead and the steep slope opposite were a jumble of grey rocks and grass-trees.

Unaccountably Roger felt uneasy. The hair on the back of his neck bristled and he shivered. He looked around him but there was nothing but ordinary bush.

When they reached the tunnel they halted. The other end was visible about two hundred metres away but the middle was dark. Graham bent down and moved a rock. He straightened up holding a plastic bag containing an oblong of yellow cardboard.

"The clue," he said.

Roger was so tired he did not really care. He leaned on the side of the cutting and eased the weight of his pack on the rock face.

Graham read the clue aloud. "Seven Pines; Mount Baldy."

"Bugger Mt. Baldy!" Roger cried. "I'm sick of hearing about it." He felt very dejected and dreaded the ordeal of having to climb the mountain. He had had enough. All he wanted to do was lie down. He shivered again.

"Seven Pines?" Peter queried. "There were pine trees back at The Chimneys."

"A whole forest of them," Stephen added in a dry tone.

"No, a line of them beside the clearing."

Graham shook his head. "That is fifty kilometres or more back. That can't be right," he said.

Peter added, "There was a line of pine trees at the turnoff of the East Barron Road too."

Roger was too sick and tired to care. "There were bloody pine trees everywhere!" he cried in exasperation. "Let's find somewhere to camp, but not here. This place gives me the creeps."

Graham looked around. "Good spot for an ambush."

"Will we go through the tunnel or up over the hill?" Stephen asked.

"Through the tunnel," Roger said. He could face his claustrophobia more easily than he could face the probable pain of dragging himself, pack and all, up that steep slope.

Graham opened his basic pouch and took out a torch. "Might be snakes in here," he said. He slipped the clue into his map pocket, clicked on the torch and walked into the tunnel.

The others followed. Roger pushed himself upright and hurried after them, wishing he wasn't last. Ever since being trapped in the old mine at Stannary Hills the previous year he had hated tunnels. Now it took an effort of will for him to follow the others into the blackness.

The tunnel was lined with concrete which was black with soot and lichen. It was quite dry, and a strong wind blew on their backs, funnelled by the mountains. The boys' boots crunched loudly on the gravel and Stephen could not resist uttering chuckles and making loud noises to hear the echoes.

"Shut up Steve!" Roger snapped. He was in no mood to be frightened by Stephen's silly games.

After 2 minutes they emerged from the other end into another deep cutting that curved right. The sides slowly levelled out. Ahead was a line of mountains on the other side of the pass. The sun had just dipped below them but still shone on the upper slopes up to their left, rear.

The railway ran straight for several hundred metres through an open forest of short grass and she-oaks. Ahead of them a truck suddenly roared across, showing where there was a level crossing.

"Will we camp here?" Stephen asked, indicating the open bush on either side.

"Too close to the road," Graham replied. "Let's walk to the level crossing and have a look."

Roger groaned but plodded wearily on. He now didn't care where they camped, as long as they stopped.

The south side of the pass was a forested valley about a kilometre wide, a long gentle slope which the railway ran across to the western side of. The highway came down from the saddle on their right rear in a wide, sweeping curve through open grass to cross the railway, then dip down across a small creek before climbing over a long, gentle rise to the south.

The valley leading to Herberton was much flatter and wider than that to the north of the pass. On either side forested slopes rose several hundred metres to vanish in cloud.

As they reached the main road Graham pointed to his right to a dirt road going off to the west through a dense clump of she-oaks. "Let's look in there," he suggested.

They waited for two cars to race past then walked across the bitumen and along the gravel side road. It dipped slightly across a small dry creek and crossed a cattle grid in a boundary fence. A sign informed them it was State Forest and entry was only permissible by permit. Ahead the road ran around the lower part of a wide spur through open bush.

"We've got a permit," Graham said. "It's in the bundle of papers Captain Conkey gave me. I'm sure we are all right. He wouldn't send us here unless we had approval."

So saying he led on across the cattle grid and up the gentle slope. As the road curved out of sight of the highway he stopped.

"This will do," he said. There was a side-track there and only short grass. He walked down the track 20 paces and stopped. Roger limped down to join them. Packs and webbing were dumped. Roger sighed with relief and flopped down to lie on his.

"We will need water," Peter said.

"There is a creek just down there. It might have some," Graham said.

"Let's have a look," Peter agreed.

Graham looked at the others. "Roger, you and Steve collect some firewood while we check the creek. Give us your water bottles," he said.

"Stuff the firewood," Roger groaned. He closed his eyes and shivered. Carefully he eased his limbs, fearful of cramp. He seemed to be trembling in every muscle. His body felt like one huge mass of throbbing aches.

For 5 minutes Roger just lay with his eyes closed. Stephen disturbed him when he threw down an armful of deadfall near him.

"Come on, Roger. It will be dark soon. Don't just lie there like a slug!"

Roger opened his eyes. With difficulty he bit back a retort but still felt hot resentment. Slowly he sat up and hauled himself to his feet. Stephen had already walked away. A glance around showed that the sunlight only tinged the top of the cloud on the mountain across the pass. There was also some cloud on the peak to the north of them, but overhead was clear blue sky. Evening was definitely upon them and Roger felt a distinct chill in the air. He hobbled off down a gentle slope to where he could see some deadfall near the old railway.

Almost in tears from the effort he dragged back a sizeable dead branch, just as Graham and Peter returned from the creek. Stephen came in with another armful of sticks at the same time.

Graham put down the water bottles he was carrying. "There is water in the creek. Not much, just a trickle, but it smells and tastes okay," he said.

"I'll light the fire," Roger offered. Stephen did not dispute this but dumped the sticks and went off with Peter and Graham to collect more. Roger limped around collecting tinder and tiny sticks for kindling. Then, with stiffness in seemingly every muscle, he knelt and cleared a space on the dirt track. The sticks and logs were sorted into piles of different sizes. A small pyramid of twigs was constructed over a handful of she-oak needles and gum leaves. One match set this aflame. Roger crouched beside it to carefully add pencil thin sticks and to fan the flame with his hat.

The fire accentuated how dark it had become. Graham and Peter returned and added more sticks to the pile. From out in the darkness Stephen chuckled loudly then called, "Well, I've found it. We can all go home now," he said.

"Found what?" Peter asked.

Stephen walked into the light grinning. With a flourish he held up a huge bone about half a metre long and so thick he could not get his fingers around it. "The Thigh Bone of St Joris."

This produced a shout of laughter from them all. Even Roger thought it a good joke. It was so obviously a bone from a dead cow that it did not bother him.

Stephen tossed the bone aside and dusted his hands. "Will we eat first or put up hutchies?" he asked.

"Hutchies," Graham answered. "We won't feel like it later."

"I don't feel like it now!" Roger groaned.

"Why bother?" Peter asked. "There are stars coming out."

"That cloud on the mountain could build up," Graham cautioned.

They set to work clearing sticks and rocks from between trees selected as suitable for erecting the plastic shelters. It was nearly dark by then. As the shelters were being tied to the trees Peter bent down and picked something up.

"Sorry Steve. We have a problem," he said. He held up another large bone. "We have another Thigh Bone for St Joris. One must be a fake. How will we tell which is the authentic one?"

"Ass!" laughed Graham.

"No. Ox," Stephen corrected.

They all laughed.

As soon as the two hutchies were pegged down the boys returned to the fire and sat down. Roger undid his bedroll and sat on it. Then he unlaced his boots.

"Ah! That's better," he sighed as he pulled off his socks.

"Phew! What a pong! Put them on again Roger," Stephen cried.

Roger ignored him and gently massaged the toes and soles. To his surprise there were no new blisters, but his feet were certainly red and tender in places. "My poor feet! How far have we walked today? Must be thirty kilometres," he said.

"A bit over," Graham replied.

"At least it is all downhill tomorrow," Roger said.

"Don't forget old 'Baldy'," Peter reminded.

Roger swore, but only half-heartedly. He felt immensely pleased with himself as the realisation dawned on him. *I have walked more than thirty kilometres!* he thought. And he had kept up all day! *I will make it through the hike now!* he told himself. As he rummaged in his gear for food he began to hum happily.

Darkness set in. Apart from the occasional vehicle on the highway they seemed to have the world to themselves. A gentle breeze sprang up. It developed into a very pleasant evening. Only as he was finishing his desert did Roger feel cool enough to put on his pullover.

He ate a huge meal of chicken soup, rice and savoury mince, Milo, peaches and condensed milk, more Milo, then a chocolate and another cup of Milo. He slowly relaxed and, while his muscles trembled from time to time, he did not suffer any cramps.

The friends sat around the fire talking for a while, but all were tired. By 8pm Roger was yawning. Soon after that he excused himself and moved his gear and bedding into the hutchie he was sharing with Graham. 10 minutes later he was asleep.

Chapter 24

THAT TIME OF MORNING

Roger hardly stirred all night. So soundly did he sleep that when he woke he found his left arm was numb. As he blinked in the darkness, he found he was shivering with cold and was half out of his sleeping bag. He snuggled down to get warm and checked his watch. It was 0525hrs. Time for another hour's sleep he decided, but then found that sleep would not come. To add to his exasperation Graham lay beside him, breathing the slow, steady breaths of deep sleep.

Roger shifted position. He lay on his side and adjusted his pack to make it a more comfortable pillow. But the more he tried, the more wide awake he became. Equally annoying was a growing and persistent urge to go to the toilet. After 10 more minutes, Roger gave up. He crawled quietly out and pulled on his socks, tipped his boots upside down to check for scorpions or spiders, then pulled them on. He laced them tight and gingerly stood up.

To his surprise, he felt stiff but not too sore. The air was quite chilly, so he added his field jacket. It was still dark but a faint lightening in the sky indicated dawn was not far off. The low, dark shape of Peter and Stephen's hutchie was just visible between two nearby trees. The fire had burned itself down to grey, black ash.

After retrieving his toilet paper from his webbing Roger walked quietly up to the gravel road. He paused to listen. Not a sound; not even wind in the trees. The air was completely still and there was a light mist. He stared up and down the grey ribbon of road.

Which way? Right or left?

Right, he decided. There was a bit of a thicket near the cattle grid which was well away from the camp and offered some privacy, Roger being sensitive about such things. He walked that way, his boots crunching on the sand and gravel. Once across the grid he made his way among the she-oaks and ferns a few metres off the road to do his morning business.

While he squatted there it grew rapidly lighter. The sound of a car coming from Herberton along the Highway disturbed the stillness. Roger watched its headlights flicker through the trees. It raced past and out of sight up towards the pass. Silence settled again as the vehicle went over the crest.

Roger had finished and was buttoning his trousers when he heard the quiet crunch of footsteps coming from the direction of their camp. He looked and could just make out two figures in the misty half-light. Was it Graham and Peter? Or Stephen and Peter? In the gloom he could not tell. Still adjusting his clothing he walked out onto the gravel road and stopped in surprise, a cheerful greeting left unsaid.

Two armed men in dark uniforms were at the grid. Both men carried rifles. The front one was looking down watching his footing but the one behind saw Roger and cried out in alarm.

Roger froze in shock. His mind took in the weapons, webbing, dark green trousers and jacket and a green cloth forage cap with some sort of badge on it. He saw the first man look up, his eyes and mouth open in surprise. Then the second man cried out again.

"Soldat!" he cried as he threw up his weapon.

KSS! Roger's mind shouted.

In panic he threw himself sideways. His eyes registered a flash from the rifle. The sharp crack of the bullet was overlaid by the duller bang of the weapon going off. At the same moment there was a loud cry of fear, followed by a scream.

Roger rolled into a low ditch among some ferns as another bullet tore through the undergrowth beside him. His whole being gripped by terror he yelled, "Graham! Graham! Peter! KSS! Help!"

There was a thumping and rustling noise near the fence and another scream of pain. Roger glimpsed the first man writhing on the cattle grid. The second had dived for cover into the grass beyond the road.

To Roger's immense relief, he heard Graham yelling. "Roger! Roger! What's going on?"

Roger saw the man in the grass jerk his head round in surprise at the sound of shouts from his rear. There was another piercing yell of agony from the first man, who was still in a struggling heap on the grid. Roger scrambled behind a log. He was on the edge of panic.

Again he yelled, his voice cracking with near hysteria. "Graham! Help! Two armed men. Be careful. They've got guns." His voice went high pitched on that last bit and he flushed with shame. As he shouted, he saw the second man spring to his feet and look his way. For a moment Roger dissolved in terror as the man swung the rifle round. Then the man ran to his companion and reached down to haul him to his feet. This provoked an even shriller scream of pure agony.

There were more yells from Graham and the others and Roger heard their boots thudding through the bush. The second man heaved at his companion who had now slumped unconscious. Failing to free him, the second man darted fearful glances towards Roger's hiding place and over his shoulder, then released the injured man and fled. Roger glimpsed him bolting up the slope through the she-oaks.

Dark figures flitted through the trees from the direction of the camp, then vanished as Graham ordered them to take cover.

"Roger! What's going on?" he called.

Roger tried to reply, but his voice quavered too much and he had to pause and wipe spittle and sweat from his mouth.

"Th... Th... There are two men... with g... guns. One has run up the hill to your left. The other is here at the grid. I think he's hurt himself."

This was confirmed by the man emitting a loud groan and calling angrily after his companion in a foreign language.

Kosarians?

"Keep down!" Graham yelled. "What is he doing, Roger? Can you see?"

Roger was shaking with fright and did not want to look but he raised his head. He saw the man's rifle lying on the road at least a metre from his clawing hands. The man groaned again then called out. Then he swore; or it sounded like it to Roger.

There was a rush of boots and Graham appeared at the fence. He went under it in a diving roll and was on his feet and running in an instant. Passing Roger he scooped up the rifle and kept on going, to dive behind a tree on the other side of the track.

"I've got his rifle. Wait a minute while I work out how to use it," he called.

Roger let out a great sigh and shuddered. He wiped cold sweat from his eyes and crouched, ready to run. His eyes searched the bush in all directions for any sign of more of the men. The man on the grid moaned again and curled up.

Graham called, "Can anyone see or hear the other man?"

"No," Roger croaked in reply.

"Steve, you watch back towards our camp and up the slope. Roger, you watch out towards the highway and down the slope. Pete, you come and search this bugger. I will cover you," Graham ordered.

Graham moved into a kneeling fire position among the ferns near the grid. Peter rose from the grass 20 metres away and walked forward. He approached the man very cautiously and looked all around before bending down to start searching the web equipment the man was wearing.

Peter looked up. "He's fainted. He's got his leg jammed in the cattle grid. I think he has broken it."

"Get his webbing off and search his pockets, quickly," Graham ordered. He looked around in momentary indecision, then turned to Roger. "Roger, help Peter. Empty everything out of his pockets and put it in a plastic bag or something."

Shakily Roger got to his feet. He licked his lips and wiped sweaty palms. He felt chilled and was shivering all over. Despite his fear he found himself walking toward the man while half his mind rebelled. The reality of it was only now sinking in.

Search a man! he thought. He had been trained to do it and had done it often enough on cadet exercises, but this seemed quite different.

Peter called out as Roger reached him. "I can't find any other weapons, only a pocketknife. There is live ammo in these basic pouches though," he said. He pulled the webbing off and tossed it to the edge of the road near Graham.

Reluctantly Roger knelt and felt the man's shirt pockets, every nerve tensed for flight. He forced himself to unbutton the pockets and to push his fingers inside. With shaking fingers he scooped out a pencil, notebook, pen, some coins and a compass from one pocket and a wad of folded papers and a notebook, all in a plastic bag, from the other. He placed these on the ground.

Peter pointed to the man's shirt collar. "Look at those badges," he said. Roger looked. Two rhomboid shaped gold lozenges, each with a small silver 'pip' in the centre, were pinned on, one on each lapel.

From where he crouched behind a tree Stephen called, "KSS?"

Peter shook his head and picked up the green cloth peaked cap from the dust. "Don't think so. This bloke is all dressed in green, and look, this badge on his cap. It is a gold eagle with a crown on it," he said.

Roger stared at the badge. The eagle had its wings bent down, just like the one on the cover of the history book. His pulse raced with interest. "Kosarian Royal Guard," he said with certainty.

"Could be."

Peter emptied a map pocket on the man's trousers: map, toilet paper, an Aide Memoire book. Roger dug in the right trouser pocket and fished out a dirty handkerchief and some coins. Then he felt in the man's right map pocket. The man moved and emitted a groan.

Roger sprang back.

Stephen chuckled. "That was good Roger. Do that again!"

"Get knotted!" Roger retorted, his heart hammering a frantic tattoo.

"His leg is broken alright. Badly by the look of it," Peter observed. "Let's get him out. Give us a hand Steve."

Peter tossed the man's wallet down to join the other belongings littering the road. Roger pulled out the plastic bag he kept his toilet paper in and began placing the items in it. Stephen joined Peter while Graham remained crouching on guard, holding some sort of black automatic rifle.

As Peter and Stephen tried to lift the man by his arms he woke up. His eyes rolled around, and a ghastly moan escaped from his lolling jaw. The boys nearly dropped him in fright. The man's face looked horrible, all pale and sweaty. As they tried again the man groaned in agony and slumped into unconsciousness.

"We can't lift him. His leg is caught," Peter cried. "Help us Roger."

Roger put down the plastic bag and moved to the grid. He then saw just how badly the man's leg was broken. It was snapped below the knee and was twisted almost at right angles. He had to nerve himself to kneel and grab the injured member. With trembling hands he guided it up between the steel rails of the cattle grid while Peter and Stephen lifted.

"It's out," he called, feeling so nauseous he thought he was going to black out. They dragged the man clear of the grid and stretched him out on the road.

"Phew! Broken alright," Stephen whistled.

"Just as well he was out to it," Peter commented. He knelt and felt gently along the twisted leg. The unconscious man moaned and thrashed feebly.

Graham walked over to join them, his eyes still searching the bush in all directions.

"What are we going to do?" Roger asked.

"Let's get out of here before that other bloke comes back," Stephen suggested.

Peter shook his head. "This joker needs hospital treatment," he said. "We can't just leave him."

"Bugger him. Leave him for his mates," Stephen replied.

Roger's conscience rebelled at that. "We can carry him out to the road and wave down a car," he said. "Then we could get him to hospital in Atherton."

Peter nodded. "Or Herberton. There's a hospital there too I think," he suggested.

Graham looked around. "We have to call the police too," he added. He paused for a minute and scanned the surrounding bush. Then he spoke firmly. "Pete, you and Steve carry out First Aid. Immobilise the leg and make him comfortable. Roger, you sort out what we have found. I will keep guard."

That suited Roger. He didn't want to touch the injured man again. He was still trembling with shock but at least his heart rate had slowed.

Graham moved into a kneeling fire position at the base of a large ironbark and faced up the hill. "What happened Roger?" he asked.

"I'd just gone down there for a crap," Roger explained. "I was finished and as I walked back onto the road these two blokes came along."

Stephen snickered. "Just as well you'd had your crap before you met them," he called.

Roger flushed with embarrassment. It was too true to be funny. He remembered the moment of stark terror when the second man had raised his rifle and fired. Then he remembered the humiliating experience in the jungle at Mobo Creek. In response he just gave a wry grin and pretended the jibe didn't hurt.

Graham asked, "Which way did they come from? From the highway?"

"No. From the other way, past our camp. That's why I thought it was two of you," Roger replied.

Graham frowned and bit his lip. He dug out his map with one hand and looked at it. It was fully light by this time. "This gravel road goes right up to the top of the mountain."

Roger looked up through the trees to where the mountainside vanished from view amongst trees and cloud.

Cloud!

"Cloud!" he said. "Assembly Area Cloud. I'll bet it's up there."

They all looked up in alarm.

Stephen looked anxiously along the road. "So there must be more of them. Let's get out of here," he cried.

"A whole company, if that message was right," Peter added soberly.

"Get a stretcher made, fast," Graham ordered, a worried frown creasing his brow. He put his map back and removed the magazine from the rifle and cocked it. A shiny new bullet flicked out onto the road. He picked this up and then studied how the weapon worked before re-inserting the round in the breech and easing the working parts forward on it. Then he replaced the magazine. "Heckler and Kock G3, German," he said.

Roger met his eyes and he gave a grim smile. "Keep sorting Roger."

While Peter finished cutting the man's trouser leg open Stephen returned to their camp to get twine and bandages. Roger sat and spread out the contents of the bag. He quickly sorted the personal items, then looked in the wallet. There was a Queensland Driver's Licence with a photo of the man.

"His name is Otto Witorski," he said. There were credit cards and several printed cards which appeared to be business cards. The notebook was in German and in crabbed handwriting which he could not read but inside the cover was printed in neat block letters:

KRA10612 LT O. M. WITORSKI

6 . B . 3 KPLG

"There is what looks like a number, rank and name here. He is a Lieutenant, I think. Then it says six dot 'B'; that is Capital BRAVO, dot three; then block letters KPLG. I wonder what it means?"

"Kosarian Palace Guard?" Graham suggested.

"What about the 'L'?" Peter asked.

"Never mind. We can work it out later. What else is there?" Graham asked.

Roger put the notebook down and picked up the man's map. "There is a pencil triangle at a track junction about a kilometre up this road; and a pencil circle at some ruins on top of the mountain," he said.

"Their camp, I'll bet," Graham said. Roger picked up a small-printed book. On the cover was a set of letters and numbers: KPLG KB, 2 6109

He opened it. Each page had a number at the top, then rows of random 'trigrams', with letters of the alphabet, words or numbers beside them.

"This is a code book. Like we use for signals training. One of those 'once only' tear, out pads," Roger said. He flicked through it, feeling his curiosity and excitement mount. They were back in the mystery again! He picked up several folded sheets of paper and unfolded them. As he smoothed them out, he got another kick of excitement.

"These are Message Forms with a message written on them!" he said.

"Is it in code?" asked Stephen, who had returned and was helping Peter.

"It was, but it's been decoded. Now it's only in what looks like German."

"In German!" Graham echoed.

"Oh bugger!" Roger said. He had wanted to read the message as he felt it must be important.

Stephen held out his hand. "Give me a look," he said. Roger passed him the sheets.

Graham called softly. "Roger, you help Pete. Bring the message here Steve."

Reluctantly Roger did as he was told. Peter walked into the bush a few metres and began to hack down a sapling with his sheath knife. Roger knelt beside the injured man. He averted his eyes from the ugly blue, black swelling and listened to Stephen and Graham.

Graham studied the message and nodded. "It is a signal form alright. I wonder what KKG oblique 'R' means?" he murmured.

"Kosarian King's Guard?" Stephen suggested.

"It's in German remember."

"So? King is Konig and Guard is spelt in the French way: G, A, R, D, E," Stephen replied.

"You could be right. Well, the security classification is 'Secret' and this says, 'Officer only'."

"So he is an officer," Roger said. He looked down and touched one of the gold lapel badges.

"The 'Action' is BLITZ, Flash or Lightning."

"So it must be important," Stephen suggested.

"I'd say so. Now, Date, Time. it was sent at 0300 this morning and this bit says 'Handling Instructions', Hmmm. KODEX KPLG KB, 2."

Roger looked at the cover of the code book. "That is what is on the cover of this code book," he noted. He bent and picked it up. "KPLG KB, 2 6109."

"That makes sense. Now then, it is from the 'White Falcon'; whoever he is; to the Kommander KPLG PL 6 KKG."

Stephen snapped his fingers. "I know. KronzPrinz Leib Garde, the Crown Prince's Life Guard," he said. "Some of those model soldiers I make from alloy castings are Leib Gardes."

"Makes sense," Graham agreed.

Roger felt another surge of excitement. "So the Kosarian Crown Prince must be near here!"

"Why Roger?" Stephen queried.

"If the commander of his guard is here then he must be. It stands to reason," Roger replied.

"Not necessarily. This is to Commander 6 Platoon," Graham said.

"Are you sure?" Stephen asked.

"No. But it might be," Roger cried. "That's what it says inside his notebook. Here. 6 dash BRAVO dash 3."

"6 Platoon, 'B' Company, 3rd Battalion," Graham suggested.

Peter asked, "Why 3rd Battalion?"

"I read it the other night. The 1st Battalion of the Royal Guard is the King's Guard; the 2nd Battalion the Queen's Guard and the 3rd Battalion is the Crown Prince's Guard," Graham replied.

Roger felt his chest tighten with excitement. "So we might bump into Prince Peter the fourth!" he squeaked breathlessly.

"Peter the Fifth," Peter reminded as he returned with a trimmed sapling.

"Or sixth," Stephen added.

Peter looked serious. "If we do bump into Prince Peter, they might bump us off," he said.

Graham nodded. "By Jove yes! We will have upset their plans and we know too much to let go," he added. That thought made Roger feel so afraid he began to tremble.

Peter gestured to the injured man. "Here Roger, hold this man while

I secure his leg," he ordered. Roger did so. Peter gently moved the broken limb beside the other. The man uttered a groan and writhed feebly. Roger felt so nauseous he thought he was going to be sick.

Peter frowned. "Not so good. We will splint it like that. I don't want to try straightening the broken bone in case it cuts an artery or something. He's got some bandages in his webbing. Use those," he said.

"Are we going to make a stretcher?" Roger asked.

Peter shrugged. "I suppose so. We can easily enough."

Roger nodded. "Yes. But is it worth the effort, just to carry him a hundred paces. The ambulance can drive in here easily enough. It would be better if one of us hitch, hiked down to Atherton to get help."

Peter considered this. "You are right. Who should go?"

Graham looked up from writing in his notebook. "We have to tell the police as well."

"That's alright. I will go," Peter offered.

"Shouldn't two of us go?" Roger cautioned.

Graham shook his head. "No. One is enough. You keep watch for us while we work on this," he said.

Peter stood up. "I'll get going then. I will just get my hat and lace my boots up," he said. He walked quickly back to their camp.

Roger looked at his watch. It was just on 0630hrs. The sun was touching the treetops. He bent to the unpleasant task of bandaging the man's legs together with the splint on the outside. Every time the man winced or moaned, Roger stopped. He thought he was going to be ill. Gingerly he pushed padding between the legs. The task was completed by the time Peter returned.

"See you in an hour or so," Peter called as he walked past towards the highway.

"Take care," Roger called after him.

He watched Peter walk out of sight and felt suddenly afraid.

Chapter 25

A RACE AGAINST TIME

Roger watched his friend vanish among the trees with deep concern. In the aftershock of his own fear, he was gripped by a nameless dread which overlay his excitement. Graham and Stephen still sat side by side on the edge of the gravel road with their heads together over the captured Signal.

Graham looked up and held out the automatic rifle. "Here Roger, take this and keep watch."

Roger licked his lips and stood up. Nervously he walked around the injured Royal Guard and took the weapon.

Graham held the rifle vertically. "It is on 'Safe', and in the 'Action' condition," he stated. Roger turned the weapon over and examined it. His mind ticked off the items as he identified them: safety catch, cocking handle, foresight, backsight and... and ah yes! There it was, the magazine release catch. He was satisfied he could use it, if he had to. The weapon felt heavy and cold, and knowing it was loaded with live ammunition made Roger tingle with apprehension. He crouched behind a tree near the other two and looked carefully in all directions, peering through, not at, the bush.

Somewhere out there was a second armed man; the one who had fired at him; who had tried to kill him. And, if the injured Royal Guard was indeed a lieutenant, and a platoon commander, then there could be the rest of his platoon, 20 or 30 soldiers. They would certainly come to rescue their leader as soon as the other man got back to them. It was only a kilometre or so.

A fit soldier could run that in five or ten minutes, Roger thought. *He could be there already.*

Roger licked suddenly dry lips and wished Graham and Stephen would hurry up. "Graham, this bloke's platoon could be here at any moment. Can't we move and finish that later?"

"We shouldn't leave him," Graham replied, gesturing towards the unconscious man. "Ah! Sounds as though Peter has been picked up."

They heard the noises of a car accelerating through its gears out on the highway.

"Towards Atherton," Stephen said.

"Good," Graham nodded. "Now; the Red Eagle *fahren*, that is travel or is travelling, from Atherton to Herberton between 190800K and 190900K."

"That is today. In just over an hour's time," Stephen said, glancing at his watch.

"Red Eagle? Who's he?" Roger asked.

"Don't know," Stephen answered. "Now; Paragraph Two. 'Hinterhalt ihm nach das Gipfel GR321819'. What is 'Hinterhalt'?" he read.

Graham spoke. "That GR could be a Grid Reference. Roger, have a look on the map for GR321819."

Roger stood up and pulled out his map, mumbling the numbers to remember them.

Stephen kept muttering. "Hinterhalt? Hinterhalt ihm at the Gipfel. What the devil is a Gipfel? I wish we had that German Dictionary"

"Well, halt means stop or halt," Graham pointed out.

Roger looked up from the map. "Hinter means behind doesn't it? Like in Geography, Hinterland."

"Behind halt. Behind stop. Stop behind at the Gipfel. Stop Red Eagle at the Gipfel," muttered Graham, trying various combinations. "Maybe, but I don't understand it. Where is this Gipfel thing Roger?"

Roger bent back to where his thumb had followed a northing across the map. When his mind registered what his eyes saw he sucked his breath in sharply. "It's only about a kilometre away. No, less. Only a bit over five hundred metres. It is on the highway just near the railway tunnel."

They all turned to look in that direction although the trees obscured the view. The rising sun shone full on their faces.

"That's where the highway crosses the saddle at the Pass," Graham observed.

"Gipfel, Pass?" Stephen suggested.

"Stop behind him, that's the Red Eagle, at the Pass?" Graham said in a puzzled tone.

Roger had an idea. "What about 'Hinder', meaning delay or interfere with? Interfere with the Red Eagle at the Pass," he suggested.

Graham looked up. "Ambush!" he said, as though not wishing to think the word. He bent back to the message. "Look at the next paragraph. 'Er toten muss.' He must be killed! It is an ambush!"

Roger felt a sharp chill. Ambush. He must be killed! It had a terrible reality and finality to it. But this was peaceful old Australia! That sort of thing didn't happen here! But then he knew it did. Images of Captain Krapinski's corpse rose mockingly into his thoughts.

Stephen scribbled and read aloud. "Paragraph Four. There will be four autos. Cars they mean. Red Eagle will be in the second auto."

"So they know which car to hit," Graham said. They were all silent for a moment.

In his imagination Roger saw the four cars winding up the mountainside. In the first would be bodyguards. It would drive past, then the men in green uniforms crouching behind rocks and trees would aim at the second car. A savage rattle of automatic fire...

Graham shook his head, a grim expression on his face. "What else does the signal say?" he asked.

"'Andern'. 'Andern'? That is 'after'. After the ambush 'zuruckziehen nach Sammelplatz Wolke'."

"Concentration Place Cloud!" Graham cried.

"Up there I'll bet," Roger said, pointing up the slope to the north.

Graham nodded. "After the ambush go back to Concentration Place Cloud," he repeated.

Stephen then queried Paragraph Six. "What do you make of this? It says 'Bewachen', beware or be awake, 'gegen', against."

Graham frowned. "You sure?"

"Yeah. The Germans used to sing a song called 'Wir fahren gegen England'. 'We sail against England'. It's on a DVD at home," Stephen replied.

"Okay. Beware or watch out for or against KOSPUSS oder, that's 'or', or KOSPAR. Both words all in Block Letters. What the hell is a KOSPUSS?" Graham asked.

Stephen pushed his glasses up his nose. "Some sort of a big cat?" he replied.

"Don't joke Steve. This is deadly serious," Graham chided.

Roger had returned his map to his pocket and crouched down again. "Is it an Acronym? You know, a word made up of the Initial letters of other words?"

"Might be. I'm sure I've heard it before," Graham said. He chewed the end of his pencil thoughtfully.

Roger was now very curious as well as anxious. "What else does the message say?" he asked.

"It says 'Ende' and is signed by Stiltz, Adjutant from the Operations Branch; and there is a file number and date," Stephen read.

Roger turned to look at them. "Stiltz, Adjutant. He was in that other signal. He was one of the men in the grey Mercedes with the White Falcon," he said.

Graham nodded. "That's right. So we have the adjutant of the White Falcon sending an order to the Royal Guard to ambush and kill the Red Eagle. Who is the Red Eagle?" he asked.

Stephen answered at once. "Red, Communist. Prince Peter the whatever is the White Falcon. That is his badge. The Red Eagle is a communist leader; his enemy."

Roger clicked his fingers. "The Inspector told us the other night. The Kosarian government is Communist. He said their Embassy were very worried about the KSS because the Kosarian Deputy Premier was on a visit to North Queensland."

Graham nodded. "Yuri Stinkibitz."

"Do you mind! Keep your vile habits to yourself," Stephen said.

"Don't be flippant Steve! That's the bloke's name: Yuri Stinkibitz, Deputy Premier."

"I know. The Inspector went mad at me for laughing at it. If it was me, I'd change it," Stephen replied.

Roger was puzzled. "But why does the White Falcon want to kill him?" he asked.

"Because Communists and Royalty are natural enemies," Graham answered.

"More than that," Stephen said. "Remember what the Inspector told us? Kosaria has been ruled by the Communists for more than half a century, by that dictator, Slimy Turdorov or something. He's an old codger, nearly ninety. He is sick and ready to kick the bucket. Stinkibitz is his number two, so probably next in line for the top job. If he is bumped off it might precipitate a crisis; a power struggle, in Kosaria."

"That sounds right," Graham agreed.

Roger nodded. "Yes. And I'll bet the Royalists have a plot ready to start a revolution to put the king back on his throne. That's what 'Operation Return' must be all about," he said.

Graham pointed at the unconscious lieutenant. "They have formed a secret army overseas, like here in Australia, and will move it back to Kosaria," he suggested.

Stephen shook his head. "More likely most of their supporters are in Kosaria already, in some sort of secret organisation. They couldn't smuggle an army halfway round the world and into the country. Probably it is only the Prince and his bodyguard who have to do the returning."

"That sounds likely," agreed Roger. "But where do the KSS come into this?"

For a moment the boys were silent. The thing had too many sides. Stephen spoke first. "Obviously, Prince Paul also wants to be king. Peter is his rival in the family feud. The KSS have infiltrated the Royal Guard and know their plans."

"How do you know that?" Roger asked.

Stephen shook his head. "Oh Roger! We spent hours translating that other signal. Dorkoffsky is a KSS man, but he was also the contact man between Captain Krapinski and the Royal Guard."

Roger flushed. "I forgot. Strewth! This neck of the woods must be crawling with the foreigners having a three-sided civil war!"

The thought made him look around nervously. Stephen then posed another question. "But why this 'Flash' signal to bump off the Red Eagle now? I mean, if it was part of the plan it wouldn't be set up that way."

Graham nodded his head. "You are right. I think they are just seizing an opportunity. I don't think it was part of their original plan at all." He returned his notebook to his pocket and looked at his watch. "It is ten to seven. That ambush is due to be sprung in about an hour."

"Maybe it won't happen now," Stephen suggested. He pointed to the injured man who was moving his head slowly from side to side and moaning. "If he is the platoon commander he was probably on his recce and hasn't even made a plan, much less given orders to his troops. His men are probably waiting back in camp for him."

Roger agreed, "Yes, and when that other man gets back and reports he was captured by soldiers they will know their secret is discovered and give up the idea."

"Why should he report we are soldiers?" Graham asked.

"When he saw me he called out 'Soldat'," Roger replied.

"I see. Yes, that will have them worried. In that case I doubt they will come here looking for their boss. I reckon having a battle with an unknown number of Australian soldiers wouldn't be part of their plan. It would blow their whole secret."

"But where have they all been hiding?" Roger wondered.

"I don't know about 'all'. There may only be a handful; just a cadre of trained leaders. And I don't think they've been hiding. I think they have been like Captain Krapinski; just living normal lives and doing some part, time training in secret."

"Or even serving in our army to get training," Stephen suggested.

"Probably. They seem to use a lot of procedures we understand," Graham agreed. "And now, with their plan due to start on the nineteenth of June, they have all come together at the Concentration Area."

"The nineteenth, that's today!" Stephen said.

Roger felt a sharp stab of excitement tinged with apprehension. "So it is! Quick! We must do something. We must tell Inspector Sharpe," he cried.

"We've already sent Peter to do that," Graham reminded him.

Roger felt foolish for a moment, then said, "But Peter didn't know about this ambush."

"I don't think there will be one now," Stephen said. "Besides, what else could we do?"

Roger resented Stephen's tone. It made him stubborn. "We can't just sit here hoping it won't happen. People could get killed. We can't take that risk."

Graham shrugged. "I don't care if Communists get killed," he said.

Roger felt anger flare. "Other people could get killed too, innocent people. Besides, even if Comrade Stinkibum is a Commo he is a guest in our country and it's Australia's responsibility to keep him safe."

Graham looked at Roger in surprise and had the good grace to blush. There was a short silence while each considered what to say next.

Stephen spoke first. "We aren't the government. We aren't the army. Cadets aren't soldiers."

Roger shook his head. "Doesn't matter. We are Australian citizens, and we know. We have a duty to do something," he replied. He scrambled to his feet, still clutching the rifle.

"But what?" Graham said. "We've already sent Peter to get the police."

A dreadful thought struck Roger. "But they won't know about the ambush. They could drive into it. Peter could get shot." He meant killed but couldn't say it. Graham looked uncomfortable. He also stood up. So did Stephen.

Graham spread his hands. "But all we can do is send someone else to warn them."

Stephen looked around. "Perhaps we could warn them to go another way, to Herberton, so they don't have to pass through the ambush. We could go to Herberton and telephone a warning to Atherton," he suggested.

Roger thought about this. He did a quick sum in his head. "Peter must be in Atherton now. He could even be on his way back already. There isn't time. We must go and warn him."

"Warn him? How?" Graham asked.

"Go up to the pass and sneak past the ambush," Roger said.

"Get real Roger. We don't know how far the ambush might extend. They could have a cut-off a kilometre down the road. You would have to circle right up over the mountain or maybe go down the railway, then across the valley. There isn't time," Graham said. He also began to fidget anxiously and again looked at his watch. Roger glanced at it and felt a stab of anxiety, nearly 0700.

The sound of another vehicle passing out on the highway decided Roger. "Well, we can't stand here talking. Time is running out. I'm going, even if you aren't."

"Roger! Don't be silly. You could get shot!" Graham cried. He placed a restraining hand on Roger's arm as he went to leave.

Roger shook him off. "I don't care. I don't want to have to live with myself with innocent people's deaths on my conscience. I'm going." He began walking towards the highway.

"Wait Roger! At least get your hat and your webbing," Graham called.

That made sense, Roger decided. His webbing included a field dressing, a small first aid kit, and water bottles. *I might need all of them,* he thought. So he turned and walked back.

"What about you two?" he asked.

"I'll come," Graham replied. "What about you Steve?"

Stephen shrugged. "What about this guy? He's starting to come round. I don't think we should go."

"Then you stay here and watch him," Graham said. "You can pack up our gear while you wait." He pointed to the litter on the road. "Roger, pick up all that stuff."

Roger did so. Graham picked up the man's webbing and the three of them walked back quickly to their camp. Roger realised he had not had breakfast, but he pushed the thought out of his head. Stephen was very agitated, but Roger ignored his pleas to stay. He had a big drink and swung on his webbing.

"I'll take the rifle," Graham said, holding out his hand. Roger hesitated. Graham then spoke in a determined tone. "Give it to me Roger. Captain Conkey put me in charge. I am responsible. If anyone is to do any shooting, I will do it."

Roger handed over the rifle with a feeling of relief. He knew Graham wouldn't back out now and was better with weapons than him. Graham looked very much the grim-faced Sergeant Major preparing to go into battle as he emptied his basic pouches of food tins and odd items. His camera he slung over his shoulder and into the empty pouches went the three full magazines from the prisoner's webbing. It gave Roger a sickly thrill to glimpse the shining brass of real bullets.

Graham stood up and checked his watch, then studied the map. "Ten past Seven. It is about seven hundred metres. That should only take us ten or fifteen minutes."

Stephen gave him a sulky look. "This is stupid! Someone could get killed."

Graham nodded. "Probably. We are going anyway. See you later," he replied. Then he started walking.

Roger followed. He and Graham walked back along the gravel road towards the highway, leaving a very unhappy looking Stephen standing alone in their camp.

Chapter 26

IN THE CLOUD

As they walked past the injured Royal Guard the enormity of what they were going to do hit Roger. It made him sick with fear.

"Which way will we go?" he asked.

"I've been thinking about that," Graham replied. "I've read that the best place to set an ambush on a road is on the outside of a bend so you can fire both ways along it. And you don't want any 'dead ground' or cover for the enemy. It is better to be level or only slightly above them, so they have no escape by going over the bank and downhill."

"That little hill above the railway tunnel. It looks right back down to here as well as down the road and railway," Roger suggested.

"Yes. And it covers the re-entrant and hillside above the road. I reckon that is the place to start looking," Graham agreed.

The sound of a vehicle coming from the direction of Herberton reached Roger's ears. "There's a car coming. Should we stop it?"

Graham shook his head. "No. Let it go."

Roger wanted to get away from there but knew that Graham was right. With a twinge of regret, he watched the car rush past along the highway. It appeared as a flicker of blue through the trees. For a moment it was clearly visible along the cleared lane of the road. Then it went up the slope towards the pass and was soon out of hearing.

"How will we go about it?" Roger asked.

They were across the grid by then and in sight of the highway. Both halted a couple of metres back from the edge of the bitumen, from where the railway level crossing and small hill in the pass were both visible. It was mostly open ground all the way to the hill half a kilometre away.

"I think we should just walk straight up to it in the open," Graham said as he carefully scanned the hill and the mountainside to the left of it.

"Shouldn't we creep under cover?" Roger asked.

Graham shook his head. "No, we won't try creeping up. I reckon we will be a lot safer if they see us at long range and we don't suddenly surprise them. I am hoping they will think we are soldiers and that will worry them. They won't know how many of us there are, and I am banking on them not shooting at us. They will either think that the army is doing a security operation; or that their plan has been discovered. If they've any sense they will then pull out before we arrive, rather than risk a fight. If we sneak up and suddenly bump into them at close range with no warning, they are liable to shoot first and think later."

Roger gulped. His mind told him that Graham was right but suddenly he felt almost paralysed by fear and realised he was trembling. He wiped sweaty palms on his trousers. "I hope you are right." he said.

"So do I!" Graham replied with a wry grin. "Now, pick up a stick that looks like a gun. We need to appear armed."

Roger did as he was told. It made him feel even more defenceless and slightly foolish.

"Make sure the safety catch is on," Graham quipped. Then he walked forward into the open, looked both ways along the highway and strode across. Roger took a deep breath and followed.

As he crossed the road, Roger could see all the way up to the top of the pass. The highway went up in a wide sweeping curve, with the forested mountainside on the left above it. On the right, between the road and railway, was about four hundred metres of gentle slope covered with short grass. The small hill was covered with a scattering of trees and rocks. Having fired rifles at the range Roger knew with sickening certainty that a person on that hill could strike them dead even now. The thought chilled and almost paralysed him.

Graham angled over to the fence beside the railway. Roger watched a heavily laden truck come grinding into view over the crest. It came growling down towards them at an ever-increasing pace. The driver glanced at them curiously. That gave Roger an even greater sense of unreality. Here was this man calmly going about his daily business while he and Graham were walking forward in fear of their lives.

Roger swallowed to ease his fear and said, "If those characters are really up there, they must be able to see us now."

He was finding it harder and harder to keep walking towards the pass. His flesh seemed to be rippling as it cringed in anticipation of being struck by a bullet. But despite an almost paralysing fear he made himself keep pace with Graham, moving 10 metres out to his left. The hill loomed larger and larger.

We are well within effective rifle range now, he told himself. *If they are going to shoot it will be soon or we will reach those trees.*

Two hundred metres to go. Keep walking. Breath coming in rasps. Sweat dripping off the nose and upper lip. Walking directly towards the sun. One hundred metres to go. Roger wanted to stop, to go back. He screwed his eyes up against the glare and anxiously searched the slopes for any sign of the ambush.

Graham kept beside the fence and this led them slowly further away from the highway. By the time they reached the first trees and began to climb the hill they could no longer see the actual road, which went into a cutting between the small hill and the mountain to their left. Roger approved. Graham had led them into dead ground, although a smart enemy who knew his job would have flank and rear security deployed watching the way they were coming.

Down to his right Roger glimpsed the deep cutting that led the railway into the tunnel. Graham led him to a grassy saddle almost above the tunnel and Roger saw the railway continue on down the mountain. He shivered and remembered his apprehension the previous day when they had stopped just down there. Perhaps the ambushers had been watching them through their rifle sights even then?

The small hill turned out to be steeper and larger than Roger had expected. As they went up it he began to puff and pant. He wiped sweat from his eyes and kept looking down to see where he was putting his feet. The route Graham had followed led them up into the rear of where he had suggested the ambush be set. As they neared the top and nothing happened, he began to relax. A breeze came through the gap and cooled him. He got glimpses out over the Tablelands in the distance.

Graham had drawn ahead as they climbed. Soon he was 20 paces in front. As he reached the top and began to angle over towards the cutting, he suddenly went down in a crouch.

At first Roger thought he must have tripped he went down so fast, but then he saw him look cautiously around a tree. His left hand went out, thumb down—Enemy!

Roger froze. For a moment he was unable to move. His mind refused to accept the field signal. Enemy! It couldn't be true! But it must be. Graham began scrambling through the grass, rocks and grass-tree.

Blood pounded in Roger's temple. He twisted the stick he held in his sweaty hands, then scuttled over to a solid looking tree. As he reached it Graham rose and signalled him forward with urgent gestures. Roger did not want to move but he obeyed.

"Quick!" Graham hissed. "Look, there they go. Five of them at least."

Roger was just in time to see an armed figure in a dark green uniform run across the highway at the next bend about a hundred metres away. He glimpsed others scrambling up the steep slope above the road. Quite distinctly he saw the shape of an armed man go back over the crest of the spur into the re-entrant beyond.

"So they were here!" he said incredulously.

"Yes. And they obviously saw us coming and bugged out. I wonder where they are going? Come on! We had better follow them."

"Isn't that dangerous?" Roger asked. "After all, we've sprung their ambush."

"Very dangerous," Graham agreed. "But we have to be sure they don't just move and set the ambush further down the road."

Roger looked over his shoulder. He could see all the way back down to the junction of the Forestry Road where they had come from. Beside him was the cutting, at least 5 metres deep. Beyond it, in the direction of Atherton, the highway curved left to go out of sight behind the spur about a hundred metres away. There the road had a cut on the left and a steep drop on the right. The slope led down into the re-entrant which widened to become a valley further on. Up on the opposite slope away to his right he could clearly see the railway they had walked up the previous day. The highway wound its way down the mountainside, its next bend barely visible through the trees. The slope above the highway went up through an area of rocks and grass-trees into a steep, grass-covered ridge with an open forest of tall, white, trunked eucalypts on it. Above that was shrouded in cloud.

Graham grunted with approval. "Bloody good spot for an ambush alright," he said admiringly.

"Here comes a car," Roger said, hearing the sound of an engine climbing the range from Atherton.

He hoped it was Peter with the police. To his sharp disappointment he saw it was a snappy, electric-blue sedan driven by a smartly dressed young woman. She did not even see them, and the car sped through the cutting and on towards Herberton.

Graham began walking along the top of the cutting in the direction taken by the Royal Guards. Reluctantly Roger followed him, wondering how he could stop him. When they descended to the road they did not cross over as the steep rock face of the cut continued on the other side and was far too high to safely climb. Instead the boys walked quickly down the side of the road.

Roger was acutely aware that they were now in the intended 'Killing Ground' of the ambush and his eyes searched the slopes above them anxiously. Once again, he felt his flesh cringing and tingling in anticipation. Graham went first, eyes also searching, the rifle carried at the ready, pointing up the slope.

A red car came from behind and raced past. The driver, a young man in a white shirt and tie, gaped at them and called something rude. The vehicle vanished around the bend.

"I wish Peter would hurry up," Roger said.

He looked at his watch. It was half past seven. Peter had been gone three quarters of an hour; ample time surely?

Graham reached the bend. The road curved sharp left into the re-entrant, then sharp right around the side of the next spur before another sharp left took it out of sight. After a searching scrutiny of the mountainside, Graham strode across the road and began clambering up the steep slope beyond.

"I think I can see them. Yes, there's one," he called, pointing up amongst the trees. He continued on.

Roger crossed the road and began climbing. He looked but could see no sign of the Royal Guards. "Wait Graham," he called. "Shouldn't we wait here to tell the police?"

Graham stopped and looked back. "But they will get away."

"We know where they are going. It will be to that ruin on top of the mountain."

"They may not. You stay here and tell the police. I will follow them," Graham replied.

Roger felt very uneasy. "That's not a good idea. Instead of a group of four we would then be four individuals scattered all over the place. Remember Stannary Hills."

Graham hesitated. He moved restlessly, wiped sweat from his eyes with his sleeve, looked up the mountain in frustration; then put the safety catch on and swore. He took out his water bottle and had a big drink. Roger did likewise, feeling immensely relieved.

There was a cool breeze on that side of the slope, funnelling through the pass, and it chilled their sweat. Graham put his water bottle away and took up the rifle. "Okay Roger, you walk back to Stephen. When the cops arrive tell them what is going on. I will meet you at the ruin on top."

"Don't be silly Graham!" Roger cried.

He shook his head in annoyance at Graham. He knew he could get very stubborn and was apt to do things from sheer bravado. "We have taken enough risks. Someone could get killed."

Graham turned and began walking rapidly up the steep, grassy slope. Anger welled up in Roger. "Don't be such a bloody stubborn idiot Graham! We've stopped the ambush. Leave it to the police. Besides, what will Captain Conkey say?"

To his frustration Graham ignored him and kept on climbing. Roger swore and fidgeted in indecision. He had horrible thoughts of Graham being caught by the men. They would probably shoot him, and his body would be dumped in the rain forest, never to be found.

"Oh blast you, you stubborn idiot!" Roger cried. He began climbing as well. "I can't let him go on his own."

Graham was 50 metres ahead by then. He glanced back and Roger saw his face darken with anger. He waited till Roger had struggled to within about 10 metres of him.

"I told you to go back to Stephen to tell him what is going on," Graham snapped.

Roger leaned on a tree, gasping for breath. His heart hammered so fast he feared he was going to have a heart attack. "Ya... you... puff, puff... you can't follow... puff... them on your own. Puff... cough, cough... puff. Something might happen to you."

"Go back. That's an order."

"No. I will, if you do," Roger replied.

"Then you are as silly as I am. Don't slow me down. I'll meet you at the ruin," Graham snapped angrily, his chest heaving. He hefted the rifle to ready and went on up the slope as fast as he could walk.

Roger watched his departing back with anger and resentment. Then he resumed plodding upwards through the waist high blady grass, even though his pulse rate was still well above normal.

After a few minutes he had to stop again. Gasping for breath he leaned on a tree, alternately sweating and shivering. Anxiously he watched Graham vanish over a false crest a hundred metres further up. As he looked around he got another shock. He was enveloped in cloud.

The white vapour came seeping through the trees, cutting out the view down into the valley and limiting visibility to about a hundred paces. *Stephen is down there,* he thought. Then other worries came to him: Was he alright? Had any of the Royal Guard turned up and taken him prisoner? *He must be feeling very lonely and wondering where we have got to.* He saw by his watch they had now been gone more than an hour. Would Stephen be able to work out where they had gone? Yes, the ruin on top was the logical place. What was the ruin?

Roger had a drink and slogged on up. He only just reached the false crest before he had to stop again. The cloud closed in, cold and clammy. It did not effectively restrict his visibility which was affected more by the trees and bushes, but it gave things a creepy, eerie atmosphere.

With relief Roger saw that the next section of the mountainside was not as steep. It went up for at least two hundred metres to another crest, dimly seen in the mist. Was that the top of the mountain? He hoped so.

After resting for a couple of minutes, Roger continued walking. He found his trouser legs getting wet from the condensation forming on the grass and he was soon soaked from the waist down. There was no sign of Graham. The trees were much smaller now and formed a real thicket, being interspersed with masses of bushes, lantana and ferns.

Abruptly Roger halted. He looked down, then left and right. He had stepped onto an old vehicle track running up the spine of the ridge from his left, from the direction of their camp. It was just two wheel tracks and had not been used for a long time.

After a careful look around Roger began following the track. A quick check showed it wasn't marked on the map but he guessed it would lead to the ruin, which he surmised should be only a few hundred metres ahead. The slope gradually levelled out and the track entered a thick belt of chest-high ferns and small bushes that formed a jungle under the trees.

Roger slowed down and began scouting cautiously forward. As he reached the gentle crest of the slope he heard voices. He froze for a moment. The sound came from down to his right-front. The belt of scrub appeared to end about 50 paces further on so Roger crept forward.

"Pssst! Roger!"

Graham's voice from right beside him made Roger jump in fright. He looked down. Graham was crouched in the bushes. He reached up and grabbed Roger's sleeve and roughly pulled him down.

"Get under cover before that sentry sees you," Graham hissed.

Roger went down on hands and knees. "What sentry?"

"The one beside the track on the edge of the scrub," Graham replied.

"I didn't see anyone."

"He's there alright. It's a wonder he didn't see you. And he's got a mate patrolling on the edge of those ferns."

Roger cautiously raised his head and peered through a bush. For a moment he could see no-one. Then a movement attracted his eye and he clearly saw a soldier dressed in the green uniform. The man had put the butt of his rifle down and was adjusting something on his webbing. Realisation of how close he had come to disaster made a chill sweep over Roger. His mouth went dry and his heart began to pound with excitement.

As they watched, there was a faint rustling in the bushes and a second man appeared from their right-front. He was carrying a sub-machine gun. The soldier crossed the track and spoke to the sentry for a moment, then went on into the scrub.

"Come on," Graham whispered. He started crawling to their right. Roger followed, his mouth dry with fear.

They crawled about 20 metres until Graham was sure the sentry could not see them. Then he rose and began 'Ghost walking', the rifle held ready. Roger did likewise. The pair angled down through thick scrub towards the sound of voices.

Roger wanted to call Graham back. He knew that what they were doing was deadly dangerous and stupid. If they met a sentry unexpectedly it would be 'shoot first, ask later'. But his fear battled with the fear of being ridiculed or thought a coward. And he was curious. Was it the Royal Guard hideout?

Maybe I will see the Prince? he thought.

So he continued to creep along 5 paces behind Graham. There were a lot of dead twigs in the long grass but luckily things were so damp from the mist that these did not make too much noise when trodden on.

After a few minutes they reached the edge of the scrub, about 50 metres to the right of the sentry post. Ahead of them was a mass of ferns about a hundred metres across. These were waist high and covered a gentle down, slope, ending at a clearing. Beyond the clearing was a dark wall of pine trees and rain forest. Low cloud drifted past, shrouding everything in mist. There was constant dripping of condensation from the leaves.

They could not see into the clearing very well as several bushes and small trees obscured the view, but they could see people, at least their top half. Roger was amazed. There looked to be a dozen or more, all in the green uniforms and most with guns. One, with the gold collar badges of an officer, was busily giving orders.

Graham leaned in. "They look like they are packing up," he hushed. "Let's go down to the right and see if we can get a better look."

Roger didn't agree and shook his head, but Graham ignored this. He set off back into the scrub and began a wide semi-circle downslope. Roger reluctantly followed. They crawled most of the way, under bushes, between trees and through long grass.

All the while Roger was straining eyes and ears not only for the first sign of a Royal Guard, but also for any snakes. He was sure the repulsive reptiles would love this environment: wet and damp; lots of frogs and small animals! And he was right. Once Graham hissed and pointed. Roger looked, in time to see half a metre of black snake slither into a clump of grass, just like a hundred other clumps he had just crawled through. He shuddered and kept moving. Nearly 5 minutes creeping brought them back to the edge of the ferns.

Graham pointed down. A line of trampled ferns made a rough foot track. "The sentry on patrol. Keep alert," Graham whispered. Roger nodded and looked to his left.

His heart stood still. His voice choked up and he could only grunt as he grabbed at Graham. The soldier was coming their way and was not 20 paces away!

"Back! Hide!" Graham hissed.

Roger turned and crawled back behind a bush, using all his training and will power to resist the urge to run, or even to crawl quickly. As soon as he was behind the shrub, he pressed himself into the long grass and leaf, mould. Rising terror drove the thought of snakes out of his mind.

He curled up his legs and lay still.

Chapter 27

ON TOP OF THE HERBERTON RANGE

Roger strained his ears to listen but all he seemed to hear was the surging and pounding of his own heartbeat. The crackle of breaking twigs and swish of ferns on cloth made him hold his breath. Out of the corner of his eye he saw movement, the Kosarian soldier.

Quite distinctly Roger could see the Royal Guard badge on the man's cap. The soldier was walking slowly, eyes searching the bush, finger on the trigger of an Uzi. Just as he drew level with Roger he stopped. Roger felt fear shrivel his insides.

A voice called from the clearing. The soldier abruptly turned and raised a hand in acknowledgement and walked quickly back the way he had come.

Graham whispered, "Whew! That was close."

"Let's get out of here," Roger replied, his throat dry and constricted.

"Not yet. Something's going on. Let's go closer," Graham replied. He turned and crawled further into the scrub, then stood up and began walking cautiously along, moving parallel to the patch of ferns.

After several minutes of careful stalking Graham stopped and pointed ahead. Roger joined him and cautiously peered through the bushes. On the edge of the clearing about 50 paces away were two mango trees. Parked under them were three Toyota Landcruisers. These were painted a dull green. Men were busy around them and even as the friends watched one vehicle started up and reversed into the clearing. Men climbed into the others and they were also started.

The clearing was a rectangle of lawn. On the uphill side were a concrete fireplace and some fruit trees. Roger looked around for the ruin. There was no sign of any walls. He surmised that the fireplace was all that remained of whatever building had once stood there. A short access track led through long grass past a line of tall hoop pines to a gravel road. Roger knew this was the same road they had camped beside the previous night. On the other side of the road was a wall of dark jungle.

In the clearing stood a group of Royal Guards with their packs and webbing. Six of them Roger counted, including their officer. Even as he watched the soldiers began loading their gear into the backs of the vehicles. Two more soldiers came walking into view through the ferns on the opposite side of the clearing. Roger recognised the sentries.

These collected their gear and clambered into one of the vehicles. The officer looked around, walked to the first vehicle and spoke briefly on a radio, then climbed in and slammed the door. With a growl of motors the three vehicles drove down to the road, turned right, and accelerated. The road then curved left and around the side of a small hill, jungle on the left, open forest on the right. In a minute the vehicles were out of sight over the crest, heading north.

After waiting a few minutes, Graham walked forward into the clearing, searching the ground. Roger followed more slowly, shaking with reaction and cold. Marks in the grass showed where a row of small tents had stood and there was some litter, but it was all packets and tins of locally purchased food. There had been a fire in the old fireplace, but it was now just grey ash.

"Not much of an army," Graham said derisively, although whether he was referring to their evident poor discipline; or their small numbers Roger wasn't sure.

"Eleven of them, including the officer," Roger commented.

"Twelve if you count the officer we caught. Not even a full platoon."

"But, if this is 6 Platoon there may be more in other camps," Roger pointed out.

Graham nodded. "That's possible. But why two officers? I reckon this organisation is only a cadre and they will bring it up to strength when they get back to Kosaria."

"What do we do now?" Roger asked.

"Wait for the police I suppose. I don't know what is delaying them. It's ten to nine. That is two hours since Peter left," Graham replied. He began walking towards the road.

Roger followed. There was a spatter of raindrops and cloud swirled around them. He shivered and swore and put his hand up to turn up his collar. The hand hurt as the stinging tree bite was aggravated by the damp.

"Strewth it's cold! I wish I'd left my jacket on," he grumbled.

Graham laughed. "Well, we are on top of the Herberton Range," he commented. "We are about as high as you can get in this part of the

239

world. Eleven hundred metres. And Herberton is the coldest place in North Queensland."

"Yes, well... Aargh! Uuk!" Roger cried out. He scraped at his neck and stared aghast at the bright red blood drenching his fingers.

Graham turned in alarm. Then he smiled. "Leech. Big bastard too," he said. "Hold still and I'll get him off. No. Too late. You've scratched him off."

"Urk! Ah yuk!" Roger cried as he flicked a bloated leech the size of his little finger onto the grass. With a savage grunt he ground it under his boot heel. Blood spurted to mix with the mud and grass.

Graham smiled. "He had a good feed out of you mate. Hold still while I look at the bite," he said. The leech bite did not hurt but it was bleeding profusely, bright red blood.

Roger pulled out his handkerchief and pressed it over the bite. He wasn't really worried. Over the years the friends had experienced so many leeches that they were just accepted as part of the deal. "I bet I picked it up in those ferns," he commented. Ferns were a favourite habitat of the creatures.

Graham flicked another leech off Roger's shirt. "There's another of the little mongrels. Huh. Is that a vehicle?"

"Yes. Coming this way. Must be the police," Roger replied.

The two boys stood beside the road and listened to the sound of the approaching motor. Roger dabbed at the bleeding and kept looking in amazement at how much blood there was on his handkerchief. Then an awful thought came to him.

"What if it's not the police?"

"Strewth! I never thought of that. Quick, hide!"

The boys ran back up the short track.

"Here it comes. Get down!" Graham cried as he threw himself flat in the grass beside the track. Roger did likewise, aware that if the vehicle turned into the clearing they would probably be seen. In fact he was horrified to discover he could easily see the road through the grass. But it was too late to move. Heart thumping and mouth dry with fear he lay still.

A dark green Land Rover roared across his field of vision, accelerating as it reached level ground. As the vehicle raced past Roger saw green shirts and green caps with gold badges: Kosarian Royal Guards!

And we were just standing in the middle of the road! he thought.

The vehicle tore through a puddle and hit several potholes so hard the men in the back all cried out as they were violently bounced around. The driver slowed, but only fractionally. The vehicle vanished over the crest heading north.

Graham stood up. "Royal Guards. We would have looked a prize pair of geese if we had flagged them down."

Roger shuddered again and wiped his brow. He thrust his handkerchief away and began walking out onto the road.

Graham called, "Where are you going?"

"Something fell off that Rover when it hit those bumps," Roger replied. He walked down past the line of pine trees to where a bundle lay in the grass beside the road.

"It's a pack," he called, kneeling to examine it.

"They might come back to look for it," Graham cautioned as he joined him. They both listened but the only sound was the wind in the trees and the spatter of raindrops.

"You keep watch while I have a look," Roger replied.

"Not out in the open. In the jungle just there," Graham said, pointing to his left.

Roger lugged the pack over into the cover of the jungle and crouched to open it. Graham stood nearby, rifle at the ready. It was a soldier's pack similar to their own. Inside the bottom half was a groundsheet and sleeping bag. "Someone is going to bloody cold tonight," he said, very aware that he was starting to shiver himself. He opened the top flap.

In a plastic bag were a field jacket, a dirty green shirt, spare socks and underpants, and other personal items. Most had name tags sewn inside them. "The owner's name is Zumpitch," Roger read. He then looked inside one of the side pockets. It was full of tins of food. He pulled out the top one. "Braised Steak and Onions. I could go them. I'm starving." He was also aware he had not yet had breakfast.

Graham laughed quietly. "Anything else?"

Roger opened the other side pocket and dug his hand in. There was a small pocket of some sort sewn on the inside. He pushed his fingers in and fished out a cloth cap.

It was a blue forage cap, quite unlike those worn by the Royal Guards which had a peak and a brim, similar to the Austrian *Bergmutze*. This one

241

was meant to be worn 'fore and aft' and on the front was pinned a red star. Roger fingered the metal star in puzzlement and looked at Graham.

"This is odd. I thought these were Royal Guards, but this is a communist badge. Aren't the Communists their enemies?" he asked.

Graham nodded. "Yes they are. Perhaps it is a souvenir; or a disguise; or used to mark the 'enemy' in training exercises?" he suggested.

Roger opened the cap and looked inside. "It's got the same name sewn into it as the other clothes: Zumptich."

Graham shrugged. "I don't understand it. Keep it. The Inspector might find it useful."

Roger opened his basic pouch, rolled the cap up and pushed it in. He then turned back to the pack and dug into it again. "A battery. Radio battery I reckon. And this." He held up some papers in a plastic bag.

Graham crouched to look, "Let's see what it is."

Roger dried his fingers on the shirt then extracted the papers. Immediately a heavy raindrop went splat on them. Roger swore and hunched over to keep the papers under the brim of his slouch hat.

"It's another code book. And this looks like instructions on how to use some sort of radio." He passed the printed booklet with its pages of diagrams to Graham.

"The bloke must be a sig," Graham said.

"And here are some notes, in German though." Roger held up two pages torn from a pocket notebook with handwriting on them.

Graham took them. "S. O. Is," he said. "Signals Operating Instructions, from a set of Orders. Look. It says '5. Komd. und Sig.' Command and Signals; same as in our 'Headings for Orders'. And this, under 'Funk', that's 'Radio'. It must be a Net Diagram."

Roger looked and saw that there were five small circles in a semi-circular pattern, all connected to a larger circle underneath with 34WF printed inside it. The circles on the 'net' were numbered: 34R, 34M, 34S, 34W, 34Z.

Graham said, "These will be their call signs. And these are the frequencies: 'Primary; 44.60; Alternate; 46.90'. And the code to use: 'Ratsel Nummer Fier'."

"Parole," Roger read. "That's French. It means, pass, or..."

"Password. It is the same word in German," Graham cried. "Falke Festung: Falcon's Fortress!"

242

"Great. I hope we don't get close enough to need to use that," Roger replied. "What is this where it says: 'Standort vom HQ'? Oh! I can read the next bit: 'Karte: Atherton 1:100 000. Grid Reference 324868. Is 'Karte' a map?"

"'Karte'? Yes. A chart or map," Graham replied. "But I can't remember what 'Standort' is."

Roger felt a surge of excitement as he pulled out his map and unfolded it. "I can work it out. In our 'Headings for Orders' the heading would be 'Location of Headquarters'. That's it. We know where their HQ is."

"Only until 1200hrs today," Graham replied, pointing to the timings.

Roger ran his finger over the map. "Here, where this road along the top of the mountain range dips down to cross the headwaters of the Walsh River. It's only about four kilometres in a straight line."

"Look how that road wriggles along the crestline. It would be twice that."

Roger replied, "Eight kilometres. We can do that in two hours."

Graham looked at him in surprise and grinned. "Is this really Roger? Wanting to march eight Ks over the mountains in the rain?"

Roger ignored him. He was too excited. "Come on. We can make it in time."

"Slow down Roger. Firstly there is no guarantee they will stay, now they know, or think, that the army is in the area. Secondly there are other roads by which they can leave. Look, there's one that loops out to the west then comes back as two roads on either side of the Walsh. And there are those two going east to join up at the 'Hope of Atherton' mine. There's another road that goes down the mountain to Atherton past the rifle range. And thirdly; we should wait for Peter and the police. We can't just charge off into the jungle."

"We could leave a note," Roger suggested.

"They might not find it."

"What if we put this pack in the middle of the road and pin the note to it?"

Graham shook his head. "Great! What if those Royal Guards come back looking for the pack? They get the note and come hunting us."

Roger felt a bit sheepish. He cast around for an idea. More than anything he wanted to follow the Royal Guards. "Could one of us go and one wait here?"

"No. You'll just get bloody well shot. We were lucky earlier; and I was stupid. We should both walk back down to Stephen. He must be worried sick. It is only a ten- or fifteen-minute walk. Besides, he might be in trouble. That other bloke might have watched us leave and come back to rescue his boss."

Roger was appalled as the implications of this sank in. Reluctantly he agreed, "Okay. We'd better go back. What will we do with this pack?"

"Repack it and dump it beside the road. Keep those notes though."

Roger added the notes to his left basic pouch, then repacked the pack. He then carried it out and placed it beside the road.

Graham grunted, then said, "Okay, let's go back to Stephen." He looked along the road to the north, then clicked on the safety catch.

"Which way will we go?" Roger asked.

Graham pointed up through the ferns. "Down the ridge that leads from here to where we camped. That will be quicker and safer than walking along the road. That way we will keep well away from that sentry post they have marked on their map," he said.

That brought an awful thought to Roger's mind. "But what if Pete and the police drive into the sentry post? They could get ambushed. We need to be able to warn them," he replied.

Graham nodded as he started walking. "You are right. So we will walk through the bush near the road and be ready to run out if we see a police vehicle. We know where the sentry post is and we will cut across that big loop in the road to by-pass it," he said."

So the boys walked back across the road past the grassy clearing. Then they entered the open bush on the left and went westwards down the slope. They kept the road just in sight. The walking was easy enough, but the grass was wet and once again Roger found his boots and trousers soaked. But that didn't worry him as much as fear of meeting more armed men, or of stepping on a snake.

Graham led and Roger thankfully followed in his footsteps. As always it seemed further than the map indicated and Roger felt they were trudging through the bush for a long time, stepping over logs and detouring around trees and clumps of lantana.

After a few minutes' walk they came out of the cloud. Away to the west Roger could see the next mountain. It looked to be much drier country, almost open savannah, unlike the thick scrub and ferns they were pushing through. The boys walked in silence one behind the other. From time to time Graham stopped to study his map. By then Roger was feeling tired and hungry.

After 10 minutes' walk Graham stopped and took a compass bearing, then pointed to the left. "That sentry post should be a couple of hundred metres ahead of us. We will cut across the bend here," he whispered.

Carefully the boys moved forward, now angling to the south. The slope became much steeper and the bush opened out to savannah woodland with almost no undergrowth. The road came into view again. It was a few hundred metres ahead and below them. Through the stands of tall trees Roger saw that they were now in the head of a forested valley.

Graham stopped and scanned the road and bush ahead of them, then back to his right. "The road junction with the sentry post should be back up there on a saddle on the edge of this open timber," he whispered.

"Can they see us?" Roger replied, straining his eyes to study the trees behind his right shoulder.

Graham shook his head. "No, this small spur here should be blocking the view. Come on, let's get down near the road in case the police arrive."

Roger agreed. The whole time they had been cutting across the bend he had been worried about just that. So he hurried along behind Graham who contoured down the grassy ridge until he was just above the road. Here he paused and cradled the rifle in both arms while he studied the map.

Roger looked down at the gravel road 10 metres below. "It will be quicker if we use the road," he suggested.

Graham shook his head. "Yes, but not safer. We will look like a pair of prize idiots if we run into that other fellow who ran way," he replied as he slid the map back into his map pocket.

Roger could not answer. He could only grab at Graham's sleeve and gape, his gaze riveted on the rifle barrel pointing directly at him: a tiny black hole of the most startling clarity.

As he came to a standstill and Graham looked up in surprise a voice up to their left cried, "Halt!"

Fear seemed to root Roger to the spot. He instinctively put his hands up.

"Hand up!" the man's voice commanded; a harsh, guttural voice. "Put der rifle down or you is ver dead!"

For a moment Roger thought Graham might try to fight back and a stab of pure dread lanced through him. To his mingled relief and regret Graham did not. With obvious reluctance he placed the rifle on the ground and raised his hands.

The man spoke again. "Move away from der rifle. Keep apart and keep der hands high," he ordered.

Glancing fearfully at the man Roger recognised the uniform. "He is a royal guard," he muttered to Graham.

The royal guard heard him. "Silence or I shoot!" he snarled.

Once the boys were well clear the royal guard halted them again and then moved to pick up the rifle. He studied it for a few seconds, a frown creasing his brow. "Ver you get zis rifle?" he queried.

Roger answered. "Off your lieutenant," he replied. By this time he was shaking with fear as well as a cold.

"He der prisoner is?" the royal guard asked.

Graham answered before Roger could. "Yes. And you may as well surrender too because the police are on their way up here."

Roger saw an anxious look on the man's face. For a few more seconds they stood there, the royal guard obviously trying to decide what to do. As they did realisation came to Roger.

This bloke is a sentry watching down the valley. We have just blundered into him by sheer chance, he thought. He studied the situation trying to come up with a plan that might keep them alive and set them free.

But no idea came to him and the man pointed down to the road. "Go zat vay," he ordered.

Graham looked at him. "Your mates have gone. They have bugged out," he replied.

"Bugged out?" the man queried.

"Gone. Run away," Graham replied.

The man looked anxious then shook his head. "No matter. Ve go zat vay. Move!"

Reluctantly they did. They made their way down onto the road and were told to start walking up it. "And keep your hands on heads!"

So, even more reluctantly, they started marching up the road, the royal guard following at such a distance that there was no chance of jumping him.

And in this open bush there is no chance of making a run for it without being shot, Roger noted.

For the next 5 minutes they trudged up a slope that was much steeper than Roger had expected, and the effort had him panting and perspiring. With every step his mind roved over the dreadful possibilities of the situation and he became so afraid he could hardly make himself keep putting one foot in front of the other. Even the effort of keeping his hands on his head almost became too much.

Another call to halt sounded from behind a tree at the bend ahead. Roger and Graham at once halted. Roger saw another rifle muzzle being aimed at him and felt his bowels weaken with terror. The royal guard behind them shouted back and a rapid conversation in a foreign language followed.

"Advance!" called the man behind the tree.

Gasping with fear and over, exertion Roger did so, Graham keeping level beside him. They rounded the bend and came to a road junction. As they did Roger glanced out of the corner of his eye at the sentry and noted that he was also dressed in royal guard uniform.

We have really mucked this up, he thought miserably.

Then Roger saw a second royal guard kneeling behind a large tree on the other side of the road junction.

"Halt! Keep your hands up!" A hard, faced, middle-aged man appeared out of the scrub in front of them. On both sleeves of his green uniform shirt, just above the elbows, were pinned diamond shaped yellow metal badges with three black parallel lines across them. The man had a sub-machine gun of some sort, a wicked looking thing with an air cooling casing around the barrel. Roger did not know what type it was, but he could see that the man had his finger on the trigger.

The soldier pointed with his left hand. "You, take off your vebbink. Lie down over dere. Und you, over dere."

The boys did as they were told. Roger was shaking with fright. He felt sick and was very conscious that the other soldier had his rifle aimed at his head from only a few metres away. A third appeared from behind a tree. The middle-aged soldier began to question the man who had captured them. Roger could not understand a word of what was said but got the impression that the middle-aged man was very angry and not at all impressed with the explanation the soldier gave him.

The middle-aged man then walked over and stood beside Graham. "Are dere any more off you?" he snarled in heavily accented English.

"Might be," Graham replied.

Thud!

To Roger's horror the man took a step forward and kicked Graham hard in the ribs. "Don't be smart-alek bastard boy! I ask you. You tell me; or else." He bent and peered at the badges on Graham's sleeve, then turned and spoke rapidly to the other two soldiers in a foreign language. The only words Roger understood were 'soldats' and 'kadets'.

The man spoke again, and Roger heard boots crunch on the gravel near his head. He tensed for a blow.

"Put hands behind back," he was ordered. He did so, his face then resting on the wet sand and stones. The second soldier quickly tied his wrists together with thin nylon cord. It hurt but Roger made no complaint. It was all he could do not to cry, so great was his fear.

Graham was similarly tied. Roger watched the royal guard do it. The man had a wicked looking sheath knife and used what looked like army green nylon cord. Graham was then searched and his pockets emptied. Roger suffered this next. He had had it done to him in training exercises, but this had an entirely new and unpleasant dimension of fear, pain and indignity. The man hauled him roughly onto his back so that his weight was on his left arm and wrists. Then his pockets were emptied.

Roger heard the man grunt and say something. He held up Roger's jellybeans and grinned, then popped one in his mouth and tossed another to the man with the SMG. The man wasn't amused and snapped something back.

Maps and notebooks were collected. The compass tied to his pocket was left hanging. His protractor fell to the ground. The man with three stripes (a sergeant?) bent over Graham and put the muzzle of the SMG near his nose. Roger could see a muscle in Graham's neck twitching, but his face looked calm enough.

"Now boy, answer me and tell zer truth or ve shoot you und zen ve ask der fat kaporal."

Fat corporal! Roger felt a surge of hot resentment even in his state of near collapse.

The man asked, "Are zere any more of you?"

"Yes," Graham replied.

"How many?"

"Four. No. Three. One has gone to get the police."

"Der police! Vy?"

"Because we saw you people."

"So? Ve could be anyvon."

Graham shook his head. "We know who you are."

"Oh ja! Who are ve den?"

"Kosarian Royal Guards."

The man's face was a picture of genuine astonishment. Then it darkened into anger and worry. "How you know zat eh boy? You are kadet Ja?"

"Yes, I am a cadet."

"How you know?"

"We. Roger there, pulled Captain Krapinski's body out of Tinaroo Dam. And we helped the police search for clues as to who killed him and why."

Again the man's face registered astonishment, even shock. "Krapinski! You know ver he is?"

The other men began talking rapidly in their own language with Krapinski's name cropping up several times. The man doing the questioning was Feldwebel Stegberg or something Roger deduced.

The feldwebel grabbed Graham's shirt front and spoke harshly to him, "Vot is dis about Krapinski's body? You say his body vos in a dam? You mean he is dead?"

Graham nodded. "Yes. We pulled his body out of Lake Tinaroo four days ago. He had been shot."

"Shot! By who? By you?"

"No. By Dorkoffsky."

"Dorkoffsky!"

The man seemed even more astonished. Again the men began talking in their own language. The feldwebel turned to Graham again, holding the muzzle of the SMG right under his nose.

"Zut! How you know Dorkoffsky? How you know he shoot Krapinski?"

"Because we were there when the police arrested him and the other KSS men," Graham replied.

"KSS!"

The feldwebel sprang to his feet in agitation. The four men almost gabbled at each other, 'KSS' punctuating every sentence. The man knelt beside Graham again. He was clearly both very worried and confused.

"Vot you know about der KSS?"

"There were five of them searching for something in the jungle in the Danbulla State Forest," Graham replied.

He quickly described their encounter. Now all four of the royal guards crouched listening and the SMG was no longer pointed at him. Roger watched the men's faces. He could see they had received a real shock. Their muscles were quivering with tension. When Graham described the KSS badge Roger had found the men all hissed involuntarily and Roger saw the feldwebel's fingers fidgeting nervously with the SMG. The royal guards had another rapid discussion in their own language.

Then the feldwebel went and picked up the rifle Graham had been carrying. Again he gasped in astonishment and turned it over to look at its serial number.

"Ver you get zis?" he snarled at Graham.

"From Leutnant Witorski," Graham said, pronouncing the rank in the German way.

Roger wouldn't have thought the men were capable of further astonishment, but they gasped and gabbled at each other. He wished Graham wouldn't tell them so much and tried to catch his eye to frown his disapproval. Not only was he very afraid but he was also getting very cold and uncomfortable.

The feldwebel asked, "Ver is Leutnant Witorski? How you know ihm?"

"We captured him. He was injured. The police have him now, in hospital," lied Graham. "They will be here soon."

"Vot did Schutzer Nitsky do?"

"If he is the bloke who was with the leutnant and who just captured us then not much. He fired a couple of shots at Roger and ran off into the bush."

One of the men spoke in a 'told you so' tone and Roger saw the feldwebel scowl several times while the others made comments in a derisory tone.

Sounds like the silly bugger can't navigate, he thought.

The feldwebel shrugged and the men began a discussion which

seemed to be over what to do with their prisoners. Roger began to dissolve in fear again as he realised they could well be shot.

Then the felwebel made up his mind. He gave rapid orders. One man ran off and returned a minute later with a chain saw. The feldwebel picked up a radio and began typing on a small keyboard on its face. The other man scooped up their belongings and shoved them roughly back into their map pockets. Then he picked up their webbing and the rifle and carried them down to where Roger now saw a Land Rover under a camouflage net. The soldier rolled the net up and then came back and with another soldier hauled Graham to his feet and pushed him towards the vehicle. He was shoved up into the back.

Then it was Roger's turn. It hurt to be wrenched to his feet by one arm, but it was also a relief. Clearly, they were being taken somewhere and would not be shot immediately.

Chapter 28

CAPTURED

Roger was pushed into the back of the Land Rover beside Graham. The soldier, a kaporal, climbed in and sat opposite, with his rifle across his knees.

"No talk," he cautioned.

Through the front Roger could see the feldwebel at the radio. The man stood up and called something, then picked up the radio and walked towards them. The soldier who had captured them scrambled in the back and sat beside Roger. The third soldier sparked the chain saw into life and began to attack the base of a large tree. By the time the feldwebel had put the radio into the vehicle and climbed in the tree had been cut through. It fell with a crash of splintering branches so that it lay diagonally down the road, completely blocking it. The harsh clatter of the chain saw died and the man began walking towards them.

Suddenly he stopped and half-turned, then broke into a run, shouting. Roger understood the words 'Polizei' and 'kommen'. He writhed with mortification. The police were coming but they were too late!

The soldier heaved the chain saw in the back, hitting Roger's leg with it as he did. He then ran and jumped into the driver's seat, handing his rifle to the feldwebel. The engine whirred and burst into life and the vehicle lurched out onto the road.

They swung right towards the top of the mountain and rapidly accelerated. The driver ignored the bumps and ruts. The vehicle bounced and swayed violently so that gear clattered and tumbled. Roger felt his elbow whack against the side so hard he yelled in pain. The chain saw dug sharply into his ankle. He tried to grip the seat behind him, but his hands had gone numb.

He was also terrified that the soldier opposite would accidentally pull the trigger as they crashed and bounced over the bumps. To his relief, he saw the man take his hand away from the pistol grip to hold on. The soldier shouted something and the feldwebel also shouted. The vehicle slowed down.

Roger glimpsed the grassy clearing as they roared past and then the feldwebel called out again. The vehicle braked violently. The feldwebel got out, to reappear at the back with the pack in his hand.

"Zumpitch," he said, reading the name tag on the pack.

He tossed it on Roger's feet and returned to the cab. Roger met Graham's eye but tried not to look as though the pack meant anything to them. The drive resumed.

They were back in the cloud and a cold wind swirled through the vehicle, rapidly chilling Roger so that his teeth began to chatter. The windscreen wipers were turned on as they encountered rain. The vehicle roared down a long, greasy slope too fast for safety, sliding so much that the feldwebel spoke sharply to the driver who, much to Roger's relief, slowed down.

As they drove along, Roger tried to visualise the map. He was sure where they were going, to the Royal Guard HQ at the Walsh River crossing. The road wound down steeply to the left with thick jungle on both sides. They dipped below the cloud briefly before starting up a long, slippery uphill grind in low gear.

At the top, the vehicle stopped and both driver and feldwebel got out. The motor was left running. A steady drizzle started. Fear clawed at Roger. Were they to be shot and their bodies tossed over the near, vertical side of the ridge to rot in that tangle of jungle?

The driver leaned in the back, swore, tossed the pack and loose items aside and hauled the chain saw out. He walked back into the swirling mist to where the feldwebel indicated a large tree. Roger relaxed and allowed misery to engulf him. He began to shiver so much his teeth started to chatter. The guard looked at him and shrugged sympathetically. He was cold too.

The chain saw screamed into life and the driver went to work. In a couple of minutes a huge hardwood fell with a crash across the road, bringing down a mass of creepers and vines with it. The two men walked back to the vehicle. The chain saw was dumped on Roger's boots and the journey resumed.

Roger looked back glumly at the tangle of greenery blocking the road. *The police will never get through that in time!* he thought.

The Land Rover ground on, half-bogging from time to time in muddy patches, swerving to avoid fallen logs (and going so close to the edge that Roger's heart leapt into his mouth in fright), and bouncing and slipping up greasy pinches in 4WD. The road levelled off for about a kilometre, cutting around the western side of a jungle covered mountain. *We are definitely going north along the spine of the Herberton Range,* Roger decided.

The vehicle slowed and swung around a hairpin bend and began to descend. Roger caught a glimpse of a green clad man with a machine gun, an MG55 or MG3. The soldier had a belt of shining ammunition draped over his shoulder. They passed another 4WD parked beside the road with more royal guards in it.

That vehicle began to follow them. Roger was in a state of near collapse by this. His hands and arms were numb, his body frozen, and his brain a maggot's nest of fear. Graham appeared to be sitting there calmly, observing everything. Roger wondered if it was just a front and tried to control his own face.

At least I can try to die with a bit of dignity, he told himself.

The vehicle slowed, to slosh through a muddy hollow where water was flowing across the road. Its wheels crunched over a rotten log. Vines and leaves slapped and scratched at the vehicle. The road was obviously not used much, and the jungle was encroaching on it.

Up a muddy slope, around and down past a road junction and another 4WD, a brown one. A royal guard in a raincoat stood beside it holding a radio handset. Roger wished the journey would end so that whatever was going to happen could.

Then they were bumping and grinding through a swiftly flowing stream of crystal-clear water.

"Walsh River," Graham murmured.

The guard looked at him but said nothing. Roger felt all his muscles tense up. Won't be long now!

Bump! Crash! Roar! Bump!

The rover lurched over rocks and runnels as it clawed its way up the far bank. The vehicle growled up a long, slippery slope, the wheels spinning and spraying mud. Roger watched the following 4WD splash into the creek behind them.

The vehicles ground up a long, muddy slope. Then their brakes came on. They were stopping!

Roger looked through the front and saw more vehicles and at least half a dozen royal guards. Suddenly his mouth went dry and his tongue felt too big for his throat. He wanted to cry out but restrained himself. He also urgently wanted to do a pee.

The vehicle stopped and the motor died. The kaporal dropped the tailgate. The feldwebel came to the rear and reached in to grab Roger's sleeve.

"Out!"

Roger had to wriggle over the pack and chain saw. His arms and left leg had 'gone to sleep' so that he slid to the ground and fell in a heap on the muddy track.

Thump!

The feldwebel kicked him in the thigh and hauled him to his feet. Another royal guard, with one stripe on his sleeve and a bayonet fixed to his rifle, appeared and pointed. Roger stumbled up the track to where a group of officers in overcoats stood. The lance corporal pointed to the side of the track. "Sit there."

Roger did as he was told, slumping down on the wet soil a few metres behind another green Land Rover. Graham joined him. Their webbing was tossed down near their feet. Roger was aware of other vehicles arriving, of engines switching off, doors slamming, voices, commands.

The feldwebel marched up to a tall young officer with a moustache, snapped to attention and saluted, clicking his heels while he did so. There were three other officers there and two senior NCOs: one with three stripes across and one down though their centres, and the other with a gold crown: A sergeant major?

The feldwebel talked rapidly for several minutes. The officers listened intently, their faces worried frowns. From time to time they looked surprised or shocked and glanced at the boys.

Roger tried to breathe slowly to calm his heartbeat. He looked around. In the back of the Land Rover on his left was a signaller wearing earphones connected to a large radio mounted in the back. Nearby were two infantrymen lying behind an LMG facing into the jungle. Other soldiers were just visible further along, crouched behind trees. The misty rain continued to fall and there was a continual heavy dripping from the leaves.

The squelch of boots made Roger look up in alarm. The officers and senior NCOs now stood facing them. Roger licked his lips and pressed his legs together to stop from wetting himself. He felt faint and shook with fear.

The officer with the moustache spoke to Graham. His English was excellent and he sounded like an upper-class Englishman. "Tell us who you are, what you are doing here, and what you know," he said.

Graham proceeded to tell the story of the hike, explaining they were only cadets doing a map reading expedition. He described how they had started from Tinaroo and how Roger had seen Krapinski's body. At that all their eyes turned to Roger. He met some of them and knew he had never seen harder or more hostile eyes in his life. He was terrified. A vivid recollection of Krapinski's corpse rose in his mind and fear of death so gripped him that for a few minutes he was speechless.

The young officer spoke. "Speak boy! Tell us. How did he die?"

"G... G... Gun... Gunshot sir. In the... the... h... h... head," Roger replied.

He sobbed and took a deep breath and recounted how they had helped the police search at Platypus Rock; then of the meeting with the two KSS men at Robsons Creek and the finding of the badge.

The officers exchanged worried glances and the young one snapped, "Describe the badge."

Roger did so. He saw that the audience was intensely interested, and they all nodded in unison.

The young officer asked, "Do you have the badge? Where is it?"

"Inspector Sharpe has it. He took it," Roger replied. He was trembling but managed to keep talking. He described meeting the Inspector at The Chimneys, then with the four KSS men in the jungle on Python Ridge.

The young officer frowned. "They were digging you say?"

"Yes, sir. They were searching for something."

"Did they find it? What was it?"

Again, Roger sensed the question was of vital importance to these men and he could not see how lying or withholding anything would help in any way. He shook his head and replied, "They did not find it sir. We don't know what they were looking for. We thought it might be a treasure; perhaps the missing crown jewels or the Thigh Bone..."

He suddenly stopped, realising he shouldn't have mentioned these things. He glanced at Graham who gave him a look of disapproval.

A middle-aged officer with a thick grey moustache bent down and grabbed Roger's collar. "You know of the sacred Thigh Bone of St Joris? How?"

The group had broken into excited chatter. They turned back to hear Roger's answer. He swallowed and broke into a cold sweat. "We didn't know then. We thought it must be treasure they were looking for." He described events at Mobo Creek.

The young officer asked in a sad voice, "You say Dorkoffsky was one of the KSS men arrested?"

"Yes, sir. We spent the night in his house at Yungaburra," Roger replied. Then he looked up. The face of the sergeant with the cross, stripe suddenly jogged his memory. "You! You are the man I saw outside our room that night. You walked off into the fog. I chased you."

The man looked most uncomfortable. The others all turned to look at him. The older officer snapped, "What is this Zumpitch? What happened?"

Zumpitch replied in what Roger assumed was Serbo-Croat, the only word he understood being the rank of Colonel. So the older man must be Colonel Von Krapnoff. The men listened to Zumpitch but Roger couldn't follow the by-play. They turned back to the boys.

Colonel Von Krapnoff asked, "You are sure Dorkoffsky was with the KSS?"

"Definitely. In a black uniform; and with one of those Iron Claw badges on his collar," Roger replied.

"Iron... Claw!" the young officer hissed. "Describe it."

Roger did so. He even mentioned that it had a number engraved on the reverse. The young officer shook his head as though he could not believe it. "How could he! We trusted him," he said sadly.

"Perhaps it was a mistake, Your Highness," a handsome captain in his twenties replied.

Your Highness! Roger's mind raced. So the young officer with the moustache must be Prince Peter. Without thinking he asked, "Excuse me sir, are you Prince Peter?"

The group turned in stunned silence.

"How did you know?" snapped the Colonel.

Graham spoke. "The captain there just called him 'Your Highness'. And you must be Colonel Von Krapnoff, Kommandant of the Royal Guard."

There was another astonished silence. The Colonel visibly recoiled and blinked. Then he drew a pistol and aimed it at Graham.

"You boys seem to know an awful lot. How is that?"

Graham eyed the pistol but replied without a tremor in his voice. "Because we translated a secret message of yours which one of the KSS men had in his pocket."

"Untersturmfuhrer Jablonski," Roger put in.

"Tell us. Tell us all of it," the Colonel snarled, shaking the pistol in Graham's face.

Graham did so, aided by Roger who explained how he found Jablonski's jacket. That reminded him of his shame, and his current need.

"Can I go to the toilet please?" he croaked.

"Take him!" Prince Peter ordered.

The soldier with the bayoneted rifle who had been standing behind them grabbed Roger and marched him down the road past the last Land Rover and pointed. Roger indicated his hands were tied behind his back. The soldier clearly wasn't going to unbutton Roger's fly and hold it for him.

"You're lucky I'm not one of those," the soldier said with a grin. He put his rifle against a tree and drew a pocketknife. "Don't try anything silly," he warned, indicating other royal guards who were lying in the jungle watching.

The soldier cut the bindings. For a minute Roger could not use his hands. They had gone nearly black. The pain as the circulation returned was so painful he burst into tears. He rubbed his hands on his wrists and slowly clenched and relaxed his fingers.

Then he was shaking so much he could not unbutton his fly for a while. He wiped tears away and was so embarrassed by the men watching that for half a minute he could not start. At last he managed to, but he was quite upset by the time he finished.

The soldier retrieved his rifle and motioned him to go back to where he had been sitting. He did not re-tie Roger's hands and Roger fervently hoped no-one would notice.

Trying to pretend he wasn't scared, he walked back and sat beside Graham.

Chapter 29

TREACHERY

Prince Peter looked at them and shook his head. "So Dorkoffsky really was a traitor," he said. "And he was our most trusted courier! We must assume that the Archduke Paul knows all our plans."

Colonel von Krapnoff scowled. "And the Australian Police Your Highness. Thanks to these interfering cadets," he snarled.

A tall, thin officer spoke. "We should leave this area and disperse at once Your Highness. Then we must recast our plans."

"Yes Stiltz. You are right. How long before the police arrive do you think?"

Adjutant Stiltz. Roger realised he should have guessed it. The man was a captain and was as thin as a stick.

Adjutant Stiltz replied, "It depends whether they have chain saws to clear the road. Several hours probably. But the real danger is that they will set up roadblocks on all the roads out of the area. We need to move at once."

The Prince nodded agreement, "What do you suggest?"

Colonel von Krapnoff then spoke rapidly in their language. As he did, another person joined them. Roger looked up and noted with surprise that it was a girl. She wore a green jacket and long green trousers, but was still obviously a girl. She had been sitting in a white 4WD parked in front of the green Land Rover.

Roger stared at her in wonder. She was only about 15 or 16 years old and had a perfect heart-shaped face, glossy black shoulder length hair, and hazel eyes.

She is beautiful! he thought. *The most beautiful girl I have ever seen!*

"Why must we suddenly go?" she asked in English. Her voice sounded like music and stirred emotions deep in Roger's soul. For a moment he forgot to be frightened.

"Because the police are coming, Your Serene Highness," Colonel von Krapnoff replied.

She must be the missing Princess Karena, Roger thought. *No, that's silly. If she went missing in 1941, she wouldn't look fifteen. Still, she must be a princess.*

The princess pointed at Roger. "How do the police know we are here? Is it because of these boys?"

"Yes, Your Highness."

"How do they know to come here?"

Prince Peter turned to Graham, "Yes. How do the police know to come here, in the jungle? We only arrived yesterday."

As Graham explained the secret message mentioning Concentration Place Cloud and the grey Mercedes with four men in it, Roger studied the prince. He couldn't see any family resemblance between him and the princess. Roger now noted that the prince wore a dark green shirt under his field jacket. The shirt had white collar tabs and pinned to them were gold and silver badges. Real gold and silver he decided, from the way they reflected the watery sunlight. The badges were a crown surrounded by oak or laurel leaves.

Prince Peter asked, "Yes, but how did that tell you where Sammelplatz Wolke was?"

"Because of Leutnant Witorski," Graham replied.

"Ah! Witorski. How did he come to tell you?"

"He didn't sir. He broke his leg and got stuck in a cattle grid. He was unconscious. We got him out and gave him first aid. When we searched him, we found a radio signal and his map, which was marked."

Colonel von Krapnoff spoke loudly in his own language, a curse or expletive from the sound of it. He bent and pulled maps and papers out of Graham's pockets and quickly sorted them. While he did this Adjutant Stiltz gave rapid instructions to the other captain and the three senior NCOs.

"You and Stegborz had better get moving. Take the western route. Hauptman Ritnik, would you please escort the princess to her vehicle. You and Unteroffizier Klotovich take her down to Atherton. Go now. Zumpitch, you remain with us."

The feldwebel who had captured them went to his vehicle and came back. He tossed a pack at the feet of the solid, square-faced feldwebel, "Your pack Stabb," he explained. "We found it lying on the road."

So he is a Staff Sergeant, Roger decided.

Zumpitch grunted thanks and walked forward, picked the pack up and took it to the green Land Rover. He spoke to the signaller there who climbed out with a rifle and took over guarding the two cadets. Zumpitch climbed in and placed the earphones on his head.

The good-looking captain led the princess to her vehicle. Roger experienced a twinge of envy. Then the fear swamped back as Colonel von Krapnoff began to snarl. He had found the radio signal taken off Witorski and was waving the paper at Graham.

"Did you read this?"

"Yes. We had enough German between us," Graham replied. Roger wished he had lied.

"So it was you and not soldiers who broke up our ambush?"

"Yes, that's right."

"You interfering little swine! I should have you shot! What gives you the right to interfere in our affairs?" Colonel von Krapnoff shouted.

"I'll tell you what right," Graham replied loudly. "The Kosarian Deputy Premier is a guest in this country and you people have no right to commit murder here. It would make Australia look pretty poor. Besides, most of you have been living here as refugees and migrants for years and I think that it is a very poor way to repay Australia. So take your dirty bloody civil war somewhere else!"

Colonel von Krapnoff said nothing for a moment but he was clearly very angry. Prince Peter looked abashed and so did Stiltz. They began to argue in their own language and Roger guessed there had been a strong disagreement over the ambush plan.

While this was going on commands had been given and soldiers had been emerging from the jungle and climbing into vehicles. Engines started and vehicles began driving off. Two went on along the road northwards including the white 4WD. Three others, including the Land Rover they had travelled in, drove past and turned left along a side-track. That left only the Land Rover next to them and a Toyota Landcruiser in front of that. Roger scratched around in his memory and decided there was still another vehicle back at the last road junction the other side of the Walsh.

Eight vehicles with four or five in each. That is about forty men, he calculated.

He now looked around. There did not appear to be any soldiers left in the surrounding jungle. Was there a chance of escape? Not really, he decided. There were still the prince, the colonel and Adjutant Stiltz, all with pistols, plus the guard standing on their right aiming his rifle at them, Zumpitch sitting in the back of the rover using the radio but watching them, and another soldier acting as sentry further up the track.

As the sound of the departing vehicles died awa,y the officers ended their argument at the insistence of Prince Peter.

"We must get going," he said

"What about this pair?" Colonel von Krapnoff asked.

The moment Roger had been dreading had arrived.

"We should shoot the interfering little shits!" rasped Zumpitch.

Roger went ice, cold. Terror constricted his stomach and chest. Zumpitch had climbed out of the Rover and held a sub-machine gun which he pointed at Roger's head. The muzzle seemed to grow larger and Roger wished he could faint. His skin crawled as he tensed in terrified anticipation.

Zumpitch gestured with his left hand. "Get in the vehicle Lurkoff," he ordered. The soldier guarding them moved to obey.

At that moment Prince Peter called out. "Stop Stabbs Feldwebel. There will be no murder," he commanded.

"But Highness they know too much. We cannot let them go," Zumpitch replied in a surly tone.

Roger was breathing very rapidly and felt panic rising, but he found his voice, "The police already know almost everything. Our friends have told them. Killing us won't change that."

Adjutant Stiltz spoke up, "The boy is right. We gain nothing by revenge; and would lose much more; our moral strength."

"There will be no murder," Prince Peter repeated. "They come with us as prisoners. They can..." He stopped and spun round. From the north came the unmistakable rattle of automatic weapon fire. "The princess! An ambush! But... but... surely the police would not?" he gasped. He went very pale.

Colonel von Krapnoff stepped across and called to the signaller who was now back in the Rover. "Call Hauptman Ritnik. Find out what is happening."

"Sir!" the sig replied. "He has just called us. He only said 'Ambush' and 'Partisans'."

"Partisans!" the three officers cried simultaneously.

They looked at each other in consternation, then back in the direction of the shooting, which sounded about a kilometre away and had become sporadic, occasional bursts and odd single shots.

"Call Oberleutnant Markoff. Get his group back," Colonel von Krapnoff ordered, as he walked towards the Rover.

"Partisans!" Prince Peter cried again. "How did they know we were here?" He turned to face Stiltz, who shrugged.

A ghastly thought had swum up through the murk of Roger's mind. Without thinking he voiced it, "Treachery."

"Eh!" They all turned to stare at him.

"They were told. By radio."

"By radio! But who?" Colonel von Krapnoff cried, turning an accusing glare at the signaller who looked appalled.

"Zumpitch," Roger said, looking up at the man.

Zumpitch's face went hard and he spluttered, "What rubbish! You lie boy!"

Adjutant Stiltz looked from one to the other, then asked Roger, "Why do you make that accusation kadet?"

"Because we found his pack on the road," Roger explained, jerking his head towards Zumpitch. "In it was a..."

Zumpitch let out a snarl. He suddenly crouched, swinging the sub-machine gun up as he did.

Tat-a-tat-a-tat-a-tat-a-tat-a-tat!

The gun rattled. Cartridge cases flicked into the air. Adjutant Stiltz just had time to push Prince Peter aside, but the burst took him full in the body. He and Prince Peter went down in a sprawling heap on the muddy road.

Colonel von Krapnoff let out a yell of rage and clawed at his pistol. Zumpitch swivelled the gun and fired again. Bullets slammed the colonel back against the vehicle. He fell in a crumpled, bleeding heap. Beyond Zumpitch's legs Roger saw the signaller, his mouth open in shock. Zumpitch fired again. The bullets smashed into the man, knocking him backwards against the radio. Bullets whanged off metal and punched into the set.

As though in slow motion, Roger saw the sentry further up the track turning to shoot and Prince Peter scrambling to his feet. Zumpitch swung the gun towards the prince. Roger sprang up, cannoning into Zumpitch.

The gun went off. Roger saw Prince Peter dive flat.

Zumpitch swore and swung the gun. It struck Roger a sharp blow on the side of his face. He fell sideways. *Dead!* he thought. *I'm dead! I shouldn't have done that. Now he will kill me for sure.* Yet he knew instinctively that he had no option. A man like Zumpitch would not leave any witnesses.

But Zumpitch turned back to face the sentry and sprang sideways as the man's rifle cracked. Zumpitch fired a burst at the sentry who twitched and rolled behind the Toyota. By then Prince Peter was on his hands and knees. He scrambled frantically for cover behind the front of the Land Rover. Zumpitch fired and missed, bullets smacking through the steel. Then his gun stopped, and he swore.

Zumpitch tore off the empty magazine and dodged for cover behind the Rover as the sentry bobbed up to shoot. Zumpitch scrabbled in the back of the Rover and pulled out another magazine. In a moment he had clicked it in, cocked the gun and come up firing.

The bullets punched through the Toyota. Glass broke. Ricochets screamed off into the jungle. Acrid smoke hung in the air. The sentry cried out and went down. Zumpitch stepped to the left to fire around the other side of the Rover.

Crack!

There was a single pistol shot. Zumpitch staggered back and ducked behind the Rover. He began firing through it.

Thud!

There was Graham!

He had struggled to his feet and run forward the slam into Zumpitch. The shock slammed Zumpitch hard into the back of the vehicle and they both went down in a struggling, swearing heap.

Zumpitch tried to roll free. He kicked and beat at Graham with the gun. Graham tried to shield himself, but his hands were still tied behind his back.

"Roger!" he cried.

Roger scrambled up, senses still reeling from the blow he had received. He ran at Zumpitch, yelling as he did. Zumpitch saw him and rolled on his back. Roger saw the sub-machine gun swing in his direction. He was 3 paces away!

I won't make it in time! his mind screamed.

Crack!

Zumpitch twitched and flopped down. Roger stomped on the hand holding the gun, gaping at the blood spurting from the man's skull.

Zumpitch lay still. Roger looked up and saw Prince Peter crouched at the back of the vehicle, a smoking pistol in his hand.

The two stared at each other. Roger gasped for air. The pistol swung to point at him.

Dead this time, he thought. *Well, at least I died fighting!*

Chapter 30

DUTY FIRST

Roger's vision blurred. His heart thumped wildly. He was aware that the sentry had emerged from behind the Toyota and was walking towards them, but he was staggering and obviously hurt. Then Roger saw things with total clarity. Prince Peter was wounded too. Blood was soaking the shirt over his left shoulder.

Roger stood up. "You've been hit sir," he said.

A vehicle was coming up the slope from the Walsh. *More royal guards, coming to investigate the shooting,* Roger thought.

He considered escaping but at that moment the sentry dropped his rifle, fell to his knees and pitched forward onto the track. Roger pointed. Prince Peter nodded and lowered the pistol. He looked hard at Roger and said, "You saved my life. Thank you for that."

The vehicle ground to a stop. Roger looked and saw, with surprise, that it was a white Queensland Police Landcruiser. From the passenger seat Inspector Sharpe sprang out, pistol in hand. DS Crowe jumped out from the other side. From the back appeared Detective West. In the vehicle were a uniformed constable as driver, plus Peter and Stephen.

For a tense moment nothing was said. The police levelled their guns at Prince Peter. They appeared dumbfounded by the scene. Inspector Sharpe then spoke. "Christ! There's been a battle alright. It certainly sounded like one. You, drop the gun!"

Prince Peter did as he was told.

Inspector Sharpe gestured to his men, who were joined by the constable. "Collect the guns and check these bodies."

Roger suddenly felt weak at the knees. Nausea welled up and he thought he was going to faint. He knelt down and found he was beside his webbing. Graham lay nearby, his nose bleeding but a grin on his face.

Moving as though in a dream Roger felt in his webbing and extracted his pocketknife. He opened it and walked over to Graham.

"You okay, mate? Roll on your side so I can cut you free."

A minute later Graham was standing up rubbing his wrists and alternately cursing and moaning. Peter and Stephen joined them and helped the police collect the guns. They checked them 'safe' and lay them in a line along the side of the road. Stephen then leaned on a tree and vomited.

Roger blinked and rubbed his eyes. He looked around. There seemed to be bodies everywhere. And blood. Lots of blood, all mixing with the mud and even dripping from the back of the Land Rover.

Inspector Sharpe walked over. "Are there any more?" he asked, his pistol still pointing at Prince Peter.

Roger shook his head. "No sir, but some might return along that track. Three vehicles and about fifteen of them. I don't know if the signaller had time to call them back or not." He indicated the crumpled form in the back of the Rover.

Inspector Sharpe looked around. "Who are they? Who are you?" this last directed at Prince Peter.

"I am Prince Peter the Seventh of Kosaria," Prince Peter replied with stiff dignity. He was holding his arm and was clearly in pain.

Inspector Sharpe blinked and bit his lip. DS Crowe muttered, "Bloody hell!"

"What on earth happened?" Inspector Sharpe asked. He shook his head in disbelief, then turned and snapped, "West! Get on the radio to Headquarters and tell them to get reinforcements and a couple of ambulances up here fast."

Roger remembered something. "Sir, if they come from Atherton up the road behind Mt. Baldy tell them to watch out for Partisans. They just ambushed the princess and her escort up that way." He pointed north along the road.

"The princess? Partisans? What the devil is going on?"

Prince Peter replied. "Princess Mareena," he replied. "She is my cousin." He swallowed and looked very distressed.

"And who are these bloody Partisans who have ambushed her?"

"Communists," Prince Peter replied.

"Tell me what is going on!" Inspector Sharpe demanded. "Bell and Bronsky, get to work with first aid on that joker. He's still alive." He indicated the sentry. "Crowe, check who else is alive. Leave the dead ones where they are till we can photograph them. Constable, get a camera and get to work."

Prince Peter suddenly swayed on his feet. Roger stepped forward and steadied him. "Sit down sir. Let me look at the wound. Graham, get your First Aid kit."

Roger helped Prince Peter to remove his jacket and sat him on the front fender of the police vehicle. Inspector Sharpe walked around, shaking his head in disbelief. He then came back and Graham outlined what had happened while Roger opened the Prince's shirt and examined the wound.

"The bullet has gone right through sir, er Your Majesty, er..."

Prince Peter gave a wry smile, "Your Highness," he corrected gently. "But don't worry about it. I am not your prince. And I am very much in your debt. You saved my life."

Roger felt embarrassed and shrugged. He pretended to concentrate on bandaging the wound with two field dressings Graham handed him. "I don't like people who are disloyal," Roger said.

Actually, he had begun to have severe doubts about what had happened, wondering if he was to blame for all the killing by speaking while Zumpitch was there with the sub-machine gun.

Prince Peter nodded and winced with pain. "How did you know Zumpitch was a traitor?" he asked.

"The radio. He went to the Land Rover and took over on the radio just after your people received their orders. Feldwebel Stegborz had given him back his pack just before. That reminded me. We found Zumpitch's pack on the road, Graham and I. It had fallen off a vehicle. We looked inside and found signal codes and things, so we knew he was a signaller. And we also found a blue cloth cap with a red star on it and his name inside. We didn't know what it meant but the moment the signaller called 'Partisans' I realised."

"This blue cap, you are sure? Where is it?" Prince Peter asked.

"In my left basic pouch. Here Graham, take over and wash off the blood. It's only a flesh wound sir," Roger said.

He turned and walked over to his webbing. The others had gathered to listen and watched in silence as he opened the basic pouch. As he touched the cloth Roger wrinkled his nose in distaste. The cloth now seemed tainted by the treason of its owner. Shaking his head he took the cap out and unrolled it and took it to the prince.

Prince Peter held the cap across both hands and looked at the badge and then the name inside. He gave a sigh and shook his head sadly. "Two traitors. And in such a small group! All our plans turned to ashes; and such good people dead as a result!" he cried, gesturing to where Colonel von Krapnoff and Adjutant Stiltz lay sprawled on the muddy track.

Roger didn't know what to say. He shrugged and began to shiver. And then tears came. He turned away and went and leaned on a tree and sobbed. What ugly things humans can be!

The others pretended to ignore him. Graham went on bandaging Prince Peter's shoulder. Peter and Stephen continued with First Aid on the sentry. He had a bullet in the chest and another in the leg.

DS Crowe looked up from where he bent over Colonel von Krapnoff. "This bloke's still alive boss," he called. "But he needs medical help real fast or he is a goner."

"Any others?" Inspector Sharpe asked.

The constable called from the back of the Rover, "This bloke might live if he gets to a doctor. He's got at least three slugs in his chest and he is coughing up blood."

Detective West climbed out of the police Toyota. "Can't get anyone on the radio sir. Too much screening." He indicated the jungle. "And we are down in this valley. We might get through when we get up on the crestline."

Inspector Sharpe rubbed his jaw, then gave rapid orders. "Right, clear the back of our vehicle Constable. Crowe, check if any of these vehicles work. Prince, do any of your radios work on civilian frequencies?"

Prince Peter shook his head. "No, they are military radios on our own frequencies."

"Too bad. Roger, sit with the prince, over there. West, help Bell and Bronsky to load these three wounded men into our vehicle. You will drive. Crowe, you stay here. Constable, you go in the back with the two worst casualties. Stick that guy in the front and strap him in."

"What about the prince?" DS Crowe asked.

"He can wait. He won't die from that. We must get these others to hospital as quickly as possible. Come on, move!"

Stephen scrambled into the vehicle and tossed out their packs to make room.

"Blankets," Peter suggested. "From these packs." He indicated gear belonging to the royal guards.

"Good idea," Graham agreed.

He bent to Zumpitch's pack and hauled out his sleeping bag. Peter and the policemen lifted Colonel von Krapnoff into the back of the police vehicle and laid him down. Graham placed a pack under his head and tucked the sleeping bag over him. The wounded signaller went in beside him and was also made comfortable. The sentry was lifted into the front passenger seat and the constable clambered in the back.

Inspector Sharpe pointed along the road. "Okay, get going West. And get more people up here ASAP. And tell those Federal buggers, that bloody Commander Simkins, what is going on," he ordered.

Roger stepped forward as the vehicle's engine was started. "Sir, don't drive on that way. That is where those partisans set their ambush. They may still be there and could kill them."

Inspector Sharpe looked up the track in disbelief.

Prince Peter joined them. "Believe me sir. Don't go that way. These are desperate men. They will not hesitate to shoot policemen," he said.

"Okay. Turn around West and go back the way we came. Blast! That adds half an hour to the driving time. Get going!" Inspector Sharpe cried.

The vehicle went forward to the track junction where it did a three-point turn. Rain began to fall so that it needed its windscreen wipers by the time it roared past on its way back.

As the vehicle went slowly down the muddy slope towards the Walsh River crossing Inspector Sharpe turned to Prince Peter. "Now sir; you are under arrest for at least a dozen offences. You are not obliged to say anything, but anything you do say may be taken down and used in evidence. Do you understand? Do you speak English well enough?"

Prince Peter nodded. "Yes, I speak English. I have lived most of my life in England and went to school there. I understand. I have only been in Australia for a week. Please, may I have my jacket?" he replied.

Roger looked and saw that Prince Peter was quite blue with cold around his mouth. He then realised he was shivering himself, although he guessed as much from shock as the lowering temperature. He passed Prince Peter his jacket and helped him to put it on. Then he found his own pack amongst the litter of gear.

Inspector Sharpe nodded agreement. "Good idea," he said. Both he and DS Crowe were only dressed in grey business suits which now looked quite incongruous in the jungle. "See if you can find me a raincoat," he asked. He put his pistol on safe and slipped it into his shoulder holster.

Graham shrugged on his own jacket and then scooped up his maps and notebooks from where Colonel von Krapnoff had dropped them. After stuffing them into a plastic bag he asked, "Why didn't you bring more vehicles sir?"

"We did. We had five vehicles including an ambulance, but the others weren't 4WD and couldn't get along that road. And we didn't expect to run into a full, scale war!"

Roger pulled on his field jacket. Stephen passed Inspector Sharpe a grey plastic raincoat and Peter gave one to DS Crowe. The rain grew heavier and the temperature plummeted noticeably. Inspector Sharpe buttoned up the coat and turned to Prince Peter again. "Now sir; do you have any identification?"

"Yes. In my briefcase. In that vehicle," Prince Peter replied.

"Get it Crowe."

Roger zipped up his jacket and turned to watch as the DS looked in the vehicle. A movement further up the track caught his eye. It was a green clad figure running, or rather staggering, towards them. "

Sir! Inspector!" Roger called, pointing.

"What the devil?" Inspector Sharpe cried, whipping out his pistol.

The man was a Kosarian Royal Guard and even at 50 paces they could see that his face was covered with blood. He was clutching a pistol and Roger saw that he was an officer.

As the wounded officer got closer DS Crowe crouched behind the front vehicle and levelled his automatic.

"Halt! Stop or I shoot!" he yelled.

The officer stumbled, then lurched to a standstill. He wiped his sleeve over his face to clear the blood from his eyes. He blinked and stared at the litter of bodies and equipment and the bullet riddled vehicles. A look of horror crossed his face.

DS Crowe called again, "Drop the gun or I shoot! This is the police."

Prince Peter stepped forward. "Hauptman Ritnik, drop your gun," he called.

"Prinz Peter?" Hauptman Ritnik called, swaying as he stood there.

"Yes. It is me. Do as the police command."

Hauptman Ritnik dropped his pistol and with a visible effort stood up straight. He appeared to focus his eyes, then marched forward as though on parade. He halted in front of the Prince, clicked his heels and saluted; then bowed from the waist.

"Your Highness, I have failed in my duty. The Partisans have captured the Princess Mareena. They are headed this way. You must leave at once. I will delay them," he said.

With an obvious effort Hauptman Ritnik straightened up, opened his mouth to speak again then slid to the ground unconscious. Roger stared aghast at the blood welling from what appeared to be a huge bullet wound in Hauptman Ritnik's left temple. He saw he had also been shot in the left forearm.

Prince Peter knelt in the mud and cradled Hauptman Ritnik's head in his lap. Very tenderly he wiped mud and blood from his face. "Please help me."

Roger and Peter both knelt beside him. Graham moved to watch up the track. Stephen just stood staring alternately at Hauptman Ritnik's wounds and at the dead bodies nearby.

Inspector Sharpe pocketed his gun. "Crowe, do any of these vehicles work? Try them quickly."

He walked over and picked up Hauptman Ritnik's pistol and checked it, then thrust it into the pocket of his raincoat.

DS Crowe climbed into the brown Toyota but at once got out again. "Dieso everywhere, sir. Looks shot to buggery. The fuel tank is riddled," he said. He walked over and handed a black leather brief case to Inspector Sharpe, then went to the Rover. A turn of the key produced no response. He lifted the bonnet. "Batteries smashed. Wires cut and radiator holed," he called.

Roger was only dimly aware of this, most of his attention being concentrated on Hauptman Ritnik's wounds. The rain was causing the blood to smear and run in long trickles down his throat and into his shirt. Roger grabbed his water bottle and a handkerchief and quickly swabbed the wound on the temple. He could hardly bring himself to touch the blood-matted hair.

"Not as bad as it looks," Peter muttered. "The skull might be cracked but the bullet hasn't gone in. He has only been creased."

"Be concussion probably," Roger replied. He applied more water and dabbed. Hauptman Ritnik moaned and rolled his head from side to side. Peter tore open a field dressing and deftly bandaged it around Hauptman Ritnik's head.

"He will live?" Prince Peter asked.

Peter nodded. "I think so sir. He may have internal bleeding and an impacted fracture but if we get him to hospital quickly he should be alright," he replied. He turned to look at the arm wound.

"Is he related to the General Ritnik sir?" Roger asked.

"You mean Field Marshal Ritnik who died in the great retreat of 1915? Yes. Yes, he is. He is the great grandson," Prince Peter replied.

Inspector Sharpe came over. "I am sorry but neither of the vehicles work. We are going to have to walk. I have your briefcase. Is there anything else we should take so these partisans don't get it?"

"What about Hauptman Ritnik? We cannot leave him," Prince Peter replied.

"We will have to make a stretcher and carry him. Can you cadets do that?"

"Easily sir. Pete, Steve, start making a stretcher, fast," Graham said.

Roger sat back on his heels and wiped rain from his face. He felt distinctly queasy. A second bullet had lodged in Hauptman Ritnik's arm causing a horrible purple swelling. Biting his lip to suppress the nausea Roger set to work bandaging it.

"Bugger the rain!" he muttered.

Hauptman Ritnik opened his eyes. For a moment he looked puzzled, then alarmed. "Your Highness, you must get away from this place. The partisans thought I was dead, and I overheard them talking. The princess is to be tortured to reveal the secret, but their real mission is to kill you."

"How many are there?" Inspector Sharpe asked.

"I counted five. But they were talking on a radio to at least one other group."

"How soon before they get here?"

"Not long. I don't know. They ambushed us at the top of the mountain, a log across the track. It was so unexpected. But they knew where the princess was sitting and did not hit her. They stepped out of the jungle and fired at point blank range. I would like to know how they knew we were coming."

Prince Peter looked grim. "Treachery. Zumpitch radioed them," he replied bitterly.

"Zumpitch! He was…"

Inspector Sharpe cut in. "How soon before these partisans arrive?"

Hauptman Ritnik thought, "I crawled out of the wreck. They saw me and chased me. I shot one. Two others followed me but very cautiously. I suppose they must be expected at any minute."

"How are they armed? What do they look like?" Inspector Sharpe asked.

"They are in partisan uniforms: brown jacket and trousers, blue cap, red star. They have sub-machine guns, PPSh 1941s, or AK47s," Hauptman Ritnik replied.

DS Crowe swore. "In bloody uniform! Here in Australia! The cheeky bastards."

Inspector Sharpe tugged at his chin thoughtfully. "They mean business then," he said. "How is that stretcher coming along?"

"Not long sir," Peter called. He had hacked down two small trees and was busy pushing them through the belts and straps of four sets of webbing. Stephen helped and tied the end sets on.

Inspector Sharpe looked anxiously up the track and checked his pistol. "You keep watch up the road young Kirk, and get under cover."

"Yes sir," Graham replied.

He moved to the far side of the track to get a better view along it. As he did he glanced down to his right towards the Walsh River. His mouth opened and he pointed. Roger saw Graham throw himself flat.

Then he jumped with fright as an automatic weapon fired a burst from behind him.

Chapter 31

INTO THE JUNGLE

Graham yelled, "Partisans!"

He rolled sideways and Roger saw him scrabble in the wet leaves. Graham's hand came up with one of the rifles that had been placed there. Several more shots cracked past or thudded into the trees beside him. With frantic haste Graham brought the weapon to his shoulder, clicked off the safety catch and pulled the trigger.

Bang! Bang! Bang!

Graham snapped three shots, then rolled the other way.

Near panic seized Roger. He dived flat, his whole being flooded with terror. So did the others, except DS Crowe who went into a crouch and squeezed off two shots from his pistol in quick succession.

"Into the trees!" Inspector Sharpe cried. "That way!" He grabbed Prince Peter and hauled him into the jungle. Roger scrambled on hands and knees behind the nearest tree. Graham sprinted across, grabbing his webbing as he passed.

Through eyes blurry from fear Roger looked anxiously around. He looked back and saw that the Hauptman was crawling to join them. "Hauptman Ritnik!" he cried. Fearful lest he be hit again, Roger scuttled out and hauled him under cover.

Bullets began to thud into trees around them. One struck the Land Rover with a metallic whang! Others cracked past along the road. Roger could see no partisans, but he could hear shouted orders from about 50 metres down the slope. By then his heart was hammering hard and he was almost frantic with fear.

Inspector Sharpe turned to Graham, who now lay facing down the track in a fire position behind a tree. "How many?" he queried.

"I saw three, sir. But I reckon twice that many from the sound," Graham replied.

Inspector Sharpe looked around at them. "Is everyone okay? Is anyone hit? No? Good, okay, let's get out of here. Crowe, you lead. Go that way," he instructed.

"Sir," Graham called. "That is west. Atherton is the other way."

"I bloody well know that. But it is too dangerous to cross back over that road; and we can't go north because there are more of the bastards that way. Now move! I will come second, then the prince. You kids help the Hauptman. Kirk, bring up the rear. And for Christ's sake don't shoot anyone if you can avoid it."

"Particularly us," Peter added.

Graham sniffed at this implied doubt as to his ability and moved into a kneeling fire position. He placed the rifle down and hauled on his webbing, then picked the rifle up again and began to carefully scan the jungle.

Prince Peter pointed back. "My briefcase!" he cried in alarm.

"I have it," Inspector Sharpe replied.

"Please, I beg of you, do not let the communists get it. If they do, many good people will lose their lives," Prince Peter said.

Inspector Sharpe nodded. "More secrets eh? Okay. Crowe, get moving. Take it carefully. Angle up hill and away from the road."

There were more shouted orders down in the jungle and Roger heard the sounds of men crashing through the undergrowth as fast as they could force a passage. The sounds were coming up hill towards them and also spreading out to their right.

If we don't move fast we will be cut off! he thought. A sour taste of bile rose in his throat as the fear gripped him. *Trapped!*

Impelled by a desperate urge to get away Roger rose and helped Hauptman Ritnik to his feet. The Hauptman was so unsteady that Roger feared he would collapse but he started walking after the others. Roger followed. A glance behind him showed Graham following. Another 20 paces brought them to the side road going west. It was an old timber road but had been used recently and was a clear path. It curved around the gentle slope.

Inspector Sharpe pointed along it. "Get out on this track. Go left and run," he called. "Don't stop till I say, then get off the track on the right. Come on, move! It is our only chance to make a break. Go!"

They burst out onto the track and began to run. There were yells from down in the jungle to their left and a sub-machine gun rattled. Roger heard the bullets thudding into trees and one snipped a leaf just in front of his face. His whole body twitched, and he ran faster than he had ever run before. He quickly caught up with Hauptman Ritnik, who was starting to stagger.

"Come on sir," he called and grabbed the Hauptman's arm.

There were three loud gunshots close behind. Heart in mouth Roger glanced back. It was Graham firing into the jungle from the hip as he ran.

They pounded around the curve, boots squelching in the wet leaf mould. The group began to string out as Hauptman Ritnik and Roger slowed down. Inspector Sharpe looked back and called, "Halt! Hold it!" As they slowed, he pointed up the slope to the right. "In there, quick!"

DS Crowe pushed his way into the undergrowth and the others followed. Graham stopped and went into a kneeling fire position behind a tree and waited till they were all off the track.

Bang!

Back along the track there was a loud yell of fear followed by voluble shouting in Serbo-Croat.

"That'll slow the mongrels down," Graham cried. Roger glanced back and saw him dash into the jungle behind him, a grin all over his face.

By then they were all panting for breath and the vines and wait-a-while quickly combined to slow progress to a walk. To Roger it was like all of his worst nightmares. He wanted to run but his boots felt like they were made of lead, and vines kept snatching at his ankles and legs to entangle and trip.

After a few frantic minutes, when they had gone about 50 metres, Inspector Sharpe called a halt, "Okay. Stop! Now everyone keep quiet and listen. No talking," he whispered.

They all crouched or leaned on trees, sweat pouring down their faces and chests heaving. Roger's throat felt dry and hot. He wanted to be sick. He was very scared.

Voices were still calling out behind them, from on the track they had just left. Inspector Sharpe knelt down and said quietly to Prince Peter, "What are they saying?"

Prince Peter shook his head and beckoned Hauptman Ritnik. "My Serbo-Croat is not very good. The Baron will translate."

A baron! Roger noted, looking at the Hauptman with even greater interest. *A real live baron!* It was like seeing a Triceratops unexpectedly.

Hauptman Ritnik nodded. He said, "Several men are calling that we have run up here. Another is ordering them to follow. Now they are complaining that we have guns." He grinned. "They don't sound very keen. This boy here, the young sergeant major, has done good work." He pointed to Graham, who flushed with pleasure.

Hauptman Ritnik's face changed abruptly to ashen seriousness and he glanced at Prince Peter and bit his lip. "The leader has just reminded them that their mission is to kill your Royal Highness. He is now calling on them to report."

Roger felt a terrible coldness around his heart. These men certainly meant business.

Hauptman Ritnik went on, "Now the partisans are being ordered to spread out along the road and to look for our tracks. Now they have seen where we turned off. One of them is telling the Comrade Squad Leader. That is bad news."

"What? That they have found our tracks?" asked Inspector Sharpe.

Hauptman Ritnik shook his head. "No. That he is a squad leader. There are nine men in a partisan squad; and these are not the men who ambushed me. That means they must have a whole platoon in the area. I fear we are in most desperate trouble. They will hunt us like wild animals."

Roger wasn't sure who were the wild animals, they or their pursuers. Inspector Sharpe compressed his lips into a grim line and murmured, "We had better get moving. Have any of you lads got a map?"

"I have sir," Graham replied. He clicked on the safety catch, then fished out his map in its plastic case and moved up to join Inspector Sharpe. Roger pulled his map out as well and showed it to Peter and Hauptman Ritnik.

Graham pointed to the map. "That way, sir. Northwest."

"Have you got a compass? I don't want us to get lost in this muck," Inspector Sharpe asked.

Graham nodded and hauled out his compass, still attached to his shirt by its nylon cord.

Inspector Sharpe nodded with approval. "Good lad. You lead. Crowe, take this rifle and bring up the rear. Have those fellows started following yet?"

Hauptman Ritnik again shook his head. "No sir. I think they are afraid to enter the jungle. There is an argument but I cannot make out all the words. I think it is about whether to wait for reinforcements or not. Now they are using a radio," he explained.

"Fine. okay, off you go young Kirk. Keep it slow. And no noise from anyone," Inspector Sharpe ordered.

They rose and began moving at a slow walk. Graham could not walk a straight line as he had to dodge trees, weave around fallen logs and thick clumps of wait-a-while. All he could manage was a general compass bearing. The course took them diagonally up a fairly steep slope which, even at the snail's pace they were moving at, soon had them panting. Roger found he was sweating in spite of the cold raindrops and mist. His leg muscles quickly began to complain.

Each minute moved the group 25 to 50 paces further away from the partisans. Roger began to hope they would not be pursued, but this was dashed when shouts behind them indicated that the hunt had begun.

"I think they are following our tracks," Roger murmured to DS Crowe. He looked back and down and could detect a faint line of disturbed leaf mould, bent leaves, scuff marks on moss covered rocks and tree roots and crushed deadfall.

"Not much we can do to avoid it," DS Crowe replied sourly.

"Yes we can. We can 'Break track'," Roger replied.

"Break track? What are you talking about?"

"It's something we learn in the cadets, to hide a camp in the jungle."

"Tell the Inspector."

Roger nodded and tapped Hauptman Ritnik on the shoulder. "Pass it on. Tell Graham, he is the CSM leading us, to explain 'Break Track' to the Inspector."

The whispered message was passed up the slowly moving line. Roger saw Graham stop and whisper to Inspector Sharpe, who nodded. Back came the message, "Break track Right, 50 paces."

"What does it mean?" Hauptman Ritnik asked.

Roger beckoned DS Crowe as well, then explained. "First we open out, from the rear, until we can just see the person in front and the one behind. Then, on a signal we all turn at right angles and walk 50 paces, being careful to leave no tracks. Then we turn left into single file again and close up on the front. That way, instead of one obvious track made by a group of people there are eight different tracks, all hard to find."

The men nodded.

"We are moving. You stand still Sgt Crowe and we open out," Roger said. The DS did so. Roger was scared now as he could hear the noises being made as their pursuers forced their way through the jungle. They sounded only about 50 metres away and were coming closer. A sharp cry of pain from one of the partisans made Roger grin with malicious pleasure. They were discovering 'wait-a-while'!

There was a hand signal. Roger passed it on to DS Crowe and thankfully turned and began walking up the slope, watching carefully where he put his feet. He tried to avoid crushing any sticks or ferns or snapping any sticks.

The rain helped. Big heavy drops drowned what little noise they made; and all the leaves and twigs were soggy. Roger kept looking to his right, expecting to glimpse the advancing partisans. However, apart from some crashing and rustling in the undergrowth he saw no sign of them.

After about 30 paces he realised he had been concentrating so hard on not leaving a track that he had forgotten to count his paces. He kept watch on Hauptman Ritnik on his left. The Hauptman seemed to be angling away from him so Roger kept edging in his direction. He looked around continually, both to check that DS Crowe was still in sight, and for the first sign of a partisan. It took all his willpower to keep moving at a slow walk.

Several times Roger had to detour around clumps of wait-a-while and once he had to backtrack to go around a large mass of it. DS Crowe followed him and on the far side, on a steep slope studded with large moss-covered boulders and ferns, they found Stephen and Peter waiting. They signalled to them to turn left and close in.

The group closed up till Roger could see Graham again.

"All here?" whispered Inspector Sharpe.

"Yes sir," DS Crowe replied.

"Okay, keep moving."

Graham led off again on the same compass bearing. This took them along the side of the mountain. Roger listened and was sure he could hear movement only twenty or so paces down the slope to his left. He strained his eyes but could see no-one.

For about 20 minutes they walked slowly along with no word spoken. The rain grew heavier and in under the tree canopy it was very dark and gloomy. Roger shivered with cold. They covered several hundred metres. Suddenly, far down to their left rear, there was a loud cry. They all stopped and looked that way. The man's voice called again.

Hauptman Ritnik grinned. "He wants to know where his friends are. He has lost contact with them. Ah! There."

Closer to them, but still off to their left rear, came an answering voice.

Inspector Sharpe nodded. "Keep moving. We must put more distance between us and them," he ordered.

They resumed their slow movement. The compass bearing led them down into a vine-choked re-entrant. The sound of yelling faded in the distance. Roger began to relax somewhat but the effort of moving through the tangled undergrowth took all his energy. He felt very tired and hungry. At the bottom of the re-entrant was a small creek. By common consent they halted to have a drink. The rain stopped but constant dripping continued. Graham refilled his water bottles.

"I think we have lost them for the moment," Inspector Sharpe murmured, pocketing his pistol.

"I think they have lost themselves, from what they were saying," Hauptman Ritnik replied.

Inspector Sharpe nodded. "That would be easy in this country without a map and a compass. I hope we aren't lost too. Do you know where we are young Kirk?"

"Yes sir, here," Graham replied. He was clearly not amused. Roger knew he took great pride in being both a good bushman and a good navigator.

Inspector Sharpe studied the map and cleared his throat, aware of Graham's resentment. "Which way do you think we should go?" he asked.

Graham pointed on the map as the others crowded around. "Well sir, it's only a kilometre to open forest out to the west. We could walk out there and detour right around the jungle to either the north or the south. I would say go north, to where all these roads join up here, behind Mt. Baldy."

They considered this. "That is about ten kilometres before we get anywhere near a house where we might find a telephone," Inspector Sharpe mused. "Wouldn't it be better to go east down to these farms at Carrington? That is only about three kilometres and downhill."

"Might be sir, but it is all jungle; and we'd have to cross the road," Graham replied.

"More chance of them seeing us in the open country than of us being spotted crossing the road surely?" Stephen said.

Graham nodded. "Stay in the jungle then. Head northwest up this ridge, then northeast back up this crestline. We should be able to cross the road there," he said.

"That's what I think too," Inspector Sharpe agreed. "There are about five kilometres of road and it's got as many curves as a snake. These partisans can't watch it all. They can't have that many men. Are you up to a march like that Hauptman Ritnik?"

Roger looked at the Hauptman. He appeared very pale and was in obvious pain. A thin trickle of blood was running down the side of his face. He shrugged. "Don't worry about me. Get His Royal Highness to safety, and the briefcase. You can leave me and come back for me later."

Peter spoke up, "We could leave you all here and two or three of us, the fittest, could go for help."

Inspector Sharpe considered this, then shook his head. "No, we will stay together. Are you confident of your navigation young Kirk?"

"Yes, sir. But I will use map to ground and only use the compass as a guide or we will do a lot of up and down as any compass bearing is going to cut across more of these re-entrants."

"If you reckon you can do it then okay. Let's get moving. I'm getting cold; and there's another bloody leech!" Inspector Sharpe plucked the leech from his sleeve and flung it aside. He glanced at his watch. "Not even midday."

Roger looked at his and saw it was only 1145hrs.

Peter said, "Sir, won't these partisans just clear out now they know the police are involved? Won't your men be surrounding the area?" he asked.

Inspector Sharpe nodded. "You would think so but I suspect their political masters might have given them orders to get the prince, regardless."

Prince Peter agreed. "You are right. They are playing for high stakes and a diplomatic row with a country as distant as Australia would be the least of their worries. While I live, I am a rallying point for all Kosarians who believe in freedom. These men are just pawns. They are expendable."

Hauptman Ritnik nodded agreement. "You are right Your Highness. The communists will have some hold over the men they have sent here, some way of blackmailing them. That is how they operate; by terror and coercion."

"Who are these partisans?" Stephen asked. "Weren't the partisans the guerrillas who fought the Germans?"

"Yes they were," Prince Peter answered. "They were the army of liberation. They kept the name after the war because of its prestige value. They are now just the communist regular army, the Kosarian Partisans, KOSPARS for short."

"This will be a special unit," Hauptman Ritnik added.

Peter gave a wry grin. "Not too special if they've got lost," he suggested.

"Perhaps they have been rushed here without any special training and without enough maps. Besides, all their experience will have been in pine forests. There is nothing like this jungle in Kosaria," Hauptman Ritnik replied.

"How many of them do you reckon there are?" DS Crowe asked.

Hauptman Ritnik thought for a moment. "At least a platoon. That is thirty-six men: three squads and a HQ. Could be more," he replied.

"How did they get here?" Stephen wondered.

Inspector Sharpe said, "Enough speculation. Let's get moving."

Led by Graham they set off up a steep slope thick with wait-a-while. They heard no more of their pursuers. The cloud thinned out and a watery sun could be glimpsed overhead. Roger began to feel hungry and regretted not having grabbed his own webbing. He had missed breakfast and now he would miss lunch as well!

After about two hundred metres they came out onto an overgrown snig track which ran up a spur line.

Graham pointed left along it. "It will probably go all the way to the top of this twelve-hundred-and-eleven-metre feature," he said. "It will be easier going."

"Not safer though," Inspector Sharpe replied.

"Quicker and quieter. That is safer, sir," Graham replied. "There is sure to be an old track on the crestline running parallel to the main timber road."

"Okay. Go up it then but take it slow and keep your eyes peeled."

Chapter 32

A LIFE FOR A LIFE

For Roger, the next hour was agony.

The group slogged slowly uphill through thick jungle with Graham in the lead. The old snig track was frequently blocked by masses of wait-a-while which they had to detour slowly around. The cloud closed in so they were enveloped in gloomy mist but there was no more rain. Roger alternately shivered and sweated. His leg muscles ached and his right knee developed a hot little pain on every second step. The direction he noted was roughly northeast.

Ahead of him Hauptman Ritnik struggled gamely on, but he was obviously tiring and started to weave and stagger a lot. Suddenly he slumped against a tree, shoulders heaving. Then he slid down into a crumpled heap.

"Stop! Stop!" Roger hissed urgently.

Peter heard him and passed it on. The group came to a standstill and the leaders came back. Roger and Peter moved the Hauptman into a more comfortable position. He was conscious but his eyes looked unfocused.

"I... I just... need a small rest," he croaked.

Inspector Sharpe looked at his watch. "Twelve thirty. Okay. We will rest for half an hour."

Roger sat down on the sodden leaf mould and leaned against a tree. He felt exhausted. While he sat there he watched as Peter and Prince Peter checked the Hauptman's bandages. The bandage around his head was now an ugly dark red, indicating that it had begun to bleed again. Roger shivered and looked around. He noted that Inspector Sharpe's good leather shoes were very muddy, and that he had squashed a large leech on his sock at the ankle. The sight reminded Roger to search himself for more leeches. Finding none he leaned back and closed his eyes.

Peter shook him awake. "We are moving sleepy head. Come on."

Roger groaned and rubbed his eyes. He was shivering and stiff. A glance at his watch told him he had slept for over an hour. It was nearly 1400hrs.

The group resumed its upward slog. Roger joined Peter in helping Hauptman Ritnik who had gone so pale he was blue around the mouth. Fits of shivering wracked the Hauptman's body.

After about 20 minutes, Stephen and DS Crowe took over helping the Hauptman. The Inspector was helping the Prince, who also looked very pale and drawn. Roger found it took all his strength to haul himself slowly up the slope. The cloud still enshrouded them and even though it was only mid-afternoon it was dark and gloomy.

It wasn't until 1510hrs that they reached the top of the mountain. Without a word they all flopped down to rest. Roger saw Graham and the two policemen crouching over the map but he felt too tired to care. He wiped sweat off his face and wished he had something to eat. A silent curse was offered up to the soldier who had taken his jellybeans.

After half an hour they moved on. Roger and Peter took over helping Hauptman Ritnik. They walked on either side with his arms over their shoulders. He was so weak they were almost dragging him along. There was a smear of fresh blood down his face and neck. The smell and feel of wet clothes and sweaty bodies, combined with apprehension over the seeping wound, made Roger feel nauseous.

At least their route now went downhill along another overgrown track heading northwest. After half a kilometre, they curved northeast along a wide, flat crestline. In this part of the jungle there seemed to be very little wait-a-while and very few vines. Instead the undergrowth comprised masses of waist high palms. There were numerous huge rotting tree trunks, presumably blown down in a storm as they were torn out by the roots, not cut down.

There was an occasional glimpse through gaps in the foliage and the drifting cloud which showed other jungle covered peaks and ridges. These caused Graham to take compass bearings and to peer closely at his map with a lot of lip biting and head shaking. Roger was glad Graham was navigating. He had great faith in him but realised there were times when his resentment at his friend's fitness and cheerful zest for adventure amounted almost to hatred.

After half an hour of slow shuffling, the ridge began to rise and progress slowed even more. A track went off downhill to the right. Inspector Sharpe pointed down it, but Graham shook his head and continued on up the slope.

Another 15 minutes of snail-like pace went by. Then Graham signalled halt. He put his finger to his lips and pointed down to his right. Roger got a glimpse of the main dirt road, about 50 metres away. Graham continued moving, angling around the slope to his left. After a time he circled back to the right. It was hard going as there was no track and the way was obstructed by half a dozen fallen trees and outcrops of rocks festooned with ferns. Roger felt so tired and cold he was almost past caring. He had Hauptman Ritnik's arm around his shoulder and was aware the Hauptman was barely conscious and was stumbling along like a zombie, murmuring and groaning from time to time.

Roger began to loathe the rain forest. He was sick of being closed in; sick of having to push through it, of having to clamber over or around things. He hated the dankness, the leeches, the prickly plants, the bloody vines which always seemed to snag.

I don't think I can go on much longer, he thought miserably.

Then, just when he was on the trembling, shameful edge of giving up Peter signalled to halt. "Okay Roger. Stop for a break," he murmured.

They lowered Hauptman Ritnik onto the wet leaves and eased their painful limbs. Graham, Prince Peter and the two policemen went into a whispering huddle. Stephen just slumped down and tried to wipe moisture off his glasses. He looked thoroughly miserable.

How I feel, Roger thought.

He noted they were on what appeared to be a flattish hilltop at another old timber track. He saw Graham get up and take the rifle from DS Crowe. Graham then headed off down the track to the right, rifle at the ready. He vanished silently from sight, his camouflage uniform blending perfectly with the mottled light and shade of the jungle.

Despite his fatigue Roger wondered where Graham was going. He could see that Inspector Sharpe did not look too happy about it. Thick cloud drifted in to give the semi-darkness an extra dimension of eeriness. Roger rubbed sore muscles and moved gingerly to ease thighs chafed by wet cloth. He was cold and worn out and was very thirsty as well as hungry.

Hauptman Ritnik groaned. Roger groaned as well. He was tired of caring for Hauptman Ritnik. Reluctantly he got up and knelt to feel his pulse. Next, he placed the back of his hand on the Hauptman's cheek. It was cold and clammy, and his pulse was very feeble.

Prince Peter looked across. "How is he?" he whispered.

"Not too good, sir. He needs a doctor," Roger replied.

"You are very good. Forgive my bad manners. What is your name?"

Roger told him. Prince Peter then asked who his friends were and then about the army cadets and the expedition the boys were on. Roger explained the Duke of Edinburgh Scheme.

Prince Peter gave a wry smile. "My people seem to have ruined your chance of completing your award on time."

"That's alright, sir. We can always go on another hike. We go on expeditions like this a lot," Roger replied.

"I am friends with the Duke of Edinburgh. Perhaps I could contact him and explain that you have done far more than required."

Roger was both thrilled and embarrassed. "Oh sir! That won't be necessary. I'm sure Captain Conkey will sort things out."

"I will anyway," Prince Peter replied.

At that moment Graham returned from his reconnaissance. He crouched near them. "We are right on the crestline of the main range. The road goes over a saddle about a hundred paces that way, but we can't cross there. A Land Rover is parked there with at least four partisans in it. They have a radio."

"Which way then?" Prince Peter asked.

"Along this ridge northwards, parallel to the road, then cross lower down," Graham said.

"This cannot go on much longer. Hauptman Ritnik is getting very weak," Prince Peter cautioned.

Graham bit his lip. "Should we split up? Some stay here with him while others go for help? I reckon Peter and I could get down the mountain in two hours," he said.

"I'd rather we didn't separate," Inspector Sharpe replied. "Commander Simkin of the Federal Police will have a grip on things by now. All the roads should have roadblocks on them and reinforcements should be moving into the area."

"It will be dark in a bit over an hour," Graham reminded him. With something of a shock Roger saw that it was after 5pm. The thought of spending the night in the jungle was not appealing.

"Then we will just have to sit it out through the night," Inspector Sharpe replied.

"Hauptman Ritnik may not last that long," Prince Peter said. "He needs medical treatment urgently."

Roger felt sick at the thought of that. Hauptman Ritnik certainly looked as though he could die. His face was an awful pasty colour.

Graham studied the Hauptman then said, "We'd better get some hot food and drink into him. I've got soup and coffee in my webbing."

"Good idea," Inspector Sharpe agreed.

"Not here. We had better get further away from these fellows and the road," Graham said.

With an effort Roger and Stephen got Hauptman Ritnik to his feet. Hauptman Ritnik was shivering all the time now and was on the edge of delirium. Graham led off down a long spur which dropped more steeply the further they went. Luckily the old timber track was relatively open and they made good progress for half a kilometre.

As the ridge levelled off Graham led them off the track for 20 paces to the edge of a steep slope. It was an area thick with low palms and ferns. He indicated a relatively flat and open area.

"This will do. We won't get any further tonight. Steve, take the rifle and go sentry just out there where you can see along the track."

They quickly cleared dead sticks to make bed spaces. Graham unpacked his webbing and lit his hexamine stove. The flame gave a very cheery glow in the dusk. Peter and the Prince made Hauptman Ritnik comfortable and checked his bandages. Roger sat near Graham. As the soup was heated the aroma made his mouth water. He wished he could have some and his stomach grumbled in sympathy. No dinner either!

Inspector Sharpe and DS Crowe stood talking quietly, looking incongruous in their torn raincoats and soiled business suits, their white shirts bright in the gloom. Roger felt very thirsty, but the only water was in Graham's water bottles and had to be rationed and shared. His share was only a mouthful. He wished he could do something to help but there was nothing, so he just sat and watched as Hauptman Ritnik was spoon fed the hot soup by Peter.

Graham then heated water and mixed a cup of strong, sweet coffee. This went to the Hauptman and the prince. Prince Peter had not complained about his wound all afternoon, but Roger could see that he also looked ready to collapse. Next Graham opened a tin of meat and heated it in a mess tin with some water. Roger knew he was selfish to wish for any, but he did.

Hauptman Ritnik appeared to revive quickly with the warm food and drink in him. He thanked them and sat back with his eyes closed. Graham cleaned his mess tins and packed them and the stove. He took back his cup and began to wipe it.

There was rustling in the undergrowth and Stephen appeared. "There are men coming down the track," he hissed. "At least three partisans. They are armed."

Inspector Sharpe gestured to get down. "Not a sound," he hissed.

Graham swung on his webbing and took the rifle from Stephen. The two policemen folded up their collars and took out their pistols. Roger rolled carefully onto his front and peered under the palm fronds.

Twilight had set in. There were a few bird noises and the gentle rustling of the wind in the trees. Then the unmistakable crunch of footsteps on the deadfall reached them. Roger glimpsed movement through the scrub. Only 25 metres away! His heart began to hammer and his mouth went dry.

What are the partisans doing here? Roger wondered.

They were obviously going slowly and searching, but surely they couldn't be tracking in such poor light? Had they seen the glow of the hexamine stove? Or smelt it? No. The wind was wrong.

Roger tried to steady his breathing and cursed when his empty stomach suddenly grumbled. The partisans were close now, near where the group had left the track. Roger saw a man with a sub-machine gun. The partisans were moving quietly, 10 paces apart, eyes searching in all directions.

Then Hauptman Ritnik groaned.

The men stopped and went into a crouch. Roger could just see the legs of the second one. They faced towards him. Blast! Roger cursed silently but then Hauptman Ritnik groaned again. Roger swivelled his head to look and saw that he appeared to be unconscious.

A metallic click which could only be a safety catch coming off made Roger's heart stop. There was a muttered command and the swish of palm fronds as the partisans began to push into the undergrowth.

A twig snapped. The men were only 20 metres away. Roger tensed his muscles and held his breath. They were sure to be discovered.

Inspector Sharpe's voice suddenly broke the silence. "This is the police. Stop or we shoot."

Tat-tat-tat-tat-tat-tat-tat!

In reply a sub-machine gun suddenly ripped out a savage burst. Roger clearly saw the muzzle flashes and heard bullets crack overhead and thud into the trees. There were shouts and another partisan also fired, a heavier weapon. It began to blast tongues of flame over to Roger's right.

Crack! Crack!

Inspector Sharpe's pistol replied. There was a shrill cry of pain, drowned out by more gunshots as DS Crowe, Graham and the third partisan all began firing.

Roger lay flat on the wet leaves, half-paralysed by fear, and half-fascinated by the flashes and noise. In the semi-darkness the muzzle flashes flared bright red. The noise was stunning. It seemed unbelievably loud. The echoes rolled across the valleys and up the mountain slopes.

Cockatoos and other birds joined in with raucous screeching. There were shouts and running feet and the shooting stopped. Roger watched Graham change magazines. The empty one was thrust into his basic pouch and a fresh one clicked on. He cocked the smoking weapon and re-aimed. The reek of the acrid cordite fumes added to the conflict of senses and emotions.

The partisans pulled back 30 or 40 paces and went to ground. There were metallic noises as they also reloaded their weapons. From the sound of whimpering it was obvious that at least one had been hit, almost certainly by the Inspector's first shot.

"Anyone hit?" Inspector Sharpe called quietly. A quick check revealed they were all safe.

"We had better get out of here," Graham said.

"It will be dark in a few minutes," Inspector Sharpe replied. "We can't move in this stuff in the dark."

"We will have to sir. If we stay here they will bring up reinforcements and surround us during the night," Graham replied.

At that moment, a voice called out in heavily accented English, "Hey Australians! We know where you are. You cannot escape us now. Give us Prince Peter and we will spare your lives."

The proposal caused a real clash of emotions in Roger. Part of him grasped at the opportunity; part of him was repelled by his own selfishness; and part of him disgusted by the whole tactic. To make people betray others! What a cowardly thing to do.

Inspector Sharpe replied. "I am Inspector Sharpe of the Queensland Police. Lay down your weapons and surrender, or take the consequences."

"Police! Hah! Fool!" the partisan cried. The sub-machine gun stuttered.

"Don't fire," snarled Inspector Sharpe to the group. "He's firing blind. He can't hit us except by sheer bad luck."

That's me! Roger thought as he hunched in a terrified huddle behind a tree.

Another partisan shouted, "Surrender policeman! Give us the prince and you can go safe."

There was another burst of firing and then silence. The men could be heard talking to each other.

Inspector Sharpe spoke quietly to Prince Peter. "Sir, you are in my custody as a prisoner. That means that Sgt Crowe and I are responsible for your safety and well-being. We will not allow them to harm you while it is in our power to prevent it."

"Thank you, Inspector. But what about these boys?"

Inspector Sharpe glanced at them in the dusk, "They can head off to safety if they like. In fact, that is a good idea."

Graham shook his head. "No, sir. You need us, and we aren't running out on you now. We've got to live with ourselves later you know."

"What's this 'we'?" Peter said with a grin.

"You can go if you like," Graham replied stiffly.

"Pigs bum!" Peter retorted. "Let's get Hauptman Ritnik up and get everyone out of here before their scaly mates rock up."

"Can you navigate in the dark, CSM Kirk?" Inspector Shape asked.

Graham looked pained. "Sir! Cadets do it all the time. It's a basic skill, but I will need to use a torch to calculate the bearings and to set the compass."

"Too risky. Can you just get us out of this area?"

"Yes, sir. Due west for two hundred paces should do."

"Okay, you lead. The rest of you crawl quietly one behind the other. I will go second last. Crowe, you go last."

DS Crowe muttered. "Always me that gets the sticky end of the stick. You wait till I'm a detective inspector!"

It was almost completely dark by then. There was just enough light to see the others as black shapes. Roger got carefully to his hands and knees and crawled over to Hauptman Ritnik. He found he was awake and sitting up, leaning on a tree. The voices of the partisans stopped. There were rustling and crunching noises. They were moving.

Roger froze to listen.

Away, up the slope. He breathed out, only to receive a shock.

A partisan's voice called loudly from closer to them, out on the track. "Give up Prince Peter. You cannot escape. If you do not give him to us, you will all die."

The man's sub-machine gun rattled again, the darts of flame lighting up the jungle.

Crack!

DS Crowe's pistol snapped a return shot from over to the left. That drew a startled oath and another burst of fire. Silence settled.

"Get moving!" hissed Inspector Sharpe. "Close up and hold onto each other."

Graham had stood up. "Roger, carry the rifle. It's on safe. I can't hold it and use the compass."

Roger stood up and took the weapon. He held it at the 'Shoulder arms' to keep it close in to his side so it wouldn't snag as much. Behind him he could still hear the sounds of people moving away up the track and decided it must be the wounded Partisan being helped away. The man with the SMG was still there though. He called again, taunting and listening.

Slowly the group formed itself into a line. "Grab hold of the person in front and don't let go. If the person behind you breaks contact stop and wait," Graham ordered.

Roger had Stephen in front of him so he grabbed his jacket. He knew Stephen would be hating every moment. Not only did he strongly dislike rain forest after being lost in it years ago, but he would have taken his glasses off and would be, for all practical purposes, blind. Inspector Sharpe groped at Roger's shoulder and gripped the epaulet of his field jacket.

Graham began moving: one careful step, feel for the sticks and vines, get balanced, bring the other foot slowly forward, feel for logs and sticks. Roger felt terribly vulnerable standing up. At any moment he expected the sub-machine gun to blast them. He found he was sweating, and his breath came in rapid, shallow gasps. The whole experience seemed to be getting worse, a nightmare come true. He just wanted it to stop.

Then a vine hooked him around the neck. Swearing silently, he unhooked the vine. Another careful pace.

293

Chapter 33

NIGHT BEHIND MT. BALDY

The group had not gone 25 paces before the sub-machine gun stuttered again. Roger flinched and crouched against a tree. He watched the flicker of the gun flashes and prayed. Even as he cringed there his mind told him that none of the bullets had come anywhere near them.

Graham nudged him. "Don't move or make a noise," he whispered. "He is just trying to pin us down and provoke us."

Roger then remembered that he had the rifle. He eased it up so he could use it but left the safety catch on and kept his finger well away from the trigger. The weapon felt cold and heavy. A whiff of burnt gun oil made him very conscious of reality.

The partisan fired again: single shots and from further down the track. Roger estimated that the man was at least 50 metres away and the gun flashes were barely visible through the jungle. The partisan began to shout.

"Surrender Peter Dragovitch. You cannot win. We know your plans. We are arresting all your criminal accomplices."

There was silence for a minute. Some small creature scuttled off, but the fugitives remained motionless. After another minute, Graham hissed for them to start moving.

As they began to slowly move, the man shouted again. "Peter Dragovitch! Surrender yourself, you dishonourable coward. Do not be so selfish as to let other people die to protect you. Give up. Your plot has failed."

What cruel words, Roger thought. They seemed to strike with physical force. He could imagine the hurt they would cause the Prince.

The man yelled again but this time in Serbo-Croat. They ignored this and kept inching down the slope.

Graham murmured, "He is on his own. The other two have gone back to the road. We need to move before they come back with more of them."

They continued the slow movement. Several minutes of silence elapsed before another single gunshot disturbed the night. Roger did not even see the flash. The bullet came nowhere near them so, after a collective wince, they continued on.

The voice yelled again, fainter now. "Give up Peter Dragovitch. Your life will be spared and so will your companions, as long as you promise not to meddle in the affairs of Kosaria."

"Pig's bum!" murmured Stephen. "Spared, my foot!"

"He sounds a bit worried and scared," Peter added.

"Sssh!" Graham hissed. "I can hear more coming."

There were distant sounds of movement and the faint flicker of lights. A man further up the ridge began yelling to the man with the sub-machine gun.

Roger was both anxious and curious. "Why are they doing that yelling and using torches?" he asked.

Hauptman Ritnik answered, "They must find each other, and they hope we will give away our position by shooting. It is one of their tactics. They don't care if they lose some men. The Kommunisti have no respect for human life, the scum!"

"Be quiet and move faster," Graham ordered. "They won't hear us over the noise of their own movement."

Roger took a firm grip on Stephen's jacket and held the rifle hard against his body so the metal would not strike a tree. But he seemed to trip or stumble every second step; or a vine caught his face or neck. After about 20 paces they stopped.

"What's wrong?" Inspector Sharpe asked.

"Bloody great log. Can't get over it," Graham replied. "I think we can get under it."

They shuffled forward. It was now so dark Roger could not see Stephen. He just hung onto him and followed. Then Stephen crouched and Roger bumped into the log. He was forced to bend lower. In the process he bumped his face on damp rotten wood. To get under he had to go right down on his belly, and even then he only just scraped under the huge fallen tree. While doing it in the pitch darkness he had to steel himself to ignore thoughts of snakes, spiders, and scorpions.

Behind him Roger could hear a distant murmur of conversation. He estimated they had about a hundred metres lead. Another huge log blocked their path. This one they clambered over. Roger felt soggy moss and slime as he slid down the other side. The rifle struck a tree with a *thunk*. Roger flushed and could imagine the glares the others were directing at him.

When all were across, they pushed on, only to run into wait-a-while. This forced them to back up and change direction. In spite of the cold Roger felt sweat trickle into his eyes. His stomach contracted in fear as voices began calling out behind them.

Suddenly the night erupted with gunfire. They all went down. Roger remembered to hold the rifle ready. At least a dozen weapons were firing but he could barely make out the flashes. He assumed that the whole partisan squad had opened fire. Terrified he crouched behind a tree, his heart beating wildly. Then he relaxed and wiped a wet thing from his face. The shots were not coming near them at all. Most sounded as though they were whistling through the treetops.

Peter gave a soft grunt. "Those buggers have no idea where we are," he said.

As the shooting died down yelling began, mostly in Serbo-Croat.

Hauptman Ritnik whispered, "They are calling insults, trying to make us angry. Do not react."

Inspector Sharpe groped his way past. "We will keep moving. We can't fight that lot."

When he reached Graham they rose and resumed their stumbling march. As they did a distant yell made Roger's blood chill.

"Peter Dragovitch, we have your cousin, the Princess Mareena. Surrender to us and nothing will happen to her. If you do not, we will prepare her for the Special Interrogator. Think about it, but don't take too long. If you do not give yourself up, we will do terrible things to her, and enjoy it."

There was a sob in the darkness. Prince Peter spoke quietly, "I must go back and give myself up."

"No, Your Royal Highness," hissed Hauptman Ritnik in a distressed voice. "It is a trick. They will not let the princess go, even if you surrender. They will kill you both."

"But I must do something!" cried Prince Peter in an anguished voice. "We must try to rescue her."

"We do not know where she is being held. She might already be dead," Hauptman Ritnik replied harshly, anger and strong emotion obvious even in the blackness.

Inspector Sharpe cut in. "Be quiet! You are both my prisoners, and nobody is giving up, or going back. Now move!"

They resumed their slow progress. The shouting went on behind them, punctuated by occasional shots.

"They aren't getting any closer," Graham observed.

"I think they're just standing along that old timber track," Peter said.

Roger thought about that. He knew he would be terrified if it was him. Only a lunatic, or a fanatic, would walk forward in the dark knowing that their first warning would be a gunshot at point blank range.

Perhaps we do have a chance to get clear, he thought hopefully.

Graham stopped and whispered, "We have come four hundred paces sir, about two hundred metres. If we get over this next log and I use my torch we can plan the next leg."

One after another they clambered over another fallen tree. On the other side they crouched in a tight group. Graham knelt and put his map on his knee and flicked on his carefully shielded pencil torch. To Roger even that weak glow was like a lighthouse.

Graham explained as he worked. "If we go on five degrees, that's Grid, so, add, no subtract seven degrees, that's 358 degrees magnetic, we will run down this spur for about half its length. Let's see... hmmm..." He used the side of the compass as a ruler. "About seven hundred metres. We'd better double that for downhill and in the dark, say fifteen hundred paces."

"Yes, alright. Do that," Inspector Sharpe approved.

Once more the group moved in single file, changing direction from west to north. Within 50 paces the ground began to drop. Roger had never imagined it could be so dark! There were muffled curses from the front and the sound of ripping cloth and plastic.

"Bloody wait-a-while!" Graham muttered.

Roger shielded his face by lowering his head. The wait-a-while snagged at his hat and pulled it back off his head. The chinstrap pulled at his throat. A tendril caught his cheek and he halted. He let go of Stephen who was swearing and squirming.

After a minute of wrestling, Stephen called quietly, "This is hopeless. We are hooked up in the bloody stuff. We've got to stop."

Inspector Sharpe replied, "No. We must not. We are still too close. They will soon catch us when daylight comes. Back up and we will try to find a way around it."

They shuffled back. There were more muffled cries of pain and tearing sounds. Roger felt blood trickling down his cheek. The scratches stung. He could feel something crawling inside his shirt. He scratched at it. Graham went right for 20 paces and tried again. Once more they encountered wait-a-while and came to a sweating, swearing stop. To Roger, it was like the worst of nightmares. He wanted to run but he was enmeshed in a tangle of thorns.

Inspector Sharpe hissed. "Stop for a while. We will have a rest for a few minutes, then back up and try again," he ordered.

They stood in silence. Roger felt sore and miserable. His stomach grumbled audibly and he licked dry lips. He seemed to be one mass of frightened aches and pains.

"Listen! They are moving our way!" Peter said.

Roger felt water move in his bowels. Peter was right. There were voices and sounds of people crashing through the undergrowth; and definitely moving in their direction.

"We must move. I'll use a torch and my secateurs," Graham said.

"Won't they see it?" Stephen cried.

"Maybe, but I doubt it. I think we are far enough away. Anyway, if they come down that ridge in extended line they will find us for sure. It is a risk we have to take," Graham replied.

"But what if we run into more of them coming the other way?" Stephen said.

"Calm down Steve. It is a kilometre or more to the next road in the direction we are going, even if they have the men, which I doubt. There can't be that many of the mongrels," Graham said.

Peter agreed. "Besides, if they are moving we will see their torches and they won't know who we are till we are close," he added.

"Kirk's right," Inspector Sharpe said. "Use a torch but don't shine it towards them. If they see it and shoot in our direction turn it off."

"But the risk!" Stephen cried.

"It is a risk either way. It is my decision. Do it!" Inspector Sharpe snapped.

Graham clicked on his pencil torch. The dull yellow beam lit up a wall of seemingly impenetrable wait-a-while. He turned left, away from their pursuers, and began walking. Roger tensed but there were no shots or shouts from the partisans. Looking back he could not see any of their torches although he could hear the partisans clearly. They were yelling and cursing loudly as they blundered through the jungle.

Graham led to the right. His small secateurs went up. Snip! A tendril dropped. He advanced a pace. Snip! Snip! They were past that bush. There was still some scratching and tearing, but they had gained 10 metres and the slope steepened downwards appreciably.

On down they went at a slow walk, clinging to each other in a human centipede. Roger stopped sweating and licked dry lips. Now he felt hot and exhausted. He itched and chafed and his muscles ached. He just wanted to lie down but fear made him cling on tightly.

In 10 minutes they moved about a hundred metres. Now they were down on the side of the mountain and only occasionally heard sounds of the pursuit. Inspector Sharpe refused to let them stop. They struggled on downwards, slipping and stumbling but making definite progress by the light of the torch. He kept them at it for another half an hour until he was satisfied they had come three or four hundred metres down the spur.

"Okay. Stop for a rest. I think we've given them the slip for the moment," Inspector Sharpe said. Graham switched off his torch. Roger sat down and leaned on a rock. Prince Peter bent over Hauptman Ritnik as Peter lowered him to a sitting position.

"How are you, Hauptman Ritnik?"

"I am feeling not too good Your Highness. My head hurts and I am very much dizzy. I feel I will fall over at any moment. I am very thirsty."

Graham groped back up and passed a water bottle to the Hauptman, who drank deeply. Once again, Roger regretted his lost webbing.

Inspector Sharpe pushed closer. "How much water do you have CSM Kirk?" he asked.

"Another two full water bottles and this one is half full sir."

"Give everyone a drink. If they've been sweating as much as I have, they will need it."

Roger was handed a canteen. He had one long swig and passed it to DS Crowe. It certainly tasted good and he felt better.

They lay there for nearly half an hour before Inspector Sharpe spoke. "Okay. It's 2100hrs. Let's move again."

How did three hours pass! Roger rubbed his eyes then groaned as he stood up. All his muscles had stiffened up. They had to wake Hauptman Ritnik who was quite disorientated for a while. He began to babble and call out till Prince Peter quieted him.

The slow movement resumed. They slithered and stumbled down the steep slope with Graham again using his torch. Twice Roger fell and once he banged his finger so hard between the rifle and a tree that he feared he had broken it. He hadn't, but it made holding the rifle painful. Another 300 paces had been covered when Graham's torch began to flicker. It abruptly went out.

No amount of tapping, fiddling or coaxing would get the torch to work again. They tried moving without its aid but after only another 50 paces they were again hopelessly ensnared in wait-a-while.

Inspector Sharpe spoke over their muted curses, "Okay. That will do. We will wait here till daylight. I want a sentry roster maintained. Prince Peter, you and Hauptman Ritnik sit next to me. Crowe, you sit beside the Hauptman. Now, you four cadets sit behind me side by side. Rest for a minute while I work out a roster."

"We can do that sir. We do it all the time in the cadets," Graham said.

"Fine. Work one out please, and keep it simple."

Graham thought for a minute, then said, "We are in two rows. We just wake the person next in line. We do two hours each, with a staggered relief, that is changing every hour so we have a fresh person and a tired person on at once. No talking, no fires or lights and no moving away."

Graham then went on to detail the timings for each person. This got a bit muddled in the dark and he had to repeat it before they were all sure who they woke up and when. Roger was fourth so he wedged his boots against a tree to stop himself sliding down the slope and lay back. He was too tired to care about ticks, mites and leeches. He just closed eyes which felt hot and scratchy and settled down as best he could. In spite of his fear sleep claimed him within minutes.

Peter shook him awake with difficulty two hours later. For a moment Roger wondered where he was and when he remembered he experienced a surge of panic. Heart beating rapidly, he sat up and rubbed sore eyes. Stephen was still awake but lay back when he was sure Roger was fully awake.

Sentry duty was something Roger was familiar with, but he had never experienced it like this before, with armed enemy soldiers hunting for him. He strained his ears but the only sound was the wind in the trees and the dripping of condensation. It was so dark that the only thing he could see was the whitish glow of luminous fungus and the faint paleness of the clouds overhead. He could not see Peter beside him. To test the old saying he waved his hand in front of his face and could not see it.

A tiny flickering light appeared further down slope. Roger tensed, then smiled. Only a firefly. When he looked for them, he saw more and also the tiny pinpoints of pale green which showed glow-worms among the rotting leaves.

Roger was surprised that he wasn't all tense over every little rustle and creeping noise but decided it was partly because he was too tired to care, but mostly because experience told him no-one could creep silently towards them in that jungle, even if they knew where they were. What did prey on his mind was how they could escape from the partisans when daylight came.

From time to time he or Peter muttered a few words. The others all sounded as though they were sound asleep. Inspector Sharpe began to snore, so Peter nudged him with his boot until he rolled on his side and the noise stopped. Time dragged slowly.

Peter checked a watch with a small light in it. "Graham's," he explained. "Okay Roger, wake up Sgt Crowe. It is zero zero thirty."

Roger shook DS Crowe. He snuffled and groaned, then sat up. "Wuzza matter? Christ it's dark! Where am I?"

"Sssh!" Roger hissed. "We are in the jungle hiding from the partisans."

"Partisans! I'll give the bastards a hiding if I get a chance," grumbled the DS. He sat up, and as he did farted loudly. "Umph! Sorry. What's the time?"

Roger told him. Peter passed Roger the watch and lay down.

DS Crowe yawned. "Thought it would be colder," he said.

"It's the cloud cover. It acts as a blanket and keeps it relatively warm. And we aren't supposed to talk on sentry duty," Roger replied.

"Hmmm. Yes. Sorry."

They sat in silence. Roger then realised he was cold. He was shivering slightly and felt feverish. He also felt extremely thirsty. The hour seemed to drag by. For a while Hauptman Ritnik muttered and groaned. Roger touched him with his hand and he rolled onto his back and began to snore. Roger and DS Crowe had to get up and make him comfortable on his right side, which was difficult as he kept sliding or rolling down the slope. Then Roger had to find the rifle again.

On one occasion an animal scampered past and gave them a fright. Lizards scuttled. More glow, worms appeared. There was a brief shower of rain. On the next ridge a dead branch fell with a crash. Time dragged. It was dark and cold.

At last 0130hrs came. Roger crawled over and shook the Inspector. Once he was awake Roger handed the watch to DS Crowe. With a sigh of relief he lay back on the wet leaves and put his hat under his head as a pillow.

A few drops of condensation irritated him, but within minutes he was asleep.

Chapter 34

BEHIND MT. BALDY

R oger was shaken awake by Peter.

His eyes were gummed by sleep and felt hot and gritty. He rubbed them open to find that it was still completely dark. Every muscle felt stiff and he shivered. With an effort he hauled himself into a sitting position. He was so thirsty it felt as though his tongue was stuck to the roof of his mouth. It took him a minute to generate some saliva.

Peter nudged him. "You awake now Roger?" he asked.

"Mmmm. Yes," Roger mumbled.

He yawned and stood up to stretch. In doing so he slipped and lost his balance. He slid down slope and was brought to a painful halt by some wait-a-while. It took him a minute to untangle himself. Gritting his teeth to hold back sobs of misery he groped his way back up, bumping into a sleeping person as he did. His hand encountered the cold metal of the rifle. That woke him up and returned him to reality. He sat down. His stomach grumbled and he felt very thirsty.

"What's the time?" he murmured to Peter.

"Just after five thirty."

"Be daylight in an hour," Roger replied.

"Hauptman Ritnik doesn't sound very well."

They listened. The wounded officer lay near Peter's feet. His breathing was irregular and to Roger it sounded as though it had a sort of choking rattle to it.

Is that a death rattle? he wondered, appalled at the thought.

"He sounds cold," Peter said.

Roger slid down and found Hauptman Ritnik's throat. With cold and trembling fingers he felt the pulse. It was very weak and rapid and the Hauptman was shivering violently.

"He's freezing," he replied.

For a moment he hesitated, as he was cold himself. Then he rebuked himself for being selfish. He peeled off his own field jacket and gently wrapped it round the wounded man. Carefully he tucked the edges under

303

as far as he could. Satisfied he had done all he could he groped his way back to sit beside Peter.

The two cadets sat in silence. Roger brooded over the events of the previous day; the shocking violence and sudden death; and on their chances of getting away. He was very scared, and very hungry.

His stomach gurgled.

Peter nudged him. "Bloody hell, Roger! That sounded like a wild pig."

"I'm hungry. I've missed three meals now. And I'm cold."

Roger's teeth began to chatter as the chill bit into him. He tucked his hands under his armpits. Heavy drops of condensation added to his misery.

As 0600hrs approached and the first glimmer of daylight showed, Peter said, "Let's wake the others."

There was a hint of greyness among the treetops. Roger turned and shook DS Crowe while Peter roused Stephen and Graham. There were a few minutes of groaning, yawning and grunting as the group stirred.

Prince Peter shook Hauptman Ritnik. "Wake up Herr Hauptman."

Roger watched the prince try to rouse the wounded man. His heart sank. Had the Hauptman died? Then Hauptman Ritnik groaned.

Prince Peter checked the Hauptman's temperature and pulse. "He is very sick," he murmured to Inspector Sharpe. "Whose jacket is this?"

"Mine," Roger replied.

Prince Peter looked at him, then unwrapped the jacket. He passed it up to him. "Put it on. He can have mine. You are very good, but you are also freezing. I can hear your teeth chattering. No, do not argue."

Roger was embarrassed. He took his jacket and pulled it on. The light was now sufficiently strong to see the others as dark shapes in the gloom. Low cloud drifted through the trees.

Hauptman Ritnik was eased up to a sitting position. He groaned and muttered. Prince Peter spoke to him in a comforting tone and held him up till he was fully awake. Inspector Sharpe helped pull him to his feet, where he stood leaning on a tree, supported by the Prince.

Inspector Sharpe said, "We must start moving."

"Which way sir?" Graham asked.

"Advise me."

"Down this spur until it gets light enough for me to read the map."

Inspector Sharpe nodded. "That will have to do. We must put as much distance as we can between us and those partisans. Let's move."

Roger picked up the rifle and peeled wet leaves off it. At the touch of the cold metal he shivered and his teeth chattered uncontrollably for a minute. The group began shuffling slowly down the slope. Within a few paces wait-a-while was snagging them but they could see well enough by this to avoid the worst of it. A tendril jagged the sleeve of Roger's jacket. He cursed and tore free, the cloth ripping as he did.

The darkness slowly changed to grey gloom. Roger began to discern colours, and then shades of colours. He felt so cold and sore his spirits were right down. Exhaustion, thirst and hunger were only dominated by fear. This kept him shuffling along.

The effort of moving, and the frustration of pushing through the jungle, began to warm him. After a time thirst became his dominant concern, even eclipsing chafing and sore muscles. This in turn was replaced by hatred for the ensnaring vines and the wait-a-while. This generated anger. Next time his jacket was hooked by one he swore and wrenched himself free, regardless of the tearing sound which resulted. This earned him a glare from both Graham and the Inspector. If his body had had the moisture to spare, he knew he would have been in tears.

At 0630hrs they halted and went into a huddle around either Graham's map or Hauptman Ritnik.

"Where do you think we are?" Inspector Sharpe asked Graham.

Graham unhesitatingly placed the point of his pencil on the map on a spur line about half a kilometre south of Walsh Falls.

Stephen made a face. "You mean we've only come about three kilometres since midday yesterday," he said bitterly.

"A bit more. About four and a half," Graham replied.

"Which way do you recommend we go now?" Inspector Sharpe asked.

"Those partisans have pushed us way off course sir. It is about half a kilometre to the edge of the rainforest anywhere to the north of us. We can go to Walsh Falls and either north along this ridge, then east; or go down where all these tracks are marked, into the valley of Sylvia Creek and past the rifle range. That would be easiest."

"But is it the safest?" Peter asked. "Once we are in the open country we are much more likely to be seen."

"Where is the nearest police roadblock sir?" Graham asked.

"I'm not sure but I would guess on the main highway where this road turns off to come past the rifle range and up the mountain to here," Inspector Sharpe replied, pointing to the map.

"What about this secondary road which goes across these hills from Sylvia Creek to Mazlin Creek?" Stephen asked.

"Probably not being watched," Inspector Sharpe replied.

Roger looked carefully at the map, then made a suggestion, "Why don't we go east and cross the timber road near this pine forest, then follow this road out to Mt. Baldy?"

Peter grinned at him. "What's this! Roger suggesting we climb over a mountain! And Mt. Baldy at that."

Stephen sniffed, "Besides, it's a dead end."

"Which means the enemy probably won't be watching it," Roger said.

"How do we get from Mt. Baldy down to Atherton?" DS Crowe asked.

Graham spoke first, "It is open forest. We could just walk down the mountain." He bent closer to the map. "That's not a bad idea. If I was trying to surround this patch of forest we are in, I would put men at this road junction near Walsh Falls; and here, where all the tracks come together. And here, at this road through the pine forest, where the track to Mt. Baldy turns off. So, we avoid them, go southeast and cross the main timber road here. We can then either go down Scrubby Creek to Carrington as we originally planned, or go to Mt. Baldy."

Inspector Sharpe rubbed his jaw. "Yes. If I was them, I'd watch all these road junctions. But how about Hauptman Ritnik? Is he up to a slog like that?"

The Hauptman was sitting leaning on a tree. He looked ashen faced but had been following their discussion. "Do not let me delay you getting His Royal Highness to safety. Just leave me, under guard if you wish. In any case I give you my parole, on my honour as an officer of the Royal Guard."

Inspector Sharpe shook his head. "We've had that argument. We stay together," he replied. He reached over and squeezed his shoulder. "You're a good lad. I wish all my prisoners were gentlemen like you. Do you think you can walk?"

"I believe I can."

"Good. okay CSM Kirk, get us to Mt. Baldy."

"Yes, sir." Graham used his compass as a ruler to pencil on a bearing, then as a protractor to calculate it. "One hundred and ten degrees Magnetic should do. We might be a bit out in our location here."

"Lead on," Inspector Sharpe said.

They resumed their slow trek. The compass bearing led them down a steep slope into a deep re-entrant choked with wait-a-while. Progress was a painful crawl. Frequent detours were necessary to avoid impassable masses of vines and wait-a-while. Even so Graham's secateurs were in constant use. Blisters began to develop on his thumb and forefinger, and he was scratched dozens of times by thorns and prickles.

After about an hour they came to a tiny creek at the bottom of the re-entrant. Small pools allowed them a chance to drink their fill and to rinse their grimy faces. The men all looked haggard and unshaven, as did the three older boys. Hauptman Ritnik looked like death warmed up and was visibly trembling. Roger washed his face and rinsed salt out of his eyes. Graham refilled all his water bottles.

When he was satisfied there was no obvious pursuit, Inspector Sharpe allowed them to sit down for a short halt. The 20 minutes' rest and water revived them noticeably. Roger noted they were just in the bottom of the cloud. A watery sun glowed beyond the foliage and mist. Roger found he was sweating again but left his jacket on, reasoning he needed it for protection against thorns. The ripped and tattered condition of the plastic raincoats worn by the two policemen showed what they had passed through in the night.

The next hour was the hardest of the entire ordeal. The route led up a steep slope and through a massive belt of wait-a-while so thick that progress was a painful snail's pace. Several times the suggestion was made to go back and detour around. Graham shook his head and continued snipping a path.

Roger swore as another wait-a-while snagged him. "I hope I never see rainforest again as long as I live," he said. Almost at once he was jagged again and he swore again. After wrenching himself free he wiped both sweat and tears from his face. It was all getting to be too much! *I just want it to end,* he thought.

Quite abruptly they reached the top of a narrow spur and all lay down, sweating and gasping.

"Halfway to the timber road, I think," Graham said. "It should be only a hundred metres up this ridge." He pointed to the map.

"Eight thirty. Time flies when you're having fun!" Peter commented.

Roger's stomach gave a long growl and Graham frowned and threw a twig at him.

"I haven't eaten a thing since tea time two days ago!" Roger wailed.

"Do you bloody good!" Stephen snapped.

"I can't help it. I'm hungry," Roger retorted.

Stephen gave a derisive snort. "We all are!" he replied.

"Shut up! Don't argue," Graham said. "Let's get moving."

They pushed on down an even steeper slope through what appeared to be even thicker wait-a-while. Ordinary rainforest seemed open and easy by comparison; something to just stroll through. Roger found a leech behind his ear and pulled it off. He was sick and sore and fed up.

After 20 minutes they had moved barely 200 metres and had reached another tiny creek. This was just a trickle through a mass of rotting leaves, but Roger still washed his face from a small pool. A scrub turkey scuttled away, giving them all a fright. They had been so taken up with their struggle against the jungle that they had forgotten their real enemies.

Then it was another testing drag uphill. Much of the time they had to actually crawl on hands and knees under the tangle of vines, ferns and thorny tendrils.

Graham suddenly halted, held his finger to his lips and pointed. Roger crouched and peered ahead to see what it was. He could not see anything and moved to one side. Then he saw it, through a gap in the tree canopy.

A pine tree.

The end of the rainforest!

Roger almost yelped with joy.

Inspector Sharpe and Graham went into a huddle. DS Crowe moved up to join them. After a short discussion Graham crawled forward out of sight. Roger sat and searched himself for leeches, then examined his scratches. Stephen made another attempt to clean his glasses, but they remained smeared with moisture and he looked thoroughly miserable. Hauptman Ritnik slumped down and lay with his eyes closed and mouth open.

Graham was only gone a few minutes.

"The road is about 25 metres ahead," he whispered. "And we've gone a bit too far left. I can see a road junction which I think is the one to Mt. Baldy. The side road runs east through the pine trees anyway; and there is a partisan sitting there. He is on the far side of both roads, about 50 paces up to our left. He is behind a log. All I could see was his head."

"So which way do we go?" Inspector Sharpe asked.

Graham pointed to the right. "We need to back up, then go right for at least two hundred paces. The road curves and it goes into a dip. We should be out of sight of the sentry there. We need to be very quiet though in case there are more of them spread along the road."

Roger groaned inwardly. He couldn't bear the thought of more jungle. Most unwillingly he followed Graham and the others back the way they had come for a hundred paces. Graham resumed slowly and laboriously cutting a path with his secateurs, and constantly checking compass bearings. They inched forward a couple of metres a minute.

0930hrs came and went. The cloud lifted and bands of sunlight shone through, making them all sweat. Hauptman Ritnik staggered from tree to tree, helped by Stephen. Roger wondered just how much more the wounded officer could endure. He knew it would be a nightmare of a task trying to carry him through the jungle.

Graham signalled again. Roger glimpsed part of the road in a bar of sunlight. It looked very inviting. Graham went forward again to scout the area. After 10 minutes he returned and beckoned them in close.

"We are on the bend. I can't see anyone. What we will do is move forward to the edge of the trees and form a line side by side. When I give the signal, we all walk across the road at once. But do not run. Sounds like that travel. Go quietly and try not to leave boot prints in any mud."

"Wouldn't it be safer to cross one at a time?" DS Crowe asked, taking out his pistol and checking it.

"No. If we all cross at once, a bored sentry may not see us, and have no time to aim if he does. If we cross one after another it takes much longer so he is more likely to see us and he can shoot the third or fourth. That would split the group across the road," Graham replied emphatically.

"Okay. All at once. You control it," Inspector Sharpe agreed.

He also took out his pistol. They crept forward to the trees on the edge of the road and formed a line. Roger crouched on the right-hand end. He carried the rifle ready to use and clicked the safety catch off. Peter was on his left. Roger crouched behind a tree and peered out. Everything was quiet. The gravel road looked damp and greasy. On the other side was the dark mass of a fully grown pine plantation, big trees 20 metres tall. Under them was a tangle of weeds, bushes and deadfall.

Out of the corner of his eye he saw Peter rise and signal.

Go!

Roger stood up and walked forward, heart fluttering and mouth dry. He had to use conscious willpower to resist the temptation to run. As he came out into the open he looked to his right. The road curved out of sight through jungle. He glanced left. The road went up over a low rise. A few more paces and he was in among the pines, bent double to get in under the low branches.

They had made it. He sighed with relief. Roger realised he was gripping the rifle tightly and that reminded him to click the safety catch back on.

The group collected together 10 paces in, and Graham held up his hand. "Sssh! Wait a minute and listen."

They crouched in thick weeds. Roger strained to listen but all he could hear was the sighing of a gentle breeze in the treetops. Graham nodded, rose and led them downslope to the right, pushing through dense, waist, high weeds at a slow walk. After 50 paces this brought them out on an overgrown vehicle track running between the pine plantation and the jungle. The track went downhill in the right direction. Without a word Graham headed along it.

Roger became 'Tail-end Charlie'. He crouched and looked back towards the timber road, then walked quickly to catch up, casting nervous glances over his shoulder.

And they were being followed!

For a moment he clearly saw the silhouette of a man against the sunlight where the track joined the road.

"Psst! Psst!" he hissed to Peter, giving the thumbs down.

Peter glanced back and saw Roger crouching amongst the weeds. He quickly passed the signal on and also took cover. Roger backed into the pine forest, all his nerves tingling. Peter and Stephen did likewise. Inspector Sharpe and DS Crowe came quickly back, pushing under the edge of the pines.

They joined Roger, who was now kneeling in the weeds behind the trunk of a pine tree.

"What is it?" Inspector Sharpe asked.

"A partisan. At the track junction. He..."

Roger stopped and his blood froze as the sound of a stick snapping out on the track came to him. Visibility was so restricted he could not see more than a few metres up the track. He lifted the rifle and slipped off the safety catch. That alone cost him an agony of conscience as the moral arguments swirled in his head. But aiming was even harder to do. Roger cradled the butt into his shoulder and tried to aim but was shaking so much the sights appeared to dance. His heart was pounding furiously, and he was terrified and knew it. He rested his finger on the trigger and licked dry lips.

Oh no! Please God! I hope I don't have to shoot!

Chapter 35

MT. BALDY

Roger crouched lower. The sound of soft footfalls came to him. Into sight walked a partisan. He wore a uniform that was more brown than green, with brown leather webbing. On his head was a blue forage cap with a red star on the front. Circular orange badges with three black lines across them were pinned to his lapels. Across his chest was slung an AK47. He carried a small radio in his right hand.

The man stopped. His eyes searched the undergrowth. Roger licked lips dry with dread and squinted through the rifle sights. At 10 paces he could not miss. His stomach churned at the thought of killing and he trembled, then moved his point of aim to the man's leg.

Then, to everyone's surprise, the partisan spoke. "Australian soldiers, where are you? I know you are in there. I saw you. Do not shoot. I surrender."

Was it a trap? A trick?

Roger saw Inspector Sharpe exchange a worried glance with DS Crowe. The partisan spoke again, "Australian soldiers, I surrender. I wish to claim political asylum." He put his hands up, well clear of his rifle.

Inspector Sharpe spoke, quietly but clearly, "Who are you and why do you wish to surrender?"

"I am Comrade Platoon Administrator Yuri Barkovitch. I am not a communist. I no longer believe. Kosaria not a good place to live. I wish to live in Australia."

"I am a police inspector. I cannot make you promises like that, but if you co-operate it will be easier for you."

"I help! I help! I tell you where other partisans are so you can escape," the partisan replied.

"Are you alone? Is there anyone with you?"

"I am alone. I was walking along to check the sentries. That is how I saw you. The others are all back on the road."

"Put down the radio and the rifle and come here with your hands up."

The partisan did as he was told. As he walked towards them, he said,

"The radio, you see it? I could have used it to call the officers, but I did not."

Inspector Sharpe stepped out, pistol ready. "Crowe, search him. Then tie his hands behind his back. Peter, pick up the rifle and radio and get back under cover. Roger, keep watch back along the track."

Roger moved forward so that he could just see along the track. Shuddering with relief he put the safety catch back on and wiped sweaty palms on his trousers.

Inspector Sharpe continued to question the man. "How many others are there and where are they?"

"We are a platoon of thirty-nine: three squads and a headquarters. I am here at this place with the Comrade Quartermaster. The two officers and their signallers are up there somewhere." He jerked his head towards the cloud-shrouded peak to the south. "I have half a squad spread out along the road to Walsh Falls. I can show you on the map."

"Map," Inspector Sharpe called. Stephen pulled his out and went over. Inspector Sharpe asked, "Are any of these men close? Will they come here?"

The partisan shook his head. "No. The nearest is two hundred metres away at the road junction over there. He will not move without orders."

"Where are the ones on the mountain?"

"I do not know for sure. They camped right on top last night. I took them a hot meal. I did hear that one of the squads is lost in the jungle somewhere over to the west. The two officers are at the top."

"Two officers?"

Hauptman Ritnik answered. He rose from the weeds to glare at the man. "Yes. They use the old Communist system, a Military Officer and a Political Officer; a Commissar who has the power of veto."

The Partisan sergeant looked at Hauptman Ritnik's uniform. His eyes took in the badges and his mouth fell open in alarm. He spoke rapidly in Serbo-Croat, a frightened, whining tone evident.

Inspector Sharpe cut in, "Speak English! What did you say?"

Hauptman Ritnik answered, "He wanted to know if mine is a Royal Guard uniform. I told him that it is." He gave the partisan a hard and suspicious appraisal.

"Why are you partisans here?" Inspector Sharpe asked the partisan.

"We were sent to assassinate Peter Dragovitch."

313

"How did you get here?"

"We were flown to Australia last week, disguised as tourists. We came in ones and twos and were flown or driven to North Queensland only two days ago. The embassy people gave us the uniforms and guns. We only came into these accursed mountains yesterday morning."

"Are you some sort of special squad?"

The partisan nodded. "We are what you would call 'commandos'. Our platoon got the job because we all speak English, and some had been to Australia."

Prince Peter stepped out from behind a pine tree and asked, "Were you sent because you knew the plans of the Royalists?"

The partisan stared at Prince Peter with frightened eyes. "Yes. We... er..," he stammered. The man licked his lips with obvious uncertainty, unsure whether he had been wise in surrendering to this group. "There have been many rumours sweeping Kosaria that the king was about to return. The people are in a state of ferment. It has even been said that Peter Dragovitch would return with the Thigh Bone of St Joris. The peasants believe that; the superstitious fools!"

"So you were sent to murder Prince Peter?" the Prince asked.

The partisan licked his lips nervously and nodded. "Y... yes... er... s... sir," he croaked, his voice quavering with fear.

Prince Peter held himself erect and opened his jacket to reveal his badges. "I am Peter Dragovitch."

The partisan's eyes opened wide. His mouth gaped open.

"Sire. I... I... Your Maj..." He clicked his heels to attention and bowed his head. His body trembled.

Prince Peter stepped forward and asked in a steely voice, "Where is the Princess Mareena?"

"Sir... Sire... Highness. I... We... She is our prisoner. She is being guarded by the other half of the squad from here. I can show you where."

The partisan looked up at Prince Peter in awe and swallowed nervously. Roger could see that strong emotions were gripping the man.

Prince Peter nodded grimly. "You had better. Has she been harmed?" he asked, icicles in his tone.

The partisan shook his head. "No! No Your Royal Majesty. She is being guarded in a hut till the Special Interrogators arrive."

"Special Interrogators?"

"KOSPUSS men Highness. A major from the Embassy in Canberra. He is due this morning."

Inspector Sharpe cocked an eyebrow. "KOSPUSS?"

"Secret Police. Like the KGB was," Prince Peter replied. He turned back to the now ashen faced partisan. "You say this morning? What time this morning?"

"I do not know Sire. He and his team had to fly up from Canberra."

"And you know where she is? Where?" There was anguish in Prince Peter's voice.

"Yes Your Majesty. She is in the hut at this end of the rifle range down there in the valley; the hut where they keep the targets."

Prince Peter snatched the map from Stephen's hand. Graham moved over beside the Inspector with his map.

"How many men are guarding her? Where are they?" Prince Peter snapped.

"Five Highness. A Comrade Squad Leader and four riflemen. I do not know their exact positions. They have put up a sign on the road into the rifle range warning people away and there may be one on guard at the entrance," the partisan replied.

Prince Peter looked at his watch. "It is ten thirty. We must hurry. We must rescue her. We must!"

Inspector Sharpe tugged at his chin. Even Roger was aware that if this incident was handled wrong it could wreck the policeman's career.

"We will try. What is the quickest way?"

Graham spoke. "If there are men at these road junctions, we have no chance of sneaking past without wasting hours, or making big detours. The track to Mt. Baldy is still our best bet. That puts us above the rifle range."

Inspector Sharpe nodded. He asked the partisan, "Are any of your men along this road?" He pointed on the map and then to the east.

"No Comrade... er... sir. Definitely none." The partisan now looked very frightened.

"Then Mt. Baldy it is. Let's start moving. Go fast, but keep the noise down."

Peter murmured to Roger, "Aren't we lucky. Mt. Baldy! But we don't have to climb all the way up from the front. We can sneak in from behind."

"Bugger Mt. Baldy!" Roger grumbled, getting to his feet. But he did not care how high the mountain was. He just wanted to move fast. He wanted to run. An intense desire to rescue the princess gripped him.

Graham led off at a brisk walk. The partisan sergeant followed, with Inspector Sharpe behind him, then Prince Peter, DS Crowe, Hauptman Ritnik, Stephen, Peter and Roger.

A couple of minutes brought them to a wall of jungle along a small creek. Pine trees could be seen beyond it.

Graham pointed to the left. "Go round. Be quicker than going through," he said. He turned left and headed up the slope on the edge of the pine plantation, trampling weeds and small bushes as he went. The others followed as fast as they could walk. Roger began to sweat and pant but barely noticed. He wanted to run. He cursed his unfit body. *We must save the princess!* he told himself.

Another 5 minutes' walk brought them to the end of the pines on the edge of a wide, grassy ridge top. The vegetation on their left was open forest with a scattering of large eucalypts, on their right, rainforest. A rough vehicle track plunged down slope into the rain forest. With barely a pause Graham stepped out onto the track and turned right.

The partisan inclined his head towards the open ground. "Our base camp is along there. It is a place called 'Tardents Lookout'."

They all looked that way but no-one was visible, so the group continued walking fast in single file. In a less than a minute they were safe inside the jungle. Roger was sweating inside his jacket. He saw that the clouds had gone and that the sun was blazing down. On their left the ground dropped very steeply into a large valley. At the far end of it, only a few kilometres away, the sunlight glinted on house roofs.

Atherton!

Roger's heart leapt. Not far now! Would they make it in time? He sucked air into his wheezing lungs and began to pump his legs determinedly up a long muddy slope.

The vehicle track wound its way on up through thick rainforest. It seemed to go on and on. False crest succeeded false crest. At each bend Roger hoped to see the top. His heart hammered in his chest cavity. His breath came in hot gasps. His vision went hazy. His muscles became one impatient ache.

The group went up the mountain with barely a word, other than a few muttered curses at the mud or when some dangling wait-a-while tendrils snagged them. After 10 minutes they reached a crest, still in thick jungle. Roger noted that the area had been deeply rooted by wild pigs, but he simply did not care about any risk from them. To his disgust the road went steeply down a churned up and muddy slope through more jungle.

They slithered and slipped from time to time. The partisan fell twice, unable to save himself with his hands tied behind his back. Inspector Sharpe hauled him to his feet each time.

The radio began to talk. Inspector Sharpe called back to Peter, "Give that thing to the prince. Do not answer it Your Highness. Just tell us what they say."

The partisan spoke. "They are calling for me," he said.

"Answer them, and no tricks," Inspector Shape replied.

He held the radio close to the partisan's face. The partisan nodded and Inspector Sharpe pressed the transmit button. The partisan spoke, watched anxiously by a glowering Hauptman Ritnik. A short conversation followed. Hauptman Ritnik translated, the gist of it being that the platoon commander wanted to know where the partisan was. The partisan replied that he was on his way back to the base camp and would be there in a few minutes after checking the sentries. The radio fell silent.

Inspector Sharpe shrugged, passed the radio to Prince Peter, and resumed walking.

Open country!

Roger cried out with relief. The track emerged onto a razor, back ridge, open timber on the left and jungle on the right. On his left he could see across the valley to more hills to the north. The forced march continued; up a small rise, then down a long slope with loose gravel and eroded runnels. The massive bulk of a feature loomed ahead through the trees.

Roger realised it must be Mt. Baldy. It looked much bigger than he had expected. He fished out his map to check. Yes. It was Mt. Baldy. He realised he had not studied the map carefully enough. He had not noticed the jungle covered peak they had just come over. With a groan he gritted his teeth and pushed himself on.

The track plunged into jungle again, then abruptly went up a very steep pinch and out onto open country. It led diagonally up around the side of the mountain on a badly eroded bench, cut. Roger found himself falling behind, gasping for breath. He felt sick in the stomach and his feet felt like lead. Grimly he plodded on.

Abruptly he caught up. Hauptman Ritnik had collapsed.

"Leave me! Leave me! Go on. You must save Princess Mareena," the Hauptman gasped.

Peter hauled him to his feet. "Help me Steve. Roger, you take this rifle and keep on going. It's on safe."

Roger paused to take the AK47. The whole world seemed to sway and whirl. It occurred to him he was going to faint. To stop it he leaned on a tree and steadied his breathing. For a few moments he stood there sucking in air. Then he resumed a slow plod up the slope.

A hundred metres ahead Graham, the partisan, Inspector Sharpe, Prince Peter and DS Crowe rounded the shoulder of the mountain and vanished from sight. Roger gritted his teeth and kept on walking, the two rifles being carried at the 'trail'. Sweat ran into his eyes. Thirst developed anew. He stopped to allow his heart to slow down. The rifles were put down and he peeled off his field jacket. A cool breeze made him shiver.

A glance behind showed that Peter and Stephen were half-carrying, half-dragging a stumbling Hauptman Ritnik between them. Roger took several deep breaths, picked up the rifles and continued on. The road was just a badly eroded track suitable only for 4WD vehicles. It curved to the right up a steep slope into a patch of rainforest on a small knoll, then left and up again.

Roger again stopped to allow his hammering heart to slow down. He bent over thinking he was going to be sick, but his stomach was too empty. While his breathing eased, he rubbed sore muscles. Then he put his head down and continued his dogged plod up the slope.

Bugger Mt. Baldy!

And then he was on top. The track levelled out to a clearing of short grass on the summit. The wind buffeted him. He tottered forward to where the others lay or sat and flopped down.

After a minute he raised his head to look. It was a most impressive view. Roger looked left, back up the valley towards the pine forest, then slowly turned. Rugged mountains ran off northwards. He could see for a hundred kilometres in that direction, beyond Mareeba to the dimly outlined mountains behind Mossman. He picked out Black Mountain up near Port Douglas, the Lamb Range and Lake Tinaroo. The distant waters of the lake twinkled in the sunlight. The Danbulla State Forest lay beyond them, the jungle appearing black with the distance.

It seems like weeks, not days, since we started this adventure there, he thought.

The eastern edge of the Tablelands showed clearly. Roger identified Walsh Pyramid and Mt Bellenden Ker. Mt Bartle Frere, highest mountain in Queensland, stood up on the far side of the Tablelands like a dark blue cardboard cut-out. Further right Roger could see out over the rolling farmland of the East Barron area down towards Millaa Millaa.

Then he picked out their route past Wongabel and across the base of the Herberton Range. The line of the old railway was just visible and led his gaze to the Pass, then back over the jungle covered peaks they had been struggling over for two days. It was the grandest panoramic vista he had ever seen.

What a fantastic view! he thought.

And there, at the foot of the mountain below him, was their objective: the rifle range. It was a long clearing in the open forest with several huts beside it. A belt of timber separated it from the town of Atherton. Only a couple of kilometres to go. Thank God!

Graham, crouched behind a small tree, called to him, "Well done Roger. You've made it up Mt. Baldy. Here, have a drink."

Roger took the water bottle and had a big drink. As he finished Peter and Stephen arrived, still supporting an ashen-faced Hauptman Ritnik. Roger took the water bottle to him. The Hauptman was eased to the grass.

Peter straightened up and looked around, then whistled. "Whew! What a view. I can see why Captain Conkey wanted us to climb up here."

"Bugger Captain Conkey! He's a sadist," Stephen grumbled, wiping condensation from his glasses.

"Who is Captain Conkey?" Hauptman Ritnik asked.

"The OC of our army cadet unit. We were going to have to come up here anyway as one of our clues," Peter answered.

"Clues?"

Peter explained their 100 kilometres expedition, and Graham stood up. "We'd better push on. That took us nearly forty minutes. It is 11:10."

"Clue!" Peter cried. "You start. We will give Hauptman Ritnik a rest and look for our clue. Come on Steve."

"Bugger the clue! You look," Stephen said, flopping onto the grass.

319

"Roger?"

"Yeah. okay." Roger looked around. Over to his right were a few bushes and a small tree. The crown of the bare hilltop was ringed by gnarled and wind, bent trees.

Graham walked over and took the Royal Guard rifle. "You lot follow us. Go down this foot track along the ridge and we will meet you at the bottom. We will do a recce. If we aren't there when you get to the bottom stop and wait. Keep away from the rifle range."

He set off, followed by the partisan sergeant, Inspector Sharpe, Prince Peter and DS Crowe. Roger got to his feet and moved slowly around looking behind rocks and in easy places. Peter walked across to the small tree and cried out, "Here it is!"

He bent and removed a rock and picked up a plastic bag with the familiar piece of yellow cardboard in it.

"What does it say?" Roger called.

Peter turned it so he could read:

BUTTS SHED
ATHERTON RIFLE RANGE

"That is where the princess is!" Roger cried.

"Suits us. We have to go there anyway," Peter replied.

"Come on. They might need us. We've got one of the rifles and we might still be in time," Roger cried. He scooped up the AK47 and started down a narrow and rough foot track which went down the eastern spur of the mountain towards Atherton.

Stephen swore but then helped Hauptman Ritnik to his feet. The Hauptman gritted his teeth but made himself walk. Peter handed him a stick to use for support and they followed.

Roger quickly found that going down was not so easy. All his muscles were thrown into reverse and the pain was sharper than on the upward slog. Graham's group had already vanished from view. The track was easy to follow but they had to watch carefully where they put their feet so as not to slip on loose pebbles, or trip on a rock or log. The slope was clothed in knee high grass and open timber and as they went down they could see the entire Atherton Tablelands. From time to time they could see part of the rifle range.

Roger paid particular attention to this and the moment the Butts Shed came into view he stopped. The shed was an unpainted corrugated iron building, set in behind the concrete retaining wall which supported the mound and the target frames. A dirt road circled in to it through a belt of trees from another road which ran along the far side of the range clearing. This road continued on west, up the valley. A check of the map confirmed it was the main timber road which they had crossed near Tardents Lookout at the pine plantation.

Roger strained his eyes. Yes! There was a person there. Two people! His pulse quickened. *Perhaps we will still be in time?* he thought.

He turned and looked back up to see where the others were. They were 50 paces back. He caught their attention and pointed. Peter gave a thumbs, up. Hauptman Ritnik nodded grimly and increased his pace.

Roger resumed the descent. Leg muscles began to stretch and cramp. His right knee started to hurt; a sharp, hot pain, on every second step.

If I can see them, can they see me? he pondered. *No. Not unless they are watching very carefully.* There were too many trees obscuring the view he decided. Then a curve in the ground hid the shed from view and he did not see it again.

The spur seemed to go on and on. Sometimes it flattened out for short stretches. The track snaked on down through the grass. Most of the time the slope was so steep there was a constant need for care to avoid slipping or stumbling.

After about 15 minutes walking, the ridge levelled out. This was about in line with the Butts. A short detour confirmed this. After about 200 paces the track dropped down over a steep, rocky section before finally ending at a low saddle down among the tops of the surrounding forest. A fence ran at right angles across the spur. The foot track joined a rough vehicle track.

Roger went left along this for 50 paces until he could just see the open grass of the rifle range a few hundred metres away through a belt of she-oaks. He was at the height where the tree canopies obscured most of the view. He stopped at a wire gate at the bottom of the slope and looked around. No-one was in sight. He was quite alone.

He fingered the AK47 nervously, then settled himself in the grass beside the track and slipped off the safety catch.

Chapter 36

THE RIFLE RANGE

Roger sat in the long grass and looked at his watch: 1142hrs. It had taken 27 painful minutes to come down Mt. Baldy. He felt pleased with his achievement but was acutely aware that the morning was slipping away. Thirst bothered him. His stomach kept grumbling, making him keenly aware that he had now missed four meals. He had never felt so tired and sore in all his life.

Nearly 10 minutes later Peter, Stephen and Hauptman Ritnik joined him. The Hauptman looked terrible. His unshaven face was very pale, making the beard stubble more noticeable. His face was grimed and streaked with dried blood, and his eyes were sunk deep in dark, ringed sockets. His wounded arm appeared badly swollen. The group sat down.

A movement in the distance caught Roger's eye. It was Graham, running towards them through the bush. He was skirting along the base of the mountain. Roger stood up and gripped the rifle.

Were they too late?

Graham raced up in a lather of sweat, pounding through the waist high grass with complete disregard for snakes and logs. He arrived with eyes gleaming and face alive with excitement.

"Come on! The princess is still there. Or at least we think she is because there are five worried looking partisans guarding the shed. They wouldn't do that if there wasn't a good reason. Switch that radio off and follow me."

He turned and set off at a run back the way he had come. Roger and the others followed. Even Hauptman Ritnik forced himself into a staggering jog. Roger felt excitement surge in his veins. He gripped the rifle tightly at the 'High Port' and ignored his sore muscles and pounding heart.

Graham led them through open she-oak forest northwest along the base of the mountain. After a couple of hundred paces, Roger could not keep up and slowed to a brisk walk. Peter and Stephen passed him and even Hauptman Ritnik was able to keep up.

After 5 minutes, Roger caught up, his heart pumping fit to burst. The others were lying on a low rise amongst rocks and trees, peering through the grass and foliage at where the roof of the shed was visible. Roger crouched and crept up to join them. He saw that they were about a hundred metres from the shed, in a dip between the mountain and the rifle range.

"There's one," Inspector Sharpe whispered, pointing up to the left.

Roger looked and saw movement: a partisan. The man was sitting with his back to a tree watching up the steep slope away from them; or would have been if he wasn't bored and looking at the ants.

Inspector Sharpe pointed again. "There is another at each end of the Butts Mound. One is looking this way, but you can't see him from here. A third one is facing down the entrance road. There's a fourth one over beyond the shed. He must be watching back up the valley. I haven't seen him but the NCO has walked around there when he has been checking that his sentries are alert."

"What about the NCO sir?" Peter asked.

"He seems to spend some time in the shed and the rest checking around outside. He has a radio," Inspector Sharpe explained. He turned to the partisan sergeant, "What are his orders? What is he to do if there is a rescue attempt?"

"He is to shoot the princess."

"So we need a plan to prevent that happening. We will move back to that gully behind us to talk this over."

They crawled back 10 metres into dead ground, then moved at a crouch into the bed of a small dry creek. Graham pointed and said, "Pete, you watch back towards the shed, Roger watch back the way we came and Steve, you watch down range."

He crouched, put the rifle down and took out his notebook and a pencil. A minute's rapid sketching produced a rough map of the area.

Inspector Sharpe looked at each in turn, "Any ideas?"

Graham nodded. "We need to hit them when the NCO is out checking the sentries," he said. "He must be our priority target."

Inspector Sharpe shook his head. "I don't want any shooting if it can be avoided. And you cadets will not be involved."

"Oh sir! I'm a good shot," Graham replied.

"I don't care how good you are. This is police business, not self-preservation like it was yesterday. You will not be taking part," Inspector Sharpe replied emphatically.

Roger felt relieved by this decision. He did not wish to shoot anyone. To his surprise Peter objected, "You won't have enough men then sir."

"I propose giving rifles to Prince Peter and Hauptman Ritnik, if they will volunteer and promise not to misuse them. That will give me four; plus the element of surprise." He turned to Prince Peter. "I must ask for your word of honour sir; that you will only use the weapons on my command to rescue the princess, not for revenge; or to try to escape."

"You have it Inspector," Prince Peter replied.

"I too can help," the partisan sergeant said.

"Yes, you can help. But I am not giving you a gun. Now, we need a plan and quickly. It is nearly midday and we don't know when this Interrogation Team is due."

Roger spoke up, "A decoy sir. Something to get their attention and to lure the NCO out."

"Good idea Roger, but what?"

Graham answered, "Attack from one direction and send in a rescue group from another?"

"No. No shooting if it can be avoided. It is too risky."

"I could call on them to surrender," the partisan sergeant suggested.

Inspector Sharpe nodded. "Good idea. Could you order them to move out, or to lay down their weapons?"

"I think not Comrade, er... sir. They were given their orders by the Political Officer."

There was a pause while they all puzzled over a solution to the problem. Peter spoke first, "Put the ideas together sir. First Roger's decoy, then, while they are watching the decoy, crawl forward so you have the drop on them and then call on them to surrender. If they shoot, then fire back and pin them down while a rescue group goes round the back."

Inspector Sharpe looked thoughtful. "Sounds promising. How do we attract their attention? What is the decoy?"

Graham turned to the partisan sergeant, "Do they know what Australian soldiers look like?"

"Yes. That is what we thought you were."

"If they saw a patrol of Australian soldiers in the distance would they shoot at them?"

The partisan sergeant shook his head, "No, they would not wish to attract attention to themselves. They would shoot only if discovered or attacked."

Graham turned to Inspector Sharpe and pointed to his sketch map. "What if your group crawl forward as close as they can, say up behind this low rise where we just were, or even up the drain beside the range. When you are in a position to see in behind the Butts and to watch the shed door, we four cadets could walk across the rifle range halfway along, to the Club buildings or caretaker's huts or whatever they are. We could carry sticks to make it look as though we are armed. If we did it at the three hundred or four hundred metre mound, we should be safe enough. Their AK47s are only sighted to three hundred. Then, when the sentries see us and call the NCO out to have a look you creep closer and call on them to surrender. If he tries to run back to murder the princess, you could shoot him."

Inspector Sharpe nodded. "You are a bloodthirsty bugger, CSM Kirk. But it sounds workable. That is what we will do. But I don't like the idea of you lads walking across a rifle range."

Graham snorted derisively. "Oh sir! I've seen soldiers firing on a rifle range lots of times. Most of them couldn't hit the side of a barn!"

At that DS Crowe chuckled and said, "Don't forget General Sedgewick at the Battle of Spotsylvania Courthouse."

"Eh?" Inspector Sharpe asked puzzled.

DS Crowe explained, "During the American Civil War sir, 1863 or 4. A Yankee general stood up to study the field and his men told him to keep down. He replied, 'Nonsense, they couldn't hit an elephant at that range,' then *Whack!* He got it right between the eyes. It's in my book of Famous Last Words."

Inspector Sharpe frowned and snapped, "Enough history, thanks. I still don't like it."

"I think it's a fair risk, sir," Graham said. "Besides, what better plan is there?"

That stumped them. Hauptman Ritnik nodded. "We can't waste more time," he said, "The Special Interrogators will be dangerous communist fanatics. We must act before they arrive."

"We could go out and get police reinforcements sir. It must be only a kilometre or so," Peter suggested.

Roger saw Inspector Sharpe bite his lip and frown in indecision. Then he shook his head. "No, no time. We must act fast and avoid a hostage situation. We will do it. Now, let's settle some details and get cracking."

After 5 minutes, with timings and signals agreed on, Roger handed his rifle to Hauptman Ritnik and followed Graham back along the base of the mountain. Graham had given his rifle to Prince Peter. Peter and Stephen followed them.

Over 500 paces down range they halted. Stephen glanced back and said, "I wonder if those Kosarians will use those rifles to get away?"

Roger was indignant. "Of course not! The prince gave his word of honour."

Stephen curled his lip. "Word of Honour! What a load of crap!"

"To you maybe!" Roger cried.

Graham cut in. "Inspector Sharpe trusts them," he said.

"I'll bet they take the opportunity to plug all the partisans they can. I wouldn't want to be that sergeant who surrendered to us," Stephen said.

That annoyed Roger as well. "Inspector Sharpe wouldn't let them. The sergeant is a prisoner in his care as well," he answered hotly. Sometimes he was quite offended by Stephen.

But Stephen persisted. "The Inspector may not be able to do much about it if he gets a 7.62mm through the back of the head," he commented.

Peter shook his head. "I'll bet DS Crowe is keeping an eye on them. And I wouldn't cross that man," he put in.

"Too right!" Graham agreed. "Well, the fifteen minutes is up. Grab a stick and let's go."

They selected sticks which looked roughly like rifles, then walked due north through the trees in single file, 10 paces apart. As they got closer to the clearing of the rifle range Roger became very tense but despite his fear he kept on walking.

Graham walked out of the trees, jumped the drain and headed for the huts on the other side at a steady walk. Roger followed. As he scrambled across the drain onto the open ground, he was unable to resist a glance to his left. The rifle range was covered in short grass, recently mowed. There was no cover at all. Roger tensed, expecting to hear the crack of bullets, or to feel one smashing into his body. Ghastly memories of the carnage he had witnessed the day before made him go cold with fear.

They couldn't hit an elephant from that range! he thought, chilling at the idea of a bullet smashing into his head. By an effort of will power he kept on walking.

Everything remained quiet, save for the sounds of distant traffic in the town. Roger glanced behind. Peter and Stephen were following, spaced well apart and pretending to be on patrol. It was only one hundred metres across the range, but it seemed much longer. They crossed about halfway along, the cleared area extending off on either side for hundreds of metres.

The sheds were closer with every step. Roger resisted the urge to speed up. Graham actually stopped on the gravel road beside the range and took out his map. He then looked around, beckoning the others to join him.

"We have to be sure they see us," he explained.

After a minute, to Roger's intense relief, Graham continued walking and they reached the cover of the sheds. The boys went behind a large club building and passed out of sight of the Butts Mound.

As they reached cover Peter wiped his brow theatrically. "Whew! Talk about ducks in a shooting gallery," he said.

Graham grinned, "That should have the mongrels in a fluster!"

"Shhh! Listen," Roger said.

Very faintly came the sound of a voice.

Graham listened then nodded. "This is it! They are calling on them to surrender. Get ready to run," he said.

The plan was for them to run away if there was any shooting. They were to go to the nearest houses to call the police. They moved to peer around the corner of the building.

Graham waved them to move. "There is the partisan sergeant standing in the open. That's our cue. Let's go."

Led by Graham they began advancing up the gravel road towards the Butts at a brisk walk, but still spaced well apart. This was to continue the bluff by representing soldiers moving up as reinforcements.

No shots so far. Had it worked? Was the princess safe? Roger found he was not as frightened as he had expected to be.

Graham pointed. "Look, they've surrendered!"

A figure had stood up on top of the mound with his hands in the air. Other figures joined him until five stood in a line. They sat down, hands on heads. Inspector Sharpe and DS Crowe walked out of the trees to cover them.

Roger got a fleeting glimpse of Prince Peter and Hauptman Ritnik running down behind the mound. "I think they have done it," he said. He felt enormously relieved and walked as fast as he could.

Then 3 minutes later the boys walked up onto the mound in front of where six partisans sat. Five had their hands on their heads and the sixth, the sergeant, still had his tied behind his back. DS Crowe stood to one side with a sub-machine gun. The partisans stared at them. One began to speak rapidly in Serbo-Croat.

"Silence!" DS Crowe rapped.

The partisan sergeant explained. "He is angry because now they see they have been tricked by boys with sticks."

Roger suddenly felt foolish and dropped his stick. Peter pretended to unload and make safe first.

"Wait there, cadets," DS Crowe ordered.

Inspector Sharpe came around the right-hand end of the mound followed by Prince Peter, Hauptman Ritnik and the princess. She was holding on to the Hauptman for support. Roger felt like cheering and looked anxiously to see if she had been harmed. There was no visible sign that she had been mistreated.

She is beautiful! Roger thought. Then he felt a twinge of envy as she kissed Hauptman Ritnik on the cheek and hugged him.

The group stopped near the boys. Inspector Sharpe indicated them. "Your Royal Highness, these are the cadets who helped rescue you."

Graham called out, "Cadets, atten... shun!"

He snapped to attention and saluted. Roger stepped over beside Peter and Stephen and stood rigid.

Prince Peter led the princess over and returned Graham's salute. "They also saved my life. They are very good little soldiers."

Princess Mareena smiled at them. "Thank you very much. You are very brave," she said.

What a musical voice! What a beautiful smile! Roger thought. He felt quite dazzled by her presence, even though she only wore a muddy Royal Guard uniform and jacket.

Inspector Sharpe then interrupted. "You must excuse us please, but there is still danger and much to be done. Can I ask you both to sit over there just inside the forest out of sight? Hauptman Ritnik, you guard their Royal Highnesses please."

As the royal party started moving Inspector Sharpe turned to the cadets. "Right, who feels like a run? I want two of you to run out to the nearest house and phone the police. It should be just the other side of those trees at the end of the rifle range. Commander Simkin of the Federal Police is the man we want."

Peter at once volunteered. "I'll go sir."

"And me," Graham offered.

"Me too," Stephen added.

"CSM Kirk, you stay. Sergeants Bronsky and Bell, you both go. Get moving!"

"Yes sir! Here, Roger, mind my jacket," Peter said as he hauled off his field jacket and thrust it into Roger's hands. Stephen did likewise. Then both turned and raced away. Roger felt sore just watching them go.

"What do you want us to do sir?" Graham asked.

"Nothing for the moment, other than keeping watch in all directions. Do you mind standing out here in the open? Your uniforms will act as a powerful deterrent to any prowling partisans."

Roger glanced nervously up the wooded slopes of Mt. Baldy. *Will a sniper's bullet suddenly strike me?* he worried. Then he wondered, *Where are the other partisans? And what are they doing?* He put down the two jackets and realised Peter's had the captured radio in a pocket. He held it up.

"Sir, we could turn this on and listen to what the partisans are saying."

"Good idea. Better still, DS Crowe send over our Comrade Platoon Administrator," Inspector Sharpe called.

The partisan sergeant came over, looking very worried. "Yes Comrade sir?"

"I want you to turn this radio on. Make contact with your officers and tell them that the prince and princess are both in the safe custody of the police. Also tell them that the Australian Army is now hunting for them and they should come out and surrender to prevent a serious diplomatic incident. Come, we will do it where the prince can hear what you say."

"Plis, can you my hands untie?" the partisan sergeant asked.

"Yes alright. Roger, untie him. Here, CSM, take this rifle," Inspector Sharpe said. He passed the rifle to Graham, who checked it was on 'safe'. The Inspector took out his pistol. Roger untied the man's hands, remembering how much the experience had hurt him the day before.

Inspector Sharpe then took the radio and motioned the partisan sergeant to walk ahead of him over to where Prince Peter and Princess Mareena sat amongst the trees. Roger noticed that when he got there the man clicked his heels and bowed from the waist.

Graham nudged Roger. "They might have been Commos for over a century, but they still haven't forgotten how to grovel," he commented dryly.

"Can we sit?" Roger asked. He felt overwhelmed by weariness and trembled with reaction.

"No. We will walk slowly up and down. Play act we are guards," Graham replied.

The two friends walked slowly across the mowed grass talking. Roger's feet and legs really hurt but he said nothing. Minutes ticked past. His stomach grumbled loudly.

"Strewth I'm hungry. I could eat a horse."

"It sounds like you have," Graham replied with a laugh.

"Well, it's 1245hrs. Lunchtime. And I have missed five meals now!" Roger said.

"So have we all, but you will have to wait. Here, have a drink."

"Thanks. Oh, look! Here comes a vehicle."

A white car had appeared out of the trees at the town end of the rifle range.

"Police car. Thank God for that!" Graham said.

The car raced up the gravel road and braked to a standstill. Four uniformed police wearing bullet, proof vests and carrying guns scrambled out. Inspector Sharpe walked over towards them, peeling off the shredded remains of the army raincoat as he did.

He gave quick orders and the police moved to guard the partisans. These were systematically searched and handcuffed. DS Crowe was called down off the mound.

"Go and disarm the prince and Hauptman Ritnik. Be polite but firm. Then guard them," Inspector Sharpe ordered. He then walked over and sat in the police car and began talking on the radio. After a couple of minutes he walked back over to where the boys stood and said, "Watch this."

He grinned and turned to look down range towards the eastern end of Mt. Baldy. A minute later, the air began to vibrate.

"Helicopters!" Graham said.

Around the end of the ridge, just above the trees, appeared the dark shapes of army Black Hawks.

"One, two, three, four, five!" Graham counted aloud. "And more of them over there." He pointed as four more appeared.

The first five helicopters came swooping down to land one behind the other along the rifle range. The valley filled with the roar of their motors and the fierce downdraught of their rotor wash blew in the boy's faces.

Chapter 37

BUT WHERE?

A s the helicopters landed, soldiers in full battle order began jumping out, hauling out radios and machine guns before throwing themselves flat. Three more helicopters roared overhead and vanished up the valley and another three swept up beside Mt. Baldy to the summit.

"Regular soldiers from Townsville," Inspector Sharpe shouted above the roar of engines.

The five helicopters rose and swept overhead and off to the north. They vanished over the treetops in the direction of Atherton. Roger stared down the range with excitement as the soldiers rose and began moving off in disciplined groups.

"Look, a mortar," Graham pointed. "And another."

Lines of camouflaged infantry began filing off into the forest on either side. A group of a dozen with several radios walked towards them, obviously a headquarters.

"Hercules!" Roger cried, pointing down range.

Three of the RAAF transport planes passed in the distance, going out of sight behind the hill on which Atherton stood. They had their wheels down and were heading for the airfield.

As the army HQ reached them Inspector Sharpe stepped forward and introduced himself. A slim looking lieutenant colonel shook his hand.

"Lawrence, CO of the battalion. Can you give me details of where these Kosarian Royal Guards are Inspector?"

"Well, there is a bit more to it than that. I think you are too late to catch any more of the Royal Guards. But I can offer you a platoon of fully armed and very aggressive Communist Partisans instead."

"Communist Partisans! What the devil is going on?" Lt Colonel Lawrence asked in astonishment.

"It's a long story but there are six of them sitting there." Inspector Sharpe indicated the prisoners. "Here, I will show you on the map. Where is Commander Simkin?"

"On his way. He is not happy. Now, tell me what you want me to do?" Lt Colonel Lawrence replied. He and the Inspector went into a huddle over a map board held by a captain. Roger stood there feeling very self, conscious under the stares of the soldiers.

Something the Inspector said made Lt Colonel Lawrence and his officers turn to stare at the cadets. Then they looked across to where the prince and princess knelt tending Hauptman Ritnik.

"A real prince! And a dinki, di princess? This is becoming unbelievable!" Lt Colonel Lawrence said, shaking his head. He took a radio handset from a sig and began explaining the situation to an obviously puzzled company commander. Then he turned to another officer. "Okay Major Pike, set up HQ over amongst those trees and secure this area. Get the RMO and his team up here at once."

Inspector Sharpe looked up. "I have an ambulance on the way, and more police," he explained.

Lt Colonel Lawrence walked over to the two cadets. Graham came to attention but lacking a hat did not salute. Roger did likewise, unable to remember when he had lost his own hat.

Anyway we are 'In the field', he decided. By custom, the Australian Army does not salute in the field.

Lt Colonel Lawrence looked them up and down, his face interested. "You are the cadets who did all this? Bloody good job. Well done!" He shook their hands. Roger glowed with embarrassment and pleasure.

Lt Colonel Lawrence then turned. "Okay Inspector, let's meet their Royal Highnesses." He walked off, followed by his adjutant and two signallers.

A nuggetty RSM came over to the two cadets. "Bloody good work CSM. And you too corporal. And you need a shave CSM."

"Yes RSM," Graham answered, standing rigidly to attention. The RSM grinned and gave him a pat on the shoulder. "Good lads. Stand easy. Now, what are your names?"

They told him. He then walked over to join his CO, leaving the two boys standing in the middle of the range unsure what to do.

Three more vehicles appeared: a police 4WD, a police car, and an ambulance. These pulled up and more police spilled out. Peter and Stephen were with them, and so was Captain Conkey, this time in uniform.

"What have you lot stirred up this time?" Captain Conkey said. "I thought I told you to keep out of trouble? Well CSM?"

"Sorry sir. It was Roger's fault. He kept on poking his nose into the Kosarian's civil war," Graham replied.

Roger sparked up at this. "Oh sir! That's not true. We were all in it together."

Capt Conkey gave a smile. "Tell me the story. Is that Inspector Sharpe over there?"

"Yes, sir."

"Who is hurt?"

Roger turned to look. The ambulance had driven across the range to where Hauptman Ritnik lay. The ambulancemen moved quickly to check his wounds. A stretcher was laid ready beside him.

"I think they want us over there, sir," Peter said, indicating Inspector Sharpe who was beckoning.

Capt Conkey and the four cadets walked over to join the group. Hauptman Ritnik looked up and said, "I just wished to thank you for saving their Royal Highnesses," he said.

Graham answered, "Thank you sir. It was a real adventure and we enjoyed it. Sorry we spoiled your plans."

"But you did not spoil our plans!" Hauptman Ritnik cried, struggling to sit up. "They had already been betrayed by traitors." He indicated the partisan sergeant standing at the rear with DS Crowe. "The partisans knew all our plans. If you had not discovered our ambush, they would have found Prince Peter and Princess Mareena with only five men guarding them."

Hauptman Ritnik slumped back. He looked haggard and very sick. Princess Mareena gripped his hand and stroked his cheek.

Prince Peter spoke. "That is enough. We can talk later. Get the Baron to hospital."

Hauptman Ritnik was lifted onto the stretcher and carried to the ambulance. Two policemen climbed in the back with him. The ambulance sped away, escorted by the police car with two more police in it.

Captain Conkey was introduced to the prince, princess, and Lt Col Lawrence. Lt Colonel Lawrence said, "Your lads are a credit to your unit Captain. They have done a marvellous job. What exactly were they doing to get mixed up in all this?"

"They were doing a five-day, hundred-kilometre expedition for their Duke of Edinburgh Award. To make it a challenge, with navigation as a major element, I put out clues for them to follow. They had to navigate from one clue to the next and had five days to do it in."

Graham spoke up. "This is Day Six, sir. I suppose that means we failed."

"I think the circumstances were such that you will have passed," Capt Conkey replied with a smile.

"That's good sir," Peter said. "Roger wouldn't like to have to go over Mt. Baldy again."

"Mt. Baldy?" Capt Conkey asked, glancing at the mountain and looking puzzled. "What were you doing up there?"

"One of your clues sent us there, sir. In fact at least two clues mentioned it," Peter answered.

Captain Conkey looked mystified. "No they didn't. All the clues were just Grid References."

The boys looked at each other in surprise. Peter dug in his map pocket. "But I've got one here sir. Look. We found this one on top of Mt. Baldy only an hour ago." He held up the clue in its plastic bag.

There was a gasp from Princess Mareena which made them all glance at her. She blushed and shook her head. Prince Peter frowned at her. Capt Conkey took the clue. "This isn't mine. As I said, mine were all Grid References and were on light blue cardboard."

"Blue cardboard!" Peter exclaimed. The boys looked at each other in astonishment.

Graham spoke first, "But sir, we followed these yellow clues all the way. I've got all the others in my webbing."

"Blue cardboard!" Roger cried. "Remember when we were at Mobo Creek? The leader of the KSS, the old man, he had a couple of Grid References on blue cardboard in that plastic bag he tried to hide, the one which had Captain Krapinski's diary in it."

"You are quite right Roger," Inspector Sharpe agreed.

Peter nodded. "They were the ones the KSS were using for their search," he agreed.

Lt Colonel Lawrence frowned. "Who are these KSS you mention; and what were they searching for?" he asked.

"Nazis from Paraguay sir," Graham replied.

Lt Colonel Lawrence looked as though he thought they were pulling his leg. "Nazis from Paraguay?" he echoed with a touch of sarcasm.

"Yes, sir. They were searching in the jungle over in the Danbulla State Forest," Graham replied.

"For a treasure," Roger added.

"A treasure!" Lt Colonel Lawrence said in an incredulous tone.

Peter spoke next. "The Kosarian Crown Jewels," he said, looking directly at Princess Mareena.

She gasped again. "Oh! We don't know. We..." She fell silent as Prince Peter gripped her arm. She bit her lip and hung her head. Every eye was on her.

"So you were searching too?" Inspector Sharpe asked.

Prince Peter nodded, mouth set in a hard line.

"What for? What is it?" Inspector Sharpe probed.

"We don't know," Prince Peter replied. "Something very valuable. Only Captain Krapinski knew. He had kept it hidden and secret all these years. It was only a month ago that he first contacted us and only last week that we received a cryptic message from him that he had something valuable for our cause. We hoped it might be the crown so that I could wear it on my return."

"And now we will never know," Princess Mareena added. "Only Count Krapinski knew what it was and where it was hidden; and he is now dead."

"Are there no clues?" Inspector Sharpe asked.

After some hesitation, during which the prince and princess looked at each other, Prince Peter replied, "Only one. It is in that briefcase Detective Sergeant Crowe is holding. It looks like the one young Bronsky has."

Inspector Sharpe called to DS Crowe to bring the briefcase while the boys looked at the clue in Peter's hand in amazement. Prince Peter took the briefcase and unlocked it. After a moment's shuffling inside he drew out a plastic bag. Inside was an oblong of yellow cardboard. Printed on it in black block letters was:

ALL FIVE
PLATYPUS LOOKOUT

"Platypus Lookout!" the boys all cried.

Roger felt a sharp chill of dread. "That is where Captain Krapinski was murdered," he said.

"It is where I put the first of my clues," Capt Conkey added.

Graham scratched his head. "But...? I don't get this," he said.

There was a short silence. Then Prince Peter said, "We received this from Dorkoffsky in a sealed envelope. By mail we received two keys. I have no idea what they open but they were fastened to a piece of the same yellow cardboard by sticky tape. There was no explanation." He held up the keys, then said, "We went to Platypus Lookout and searched but found nothing. We searched for hours."

What a mystery! Roger was agog. He racked his brains. What did it all mean?

Peter spoke first, "I've got it! Dorkoffsky read the note. He told the KSS and they came to search. They probably tried to capture Captain Krapinski too. But they found the blue clue left by Captain Conkey, instead of the yellow clue left by Count Krapinski."

"Yes! That would be it. Where were your clues sir?" Graham asked.

Captain Conkey thought for a moment, then said, "Platypus Lookout, Robsons Creek, the Chimneys. The next one was down a timber track in the rainforest; to test your navigation. So was the next one at Mobo Creek. Then there was one at the junction of the Danbulla Forestry Road and the Gillies Highway, then Lake Eacham, Lake Barrine, Malanda Falls, Bromfield Swamp, Wongabel and Atherton."

"Not Mt. Baldy?" Roger asked.

"No Roger, not Mt. Baldy."

They all laughed. Roger sniffed. His stomach rumbled audibly.

Peter spoke again, "So that must be why you could not find any clues Your Highness." He looked at Prince Peter. "The KSS took ours and we took yours."

"Knowing that does not help much does it?" Prince Peter replied.

"Yes it does sir," Graham said. "We've got them all here. We followed them all the way."

"On foot," Roger added.

They all laughed at his tone. Graham swung off his webbing and undid the pack. He took out the clues in their plastic bags. Then he held up his hand. "May I have yours sir?" he asked.

Prince Peter handed it to him. The others stood around in fascinated silence while he sorted them out and laid them on the grass in order.

Roger ran his eyes over them. They read:

ALL FIVE
PLATYPUS LOOKOUT

MT. BALDY
THE CHIMNEYS

HIGH SCHOOL
CURTAIN FIG

MICROWAVE TOWER
RAILWAY TUNNEL

SEVEN PINES
MT. BALDY

BUTTS SHED
ATHERTON RIFLE RANGE

Prince Peter studied them closely. "Are they in the right order?"

Graham nodded. "Yes, sir. That is the order in which we went to them. I am not sure about the first one though."

Peter pointed. "See, Mt. Baldy is mentioned twice," he said.

"You followed these? How?" Prince Peter asked.

Graham explained. "Well sir, we got the first one at Platypus Lookout. It said, 'Mt. Baldy' and 'The Chimneys'. We found those places on the map. The Chimneys was closer, so we walked there. There we found the next one. As we didn't know which high school, we went to the Curtain Fig. Then on to the railway tunnel and so on."

"We followed the bottom clue in each case," Peter added.

"Where were you to go next?" Prince Peter asked.

They all looked at the clues.

Graham shook his head. "I don't know sir," he replied.

"Around the top clues perhaps?" Stephen suggested.

This time Peter shook his head. "No, that doesn't make sense. We would have to go back up Mt. Baldy. We've just been there," he disagreed.

Stephen frowned. "There must be another clue then, at the Butts Shed," Stephen suggested.

"Yes, come on. Let's look," Graham cried.

They went to run off. Inspector Sharpe stopped them. "Wait a minute! Let's have something to eat and drink first. Crowe, have something brought over to the shed. I'm famished."

"Me too," Roger agreed. His stomach rumbled loudly, and they all laughed.

Graham scooped up all the clues and the group began walking across the rifle range. The captured partisans still sat in a dejected group on the mound, guarded by two policemen. A couple of the partisans glared at them, but Roger noted that at least three stared at the prince and princess in awe. Five helicopters clattered across behind them heading for the Herberton Range.

As they walked Prince Peter said, "But why did Count Krapinski lay such a complicated trail? Why not just meet us and take us to the treasure, or give it to us?"

Graham answered. "Excuse me, Your Majesty, but I can guess."

"Yes?"

"I think he was suspicious. Did he know any of you by sight?"

"No, I don't think so. But how does that explain it?"

Graham replied, "If he did not know you to look at he would want to check. So he picked isolated places where he could hide and watch who came to collect the clue. If he was not satisfied, he could have broken the trail, or stopped them."

"You may be right. But he could only have stopped someone by using force," Prince Peter replied.

Stephen frowned. "Is this thing that is hidden worth killing someone for?" he asked.

Prince Peter nodded grimly, "Yes. If it is what I think it is, it has cost many human lives."

Graham nodded. "He could easily have sprung an ambush at any of those places," he commented. Roger re-examined the places in his memory and agreed.

Peter waved his arm around. "Like here. Who would take any notice of shooting at a rifle range?"

Prince Peter nodded. "Yes. You could be right. Count Krapinski was a very good rifle shot, a marksman. When we commenced our enquiries, we discovered that he was a very keen member of the local rifle club and would sometimes come here to shoot every day. But we did not find a rifle in his house."

"Be in the lake," Roger said. Then he wished he hadn't, as the awful memories flooded back.

They walked around the end of the earth mound. Behind it was a concrete retaining wall and walkway with steel frames to raise and lower the targets. Nearby was the corrugated iron shed. It was unlocked so they trooped in and began to search. The place was full of stacks of plywood figure targets, paper patches, planks, odd tools and assorted junk. Princess Mareena remained outside.

By the time DS Crowe and two constables had arrived with cordial and sandwiches the group had searched every nook and cranny, turned over every target and looked on every beam and rafter.

"Must be outside," Stephen suggested.

"Have some lunch," Capt Conkey ordered.

Roger needed no prodding. His thirst and hunger were so acute that even the excitement of a real treasure hunt was dulled.

Within minutes they had eaten and were searching again. Lt Colonel Lawrence stood talking on his radio and conversing with the Inspector and Princess Mareena but Prince Peter joined Captain Conkey and the boys in the search. They searched all around the shed, on all the nearby trees, on the target frames and in the nearby grass. But 20 minutes of looking produced nothing. They came back together on top of the mound, where the princess sat on the grass.

Roger felt incredibly frustrated. Despite his exhaustion he really wanted to solve the mystery. "Not a sausage. I don't get it?" he said.

Capt Conkey said, "Lay out the clues again CSM. We may have missed something."

Graham did so. The others clustered around and studied them.

Roger wracked his brains to try to think of how the clues worked. "Perhaps we take compass bearings from each one?" he suggested.

"What compass bearings?" Graham asked.

Roger shrugged and felt both silly and irritated.

Stephen took off his glasses and cleaned the lenses. "Maybe we join all the places with pencil lines on the map and the treasure is where they cross?" he offered.

"Let's try that," Peter said. He took out his map and sat and began ruling lines using the side of his compass as a ruler. He snorted in annoyance and took out his other map and tried to hold them together, then gave up. He shook his head. "No, they just go all over the place."

"There must be a key," Inspector Sharpe mused, tugging at his chin. They all re-read the clues and thought hard. Inspector Sharpe said, "You followed the bottom clues to get here and if you follow the top ones it takes you back to Mt. Baldy, either way. If you go from the Butts Shed, you would go to Seven Pines. Where is that?"

Everyone shook their head. Nobody knew of any place with that name on the Tablelands.

Graham shrugged. "Might be a farm. It's not on our maps," he said.

"There were pines at The Chimneys, big ones in a line," Stephen said.

Peter laughed. "There are pines up there behind Mt. Baldy too," he reminded. "There are bloody pine trees all over the Tablelands. Sorry Miss, er, Your Highness."

Princess Mareena's face dimpled with laughter at his confusion. She said, "I went to boarding school in Sydney. I have heard Australians swear before."

Gosh she's beautiful! Roger thought. Lest his adoration be noticed he looked away. He gazed down the rifle range into the distance. *If only! Ah well! Now, where were the Seven Pines? There are some pines!*

He stared hard at the southern slope of the hill Atherton was on. Yes, seven large pine trees stood out in clear silhouette against the sky. He counted them to be sure.

"There are seven pines," he said, pointing.

They all swung to look.

Captain Conkey carefully counted them aloud. "Possibly. Now, where are all those other places? Perhaps we don't have to go to them. Where is the Microwave Tower?"

"There it is. On top of the hill to the left of the pines," Roger said.

"Good. Now, where is the High School?"

They looked but could not see it. Stephen spoke. "You should know where it is Roger. That's where we rescued you from Willy's Airship last year."

Roger shuddered at the memory. It had been one of the more terrifying experiences of his life. He looked in the correct direction, but trees obscured the view. He felt his excitement rising. Now they seemed to be getting somewhere. He was sure there was a simple key to the mystery. The answer seemed to shimmer tantalisingly on the edge of his mind.

Peter looked at his map, then down the range. "You can't see the high school from here, sir. It is hidden by those trees. You might be able to see it from the other end of the mound."

Roger looked around. There was the Butts Shed. There (shudder) was Mt. Baldy looming over them. Out there were the Microwave Tower and the Seven Pines and...

"I've got it!" he cried. "All five! You have to go to a place where you can see all five things and that is where the treasure is!"

Chapter 38

ROGER'S REMINDER

"Well done, Roger!" Captain Conkey cried.

Roger began walking quickly along the top of the mound, followed by the others. They passed close behind the captured partisans who stared curiously at them. At the far end Roger stopped and turned.

"Where is the high school Peter?"

"Over there somewhere, on the north side of the town," Peter replied.

Roger scanned the distant jumble of buildings which sprawled down the slope of the hill. "Which one is it? I can't tell."

They all looked but no-one could positively identify any buildings as the High School. Stephen pointed to the largest he could see. "What about those?"

"That is the Hospital, remember?" Graham said.

They all nodded. Roger shook his head. *We aren't likely to forget,* he thought, *not after that horrible adventure in the old mine at Stannary Hills last year when we all ended up there.*

"Give us a magnetic bearing to the school Pete," Graham asked, seeing Peter had his map out.

Peter knelt and quickly drew a pencil line on his map. He used his Silva Compass to calculate the magnetic bearing, then converted it to a 'Back Bearing'. He gave the answer to Graham who lined his own compass up.

Graham pointed. "It is through those trees there," he said.

"Perhaps we can see it from up on the side of the mountain," Stephen suggested.

"Or further down the range," Roger added.

Stephen sneered. "Don't be a dork Roger, there's nothing there," he said, pointing down the long strip of mowed grass.

The jibe stung and Roger's temper flared. "Then the treasure might be buried. You go up the mountain and I'll look down there," he snapped. He began striding down the mound. Stephen shrugged and turned to walk up the slope. The others stood and watched.

Roger kept looking to his left as he walked. His path took him right over on the southern side of the range beside the drain. He reached the 100-metre mound but still there was no sign of the High School. But a small part of the northern slope of Atherton had come into view so he continued on.

At the 200-metre mound he still could not see the school, but he could see even more of the slope. By then he was starting to feel silly, worried that he would look a fool if there was nothing, or if he could not see the high school at all because of the trees on the other side of the range. Stubbornly he kept walking. There were some weeds and small bushes ahead near the end of the 300-metre mound. He walked to them and looked.

There was nothing among the bushes, but he wondered if they grew there because the ground had been disturbed when someone had buried the treasure. Feeling quite stressed he walked onto the mound and looked.

Yes! There, through that gap in the trees. I can see the school. To check he went forward 10 paces, but the school was lost to sight. He walked fifty and it did not reappear.

Roger stopped and walked back slowly. The school came into view again as he reached the mound again. Just that one gap in the trees. He looked down. A low concrete wall about 20 centimetres high ran across the front of the mound and ended in a concrete sump just next to him. This had a rusty iron grille over it and was almost hidden by a small bush. He walked around in a circle studying the ground for signs of digging; and checking that he could still see all five objects.

Graham called out, "Can you see the High School?"

"Yes," Roger replied. He pointed.

Then he noted with some satisfaction that Stephen was walking back down the mountain side. That sent him back to quartering the ground. He quickly discovered that he could only see all five things within a couple of paces of the drain. If he crossed it, he lost sight of the pine trees. If he went up and down the drain, he lost sight of the school.

Was it the sump? It looked such an ordinary thing, half-hidden in weeds. He stopped and looked carefully at it. A few paces away was the open drain, a deep, eroded ditch running downhill along the side of the clearing. He walked to that and looked into it. A pipe led into it from the sump but was much too small for a person to crawl into.

Roger jumped down into the drain and looked up the pipe. He could see clearly up to the concrete sump a few metres away. Nothing in there. Feeling frustrated but certain that the answer was close he scrambled out of the drain, ignoring a sharp twinge in his left knee. Again he walked up and down checking that the five objects could only be seen from that one area. Further down the drain the pine trees were obscured and so was the school.

He went back to the sump. That was the only place he could see all five objects from. But he could see no sign of any disturbed earth. Puzzled, Roger studied the sump again. It looked like every other sump he had ever seen. So what was the answer? He shook his head in annoyance and studied the surrounding area. Then it occurred to him. Why was this the only mound which appeared to have a retaining wall and a sump? Why was it there? Why didn't any run, off simply flow along the face of the retaining wall and into the ditch?

Is the treasure hidden in the sump? Roger wondered.

To check he bent down and pushed the bush aside. His eyes focused on the metal grille. It was just the usual heavy, rusty iron bars resting in grooves. He brushed some grass and leaves aside, pushed his fingers through the bars and gripped them. Then he tried to lift it.

It was heavy. Roger found he was panting as he strained with exertion.

"What is it Roger? What have you found?" called Graham, who was running down ahead of the group.

Roger made no answer. He heaved again and the grille moved. Graham joined him and grabbed a hold. They hauled the grille up.

"Just a drain," Graham said, bending to look in.

Roger knelt and peered in. The concrete rim which supported the grille was smaller than the space underneath, which was at least a metre and a half deep. He could not see under the rim because of that. On an impulse he put his feet in and slid down, just as the others arrived.

There was just room for him to bend his knees and crouch. He looked around.

And there it was: a small steel door about 40 centimetres high by 50 centimetres wide, with a heavy padlock on it.

Roger stood up, his eyes only able to focus on Prince Peter.

"The big key please, Your Majesty."

Prince Peter looked astonished, then fumbled in the briefcase.

Princess Mareena took the piece of cardboard from him, ripped the key free and handed it to Roger. He crouched and had to wipe perspiration from his hands before taking hold of the lock.

The key slid in easily. The lock was oiled and in good condition. *Click!*

Roger unlocked the padlock and passed it up. He pulled the metal door by a small handle. It swung open easily. Also well oiled, he noted. Beyond was a concrete lined cavity. Almost filling the space was a grey metal container. He had difficulty getting a grip on it but after a few tries he pulled it out.

It was an oblong box almost a metre long. It was locked.

I know what this is, Roger thought with a strong sense of premonition. He suddenly shivered and found he was trembling as he passed the heavy box up to Graham, who laid it on the grass. Peter helped Roger to climb out.

Inspector Sharpe shook his head in admiration. "The cunning old devil," he said. "He built this drain, then came here almost every day for years, to guard it with a loaded rifle."

Prince Peter put down his briefcase and took the other key from the princess and knelt to open the box. He was visibly trembling and was gripped by strong emotion.

Lt Col Lawrence moved next to him. "Do you know what it is sir?" he asked.

Prince Peter shook his head. "No. Count Krapinski did not say. But I can guess," he replied. He licked his lips and wiped his hands, then inserted the key and turned it.

"I hope it's not booby-trapped," DS Crowe commented.

There was a moment of frozen pause. Then Prince Peter took a deep breath and opened the lid.

The container was felt lined and around the edges had a rubber seal. Inside was another oblong object wrapped in purple silk. The Prince reverently picked it up and gently unwrapped the silk.

"The Thigh Bone of St Joris," he whispered.

They stood in awed silence, gazing at the relic. It was in a glass fronted box of ancient, polished wood. Roger realised that the hinges, fastenings, and clamps were made of gold. The sacred bone looked thin and grey and had several splits along it.

Prince Peter stood up. He seemed to swell up as he lifted the box. In a loud voice he cried, "The Thigh Bone of St Joris!"

"Are you sure?" Inspector Sharpe asked.

"Yes! Yes, I am. Look here. It says so."

He pointed to a gold plate with engraved Cyrillic letters. His eyes blazed and he held the icon aloft. His voice rang in exultation as he shouted in Serbo-Croat.

Roger did not understand what he said but the effect on the partisan prisoners on the mound was instantaneous. To the alarm of their police guards they sprang to their feet and began shouting.

Prince Peter grasped the box to his chest, took Princess Mareena's hand and began striding up the range. The others followed in amazed silence. Inspector Sharpe picked up the prince's briefcase as he went.

Roger walked along at the rear as though he was in a dream. He felt simultaneously uplifted and exhausted.

Prince Peter walked right up to the six prisoners. He held the box out and began to speak rapidly in Serbo-Croat, ending in a shout of triumph. The effect on the men was astonishing. One threw himself at the prince's feet and went to kiss his boots. Two others knelt and put their heads on the ground. The partisan sergeant knelt and bowed his head. Only one remained standing, glaring hate and defiance.

DS Crowe moved forward to push the grovelling partisan back.

Inspector Sharpe also stepped forward. "Please Your Highness. Please move away from these men." He led the prince and princess down off the mound to the police vehicles.

Roger turned to the partisan sergeant. "What did Prince Peter say? What was that all about?"

The man's eyes seemed to glaze. He wiped sweat from his brow. "He said, 'I am Peter Dragovitch, your rightful King and, and... here is God's sign that this is so; our most sacred national treasure'," the partisan sergeant said. He suddenly raised his arms and shouted in Serbo-Croat.

Roger and the others sprang back in alarm.

The police guards raised their weapons. Three other partisans also scrambled to their feet and joined in the shouting. It was a rhythmic chant which echoed from the slopes of Mt. Baldy. The men looked towards Prince Peter who turned to face them and smiled. He made a gesture with his right hand and the men cheered.

"Long live King Peter!" shouted the partisan sergeant, tears streaming down his face.

He suddenly embraced his neighbour and kissed him on both cheeks. The others did likewise, although handicapped by their handcuffs. Only the sour-faced one did not join in. The police looked on in astonishment.

Then the partisan sergeant turned and grabbed Roger, who was too surprised to react. Before he could move the man had slobbered smelly, sweaty kisses on each cheek. He then turned towards Stephen, but he and the others retreated hastily. Roger fled after them, aflame with embarrassment.

"Lucky you, Roger!" Peter laughed.

"Bite your bum!" Roger growled.

Graham grabbed hold of the partisan sergeant and shook him. "Stop it! Stop it! Calm down! Inspector! I just had an idea. Have this bloke radio to his officers that Prince Peter now has the Thigh Bone of St Joris."

"Jolly good idea. Come down here you cadets. Constable, sit those fellows down. And keep a close eye on that surly looking brute at the back," Inspector Sharpe called.

The boys moved down with Captain Conkey to stand with Lt Colonel Lawrence and his staff near Prince Peter and Princess Mareena. A few minutes later Inspector Sharpe came walking down.

"Done that. Good. Now, who is this coming? Ah! The Federal Police at last."

Three large white cars drew up. A dozen men in suits climbed out. There was a flurry of introductions which left the boys standing in the background as interested spectators, with the army signallers and RSM.

Inspector Sharpe did the introductions. "Commander Simkin your Royal Highness. He is with the Federal Police. And this is Mr Colin Prendergast of the Foreign Affairs Department."

Commander Simkin, a hard-looking grey man with a clipped grey moustache, shook hands with Prince Peter and bowed to the princess. Then he turned to Inspector Sharpe. "Now, Inspector Sharpe, can you please explain what the blazes is going on?"

"It is a very long story, Commander. I will give you an outline now. Then I suggest we move somewhere safer and more comfortable while we cover all the details," Inspector Sharpe replied.

He then gave an outline of the events of the previous six days which produced looks of ever, increasing surprise, shock and dismay on the official's faces.

After 15 minutes, an astonished and worried Commander said, "We will certainly move from here." He looked up at the wooded slopes of Mt. Baldy with a worried frown.

Roger also glanced up at the forested slope. *He's thinking of snipers,* he thought. He began to fret lest a bullet suddenly strike down the prince or princess.

Commander Simkin went on, "Is there somewhere not too far away where we can house fifty people and isolate and protect them for a day or two?"

Inspector Sharpe tugged at his jaw. "Hmmm. Yes. I know just the place. There is a motel on a peninsula in Lake Tinaroo at Yungaburra. It has water on three sides and is surrounded by open lawns. It is a motel called Tinaburra Waters."

DS Crowe nodded agreement. "Good spot sir. A nice comfortable place too. As well as being easy to secure. 'Lakeside Motor Inn' is the name of the motel."

The Commander turned to one of his aides. "Wilkins, go and requisition that motel. Use the minister's name. If need be call him. This is most important. Do not haggle over the rates. Pay what the management ask. Arrange alternate accommodation and compensation for any guests. Have the place cleared within two hours, except for the staff. Get going. Colonel Lawrence, I want one of your companies to move there at once, surround and secure the area. Keep everyone out who does not have my authorisation, and No media! Sorry Colonel, but your little war in the mountains will have to wait."

Lt Colonel Lawrence and his staff were visibly disappointed, but he moved at once to issue the orders. Commander Simkin turned to Captain Conkey. "Captain, I must require you and your cadets to come with us. I must also insist, nay, demand, that none of you say anything to the media or your friends or families until I authorise it, which may be never."

"I must inform their parents that the boys are safe," Captain Conkey insisted.

"Yes, you may do that," Commander Simkin agreed. He turned to Inspector Sharpe. "There have been rumours for days. Half the Press Corps in the country are out there at the turn-off, clamouring to get in.

We want to keep this quiet. It is a major diplomatic incident. National Security is involved. Captain, make sure your cadets understand."

Roger suddenly felt worried and sick. He was appalled at the authority and power of this grim-faced man. He also had the awful realisation that, in discovering the Thigh Bone, he may have started events beyond his control, which he would regret.

They were kept waiting for 10 minutes before four army helicopters came roaring down to land along the rifle range. The cadets were led forward and placed aboard the third one. Even though Roger had flown in helicopters before; twice the previous year, when they were rescued from the flooded Mulgrave River in January, and when searching for Willy Williams and his airship in June, he was still excited and anxious.

The crew strapped them in. Roger was comfortably in the middle. He didn't enjoy flying but still found it fascinating. As the machine trembled with power and lifted off, he uttered a quiet prayer. Below him he glimpsed trees, a small creek, a gravel road, houses, another creek, then the roofs of Atherton. In a minute they were beyond the town and over open farmland. Roger shivered and closed his eyes.

Nearly 5 minutes later, they were circling Tinaburra Waters. The machine settled on a wide lawn beside the lake and they climbed out. The motel had not yet been taken over, but Commander Simkin led them over to it. His aide, Wilkins, arrived at that moment and a discussion began with the manager. Roger was so tired he did not care what happened next. Now he just wanted to lie down and sleep.

More helicopters roared in, to disgorge soldiers who surrounded the buildings and were placed on guard at doorways. Others were sent to patrol the shores of the lake. The boys were warned not to leave the premises and were led to two downstairs rooms by a policeman, who then stood guard on the veranda. Roger and Graham were given one room and Peter and Stephen the other. Capt Conkey had the next along, sharing with DS Crowe.

The boys were told to shower and were given fresh uniforms by the soldiers. Roger found the hot shower to be a mixture of bliss and stinging pains. He pulled on the clean clothes and flopped onto one of the beds. Just as he was drifting into sleep food was brought by a friendly woman who gave them a cheerful welcome. Roger sat up and placed one of the trays on a table and wolfed the food down. An army doctor visited them with a couple of medics and their minor ailments were treated. Then they were left alone.

Captain Conkey checked how they were, then told them to get some sleep until they were needed. Roger needed no encouragement. He stretched out on the very comfortable bed and was soon asleep.

At 2000hrs they were woken and taken to a lounge room where Commander Simkin, several other men in suits, Mr Prendergast, Inspector Sharpe, DS Crowe and Captain Conkey were all seated. Peter and Stephen joined them, and they were made comfortable in chairs. Coffee and biscuits were provided.

Once they were settled, they were required to tell the whole story and were minutely questioned on every little detail. It was after midnight before they finished and were led back to their rooms. Roger was so exhausted he just threw himself on the bed and was asleep in moments.

After breakfast next morning they were interviewed again and detailed statements taken. They were allowed to speak briefly to their parents on the telephone, saying only a prepared speech. The morning dragged by. During this time they learned that, on orders from the Kosarian Embassy, the Partisans in the jungle had surrendered ("Much to the disgust of the Colonel and his men who were looking forward to a good little stoush," explained Inspector Sharpe). Several partisans had asked for political asylum. The rest were to be deported. Diplomatic relations between Australia and Kosaria were 'very strained'. Mr Stinkibitz had cut short his visit and flown out.

Several Royal Guards had also been arrested. Most had gone into hiding. Two more KSS men had been taken into custody.

"What about Hauptman Ritnik sir? Is he alright?" Roger asked.

"Yes. He is in hospital and will recover fully," Inspector Sharpe replied.

"What will happen to the prince and princess Sir?" Peter asked.

"They are to be flown out of the country and set free."

Roger liked that. The thought of them being put in jail or something had been bothering him.

After lunch, the four friends sat on the patio. Roger relaxed and enjoyed the lovely view out over the lake. As he dozed, he heard another helicopter land. A few minutes later the boys were called by a plain-clothed policeman.

"Prince Peter and Princess Mareena wish to speak to you before they leave," he said.

They were led down to where Inspector Sharpe, Commander Simkin and Captain Conkey stood with the prince and princess at the front entrance. Prince Peter and Princess Mareena were now in civilian clothes, the prince in a light grey suit and the princess in a lovely emerald green frock.

The boys lined up, feeling very self-conscious. Prince Peter stepped forward, and said, "We have now heard the whole story of what you did. I would like to thank you again. You saved my life, and you saved my cousin's life as well. If you would be so kind I would consider it a favour if you would accept honorary life membership in the Crown Prince's Life Guard of the Kosarian Royal Guard."

He then stepped forward and handed each of them one of the Golden Eagle badges and shook their hands. When he got to Roger he added, "And a special thanks to you for helping to find the er... the object in Count Krapinski's care."

Roger felt very proud, humble and embarrassed. But what happened next overwhelmed him. Princess Mareena stepped forward and kissed him on both cheeks.

"As a special thanks for saving the prince and Baron Ritnik," she said. Then she moved along and also kissed the others.

The memory of her touch and the smell of her perfume lingered long after the sound of the helicopter died away.

And the prince did keep his word. The boys not only received their Duke of Edinburgh Award, but also received with it a personal letter from Prince Phillip congratulating them and offering his thanks.

Months later, each of the boys received in the mail a small box. Inside was a handwritten note of thanks from Prince Peter, and a beautiful silver and gold medal on a green and white ribbon. A typed letter signed by Major Ritnik explained it was the Kosarian medal of the White Falcon for sacrifice in the service of the King.

As they were foreign medals from a government which did not legally exist, the boys could not wear them on their uniforms. But for each they remained a treasured possession, and a permanent reminder to Roger of Count Krapinski and of the meaning of duty, loyalty and honour.

Enjoy more C.R. Cummings stories

The Air Cadets

The Navy Cadets

The Army Cadets

 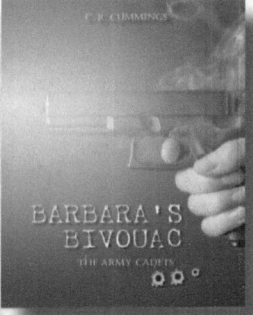 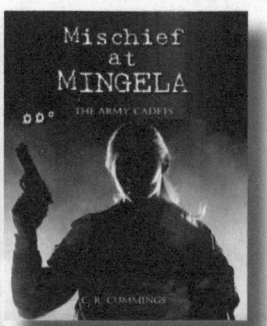